Elizabeth Missing Sewell

Gertrude

Elizabeth Missing Sewell

Gertrude

ISBN/EAN: 9783337318826

Printed in Europe, USA, Canada, Australia, Japan

Cover: Foto ©Andreas Hilbeck / pixelio.de

More available books at **www.hansebooks.com**

GERTRUDE

BY

ELIZABETH M. SEWELL

Turn to private life
And social neighbourhood : look we to ourselves :
A light of duty shines on every day
For all.

THE EXCURSION

'NEW EDITION'

LONDON
LONGMANS, GREEN, AND CO.
1886

GERTRUDE.

CHAPTER I.

IT was a calm, bright morning in the beginning of September. The brilliancy of the summer tints had scarcely begun to fade, and the warm breath of the south breeze, as it wandered amongst the foliage of the trees, and played with the flickering shadows on the turf, gave no indication that the glory of the year was departing. But there is something in the knowledge that autumn is near, which will often cast a shade over the fair face of nature, from the contrast between the charm of its present beauty and the desolation which we feel to be at hand. Lovely though it may be, we view it with something of sadness mingled with our pleasure, for, like the last sweet smile of a cherished friend, we are conscious that, even while we are yet gazing, it is passing away from our sight.

And perhaps it was a thought such as this which caused the sigh that escaped from Edith Courtenay, as she stood at the library window of Elsham Priory, and looked upon the sunny prospect before her.

The scene was one of quiet home beauty, often to be met with in England. To the right lay a cheerful village, partly embosomed in trees, and partly clustering around the base of a steep, conical hill, which had once been the station of a Roman encampment. The church, with its spire pointing to the blue heavens, and its white tombstones shining in the morning sun, stood near upon another hill of less considerable elevation, while, immediately adjoining, stretched the woods and lawns of Allingham Park, long in the possession of the elder branch of the Courtenay family. The house, an edifice of Grecian architecture, with no pretensions to beauty beyond a handsome Ionic colonnade, almost fronted the Priory ; and to the left, the eye, after passing over a few miles of wooded country, rested upon the outline of the low hills, which, receding one behind the other, formed a barrier between the valley of Elsham and the sea.

The Priory of Elsham existed now only in name, its rich endowments and lands having, in the reign of Henry the Eighth, shared the fate of the other church properties which were sacrificed to the rapacity of that monarch and his favourites. From that time the building, deserted by its former inmates, gradually fell into decay, and the crumbling walls at length entirely disappeared, as the stones were taken to form barns and stables for the farm which, in after years, occupied the spot where the Priory had stood. The modern Priory, consisting of a square front of recent date, and a long wing erected about a hundred years before, had no connection with the old religious house except that of bearing the same designation. It was of moderate size, containing the usual number of apartments—a library and drawing-room opening into each other, a good dining-room, a small study, and bedrooms in proportion, — and in its general appearance gave signs of comfort, opulence, and good taste, the latter being principally exhibited in the quiet, unostentatious style of the furniture, and the skill with which the few acres of pleasure-ground adjoining the house were laid out, so as to afford the greatest variety, and command the most striking points of view.

To the world it might have seemed that, with such a home, and in the possession of youth, health, friends, and affluence, Edith Courtenay could have had no cause to sigh ; and certainly there were no traces of sorrow in her open brow, her deep blue eye, or the half smile upon her lip. At nineteen, she was too young to have experienced the cares of the world, and too buoyant in spirit to feel more than a passing dread of its trials ; but she was not too young to have had experience in those petty everyday annoyances which are often mercifully sent us in early life, to prepare us for the real afflictions that await us in after years ; and, much as she might have been envied by many, there were circumstances in her situation which might justly have caused them to hesitate before they pronounced her happy. On this morning, however, the shade soon passed from her mind. It was only caused by the remembrance of the summer pleasures which were now almost gone ; and when she joined her mother and her two sisters at the breakfast-table, her voice was the most cheerful, and her smile the gayest of the little party.

'We are very late this morning,' said Mrs Courtenay, looking at her watch. 'Do, Jane, go into the drawing-room, and tell me exactly what o'clock it is by the timepiece.'

'It is not much later than usual, mamma,' replied Jane, in a languid tone, and not offering to move; 'I dare say your watch is quite right.'

'I beg your pardon, Jane,' said Edith, 'it is just now half-past nine; and I have been waiting at least half an hour.'

'Well,' said Jane, rather sharply, 'I suppose it will not kill you, even if you have.'

'No, not kill me,' replied Edith; 'but it is very inconvenient; I ought to be at the school by ten.'

'The school again to-day!' exclaimed Charlotte, who had hitherto been busily employed in making breakfast; 'I thought you were there yesterday.'

'So I was; but that is no precise reason why I should not be there again to-day.'

'No,' replied Charlotte, with a satirical smile, 'not in your case, though it might be in another person's. All the world are not so devoted to schools as yourself.'

Mrs Courtenay, who was still examining her watch, again spoke : 'Charlotte, my dear, I am certain that I am at least ten minutes too fast, and it really makes me uncomfortable; I wish you would look at the timepiece.'

'In a minute, mamma,' said Charlotte; and she continued to pour out the tea, and then proceeded to cut bread for the party, while Edith went to obtain the desired information. 'Ah! thank you, my love,' said her mother, when she returned; 'I thought I was wrong. It quite disturbs me in the night if I fancy that my watch is out of order; and last night I could hardly sleep at all—I was so dreadfully nervous.'

'Did you try Gertrude's remedy?' asked Edith; 'it did you good before.'

'Yes, so it did; everything that comes from Gertrude does me good; but it was not mixed, and I was obliged to go without it.'

Edith looked reproachfully at her sisters. 'I was so busy, yesterday,' she said, 'at the school in the morning, and in the village in the afternoon, and I depended upon you to attend to it.'

'I forgot it,' replied Charlotte; 'and I had no time. Miss

Forester called and paid a long visit, and I was only able to have a few minutes' walk before dinner.'

'I wish Gertrude would make me sleep too,' said Jane. 'I never have more than three hours' rest at once, and I am as tired this morning as if I had walked ten miles. I am sure Mr Humphries cannot understand my case.'

'Can any one?' asked Charlotte, whose brilliant colour and sparkling eyes differed so entirely from Jane's sallow complexion, and look of general ill health, that the family likeness was scarcely discernible. 'You have as many cases as there are days in the year—which is it this morning? Gout, rheumatism, tic douloureux, or ague? or is it all conjoined—the essence of every complaint that ever was heard of?'

'I wish you could feel as I do, only for ten minutes,' said Jane.

'Thank you, I dare say I should survive it; but remember, Jane, what I complain of is not your taking possession of any one pet malady, but making a monopoly of the whole race of diseases,—monopoly of illness implies monopoly of pity; and really I have so many little secret griefs of my own, that I must insist upon having a share in the commiseration our friends bestow upon you.'

'I would not give you much for the whole,' said Jane; 'there is not one person in a hundred who knows what real pity means.'

'Perhaps not,' answered Charlotte; 'but for everyday purposes make-believe pity does just as well.'

'No, no,' exclaimed Edith, 'nothing that is make-believe can ever be of any value.'

'Is that to be your motto all your life, Edith?' asked Charlotte; 'because, if so, you had better retire from society at once, for every one knows it is made up of make-believes.'

'That is one of your misanthropical notions, Charlotte, which you hold from mere perversity. I know that fashionable society often is pretence and show; but I never will think that there is no sincerity to be met with in a quiet country-place like this.'

'Miss Forester, for instance,' said Jane, sarcastically.

'She is an exception, and of course proves the rule. In London, I dare say she might not be remarkable; but here, the very fact of your bringing her forward, shows that she is different from her neighbours.'

'Well,' exclaimed Charlotte, 'I am thankful to say that I am neither philosophical nor metaphysical. I am willing to take the world as I find it; and if people are civil to me, it never enters my head to analyse their motives.'

'But,' said Edith, 'there is no occasion for you to do it; you determine beforehand that they are all interested and selfish.'

'Yes; and I find it is much for my happiness in the end—I am never disappointed in any one.'

'Indeed, Charlotte,' said Edith, gravely, 'I wish you would not talk in such a random way; because, I am sure, when persons are in the habit of saying the same things continually, they at last believe them to be true.'

'But that is just my case,' replied Charlotte; 'I do believe them to be true, and therefore I say them; and I am not alone in my opinion. Jane talks in the same way sometimes. Besides, Edith, we are older than you, and must know more of the world.'

'A year or two can make but little difference,' replied Edith; 'and if you were a hundred years older, I should not agree with you. I will give you some examples, and prove to you that you must be wrong. What do you say to Edward and Gertrude? You do not think them hypocrites?'

'Gertrude a hypocrite, my dears!' said Mrs Courtenay, looking up from the newspaper she had been reading; 'what do you mean?'

'Nothing, ma'am,' replied Charlotte, shortly; and then, unheeding the interruption, she went on: 'You will use such hard words, Edith; no one pretends to say that all the world are hypocrites, but only that there is a certain gloss, a French polish, over their words and actions, which does not hide, but exaggerates. As for Gertrude, I always put her out of the question when I am talking of people in general. I suppose she is— yes, she must be—sincere.'

'And Edward,' said Edith, eagerly, 'you do not doubt him?'

'No,' said Charlotte, 'not doubt exactly—he is sincere at the moment he is speaking, but what he says is not quite to be depended upon.'

'O Charlotte!' exclaimed Edith, indignantly, while the colour mounted to her cheeks, as she heard such an opinion expressed of her only brother—the very idol of her imagination.

'You need not be in such a hurry to be angry,' said Charlotte, coolly. 'Edward is my brother as well as yours, so I have an equal reason for wishing him to be perfection; but I am not blind; I can see, and so can every one else who watches him, that he is inconsistent.   You could see it if you would.'

'It may be either *can*, or *will*, which is the cause,' replied Edith; 'but I am certain I do not see it.   I wish you had heard his conversation with me when he was last here, and all his plans for doing good.'

'Excellent they were, of course, beginning with the rebuilding of the burnt cottages at the quarry, and ending with a new church on Torrington Heath.'

'And the intermediate degrees being infant, national, and Sunday schools, upon Edith's most approved principles,' said Jane.

'You may sneer at me, if you will,' exclaimed Edith, angrily; 'but if only a fourth part of the world were as good as Edward——'

'It would be a very different world from what it is,' said Charlotte. 'I quite grant, Edith, that to hear Edward talk you would believe him an angel, and that to see him act you would think him a superior mortal; but I must contend for it, that he does not show to you or to the world the average standard of his principles. Every one sees the best of him at first sight.'

'I thought you were no philosopher,' said Edith, in a suppressed tone of extreme annoyance.

'It does not require much philosophy to see the faults of one's brothers and sisters,' replied Charlotte.

'Nor one's own, either,' said Edith, recovering herself. 'I know that I have felt angry, and I am very sorry for it.'

Charlotte scarcely noticed the apology, but, rising from the breakfast-table, began to search amongst the books for something she had mislaid.

'At what time shall you be able to practise with me?' she said; 'we sang that trio wretchedly last night, and really I cannot exhibit myself in the same way again.'

'You must practise without me,' said Edith; 'I shall not be home till half-past twelve; and directly after luncheon I am going with Mrs Grantley to see nurse Philips.'

'Do let nurse Philips rest for to-day,' said Jane; 'you were with her only three days ago.'

'Six at the least,' replied Edith; 'besides, I have promised.'

'Oh! of course,' said Jane, 'all promises must be kept—those made at home excepted. You said you would try over the trio, and some of the duets besides.'

'Well, so I will, by and by; but I must go now, or I shall be dreadfully late.'

'Is Edith gone?' asked Mrs Courtenay, looking round when her daughter had left the room.

'Yes, to the school, mamma,' replied Charlotte.

'But she told me she would show me how to do the knitting from the pattern which Gertrude sent. I shall never be able to manage it without her.'

'You understand it, Jane, don't you?' said Charlotte.

'Yes; that is, I tried it once; but I should not be able to begin; and I must finish this book, for it must be sent away to-day.'

'It would not be much trouble to try the work,' said Charlotte; 'and if you succeed, mamma will be able to go on.'

'Well, I will see about it presently,' replied Jane; and she went to fetch her book, and then, seating herself by the drawing-room window, forgot her mother's wishes, till again reminded of them by Charlotte.

Edith pursued her walk to the school in no very enviable state of mind; for although daily accustomed to such a conversation as had just passed, use had not as yet become a second nature. She differed with her sisters upon almost every point, both of principle and taste; and the irritation of perpetual disagreement was at times more than she could bear with temper.

She felt something like degradation, also, in thinking of the impression a stranger would have received from the tone in which she had been tempted to reply to Charlotte's observations; and her conscience bitterly reproached her for having broken the serious resolution, made only a few hours before, of endeavouring, if possible, to spend that one day without yielding to provocation. Perhaps on any other subject she might have been invulnerable; but to speak against Edward was to touch that which was nearest and dearest to her in the world; and if her self-accusation had been less sincere, she might have found some excuse for her annoyance in the greatness of the trial; but as it was, she was too vexed with herself to complain of her sister, or to feel pained, as she often did, at the contrast between what her home really was, and what she knew it ought to be.

The school in some measure diverted her thoughts from herself. The mistress was ill, and she had engaged to take charge of the children for an hour and a half every day, till a proper substitute could be found; and the necessity of attending to them had a great effect in restoring her equanimity, as she forgot for the time that there were any other persons in the world besides tiresome Anne Godfrey, and dull little Sarah Plowden, and the rest of the half mischievous, half frightened tribe of children, whom she was endeavouring to reduce into something like order. The morning passed quickly away, for Edith had an innate love of teaching and managing, and what to others would have been the most tiresome of all tiresome tasks, was to her only a subject of interest; and she felt sorry when at twelve o'clock the children were dismissed, and she was obliged to return to the Priory—to her mother's uncongeniality, and Jane's peevishness, and Charlotte's satire. The feeling was not exactly acknowledged, but it caused her unconsciously to linger on the road, and to indulge in a day dream of happiness which could never be realised, but in which her two sisters had no share. There was another, indeed, who was always foremost in Edith's visions of enjoyment, but she was absent—living with an invalid aunt of her father's, who had taken a fancy to her when she was about fourteen, and had persuaded her parents to part with her, on the promise that she should inherit all her little property at her death. The temptation might not to some have been very great, since Mrs Heathfield's income was not more than five hundred a year; but it would at least be a comfortable provision for Gertrude, and Mr Courtenay was too much harassed with family cares to allow a dislike to parting with his child to interfere with a plan which promised well for her worldly advantage.

How Gertrude was to be educated, or what principles were to be instilled into her mind, he never inquired. Though possessed of first-rate talents himself, he considered them of but little importance in a woman. He had married a young and very pretty girl, devoid of any cultivation of mind beyond the superficial acquirements of the day; and she had implicitly obeyed his orders, and had never thwarted his wishes even by a look of ill-humour; and, though now and then irritated by her weak simplicity, on the whole he was contented;—what satisfied him must of course satisfy every one else,—he asked nothing more than that Gertrude should possess lady-like manners, a moderate share of accomplishments, a quiet, easy temper, and five hundred a year. With these advantages she would pass through life easily, and would die surrounded by friends and comforts; and then—but of what was to come afterwards Mr Courtenay never thought. This world was his home, his hope, his happiness. In the existence of another he believed—he had been taught to do so from his childhood—and in occasional moments of weariness he could discourse eloquently upon the vanity of earthly enjoyments; and when grieved at the loss of a friend, he could sigh and express a hope of meeting him again in heaven—but when the words were repeated, the feeling was gone; and Mr Courtenay returned to his easy chair, and his well-stored library, and forgot that if the heaven of which he had spoken were ever to be reached, it must be through the strait gate of penitence and faith, and by the narrow way of daily self-denial.

If left to her father's care, Gertrude Courtenay would probably have grown up the very counterpart of himself, except with superior energy of mind. She had his generosity, his good temper, and his high sense of honour; but she had also his pride, his love of command, his keen sense of the importance of the world's applause, and his delight in everything that was beautiful and luxurious. And in her own home these feelings would have been fostered to the utmost; but in the retirement of a country village, with no companion but her aunt, there was little opportunity for their development; and before she was placed in any scenes of greater temptation, she had learned to study her own heart, and to pray and strive against its weaknesses. In what way the principle of religion had first taken root in her mind, it would have been almost impossible for her to have told. It had sprung up, unnoticed even by herself, in constant intercourse with one whose minutest actions were governed by its rules; for although Mrs Heathfield, from illness and natural reserve, but seldom conversed upon the subject, there was an influence in her meek, uncomplaining resignation, and her self-denying charity, which it was impossible for a mind so thoughtful as Gertrude's to withstand.

Perhaps, indeed, the influence was the greater from the very fact of there being something of silence and mystery connected with it. When first taken to Farleigh Cottage, Gertrude had felt as if removed into a new world; new not merely in its external appearance, but in the motives and feelings of the persons who inhabited it; and when the first grief at separation from her home had subsided, she found daily cause for increasing wonder. Her aunt watched over her carefully by directing her studies;

but she was too unwell actually to superintend them. She could only recommend the books she wished her to read, and give her reasons for admiring them; and then Gertrude was left to think by herself upon the difference between her father's taste and her aunt's; and to endeavour, if possible, to discover which was based upon the highest principles. The answer, if left to her own inclination, would have been in her father's favour; but, to counteract the force of an early impression, she had daily before her eyes the picture of patience, humility, entire freedom from selfishness, and a thoughtful care which never forgot even the most distant objects of compassion. Gertrude deeply felt her aunt's goodness; she looked on it as on something surpassingly strange, almost unearthly; and she could not but believe that the subjects which interested her must be in themselves far superior to all others. And so the first bias was given in favour of religion; and the seed which had been implanted at baptism, and then buried beneath the distractions and frivolities of a careless education, grew up by imperceptible degrees into a strength and beauty unknown only to its possessor.

But notwithstanding the quiet peacefulness of Gertrude's life at Farleigh, her heart still clung to the recollection of her own home and her childish pleasures, with a tenacity which neither time nor distance could entirely destroy. There were many solitary hours in which she longed for the society of her sisters; although the letters received from them made her occasionally doubt whether difference of education would not prevent any similarity of taste and feeling between them. This doubt amounted to a painful certainty when, after an absence of three years, she paid a long-promised visit to the Priory. It had been anticipated with delight for weeks beforehand, and every passing cloud of distrust had been driven from her mind, as something unkind in herself, and unjust to her family; but when a week had been spent under her father's roof, and she had watched the tone and temper exhibited in her sisters' everyday life, the fond illusion was dispelled, and she was forced to acknowledge, with bitter disappointment, that the retirement of Farleigh afforded her infinitely greater sources of happiness than the comparative dissipations of her home. Perhaps the effect of this visit on Gertrude's mind might have been different if Edith had been of an age to be her companion; but she was then only fourteen, and not yet out of the schoolroom, and it was impossible to foresee the circumstances which contributed afterwards to form her character;

and Gertrude returned to her aunt, with the belief that there existed a barrier between herself and her sisters, far more real than any which outward separation could occasion. In her mother she had found warm feelings, but a mind so inferior to her own that there was scarcely a subject on which they could converse in common ; and in her father she had met a proud, worldly man, who saw in his children only the reflection of his own imaginary consequence, and thought but little of Gertrude when he discovered that she possessed neither beauty nor showy accomplishments, which might bring credit on himself. And yet, in spite of all these drawbacks, Gertrude still dwelt upon the recollection of her home, not indeed with pleasure, but with an interest deeper than she could feel for any other spot, however associated with enjoyment. Her aunt's age and illness were constantly before her, warning her that the time would probably soon come when she must return to it ; and even without this thought, the very names of father, mother, sisters, and brother awakened visions of happiness which she could not persuade herself it would be impossible to realise.

Two years had elapsed after her first unsatisfactory visit to the Priory, when Gertrude was again recalled from Farleigh by the sudden and most alarming illness of her father. He had been dining with a party of friends, when he was seized with an apoplectic fit, from which it was at first thought he could not possibly recover ; and although he partially regained his recollection, his mind was very much broken, and after lingering for about a week he expired, awakening, by his unexpected loss, feelings of sympathy and regard which had but seldom been accorded to him during his life. Every one exclaimed, 'How dreadful !' 'How distressing !' 'Poor Mrs Courtenay ! how much she will suffer ;' but few dwelt for more than an instant upon the awfulness of the event which had thus summoned a fellow-creature, engrossed in the pursuits of the world, to the tremendous presence of his Maker. If Gertrude had known her father better, the trial would have been much more severe ; but being ignorant of his habitual tone of mind, she could only listen to the stories which were repeated of his honourable conduct and occasional benevolence, and trust that her own judgment had been mistaken, and that these passing acts of virtue were really signs of that inward purity of heart which God requires. Mr Courtenay's fortune had always been considered equal to the style in which he lived ; by some it was reported to be two thousand a year, by others three, and some even magnified it to four or five ; and much wonder had been expressed that with such ample means he should have chosen to educate his only son for the bar. But the event of his death proved that in this Mr Courtenay had acted the part of a prudent though selfish father. He had lived much beyond his income, and he well knew it ; but he could not consent to diminish one iota of his consequence in the eye of the world ; and therefore he still kept his carriage, and horses, and paid his annual visit to the metropolis, and vied with his more wealthy neighbours in the splendour of his country establishment ; and contenting himself with providing for his wife and daughters, left his son with no expectations beyond those which were derived from high talents and the probability of success in his profession. To many young men upon their first entrance into life, this might have appeared a hardship ; but Edward Courtenay, fresh from the excitement of college honours, and longing for future distinctions, was satisfied with the knowledge that his father's death would make no very material alteration in the comfort of his mother and sisters, and considered his own situation merely an additional stimulus to exertion. Even his dreams of wealth, and his projects of benevolence, received but a momentary check ; for his expectations had never been great, and to a mind so ardent and energetic the hope of gaining riches and honour by his own efforts, and then devoting them all to good, was more alluring than the prospects of the most splendid hereditary fortune.

His wishes, however, were not destined to be fulfilled. The wealth denied by his father's extravagance was bestowed from another source ; and about two years after Mr Courtenay's death his son found himself, by the unexpected death of his cousin Colonel Courtenay of Allingham, and of his only child, a boy about six years old, the possessor of the family estate, and a fortune reported to be six thousand a year. At an earlier period, Edward's feelings at this sudden change might not have been altogether unmixed with alloy ; but four years' experience of the difficulties attendant upon a barrister's life had somewhat deadened his enthusiasm. His imagination still pictured the honours that might be gained in his profession ; but his expectations of attaining them were less vivid, and the necessity of daily economy, made him turn from his former visions of benevolence as from childish dreams, which it was in vain to imagine could ever be put in practice. At such a moment, therefore, when the first bitterness of that 'hope deferred,' which is the portion of all at some period of their lives, was just beginning to be felt, the relief afforded by the alteration of his circumstances was as great as it was unforeseen.

Had the choice been granted him, he would have preferred the acquisition of fortune by some other means; but his acquaintance with his cousin had been merely that of common courtesy; and his regret for the extinction of the elder branch of the family was soon overpowered by the brilliant prospect opened before him. Six thousand a year to one who, but a few days previous, would have considered six hundred amply sufficient for the gratification of every ordinary wish, was an inexhaustible mine of wealth; and, for the first week, Edward revelled in day dreams of enjoyment and generosity, for which even the riches of Crœsus would scarcely have sufficed.

But, with time and consideration, came the usual concomitant evils of a large accession of fortune. Lawyers, relations, tenants, and dependants flocked around him, all clamorous for attention; and, at the expiration of a month a serious doubt arose in his mind, whether his new position would indeed be the bed of roses which fancy had so fondly pictured. A second month not only converted the doubt into a certainty, but brought with it also the conviction that his wealth was not what the world believed it. The family failing of the Courtenays,—the fear of the world's ridicule, and the corresponding love of the world's applause,— had operated to its fullest extent upon his predecessors at Allingham. That which they were reported to possess, they felt themselves bound to expend. To own that there was a necessity for retrenchment, would have been to lower their consequence in the eyes of their fellow-creatures; and as Mr Courtenay of the Priory had acted on a small scale, so had his cousin Colonel Courtenay of Allingham acted on a very large one. The family estates had become every year more and more encumbered; and the income, which was believed to be six thousand a year, was not in reality more than two. Unhappily for Edward, he had had but a slight experience of the fearful evils arising from ostentation. His father's conduct had produced no visible effect upon the happiness of his mother and sisters, his own disappointment had been comparatively trifling, whilst his cousin's extravagance, though at first startling, was productive of even less apparent evil. Possibly, if any friend had been near to suggest the real motives of their actions, Edward might have been more alive to the similar defect which, unknown to himself, existed in his own character; but, as it was, he, too, yielded to what he considered the necessity of keeping up appearances, and with a secret resolve of redeeming all that others had lost through extravagance by his own strict attention to economy, he carefully kept the fact of his disappointment from his relations and friends, and suffered himself to be congratulated by all, as the possessor of a property of nearly three times its real value. To one person alone, besides his lawyers, the actual state of his affairs was confided, with a strict promise of secrecy, and this was his sister Edith; but her knowledge of the world was too slight to enable her to advise him as to his future conduct; and the reason which he adduced for concealment was so plausible, and her reverence for his opinion so profound, that she could not doubt the propriety of his decision. It certainly did appear unbecoming to publish to the world the follies of a near relation, from whom so much wealth had been derived; and, with Edward's prudence and strength of resolution, it might be possible for him, in a few years, to recover the ground that had been lost, and be in reality what he now was only in appearance. And when once the past had been retrieved, the same habits of simplicity and carefulness would enable him to indulge to the utmost his plans for the good of others; and as he said this, Edward convinced himself of his own sincerity by sketching the rough outline of a new church to be built on Torrington Heath, with a large schoolroom adjoining, and some picturesque alms-houses in the distance. Edith was quite satisfied. It was clear that wealth had made no change in her brother; he still retained the noble, generous mind, and the high religious principle which had first attracted her admiration, and afterwards mainly influenced her conduct; and the only difference perceptible was in the enlargement of his schemes of usefulness. And Edward was equally contented. Possessed of talent, feeling, and energy, he had passed through his college life with the esteem both of his companions and his superiors; his tutors had been men of real goodness; his friends chosen from amongst the *élite* of the University; he had been peculiarly guarded from temptation, and the weakness of his own heart was a lesson still to be learned; or, if an occasional misgiving as to the strength of his moral courage crossed his mind, it vanished before the brightness of those day dreams of the future which made him overlook the duties of the present. His sister Charlotte had indeed spoken the truth, when she said that he was not consistent; but it was a truth which few but herself would have discovered. It required all her insight into character, and, perhaps, likewise, a certain coldness of feeling not liable to be led astray by sympathy, to discover that Edward sometimes mistook wishes for actions, and gazed upon the promised land of holiness, till he forgot the struggles and the toils of the wearisome wilderness which must be passed before it could be attained. In the present instance his self-deception, if such it could be called, was complete; and when he left Allingham with the intention of spending a few months in London, his last words to Edith were a repetition of the plans of strict economy which he intended to practise on his return. Charlotte, perhaps, would have inquired why they were not acted upon at once; why the same overgrown establishment of servants (who, it was known, had cheated their master at every opportunity) was still kept; why the same array of hunters and dogs was still to be seen; and, above all, why a person whose professed object was retrenchment, should voluntarily choose to expose himself to the temptations of a London season. But Edith's confiding disposition shielded her from every doubt; and, amidst the annoyances of her home, her mind still dwelt upon the thought of her brother, as upon the first and greatest of earthly blessings. It was to him, therefore, even more than to her absent sister, that she looked for comfort. Gertrude's letters, indeed, were delightful, and her interest in the most minute details of home made Edith forget how little she had actually known of it; but no such intercourse could equal the charms of Edward's daily sympathy and affection; and as Edith walked slowly from the school, she began to reckon the weeks, and even the days, which must elapse before his promised return, as eagerly as a child calculates the approach of its holidays. Engrossed in her own thoughts, she passed the gate of Elsham parsonage, without recollecting that it was necessary to give an account of her morning's occupations to Mrs Grantley; and would probably have forgotten it altogether, if the approach of the person whom, of all others in the neighbourhood, she least desired to meet, had not awakened her from her reverie. The lady, who advanced quickly towards her, was of that doubtful age which is sometimes expressed as being 'no age.' Her fawn-coloured silk dress, satin mantilla, and Tuscan bonnet, with its drooping white feather, had been adjusted with every attention to that which might be most becoming; and, at a little distance, her light step, and not ungraceful figure, would have justified the belief that she was very young; but, on a nearer approach, the faded brilliancy of her complexion destroyed the illusion. The expression of her countenance was as little to be depended on as the youthfulness of her figure; for the smile upon her lips was contradicted by the keenness of her small, dark eyes, while the easy suavity of manner, which at first was alluring, excited, upon maturer observation, a suspicion that it was intended as a mask for feelings not meant for inspection. Edith's first impulse was to retrace her steps; but the motive would have been too obvious, and, earnestly wishing herself in Mrs Grantley's drawing-room, she hastened her steps, hoping to be allowed to pass with only a bow of recognition. She was not, however, so fortunate;—a hand was extended to greet her, and the lady's voice, in the blandest, softest of tones, expressed the utmost pleasure at their meeting, and then proceeded to ask after the health of her dear mother and sisters, and her absentee brother, as if the whole happiness of the speaker depended upon the information. Edith's answers were short, almost abrupt;— she was obliged by Miss Forester's inquiries, her mother was tolerable, her sisters pretty well, and her brother expected home in about a fortnight; he had been at Hastings for the last six weeks, and was now in London on business;—and trusting that this account would be sufficient, Edith would have passed on. but she was again prevented.

'You are in a hurry, I see, my dear Miss Courtenay; some errand of kindness, no doubt, as usual; but you really must spare me one moment,—on such an occasion you must allow one of your oldest friends to offer her congratulations;' and Miss Forester, fixing her eyes upon Edith, as if determined to discover the slightest change of countenance, continued, 'It is a delightful prospect for you,—such a good family; so highly connected, and so fashionable; and the young lady the belle of the season. I can imagine nothing more satisfactory in every way. Happily for your brother, money is no object, or perhaps ——'

'Really!' exclaimed Edith, with a sudden perception of what must be intended, 'you are under some very great mistake. You allude, I suppose, to some reports you have heard of my brother's marriage; we hear such constantly, but in this instance you seem to be much better acquainted with the circumstances than myself.'

'Of course,' replied Miss Forester, with a peculiar smile,

'near relations always are ignorant of these matters. There is considerable pleasure in a little mystery.'

'Not to me,' said Edith; 'I never can endure mystery, and there can be none now, for there is no secret.'

'Indeed! I must have been strangely misinformed; but you may trust me entirely. I am aware that family reasons may render secrecy expedient; and I am almost as *au fait* at keeping my countenance as yourself. I promise you not to name the subject again, since you seem so much to dislike it.'

Edith felt extremely provoked; 'I can have no wish in a case of which I am ignorant,' she said; 'if you will do me the favour to mention the report you have heard, I will give you full authority to contradict it.'

'But that is so absurd. I really cannot bring myself to repeat what you ought to have known a week since; my cousin writes me word that the affair has been all but settled for at least that time.'

'What affair?' said Edith; 'you are still speaking enigmas.'

'Oh! this marriage with Miss Howard—the beautiful Miss Howard—whom all the London world have been raving about; I see there is a little consciousness of guilt in you. It is impossible but that your brother must have named his intentions to his own relations.'

'My brother would have named his intentions assuredly, if there had been any to name,' said Edith, with a slight haughtiness of tone. 'I am aware that he is acquainted with Miss Howard, for he frequently mentions being at her father's house, and once or twice he has noticed her style of beauty; but perhaps you will assure your correspondent that this, at present, is the full extent of his intimacy or his interest. It is due both to himself and the lady to contradict the report as soon as possible.'

'Certainly, since you wish it, it shall be done; but I could hardly have supposed the subject an unpleasant one. Nothing apparently could be more natural or desirable.'

Edith did not reply to the remark, but only made a few commonplace observations on the beauty of the weather, and then saying that she should be too late for luncheon, coldly wished Miss Forester good morning. There was now a fresh subject for her meditations, but her thoughts dwelt more upon the civil curiosity evinced during the conversation, than upon the conversation itself. Reports of the kind were so common as to be mere matters of course; and Edith had entirely overcome the

awkward denial, and hesitating tone, with which at first she had
endeavoured to put a stop to them. With the certainty in her
own mind that nothing would induce Edward to marry for
several years, the credulity of her acquaintances was rather
amusing than annoying; and Miss Forester's congratulations
would have been received with total indifference, but for the
manner in which they were offered.

CHAPTER II.

'YOU have been taking advantage of this fine weather, I hope,
sir,' said Miss Forester, when she entered her father's
drawing-room, just before dinner was announced. The observation was addressed to a tall, sallow-complexioned, gray-haired
man, whose prominent forehead and piercing eye betokened
high intellect, as plainly as his compressed lips, and stiff, almost
cold manner, indicated reserve. His age it would have been
difficult to guess. At the first glance, he would have been pronounced old, decidedly on the verge of seventy; but a nearer
observation would have subtracted at least ten years from the
supposition. It was not time alone which had whitened his
hair, and sunk deep furrows in his cheek, but care, and thought,
and the turmoil of life, and the exposure to a sultry climate.
There were no signs of age in the quickness of his eye, the keenness of his remarks, or the deep, full tones of his voice; while
the calmness of his ordinary manner, though by some mistaken
for the insensibility of one to whom long experience has rendered
all things unexciting, was but the result of the habitual check
placed by necessity and principle upon feelings which in youth
had been nearly uncontrollable.

'I have been walking about the village for an hour or two,'
was his reply to Miss Forester's insinuating remark—insinuating,
rather from its tone than its purport.

'I am so rejoiced to hear you say so, for I had great fears that
you might have been too fatigued to venture beyond the garden.
Did you go far?'

The question was not answered, when Miss Forester, with
great *empressement*, turned to a gentleman who had just made
his appearance, and insisted upon his sympathising with her

happiness in finding that Mr Dacre was able to take so much exercise.—'I am sure, papa, you will be as surprised as I am. We shall have no fear now for Mr Dacre's amusement.'

There was a pause, in expectation of a compliment. Mr Dacre drily remarked, that the neighbourhood was very beautiful; but whether it had really afforded him any gratification, it would have been impossible from his tone to decide.

'We shall discuss the beauties of the scenery more at our ease in the dining-room,' said General Forester, a tall, portly man, with a pompous humility of manner, as a servant entered to announce that dinner was on the table. 'No one expects a hungry man to be enthusiastic in anything but the praises of fish and soup, Maria. Not that I can hope, Dacre, you will find anything to admire in that way with us. We are very plain, humble people in our style of living; you must have seen that yesterday.'

Mr Dacre was provokingly silent; even the recollection of the French *entremêts* and *patés*, the curry and mulligatawny on which the whole skill of the General's cook had been expended, excited nothing more than a grave, almost melancholy smile. He was as insensible to the charms of the table as to the loveliness of nature,—at least so thought Miss Forester; and she determined to explore his taste in another direction.

Why there should be so much anxiety upon this subject, might possibly have excited the wonder of the ignorant; but a slight insight into Mr Dacre's history would have solved the problem. Mr Dacre was Miss Forester's uncle by marriage,—a sufficient motive for all ordinary attentions; but he was also in ill health, and nothing could be more natural or right than the endeavour to soothe his feelings, and charm away the sense of suffering. Above all, he was rich, and if other inducements had been of no avail, there was something in the contemplation of wealth which excited Miss Forester's sympathy and interest to the utmost. In the present instance, there was an especial reason for exertion. Mr Dacre was but just returned from India, broken in constitution by the enervating effects of the climate, and broken in spirit by grief for the loss of his wife and two children. In all human probability his own life would not be long spared, and then came the important question, who was to inherit his property.

Mrs Forester had been Mrs Dacre's youngest and favourite sister, and in default of nearer ties, it seemed natural to suppose that her family would be chosen as his heirs. But there were

too many instances on record of the injury done to near connections by the plausible attentions of strangers, and both Miss
Forester and her father were too sensible of the value of the
interests at stake, to allow any unnecessary time to intervene
before taking some steps for securing them. Mr Dacre was
invited to the Grange almost immediately upon his arrival in
England. His reception was cordial and affectionate, even
beyond what circumstances demanded ; and he was pressed to
consider General Forester's house his home, as entirely as he
might have done if his sister-in-law had been still living to
welcome him. All this was very common— so common as to be
rather suspicious ; and although the General's blunted feelings
induced him to believe that nothing more was required to win
Mr Dacre's heart, except perhaps a little attention to his ap-
petite, and a few inquiries after his health, Miss Forester
thought very differently. Her hopes rested upon the daily
evidences of consideration, the actions, and not the words,
which insensibly soften the most obdurate heart ; and which
would, she was convinced, produce in time their full effect upon
Mr Dacre, notwithstanding the alarming fence of cold reserve
with which he seemed to repel them. Miss Forester knew that
her manner was soft, her voice melodious, and she believed that
her conversation was agreeable. From childhood she had believed herself a very fascinating person, and this not merely
from the consideration of her own perfections, but from the
positive assurances of relations and friends. Time had produced no change in her early self-appreciation. It had deadened
the brilliancy of her complexion, and marred the smoothness of
her skin, but its effects were visible in no other way, and, at
five-and-thirty, Miss Forester trusted as much to her powers of
pleasing as she had done at eighteen ; and in some degree
justly. The only mistake lay in thinking that she had ever
really possessed them ; in believing that suavity of manner
could compensate for an uncharitable temper, and that external
refinement could conceal the vulgarity of a low, worldly mind.
Yet it was a delusion worthy of compassion, for it had been
fostered by education and society. The loss of her mother
when she was about twelve years of age had deprived her of the
only friend likely to raise her standard of excellence, and from
that time she had been surrounded by fawning dependants and
relations, who, poor themselves, looked upon wealth and fashion
as the great objects of existence, and who, if they could not

attain the reality, contented themselves with the semblance. She had lived in an atmosphere of pretension, and every thought and feeling had been tainted by it ; and from the time when, as a young girl, she adorned herself with mock jewels, and rejoiced in the success of the deception, to the period of her introduction to Mr Dacre, the same desire had been the ruling motive of her actions,—that of making the greatest possible show in dress, ornaments, opinions, and virtues, with the least possible expenditure of money and trouble. But neither skill nor energy was lacking when the occasion demanded ; and now, carefully and thoughtfully, Miss Forester pursued the conversation, in the hope of gaining that knowledge of Mr Dacre's tastes, without which all her efforts at pleasing must be useless.

'Which way did your rambles lead you to-day, sir ? Hardly, I suppose, to the Roman hill, though there is such a splendid view from the top.'

'No, 1 was too tired to attempt it ; it is rather beyond a sick man's stroll.'

'But you must go there now, whilst the fine weather lasts. We will order the carriage to-morrow, at any hour you choose to name, and then we can drive to the foot of it, and walk up.'

'Thank you. 1 shall be glad to see it again ; I used to find some amusement in tracing out the line of the encampment.'

It was a delightful hint for Miss Forester. Mr Dacre must be an antiquarian ; and immediately, with the most simple, childlike professions of ignorance, she entered eagerly into the subject, asking the names of the most celebrated Roman stations, and begging for a minute description of the different trenches and circumvallations. But again she was foiled. Mr Dacre knew little of the subject, and was only interested in the spot from association. Antiquities, therefore, were dropped.

'I think you will find Allingham Park a pleasant distance when you do not feel equal to a regular walk. In the summer it is delightful to sit under the trees, reading ; and the Courtenays have always been such intimate friends of ours, that we are perfectly at home there, and do just as we like.'

'Mr Courtenay is absent, I think,' said Mr Dacre.

'Yes, in London, but his sister told me to-day that he would return in about a fortnight.

'He is not much of a sportsman, willingly to lose the beginning of September.'

'No,' replied Miss Forester, with a smile, 'it is said that his occupation at this moment is rather more exciting than partridge shooting.'

'Then the report is true, Maria,' said the General. 'I only hope young Courtenay will keep up things in as good a style as the Colonel. He ought to do it, with his income.'

'His sister Edith professes ignorance,' replied Miss Forester, 'but every one knows what the denial of a near relation means.'

'And what does it mean?' asked Mr Dacre, gravely. The tone was rather startling, and there was a pause before the answer.

'Of course, I don't mean to say always, but generally speaking it is;—I know, but I don't choose to tell.'

'Therefore you do not believe Miss Courtenay's words?' said Mr Dacre.

'That is so very severe, my dear sir; I only meant that I put my own interpretation upon them.'

'Oh!' was the only reply; and it was completely baffling to Miss Forester's wishes, for it was an 'Oh' peculiar to Mr Dacre. It expressed neither pleasure nor pain, neither assent nor dissent, neither surprise nor indifference—yet, that it had some hidden meaning, was evident from the frequency with which it was used, and the silence with which it was invariably followed.

'I can scarcely suppose my cousin to have been misinformed,' continued Miss Forester. 'She says that the marriage was told her as a settled thing, by Miss Howard's intimate friend; and I think she mentions next month as the time fixed for the wedding.'

'The wonder is,' said the General, 'that young Courtenay has not married before this. I should have imagined the very first thing he would have thought of, on coming into his fortune, would have been a wife.'

'He is so fastidious,' replied Miss Forester; 'nothing but a first-rate piece of excellence would satisfy him; though how he has made fashion and seriousness agree, in his present choice, it is difficult to understand.'

'What do you mean by seriousness?' asked Mr Dacre, rousing himself from an apparent fit of abstraction.

Miss Forester felt anxious. She had never been in the habit of explaining her words, and yet upon this definition what important consequences might depend? Mr Dacre might be serious himself—nothing, indeed, was more probable, considering that he had arrived at the mature age of sixty, and had lately lost his wife and two children. Her answer, therefore, was most carefully worded.

'I suppose different people mean different things by the same word. My notion of seriousness is when persons stay at home a good deal, and talk about schools and poor people, and say that they like reading sermons. I may be wrong, but that, I believe, is the general idea.'

'Perhaps so. Are Mr Courtenay's relations generally considered serious?'

'His mother is not considered anything, and his two elder sisters are just like every one else; but the youngest is the counterpart of her brother; and there is another, living with an aunt, who they say has the same turn.'

Miss Forester believed that she had so expressed herself as to give no impression of her own feelings; but even a single intonation of voice will betray volumes to a practised ear. Mr Dacre needed no further explanation of his niece's sentiments on the subject of seriousness.

'It is a great change for so young a man,' said the General. 'Six thousand a year is a magnificent fortune for a briefless barrister.'

'Not briefless, papa,' observed Miss Forester. 'Every one said that he was succeeding astonishingly well.'

'So they did; but what is a barrister's succeeding? merely the difference between a crust of bread and starvation—at least for the first half dozen years. Edward Courtenay is the most fortunate man I know.'

'What did you say his fortune was?' asked Mr Dacre, with a greater appearance of interest than he had hitherto shown.

'Six thousand a year, decidedly; it may be more.'

Mr Dacre looked a little astonished; but the expression was only momentary. If he had any reason for doubting General Forester's assurances, he concealed it under his safe mono-syllable—'oh!'

'I should have gained more information as to the wedding,' said Miss Forester, 'if I had met either of the other sisters. Jane tells everything from not knowing how to keep it, and Charlotte from not thinking it worth while; but Edith is impenetrable.'

'A valuable quality in a woman,' observed Mr Dacre.

'Yes, certainly, most valuable. No one esteems it more than

myself; but there is a manner,—some people have a much more agreeable way of being silent than others; and they say,—however, one must not speak ill of one's neighbours—but I shall not envy Edith Courtenay's husband.'

'What relation was Colonel Courtenay to the present Mr Courtenay?' asked Mr Dacre, seemingly unmindful of Miss Forester's remarks.

'Rather a distant cousin,' replied the General; 'but the elder branch of the family has dwindled to nothing of late years. Colonel Courtenay certainly was a splendid man—kept the first table in the county—he married a daughter of Sir Henry Vivian's—I think you must remember her—a poor, weak, sickly creature, who died a few years afterwards. They had some girls who never lived long; but the little boy appeared quite strong till he fell from his pony, and injured himself, and so brought out all his lurking maladies.'

'Was Colonel Courtenay a prudent man?' inquired Mr Dacre.

'As prudent, I suppose, as he had any occasion to be. I believe he gambled a little, as a young man, but I never heard of his doing it latterly. There was only this one child to be careful for, or I dare say he might have lived differently.'

'You forget the elections, papa,' said Miss Forester; 'he spent enormous sums in them.'

'You can scarcely call that extravagance; he only did what his ancestors had done for years and years before him. The Courtenays of Allingham always represented the county, and so will Edward, of course.'

'But,' observed Miss Forester, 'Mr Vivian will not give up his seat; and I should think Mr Courtenay would hardly choose to oppose a family connection.'

'Why not? one is a Whig and the other a Tory. Depend upon it, Vivian would have no chance if Edward Courtenay were to come forward. The seat has always gone with the property, and half the people who voted for Vivian only did it because they disliked Lord Montford. Vivian is not a popular man, and never will be.'

'But have you not often heard Mr Courtenay rave against the excitement and wickedness of a contested election?' inquired Miss Forester.

Mr Dacre again looked interested. 'Do you think so young a man could withstand the temptation of a seat in Parliament?' he asked.

'No,' replied the General; 'neither he nor any one else in his position; and why should he?'

'Certainly,' observed Miss Forester, with a soft smile, under which lurked an expression of a very different nature, 'it is a delightful thing for high-principled people, when duty and inclination go together. I suppose it might be possible to persuade Mr Courtenay to stand for the county as a matter of duty. I have heard him discourse most eloquently on the responsibilities of a legislator.'

'Yes,' replied Mr Dacre, more earnestly than usual, 'the duties are most important.'

'You would feel them to be so if you were in my place,' said the General. 'The first thing I shall urge upon Edward Courtenay, when he is in Parliament, will be the reduction of taxation. If something is not done, we shall all be ruined.'

'Your words will have very little effect, I am afraid, sir,' answered Miss Forester. 'Mr Courtenay's favourite hobby is the improvement of the manufacturing districts; he harangues upon it as if he were making a speech upon the hustings, and everything else is secondary in his eyes.'

'That was all very well when he was living upon bread and cheese in his chambers in London. Taxation was nothing to him then; he had nothing to be taxed for; but he will feel now that philanthropy is rather an expensive amusement.'

'For a person with six thousand a year?' said Mr Dacre, in a tone of quiet irony.

Miss Forester saw instantly that her father was upon dangerous ground. Commonplace as the conversation had been, it had yet given her some idea of her uncle's principles; and she perceived that the utmost tact would be required to prevent a collision between him and her father. Not that General Forester's sentiments were such as would shock the world in general; on the contrary, he was what would be called a sensible, good-hearted man; rather fond of eating and drinking, yet not so as to be positively ungentlemanly; rather selfish, but not more so than his neighbours; rather careless in his way of speaking of religion, yet very constant at church, and as benevolent as he said he could afford to be. If his standard of virtue were a low one, it was his own concern; and, at any rate, he had the credit of acting up to it; and, if not very strict in his life, he had the charity to be lenient to the faults of others. Perhaps the leading feature of his character was a paltry ambition—the desire of bringing himself into notice as a politician, though his fortune would not admit of his attempting anything beyond the being chairman at an election committee. It was his object, but one which he had never yet attained; and his positive assertion that Edward Courtenay would ultimately be in Parliament, might arise from the hope that, under such circumstances, he should, from his long acquaintance with him, become his adviser, and a very influential person. What Mr Dacre's opinions were could not as yet be decided, but Miss Forester felt that they were not such as she was accustomed to; and during the remainder of dinner she carefully checked every allusion to subjects of more than surface interest, reserving any further attempts at discovering Mr Dacre's character, to the more favourable opportunity of a *tête-à-tête.*

CHAPTER III.

MISS FORESTER'S gossip was repeated by Edith to her mother and sisters without exciting any greater surprise in their minds than it had done in hers. It was amusing, but nothing more. Yet, so strange is the power of a positive assertion, even when we have the strongest evidence for its contradiction, that Edith could not restrain a certain impatient curiosity when the letter bag was placed on the table the following morning; and the search after the mislaid key, with the difficulties of the patent lock, had seldom before been so provoking.

'It is Edward's handwriting!' she exclaimed, as her quick eye caught part of the direction of a letter, nearly concealed by a newspaper. 'Mamma, it is for you—do open it.'

'Edith believes Miss Forester's nonsense, I am sure,' said Charlotte.

'That would be too absurd,' replied Edith. 'I am not more eager than usual.

'Conscience doth make cowards of us all,' said Charlotte. 'I never said you were eager; but you know you were. Here is another letter from Gertrude; will not that excite your interest too?'

Edith, without answering, began looking for her mother's spectacles.

'They are in my room, dear,' said Mrs Courtenay, 'in the

lower tray of the inner drawer of my bureau—the oak bureau, I mean. Don't you disarrange my things, though.'

But Mrs Courtenay's injunctions were disregarded. Even the power of the Fairy Order herself could not have withstood the rapidity of Edith's movements, and in less than a minute she returned ; the spectacles were properly adjusted, and the seal was slowly broken. Edith watched her mother's countenance as she read, and saw directly that the contents of the letter were unusual.

' Let me have it, dear mamma,' she exclaimed. ' You never can decipher Edward's writing.'

' No, my dear, no,' replied Mrs Courtenay ; ' it is impossible. But it can't be true—he is only joking.'

' What can't be true, mamma ? Do tell us ; we really are anxious.'

' He writes so very badly,' said Mrs Courtenay. ' H—no ; it is not an H ; it must be a C. C-o-w—Coward.'

' Dear, dear mamma,' said Edith, her impatience becoming every instant more painful, ' if you would only let me have it——'

' Stop, my dear, I shall tell it in a moment ; but he ought not to have left school when he did ; I told his poor father so. Coward—it is Coward ! Miss Coward, of Oakhampton Court.'

' Howard !' exclaimed Edith, who saw directly the confirmation of Miss Forester's intelligence.

' So it is,' replied Mrs Courtenay. ' Edward is going to be married to Miss Howard. Edith, you must read it all over to me again, for I cannot quite make out what he means.'

Edith eagerly seized the letter, but her voice trembled as she began, and she was obliged to yield the task to Charlotte, who, not sharing her sister's anxiety, read with perfect composure.

' My dearest Mother,

' You must, I am sure, have been expecting to hear from me for some time ; for I have allowed my usual writing day to pass without giving you any information as to my movements. The fact is, that my mind has been so occupied with a subject of engrossing interest, that I could not turn to ordinary matters, and yet I was unwilling to mention my hopes, until I could tell you that they were likely to be realised. After this preamble, I trust it will not be a matter of astonishment to you to learn, that I have, after very serious consideration, made an offer of my hand to Miss Howard, the daughter of Mr Howard, of Oakhampton Court, in Warwickshire—a gentleman of considerable fortune, and highly connected, with whom I have lately become very intimately acquainted at Hastings. I need scarcely express to you the great happiness I experienced on receiving this morning a letter containing the acceptance of my proposals; and my only desire now is, to obtain your sanction to a step which promises so much for my future life. It would be absurd in me to attempt a description of one in whom I feel such a deep interest, but I am sure you will believe that my choice has been the result of a very close observation of character, and a firm persuasion that with no other person whom I have yet seen should I have an equal chance of happiness. Situated as I am, it was almost necessary that I should marry; and I look forward to the friendship of my sisters and my dear Laura as a source of infinite comfort to us all. It was indeed of my own family that I principally thought when first I decided upon this important step; for with your ill health it will be far better for my sisters to depend upon a sister-in-law to take them into society, than to be indebted, as they otherwise must be, to strangers; and Allingham will be a much greater source of enjoyment to them now, than it could have been when inhabited only by a bachelor brother. I shall expect your answer with the greatest anxiety, though I have not really any doubt of your approbation. Perhaps it will please you to know that Miss Howard is idolised in her own family, and considered the belle of the season. The first, however, is the only thing which is really of consequence. I do not write to my sisters to-day, knowing that they will hear everything from you, but I shall depend upon Edith's services as bridesmaid, and either Jane or Charlotte besides. Laura will be anxious to become acquainted with you all as soon as possible, and when our arrangements are made, my sisters can spend a few days with me in London, and then proceed to Oakhampton.

'The postman's bell is ringing; I have only time to add my best love to my sisters and yourself, and my earnest entreaties that you will write by return of post.—Ever, my dearest mother, most affectionately yours,   'EDWARD COURTENAY.'

'*P.S.*—Laura attained her eighteenth year the day before yesterday; so that she will be a most suitable companion for dear Edith. You will not expect any increase of wealth to the family, when I tell you that Mr Howard has seven children to provide for, and six of them sons; but happily this is a matter of no consequence to any of us. I must decide, when my sisters come, about new furnishing the drawing-room at Allingham, and perhaps the library.'

There was a moment's pause after Charlotte had finished, which she was the first to break.

'Miss Forester was right then. How she will glory in having heard the news before us!'

'It is very sudden,' said Jane. 'Love at first sight, I suppose.'

'No,' replied Charlotte; 'it was a subject of very serious consideration, decided on principally from regard to his family. I do like to see people deceiving themselves, especially, when they do it as perfectly as Edward. What do you say, Edith?'

But Edith had left the room, and was spared the renewal of the preceding day's observations.

'I do highly estimate disinterested fraternal affection,' said Charlotte, 'it is so rare. Most brothers marry to please themselves; every brother, in fact, that I ever heard of before has done it—but Edward is a solitary, glorious instance of self-sacrifice.'

'You are not sorry that he is going to be married, my dear, are you?' said Mrs Courtenay.

'Oh no, ma'am, very glad. I shall like having a sister-in-law extremely; as Edward says, it will be very convenient. And I am so pleased she is beautiful. Next to being lovely one's self, the best thing I can imagine is having a lovely relation.'

'It looks very smooth and pleasant,' said Jane; 'but if Shakespeare is true it cannot last.'

'I do not see why it should not,' observed Mrs Courtenay. 'Edward seems quite satisfied himself, and you must own, my dears, that he writes very kindly about you.'

'Very,' repeated Charlotte, emphatically. 'Marcus Curtius was nothing to him. He had the benefit of his country as a motive for his self-devotion, but Edward is going to leap into the far more dangerous gulf of matrimony, merely to give his sisters the benefit of a chaperone.'

'You are rather hard upon him, Charlotte,' said Jane.

'Not hard upon his actions, only upon his words. He is perfectly right to marry, and Miss Howard may be as likely to make him happy as any one else; but why does he not say at once that he wishes to please himself, instead of making a foolish parade of consideration for us?'

'My dear Charlotte,' observed her mother, 'you are not kind to Edward. He never says what he does not mean.'

'Indeed, mamma, that is the one thing which I am always quarrelling with him for. He does say what he does not mean; that is, he puts things in such a plausible way, that he is as much deluded as the rest of the world.'

'Exclusive of his sister Charlotte,' said Jane.

'Yes, exclusive of his sister Charlotte. I am convinced that I know him better than he knows himself. I can tell exactly what passed through his mind to induce him to write such a letter as that. First of all, he was desperately in love, and resolved upon making his offer; but, at the same time, a little anxious as to what we should say; and then—"his wish being father to his thought"—it struck him what a delightful thing it would be for us to go everywhere with Mrs Courtenay, instead of being indebted to the chance kindnesses of friends; and what pleasant parties and amusements we might have at Allingham, instead of the dull, family meetings that have been held there lately; and so, in about five minutes, these everyday advantages were magnified into first-rate blessings, and Edward made his offer, and gained his object, and piqued himself upon being the most affectionate brother in the world.'

'And he is so, my dear,' said Mrs Courtenay; 'no one in the neighbourhood is like him.'

'I quite agree with you, mamma,' replied Charlotte; 'and that makes it the more provoking. If he had not a great many real excellences, one would be less angry at his mock ones.'

'I don't see why you should be certain they are mock ones in this instance,' observed Jane.

'Simply for this reason. If he really thought so much of us, why did he not write to consult us? Surely we were the best judges as to whether our happiness depended upon having society at Allingham, and a sister-in-law for a chaperone. Just ask yourself, Jane,—do you think that Edward's determination would have been for an instant shaken by finding that we disliked his marriage?'

'No,' replied Jane; 'but it would not be natural to expect it.'

'Certainly not; but according to his own showing it ought to have been. He says that he thought of us principally, and yet he acted precisely in the way to prevent our wishes from being of any avail.'

Jane smiled. 'I suppose half the world would have done the same.'

'No, one-half would not have considered their own families at all ; and the other half would have been desirous of their approbation, yet determined upon going their own way in spite of them. There are not many who have Edward's happy knack of making duty and inclination go hand in hand.'

'There was no great duty at stake, in this case,' said Jane.

'Perhaps not, according to the usual opinion ; but Edward piques himself upon being a pattern son, scorning the ordinary modes of action ; so it might have been imagined that he would have consulted his mother before he made his offer.'

'Which of you will be bridesmaid?' inquired Mrs Courtenay.

'You must, Charlotte,' said Jane. 'The bustle and fatigue would half kill me.'

'I have not the slightest objection ; in fact, I shall like it very much. It will enable me to judge what sort of a choice Edward has made, by seeing Miss Howard in her own family ; besides, there is something awful to me in a host of unknown connections, who may prove a disgrace to you at any moment. I like to know the full extent of a matrimonial calamity at once.'

'It is no calamity, my dear, that I can understand,' said Mrs Courtenay ; 'I was very happy for a great many years, and so was my mother, and I hope dear Edward will be the same.'

'No one can join in the hope more cordially than I do,' replied Charlotte ; 'but, to make the best of it, it is a sort of kill-or-cure business ; however, that is not my affair ; as far as I am personally concerned, I am rejoiced at it, and I shall go and take a solitary walk in the back shrubbery, for the purpose of settling what my bridesmaid's dress is to be.'

'You had better consult Edith,' said Jane, 'for you must be dressed alike.'

'Oh no ! I am the eldest, and even if I were not, Edith would be entirely at a loss to decide. I would consult her upon the pattern of cotton frocks for the school children, but nothing beyond.'

'Give me my desk before you go, Charlotte,' said her mother. 'I must write to dear Edward directly.'

'We have forgotten Gertrude,' observed Jane. 'You had

better take her letter to Edith as you go up stairs ; I dare say there is nothing very important in it.'

Edith's door was bolted, and when it was opened, Charlotte's careless good humour was startled at seeing traces of agitation in her sister's face. Edith did not, however, say anything, but took the letter, and then, turning away, again fastened her door. Charlotte, in surprise, waited for a few minutes in the passage, irresolute as to whether it would be advisable to request admittance ; but there was so little sympathy between them, that it would have been felt almost as an intrusion ; and certain that Edith had some whimsical fancy with regard to her brother's marriage, Charlotte consulted her own wishes, and went into the shrubbery. It would indeed have been impossible for her to have entered into the feelings with which Edith had received the intelligence in Edward's letter ; not that she had ever supposed he would not marry eventually—on the contrary, they had often conversed upon the subject together, and built pleasant castles in the air as to the manner of life to be pursued at Allingham, and the friendship that was to subsist between Edith and her brother's wife ; and in the uncertainty of Gertrude's return to her home, Edith had looked forward to the affection of a sister-in-law, as to something that was to compensate for the want of congeniality which was now so painful to her. But the idea of a sudden marriage with a fashionable London belle, effectually destroyed these bright visions ; and, joined with other portions of her brother's letter, brought with it that most bitter of all feelings,— the first perception of a secret fault in one whom we have been accustomed to revere. Edward was not only Edith's dearest treasure, but he was also her guide and counsellor. His enthusiasm and high principles had given the original impulse of good to her mind, and his letters and conversation had daily strengthened it. Unknown to herself, she had believed him perfect ; and now, a secret misgiving, felt long before it was acknowledged, suggested the possibility that he might have been in error. It was in vain that she owned the folly of attempting to judge before the circumstances were fully known. In vain that she accused herself of unkindness, and even selfishness, in trembling at the thought of anything that was to make him happy. One thing was certain : Edward's plans of economy, and with them his plans of benevolence, must for the present fall to the ground. Even with the best intentions, considerable expense must be incurred ; and though Edith could not believe that his resolutions were forgotten, it was strange to find how soon they could be set aside. Love might excuse a great deal ; it might induce him to see excellences where none existed, and blind him to the probability of disappointment in a hasty marriage ; but it could not completely obliterate the recollection, that without constant economy he might soon be a ruined man : and the idea of the newly-furnished drawing-room, and the long upholsterer's bills, fixed itself in poor Edith's mind as firmly as that of having a fashionable sister-in-law. Unhappily, the effect produced by solitude and reflection was one not likely to conduce either to her own happiness or that of her family. This evil was but increased by consideration, and Edith's principles were as yet so new, and her feelings so warm, that she was not aware of the error which lay at the bottom of her determination to decline the office of bridesmaid ; and if her sister-in-law proved, as she expected, a mere elegant, accomplished beauty, to content herself with her usual pursuits, and to depend upon Allingham as little as possible, either for comfort or pleasure. It was the resolve of a moment of pique and disappointment, made without the serious thought which should accompany most actions of our lives, and in ignorance that the first duty of a woman is to be found in the quiet, soothing influence, exerted within her narrow circle upon her own immediate relations. She believed her sister-in-law to be a person with whose principles she could have no sympathy, and did not remember that this should be an especial reason for striving to win her affection, and lead her in the right way ; and, feeling pained at her brother's conduct, instead of patiently submitting to events, over which, since the engagement was already formed, there could be now no control, she ran the risk of vexing, perhaps offending him, in order to avoid what she considered the insincerity of sanctioning an act that her conscience could not entirely approve. The tone of Gertrude's letter somewhat softened her feelings. It was so gentle, so thoughtful, so full of consideration for every one at Elsham, that involuntarily Edith paused, and asked herself whether her sister's sentiments would resemble her own under similar circumstances,—whether she would not be likely to feel more calmly, and bear more patiently, the thought of Edward's weakness. But Gertrude could not be an example for her ; she had never given her whole affection to her brother, and trusted and reverenced him as a superior being ; and she had never looked forward to his marriage as a source of comfort amidst daily annoyances. To see an error in his conduct might be painful to her, but it could never be as trying as it was to Edith ; and the character of his wife could be but of little consequence to one who had learned to depend so entirely upon herself. With a secret doubt as to the propriety of her determination, Edith put her sister's letter aside, and went to her mother to beg that she would inform Edward that it would not be in her power to comply with his request. Mrs Courtenay wondered, and inquired, and even began to urge the subject, but Edith was firm. She had little respect for her mother's judgment, and had been permitted so long to follow her own path, that the obligation of attending to a parent's wishes did not very forcibly strike her ; while the arguments she brought forward to support her decision strengthened her conviction that she was acting rightly, and soon overcame Mrs Courtenay's remonstrances. The point was at length yielded with the usual phrase,—'Well, my dear, I do not understand these things ; people were very different when I was young ; but you must do as you choose.'

CHAPTER IV.

EDITH'S determination was received by her sisters with surprise, but without any wish to combat it. Jane professed it a matter of indifference what others did, as long as they did not interfere with her own comfort ; and Charlotte, whose fundamental principle was, that every one was the best judge of their own actions, after expressing it as her opinion that Edith was whimsical, and that Edward would be annoyed, considered the affair settled, and easily made up her mind to go to Oakhampton alone. Edith, however, was not so indifferent. Outwardly, indeed, she was tranquil and cheerful, but her brother's next letter was looked for with anxiety, and even her disappointment as to his strength of character could not render her happy in the prospect of displeasing him. But the deed was not to be recalled ; she had refused to be bridesmaid, and Miss Howard would naturally make choice of some personal friend to fill her place. It was in vain to repent of acting hastily, or to doubt whether her motives had been justifiable. Edward's anger, if excited, must be borne patiently, and she could only hope that he would trust to her affection, and not inquire too minutely

into the circumstances which rendered it so impossible for her
to leave home at that time; yet, even with this, Edith was not
contented. It was not clear that she had been wrong; but it
was not certain that she had been right. She distrusted her
motives; and, as usual in such cases, Edward's letter was to
decide the question; for Edith was young, and inexperienced in
self-knowledge. Her most glaring faults had been seen and
corrected; but the real difficulty of a Christian life—the struggle
against secret sins—was just commencing. She was not yet
aware of the slight self-complacency, and absence of the
'charity which thinketh no evil,' that had induced her to form a
hasty judgment of her intended sister-in-law; and she left the
goodness of her decision to be determined by its consequences,
rather than by an inquiry into her own intentions. Edward's
letter, when it arrived, kept her still in a state of doubt. He
expressed himself much hurt at her refusal; and hinted that all
other engagements should have given way to one so urgent.
But he did not press his wishes. His mind was pre-occupied,
and his heart full of his anticipated happiness; and two sides
of his paper were filled with plans for alterations at Allingham,
and descriptions of the style in which he intended to furnish,
not only the drawing-room and library, but a great part of the
house. Edith's pride was wounded. His indifference was more
galling than any irritation; and her aversion to her new sister-
in-law increased. She believed that her vexation arose principally from being disappointed in Edward. Six months before
his plans had been of lavish profusion in works of charity, and
the most rigid self-denial in personal expenditure. If he ever
married, his wife was to possess similar tastes: and yet, in one
week, 'the baseless fabric' of his visions had vanished. Ornamental lodges had taken the place of alms-houses; painted glass
was superseded by French windows; altar cloths and pulpit
hangings had yielded to the superior charms of silk curtains and
rich carpets. The alteration could not be in Edward himself—
it was impossible that a taste for luxury should have sprung up
in so short a time; but Miss Howard's influence must naturally
be great; and, no doubt, it was to please her that Edward now
gave such an exclusive attention to things which once he had
considered of little value. So Edith argued—and so she would
willingly have blinded herself to the fact of her brother's weakness. But in this she did him more than justice. In his barrister's chambers, Edward Courtenay sat in his easy chair, and

surrounded himself by the supposed necessaries of life, and built in imagination the most perfect church that had been erected for centuries. In his drawing-room at Allingham he reposed upon a sofa, and amused himself with books and pictures, and his church grew more splendid, and his charities more extensive. And now, he gave orders which would have accorded with a fortune double his own ; and the next minute, pictured the delight he should experience in having some one to share his plans for the comfort of his tenants, and assist in distributing his benevolence. The change over which Edith grieved was a change of circumstances, not of heart.

A polite note from Mrs Howard, containing a general invitation to Oakhampton, made Edith think for a few minutes of retracting her refusal ; but a letter from Edward, at the same time, told her that Miss Howard had already thought upon a friend whom she wished to supply her place. The wedding was fixed for an early day, and it would not do to propose any alterations, though Edith began to see that her feelings throughout the whole affair had not been entirely unblamable, and now that the immediate annoyance was over, she would willingly have been the first to conciliate. But the time was gone by ; Edward engaged to meet his sister Charlotte in London, and Edith bade her good-bye with a heavy heart, and almost the conviction that her proper place would have been by her side.

The interest of so very important an event raised the spirits of both Mrs Courtenay and Jane, and their many maladies were occasionally forgotten in the eagerness with which Charlotte's account of Oakhampton and its inhabitants was expected. But Edith felt that little comfort was likely to be derived from anything that her sister might relate. She might give vivid descriptions of Miss Howard's personal appearance, and of the general style of the family ; but where such a difference of opinion existed on the most important points, there could be no great dependence on the judgment ; and Edith trusted as little to Charlotte's estimation of character, as Charlotte did to Edith's taste in dress. Her only consolation was found in writing to Gertrude ; yet even this was far from satisfactory, while one of the chief causes of uneasiness was obliged to be withheld. It seemed absurd to grieve so much over Edward's marriage when unacquainted with his wife ; and the necessity for economy, of which Edith thought so much, was a fact unknown to all but herself.

The congratulations of the neighbourhood were soon added to

the list of annoyances, and Edith scarcely knew which was the most painful, Miss Forester's soft flattery of her brother's perfections, and ironical praises of the self-command shown by herself on a former occasion; or Mrs Grantley's earnest declaration, that 'Mr Courtenay possessed her highest esteem, and she only trusted he had found a wife worthy of him.' Praise of Edward was very different from what it had been. Once it would have found a ready echo in her own opinion, but now a feeling of distrust checked her satisfaction; and her manner became so evidently constrained whenever he was mentioned, that even the most unobservant could not fail to notice it; and the gossiping morning visitors shook their heads, and looked grave, as they hoped 'Mr Courtenay's marriage was approved at the Priory, but they had their doubts.' But the view of Allingham was that which caused Edith the greatest pain. The road through the Park could be seen from the Priory drawing-room, and she seldom stood at the window without observing some of the workmen employed in the alterations, for which Edward had already given full directions, passing backwards and forwards; or, if she failed to notice them herself, her mother was sure to call her attention to them, or Jane to remark— 'What a happy thing it was that Edward was rich, for really his ideas were so magnificent, that a man with a smaller income would soon be ruined.' Of what was doing Edith had not a very clear idea. Her mother and sister often drove to the house to note the progress of the work, but she resolutely kept from inquiries on their return, as tending to fix in her mind the thoughts she was most anxious to banish; and enough was heard in the ordinary course of conversation, of boudoirs, and ante-rooms, cornices, moulding, damask, silk, rosewood, and mahogany, and the other *et ceteras* of an upholsterer's shop, to convince her that for once Edward's dreams were about to be converted into substantial realities. From Charlotte's first letter, on her arrival in town, they found that the idea of mutual consultation as to the style of furniture had quickly passed by. Edward's impatience was too great to brook delay; and Charlotte rejoiced that she had been spared the thankless task of endeavouring to decide for a man bent upon following his own way: and said she had little doubt, from the description of what had been chosen, that Allingham would be more handsomely fitted up than any place of its size within the distance of a hundred miles.

The words sent a pang through Edith's heart, and she became more and more depressed; and feeling a difficulty in writing without restraint, she allowed the burden of the correspondence to rest with her mother and Jane; and only twice contrived to fill a sheet of paper with the commonplace hopes and fears, which might prevent Edward from thinking himself entirely forgotten. Even this was only cursorily noticed in some of his short notes. Edward's heart was engrossed; and Edith, though piqued at his neglect, was thankful to be freed from the task so easily.

Happily for her equanimity, there was at the time much employment for her in the village, and she was prevented from dwelling entirely upon one subject. Yet the visits to the cottages were often very trying. The people were so desirous of knowing all particulars; so certain that Miss Edith must be happy; so pleased at the prospect of a lady at the Hall; and above all, so curious about the grand alterations, that Edith's composure was sometimes nearly overcome. Edward's old nurse, in particular, assailed her with questions; and being ill and infirm, had a great claim upon her attention. Once a week Edith had lately been in the habit of seeing her; and it seemed unkind to make any change at a moment when there was much passing that was interesting; although the old woman's querulous disposition, and apparently unwilling gratitude, made it occasionally doubtful whether the visits were really valued.

'I thought you was never a coming again,' was the salutation, as Edith entered her cottage, after a fatiguing walk, which she had voluntarily lengthened to avoid passing through the Park; 'I sat all day yesterday expecting you, but nobody came near me.'

'I was too busy, nurse,' said Edith; 'don't you remember I told you there was a great deal to do just now, and that I could not be sure of my own time?'

'Well! I suppose there must be a good deal. Fine works there are up there at the house. It's quite right great people's business should be attended to first.'

'But indeed, Martha, I have nothing to do with the house; I never go near it.'

'Now don't you tell me that, Miss Edith. Why, all the neighbours go; my son was down here last night, talking about it. Poor Willie! he's got a hard lot of it—a sick wife and seven children. If so be as he'd gone with the rest, he'd have had less trouble.'

Martha's voice sank into a low whine, and bending over the fire, she diligently stirred the smouldering embers; and in a half crying, half muttering tone, continued her lamentations.

'Poor Charlie and Beckie! I grieved for 'em at the time; and sure, if they'd lived, things wouldn't have been like they are; and I'm so old, and so ill, and nobody comes to an old woman. But dear! Miss Edith,' and in an instant her sorrows were forgotten: 'did you see the cart go by? There's some things for the Park in it, I'll be bound. Just sit down, and tell me what they're doing.'

'I told you all I knew the other day, nurse,' replied Edith. 'Really, I have not been there since.'

'That's so contrary of you; you never was contrary before. Willie said there was a power of money spending, and he made me look across to see where my lady's new room is to be; that's the room that the Colonel's lady had: I watched Tom Slater at work there this morning. Poor Tom! he was to have married my Becky, only there—she died.'

'I am afraid he is not very steady,' observed Edith, wishing to change the conversation.

'Oh! as to that, he's just like all the others; but he's doing very fair now. I wish Willie was half as well off. The bailiff turned off in a huff when he asked for something to do.'

'My brother will assist him if he can, I am sure,' said Edith, 'when he returns.'

'Yes, I dare say he will; though Willie's been out of work a precious long time,—but I don't complain. It's not my way to find fault,—if it was I should be better off.'

Edith's patience was almost exhausted; but as she looked at the old woman's shrivelled features and bent figure, and remembered how much she had really suffered, and the warmth of heart that was concealed under so repulsive a manner, her sympathy was again excited.

'I don't think that is quite the case, Martha,' she said; 'at least I am sure, if you mean that my brother does not think of you, you are very much mistaken.'

'May be,' replied Martha, bending again over the fire, and then remaining silent.

'Come, nurse,' said Edith, 'I did not think you would be vexed with me to-day. I really put myself out of my way for you. I was very busy at home.'

'You gets busier and busier every day,' answered the old

woman. 'I suppose when the new lady comes to the Park you'll be so busy that you'll never come near me.'

Edith rose hastily from her seat, and was preparing to go, when Martha's heart softened.

'There, don't you be angry now, Miss Edith, I meant no offence. Sit down again, and just tell me a little about things. When is the wedding to be?'

'The day is not fixed,' said Edith, reseating herself on a wooden stool by Martha's side; 'but I think it will be early in the week after next.'

'And you not to go to it! really it's a shame! so fond as you were of Mr Edward. Why didn't you say you would go?'

'Because I had rather not, nurse; I shall see Edward very soon here—he is to be at Allingham in about a month after his marriage.'

'That's not like you,' said Martha, raising her keen eyes to Edith's face. 'I dare to say, now, you'd have been just as well content if he wasn't going to have such a fine new wife.'

'I shall be most contented with whatever makes him most happy,' said Edith, involuntarily sighing; and then she added, more gaily, 'It will be a nice thing for you, nurse, to have a lady so near you. It is rather a long walk for me from the Priory, but if I lived at Allingham, I should be able to see you nearly every day.'

'Tom Slater says he doesn't think I shall stay here much longer,' said Martha; 'but I told him I knew better than that— Mr Edward promised I never should move again—so I don't take what the neighbours say much to heart.'

'I don't understand you,' replied Edith; 'does he think you're ill?'

'No, no, not that. Thank God! I am as strong and hearty as any of them; but the sight from my lady's new window is not so good as it would be if the cottage was away; and the chat-tering fellow declares Mr Edward will have it pulled down.'

'There is no occasion to be afraid of that: Edward would rather have the finest view in the world spoilt, than turn you out of your home. But let me see how it comes in the way.' Edith walked to the door, and saw directly that the remarkably ugly, red brick tenement stood opposite to the front of Allingham; but how much of the view was intercepted by it she could not determine.

If any one but Martha had inhabited the obnoxious dwelling,

there was no doubt it would have been speedily removed; but
Edward's attachment to his nurse was very sincere, and he had
so often promised that she should remain in the cottage as long
as he was the owner of it, that Edith agreed with Martha in
considering any change impossible.

'Tom Slater says there 's no guessing how bad it looks from
the new room,' said Martha; 'but how should he know? He
can't tell pretty from ugly if he sees it in a book.'

'It does come just in the way of the new window,' said Edith;
and she thought of her sister-in-law, and wondered whether she
would be able to endure such a blot upon the prospect.

'But there 's no doubt about Mr Edward's promise, is there,
now?' asked Martha, anxiously. 'He told me I should stay
here—three times he said it; the very first day I came in, that
was when my poor husband was so ill, and they turned us out
of the cottage on the heath, because of the rent. I could never
go to a new place in this world; if he sends me away it will be
to another.'

'Don't worry yourself about it,' said Edith, kindly. 'It is
only the workmen's fancy. Edward is so good, you need not be
afraid.'

Martha was rather deaf, and not much alive to variations of
tone, or she would have noticed the slight hesitation with which
this was spoken. Not that Edward's kindness of heart was
really doubted, but it was no longer so implicitly confided in;
and without exactly reasoning upon her motives, Edith decided
upon returning home through the Park, in order to judge for
herself whether Martha Philips' cottage was as great a delight
as it had been described.

CHAPTER V.

THREE weeks had elapsed since Edith last visited Allingham, and in that time the improvements had made considerable progress: but the good taste displayed in everything
that Edward undertook, brought no charm to his sister's mind;
for as she gazed upon the elegance and beauty which surrounded
her, something in her own heart whispered that Edward's fabric
of happiness was insecure. It was based upon self-gratification,

not upon self-denial. A short time was sufficient to satisfy her curiosity, and to show that the offending cottage was conspicuously ugly; and after wandering over the empty rooms, and asking a few questions of the workmen, Edith sadly pursued her way homewards. The autumnal tints were just beginning to colour the foliage of the trees, adding a richer hue to the broad masses of light and shade, so peculiarly beautiful in park and forest scenery; and even Edith's melancholy reflections were beguiled, as she paused on the summit of a slight ascent, and looked back upon her brother's home. The long, regular range of buildings, the portico and colonnade, the straight walks, and the formal parterres of the Italian garden, contrasted indeed curiously with the wildness of the luxuriant oaks and beeches, and the winding glades of the Park; but, in the mellowed light of the afternoon sun, every object seemed harmonised in form as well as in colour, and the only impression made upon the mind was that of an abode of peace, wealth, and freedom from earthly anxieties. Edith leant against the trunk of a magnificent beech tree, near which she had often rested with her brother to enjoy the same view; and while recalling his tones of kindness, and his warm feelings, and noble projects, reproached herself for having ever imagined the possibility of a change. That one spot brought him more vividly before her than almost any other, for it was there they had last parted; and she well remembered the delight visible in his countenance, as he pointed to the hamlet where he hoped one day to erect a church, and calculated the smallness of the sum to which he might reduce his personal expenditure, in order to obtain the necessary means; expressing, at the same time, the deepest gratitude for having been trained in habits of prudence before he had been entrusted with wealth. For the time, Edith's feelings of confidence in her brother returned, and with it the dreams which had been a constant source of enjoyment to them both. Her eye rested happily upon the distant cottages, and her imagination pictured the spire of Edward's church appearing amongst the trees, and adding to the beauty of the scenery those associations of purity and holiness, without which the loveliness of nature can afford no perfect enjoyment. A slight rustling among the leaves disturbed her reverie, and turning suddenly round, she perceived a gentleman, whom at first sight she believed to be unknown to her; but as he came nearer, she recognised the stranger who had lately been seen at church in General Forester's pew; and about whom so m.nch curiosity had been excited, as almost to rival the interest of her brother's marriage. Edith had never been introduced to Mr Dacre, but they had met so frequently as scarcely to require the ceremony ; and she felt little surprise when he advanced towards her, and apologised for intruding upon her brother's property, saying that permission had been given him by Mr Courtenay's friend, General Forester, to wander over the Park ; and he trusted he had not presumed too far in approaching so near the house. His excuse must be the wish again to see a place which he remembered when a boy. Edith was, of couse, pleased that the Park should afford Mr Dacre any gratification ; and was certain it would be her brother's wish that it should be open to him at all times.

'For the next month,' she added, 'you will be likely to retain undisturbed possession. We do not expect my brother home yet.'

'I suppose, though,' observed Mr Dacre, 'it is a favourite walk of yours ?'

'Yes,' replied Edith, 'I never come here without admiring it : but there are so many things to be done every day, that I seldom walk merely for pleasure.'

'You should become something of an invalid, like myself,' said Mr Dacre, 'and take out a license from the court of conscience to kill time in the most agreeable way.'

'It must be a tiresome occupation,' observed Edith.

'Yes, if you really make it a pursuit ; but time may die a very innocent and peaceful death in such a place as this.'

'Provided one has a license,' said Edith, smiling ; 'but it pleases me better to have no time to kill.'

Mr Dacre sighed, and a passing contraction of his forehead showed some painful thoughts had been awakened. 'I agree with you,' he said. 'I am sure one of the great secrets of happiness is to have no moment unemployed ; but illness is a stern master, even to the most active.'

'I hope it is not wrong,' said Edith ; 'yet I think I would rather die than be condemned to a useless life.'

'Are we the best judges of what is useful ?' replied Mr Dacre. 'Don't you think we are too much in the habit of considering no actions important but obvious and exciting ones ? The moment any occupation becomes a duty, even if it is merely picking straws, it ceases to be useless, and the manner in which we do it must be of infinite consequence.'

Edith did not know what to reply, for she was surprised at the turn the conversation had taken. 'Perhaps,' continued Mr Dacre, thinking that she wished to return home, 'you would allow me to walk through the Park with you. I have been here a long time, and General Forester will scarcely forgive me if I keep his dinner waiting.'

Edith willingly assented, feeling an unusual degree of interest in her new acquaintance ; but she was too shy to renew the subject that had been dropped, and Mr Dacre did not again allude to it.

'Your brother is losing a beautiful season,' he said ; 'I can scarcely imagine any place having charms for him like this.'

Edith smiled, but it was a smile quickly succeeded by a sigh. 'You would not say that,' she replied, 'if you were as well acquainted with his affairs as the rest of the Elsham people.' She did not see Mr Dacre's face, or she might have remarked the half-serious, half-amused expression with which he answered, 'Mr Courtenay is not entirely a stranger. I have heard of his intended marriage, it is a subject of general conversation.'

'Yes,' said Edith, 'I dare say the world is acquainted, or thinks itself acquainted with the most minute particulars.'

'Even the colour of the bridal dress,' observed Mr Dacre ; 'and if so much is said beforehand, what will it be afterwards ?'

'I shall not envy my sister-in-law's position for the first few months,' continued Edith. ' I don't think women were formed for notoriety of any kind : it must always make them feel awkward and out of place.'

'Happily it will only be for a few months,' said Mr Dacre ; 'and when the excitement of the arrival is over, we may hope real happiness will begin.'

''The situation seems very enviable,' said Edith ; 'almost enough so to be alarming. Few people are permitted to enjoy uninterrupted prosperity.'

'Very few ; but I suspect the fault lies in themselves. The trial is too great.'

'And money makes a person so independent,' said Edith. 'It is seldom a rich man hears truth, even from his own relations.'

'Yes, perhaps that is one of its greatest evils. There is an indirect influence, though, which no one is beyond the reach of, and I think it is always more powerful than advice.'

As Mr Dacre said this, they reached the Park gates ; but he was plainly determined to pursue the conversation, for, unmindful of General Forester's dinner-hour, he continued his walk in the direction of the Priory.

'I don't think I quite understand you,' replied Edith: 'wh t influence do you mean?'

'Affection. A young man will often be led by a brother or a sister, when he would not listen to his father or mother.'

'Leave out the sisters,' said Edith. 'Brothers are not apt to pay much attention to them.'

'Indeed, I think you are mistaken. You speak from belief : I speak from experience. The greatest blessing of my life was the example of a sister.'

'Edward would think some wonderful change had taken place if I were to presume to offer him advice,' said Edith, laughing.

'But advice is not the necessary form of influence,' replied Mr Dacre. 'We may safely act as drags to a wheel which is going too fast, when we should be crushed in attempting to stop it.'

'Edward has chosen a drag for himself now,' said Edith, with a slight sharpness of tone, which did not escape her companion's observant ear.

'Or is there but another wheel added, which may accelerate the motion?'

'Perhaps so,' replied Edith. 'Yet it may be dangerous for bystanders to interfere.'

'Of that I can be no judge,' said Mr Dacre. 'My observations were only general. But I believe we often commit fatal errors from the belief that we have no influence.'

There was an earnestness in his manner which struck Edith forcibly. It was so different from the tone of an ordinary acquaintance, that for an instant she fancied Mr Dacre must have had some secret meaning in his remarks; but a little reflection convinced her of the improbability of the idea. They parted at the Priory Lodge. Edith walked slowly to the house, thinking of the unusual pleasure she had experienced; and Mr Dacre stood by the gate till she was out of sight, watching her with evident interest, and then, with a sigh, retraced his steps towards the Grange.

CHAPTER VI.

'A LETTER from Charlotte at last,' exclaimed Jane Courtenay on the following morning. 'Now, I suppose, we shall hear all the particulars,' and her eye ran rapidly over the crossed sheets; while a few of the principal subjects were enumerated. 'Very busy—wedding fixed for Thursday, because of an old uncle going away. The archdeacon of some place or other to perform the ceremony—Bride's dress white silk, Honiton lace veil.—Bridesmaids to be all alike—pale blue watered silk—bonnets sent for from Paris—jewels magnificent—Edward spending a fortune—carriage the most elegant affair that can be imagined—Edward a universal favourite—told to his face that he is perfection. Slight symptoms of conceit in consequence. Tell Edith this—it will please her.'

'No, indeed, you shall not tell me,' exclaimed Edith, interrupting her sister. 'Nothing is so provoking as to hear bits of a letter in that manner. Do let me have the satisfaction of reading it all quietly to myself.'

'Nay, but you must listen to this,' said Jane; 'it is just in your way. All the villagers are to have a *fête* on the wedding-day, and Edward intends giving new frocks and bonnets to twenty of the school girls, and new jackets and hats to the same number of boys; and he talks to me about the patterns of cottons and the shape of bonnets till I begin to think the wedding-dress an affair of much less consequence.'

'And what is to be done at Allingham?' asked Edith. 'I should have thought Mr Howard might have provided for Oakhamptom himself.'

'Not when he has such a long purse and such a ready hand near, to save him the trouble,' said Jane. 'Let me see, there is a postcript about Allingham. Edward has written to the bailiff to provide a dinner for the tenants; and he hopes you will all go and see them enjoy themselves.'

'There will be a sufficient occupation for you, Edith.'

'Mrs Grantley talked about the school children,' replied Edith. 'I don't mean that she intended they should be feasted at Edward's expense; but she wishes them to have some pleasure to mark the day, because many of them are the children of his tenants; and I said I was sure mamma would assist.'

'Poor little things!' said Mrs Courtenay. 'It is hard they

should not be happy one day in their lives. You arrange everything, my dear, and then tell me about it afterwards.'

'It makes me ill to think of it,' said Jane, yawning. 'Such
a quantity of trouble for such a set of dirty little creatures!
What can be the good of giving them a taste for things which
they will never have when they grow up? It will be long before they have tea and plum-cake again when they once leave
school.'

'So much the more reason that they should enjoy it now,' replied Edith. 'If your principle had been acted upon, Jane, we
should all have been miserable children, for it is impossible to
have the same pleasures at twenty that we had at ten.'

'Perhaps so,' said Jane, languidly. 'I shall be glad when it
is all over; one has lived in such a whirl lately, that none but a
strong person can stand it. How I envy you, Edith; nothing
seems to annoy you.'

If Jane had known what was passing in her sister's mind, the
words might have been unsaid. Edith had taken up the letter,
and, after turning to the account of Edward's plan for the Oakhampton school, was thinking of the reasons which could induce
him to consult Charlotte on such subjects rather than Miss
Howard. The only explanation was in the supposition that to
the latter it was an affair of no interest; and the circumstance,
though slight, contributed to strengthen Edith's predjudice. It
would have been happy if some friend, wiser than herself, had
been near to caution her against a rapid judgment, even when
drawn from facts; but the only person who could have advised
her was Gertrude, and to her Edith had only mentioned, in
general terms, a fear that Edward's marriage was hasty; and
though Gertrude, in answer, had spoken of the care and consideration which might be required in the future intercourse
between Allingham and the Priory, Edith did not apply the
observations to herself, having no idea that she was likely to be
tempted to say or do anything which would give offence.

No more letters were expected before the important one which
was to announce that the marriage had taken place, and it was
thought better to defer all rejoicing till the fact was positively
known. There were so many wonderful stories of brides and
bridegrooms dying, or quarrelling, or changing their mind, at the
very last moment, that the Committee of the Elsham National
School decided it would be less presumptuous to wait, and not
run the risk of wishing health and prosperity to Mrs Courtenay

of Allingham, when no such person might be in existence. But Edith had no fears. From the first moment, she felt that there was little hope of escape. All was easy and bright—a practical comment upon Cæsar's motto, ' Came, saw, and conquered.' And yet, when the thirteenth of October arrived, and with it the expected packet from Oakhampton, her heart beat quickly, and as her heart caught the joint names at the bottom of her brother's letter, she felt even greater pain than she had anticipated.

' You will go at once to Mrs Grantley, I suppose,' said Jane, when she had finished Charlotte's glowing account of the wedding —with the titled guests—and the carriage and four—and the school children—and the breakfast—and all the other *et ceteras* by which such events are celebrated, both by those who can, and those who cannot, afford it ; 'and we may as well send to Rayner, and ask him what has been settled about the dinner. I suppose we must drive to the Park to look at them, but I wish Edward had let the matter rest till he came home.'

' No, my dear,' observed Mrs Courtenay, ' that would have been quite wrong. In my days there used to be a great deal more done. Every poor person in the parish had a dinner when I was married.'

' Edward would have had enough to do in the parish of Elsham, to provide for the two thousand poor,' said Jane. ' I think, mamma, as you patronise the thing so warmly, you had better superintend it, and leave Edith to exercise her talents in the school feast. It will be a great relief to me if I can be left out.'

' And so it would be to me,' replied Mrs Courtenay, suddenly reminded of her maladies. ' I thought the night before last I should have been obliged to send for Mr Humphries,—I had such a dreadful pain in my shoulder.'

' Bilious, I dare say,' replied Jane. ' You know, mamma, you would eat pudding and macaroni at dinner.'

' Mr Humphries declares it is rheumatism,' said Mrs Courtenay. ' I must ask one of you to rub my shoulder for me.'

' I would, if I were not obliged to go to bed early,' said Jane. ' Edith, you don't mind being late.'

' I am obliged not to mind it,' said Edith ; ' there is no time to do anything in the day—but I heard you moving about till half-past twelve last night.'

' Because I wanted to finish a book ; and see how ill I am to-day in consequence.'

'The night before it was twelve,' continued Edith ; and then, seeing the angry flush on Jane's cheek, she stopped, vexed at having persisted in a disagreeable conversation, and seated herself at the table to calculate the expenses of the school feast.

'My dear,' said her mother, 'you are so careless. Just look, you have destroyed that nice gilt-edged paper for nothing ; why will you always write from that portfolio ?'

'I forgot,' replied Edith ; and she took up a common sheet.

'O Edith !' exclaimed Jane, 'you are scribbling on the letter I had begun, and yesterday you did the very same thing. No one ever makes such blunders as you do.'

'I did not mean any harm,' said Edith ; 'if you had as many things to think of as I have, you would make mistakes too.'

'Charity begins at home, and care ought to do the same,' said Jane. 'I do think you benevolent people are the most tiresome race in existence.'

Edith had recourse to silence—and went to her own room, with a passing consciousness that it might be better to attend more to the general comforts of the family.

The day fixed for the dinner and the school feast was unusually fine for the season ; and even Mrs Courtenay threw off her fur cloak, as she stepped into the open carriage that was to convey her to the Park, and allowed that it might be possible to enjoy a drive in the month of October. Jane declined going, under pretence of not being able to bear the excitement, while Edith accompanied her mother with a grave countenance, to witness rejoicings in which she by no means participated. The dinner was painful : for Mrs Courtenay was so little in the habit of mixing with the poor, that she was entirely deficient in the ease and cordiality which win their affections much sooner than even words or actions. With hasty steps she passed along the different tables, repeating, as a matter of form, that 'she hoped they would enjoy themselves ;' and Edith lingered behind, endeavouring to efface any disagreeable impression, by inquiring minutely after the children and the invalids of the different families.

Martha Philips was present, complaining that she was too old for such grand doings, and Edith was endeavouring to soothe her, when the old nurse suddenly recollected her fears for the cottage and began to inquire, whether Edith really thought it as ugly as she had been told ; for they said, 'that Mr Edward's lady came from a hard family, and she would be sure to have her own way.'

'Who says? what do you mean?' asked Edith, eagerly, and bending down, that the answer might not be overheard.

'Tom Slater says he heard it from one of the London workmen who knew all about them. He was at work down in their country one winter, and a weary time he had of it; but never a bit of help from the great folks.'

'Here's health and long life to Mr and Mrs Courtenay!' cried the bailiff from the top of the table, 'and we will drink it with three times three.'

Edith's heart sank within her; but she was spared the pain of such ill-timed rejoicing, by an imploring look from her mother; who, alarmed at the prospect of the stunning noise, requested that the cheers might be deferred. A murmur of disapprobation ran round the table, and the weakness of Mrs Courtenay's nerves gained her on that day more unpopularity than the kindness of weeks could have retrieved.

The poor are seldom conscious of the existence of nerves; and anything which shows an absence of sympathy with their feelings is sooner resented than even the neglect of their bodily wants. This Edith knew; and, vexed and uneasy, she hastened her mother away, and advising her to return home, walked to the school alone.

The children were all placed in order, and the tea and cake distributed; but they had waited for her, as the Queen of the Day; and she was just beginning to excuse herself for being late, when a soft voice behind her murmured, 'A peculiarly interesting spectacle, this, Miss Courtenay'—Edith turned, and saw Miss Forester leaning on her uncle's arm,—'most gratifying to you it must be in every way. I daresay you will remember your feelings on this occasion to your latest moment.' Of this Edith had no doubt, but whether the nature of the feelings was such as Miss Forester imagined, was another matter. 'I need not introduce my uncle,' Miss Forester was going to say; but she checked herself. There was a possibility that Mr Dacre might not choose to be exhibited in such an old relationship. 'I believe you are already acquainted with Mr Dacre. He gave me a most glowing account of a walk in Allingham Park, about a week ago.'

'It was a beautiful afternoon,' said Mr Dacre drily; 'we have had few like it.'

'Miss Courtenay has such powers of walking,' observed Miss Forester; 'and that is so very enviable. I should not have been able to see these little, merry creatures this afternoon, if my father had not promised to call for me in the carriage at five o'clock.' The little, merry creatures were, at that instant, looking peculiarly solemn, waiting for Mr Grantley to say grace, and Edith could scarcely repress a smile.

'You take great interest in the school, I think,' said Mr Dacre.

'Yes,' replied Edith, simply; 'it is my hobby. Every one must find something to occupy them; but of course I am only head assistant.'

'It is easy to see in these cases,' said Mr Dacre, 'what a blessing eating and drinking is. You might try for years with other things before you could make these children feel, as plainly as they do now, that they were cared for.'

'I am not sure they understand much about it at any time,' said Edith, smiling.

'We will try,' continued Mr Dacre. 'What do you say, my little fellow?' and he patted the shoulder of a flaxen-headed urchin who, with both hands, was lifting his cake to his mouth; 'don't you think Miss Courtenay is the kindest young lady you ever saw?'

'I don't know,' said the boy, still fondly clasping his treasure, and speaking with his mouth full. Edith and Mr Dacre laughed.

'Oh! but that is rude,' said Miss Forester, who had been standing close behind: 'put your hands down, and tell us if you are not extremely obliged to all the ladies and gentlemen whc take so much interest in your welfare.'

The boy stared, and understanding only that he was to put his hands in his lap, quickly moved them.

'There's a good boy!' said Miss Forester, patronisingly, and advancing as near to the table as she dared without touching it. 'It is quite delightful to see them brought up in these habits of obedience. You must be very fond of all the ladies and gentlemen, I am sure, my dear?'

'He is more fond of his cake than of anything else just now,' half whispered Edith; 'you had better let him go on.'

The child, seizing upon the permission, snatched up his cake; and then, lifting his cup to his mouth with an awkward jerk, divided its contents between Edith, Miss Forester, and the floor

Miss Forester started back with an exclamation of disgust, which included not only the little culprit before her, but all others of his race ; while Edith wiped her dress, and began to assure the boy that no one would be angry. In an instant Miss Forester had caught the words, and with the prospective view of sufficient wealth to purchase the most splendid silks in Waterloo House, thought it worth while to sacrifice her fawn-coloured satinet, for the sake of appearing amiable in Mr Dacre's eyes. 'These sudden frights make one nervous,' she said ; 'but one would bear anything rather than mar their enjoyment. Don't think anything more about it, my dear. Certainly it is a beautiful dress spoiled !'—and her voice became louder, and her countenance flushed, as she gazed at the large, greasy stain. 'It was a present, too, from my father, only a month ago ; and you know,' she added, with a pleading apologetic look at Mr Dacre, 'we are often annoyed at these misfortunes for a friend's sake, when we should not care about them for our own.'

'It is rather a handsome dress for the occasion,' said Mr Dacre, as his eye glanced upon Edith's dark silk and straw bonnet.

Miss Forester perceived the comparison, and her previous dislike to Edith was not a little increased. 'It is rather better, perhaps, than was absolutely necessary ; but I was afraid of keeping you waiting, my dear sir ; and therefore chose the first dress that was at hand. A poor woman detained me, or I should have gone to my room sooner.'

'Oh !' was Mr Dacre's answer ; and he walked away, and began a conversation with Mr Grantley.

Miss Forester remained with Edith, and pertinaciously devoted herself to her for the rest of the afternoon. The appearance of interest in Mr Dacre's manner had alarmed her, and she was resolved there should be no more *tête-à-têtes :* not that she had formed any positive plan for preventing him from becoming intimate with other persons—she acted merely from the impulse of the moment ; and perhaps, if her motives and objects had been placed before her in words, she might have acknowledged them to be wrong. But Miss Forester had never entered upon the task of self-examination. The outward world, with its pomp and pride, its cares, its business, and its pleasures, was to her all in all ; and, engrossed in its pursuits, she was passing through life without devoting one moment to the consideration of that busy world within—that tumultuous crowd of thoughts and feelings, which at every moment are born, and die, and are forgotten, but upon which God has stamped the seal of immortality.

CHAPTER VII.

THE dinner and the school feast, the congratulations and the visits, passed quickly, as all human events must pass ; and left upon Edith's mind only the recollection of the effort it had been to keep up appearances, and avoid betraying to the world the uneasiness lurking in her heart. But a greater trial was now approaching. The letters from the travellers spoke of their wish to return home earlier than they had at first intended. The weather was unpropitious for excursions ; and the beauties of Normandy and the Seine lost much of their charm under the depressing influence of a November sky. Not, indeed, such a sky as that which weighs down the spirit of an unfortunate Englishman, in a country village, without resources in himself, or interest in his neighbours ; but, nevertheless one sufficiently gloomy to make even a bride and bridegroom sigh for a blazing fire, and the cheerfulness of home society. Why they should have visited the Continent at all, in the autumn, for so short a time, was a subject of astonishment to their friends. But Edward was married in October,—a month proverbially fine ; and under the influence of a clear sky, a bright sun, and a happy heart, he had, as usual, allowed the brilliancy of the present to hide the coming shadows of the future, and persuaded himself that nothing could be more agreeable than to give Laura a foretaste of the pleasures of a foreign tour, preparatory to a longer residence in Italy the ensuing year.

The dulness of the weather did not, however, appear to have brought any change in their real enjoyment. Both were evidently perfectly happy ; and even Edith, as she read Edward's amusing lamentations over their disappointments, and Laura's affectionate assurances that she was too well satisfied to find fault with passing storms, could scarcely tremble for the prudence of the step her brother had taken, or doubt whether he had chosen a wife suited to his character. Charlotte was still absent, paying a round of visits in the neighbourhood of London; there was therefore no opportunity of gaining from her any of the minute details which can only be learned in conversation, and with which Edith longed to be acquainted; and she was obliged to summon all her patience, and occupy herself in her ordinary duties, while she waited for the day on which Edward and his bride were to be welcomed at Allingham.

It was on a chill, gloomy evening, when the fog that had hung over every object during the day was turning into a drizzling rain, while the moaning wind among the leafless trees, and the thick bank of leaden clouds, partially gilded by the setting sun, portended a stormy night, that Edith paced the gravel-walk from the house to the carriage-drive through the Park, anxiously listening to every sound, and regardless of the weather, from the excitement of her feelings; for now that she was about to meet her brother, she remembered her offences against him, and doubted whether he could so entirely have excused her neglect of his wishes as he appeared to have done. Mrs Courtenay and Jane had thrown themselves, one upon the sofa, the other into a large arm-chair wheeled close to the fire, and were contriving to banish the weariness of delay by occasional complaints of the season and the state of the roads; to which Jane added a few remarks upon Edward's want of punctuality, that were by no means responded to by her mother. Even these topics were, however, at last exhausted : and, in default of conversation, Jane closed her eyes, merely, as she said, because the firelight was painful; and in a short time, Edward and Laura, and all outward circumstances, were forgotten. Edith, too, was tired of her solitary walk, and began to be sensible that a November mist might as well be avoided. She resolved upon taking one more turn, and then attending to her mother's request, sent about ten minutes before, that she would on no account stay out any longer. The resolution was scarcely made, when the distant sound of bells reached her ear. It was a joyous peal from the old village church, yet something of a saddened undertone seemed blended with it, as the wailing autumnal wind bore it towards her, now loudly and merrily, and again so faintly as nearly to be inaudible. In Edith's melancholy mood, she could almost have fancied it a token of the consequences that would follow upon her brother's marriage; an event regarded by all but herself with unmixed satisfaction. But the certainty that Edward was arrived, put a stop to any longer reverie; and she had only time to give her mother the information, when the

carriage was heard approaching the house. The next minute
Edward was in the hall, receiving his mother's blessing, and
presenting to her his young and beautiful wife.

'She is your youngest child, my dearest mother,' he whispered,
'and you will love her very dearly for my sake.'

Laura withdrew her arm from her husband, and advanced to
receive Mrs Courtenay's kiss.

'For your sake, now,' she said, as she looked in Edward's face
with a sweet, bright smile; 'for my own, I trust, soon.' And
then turning to Jane and Edith, she added, 'May I not be introduced to your sisters?'

Edith's warm affections were in a moment roused. The tone
and manner were so simple and winning, that it was impossible
to retain any feeling of coldness; and as her eye rested upon the
slight, fairy-like form, and childish, but exquisitely lovely face
before her, all Edward's offences were forgotten. His love was ac-
counted for, and his extravagance seemed but the natural homage
paid to the captivating grace of the object of his choice. Laura
indeed appeared born to receive and enjoy all that wealth and
affection could lavish upon her, and even the most foreboding
mind could hardly have associated any idea but that of happiness with her sparkling, hazel eyes, laughing mouth, and brilliant
complexion. At the first glance, whilst she was standing en-
veloped in shawls and furs, Edith was fascinated with her beauty;
and when, on entering the drawing-room, she carelessly threw off
her bonnet and cloak, and showed the delicately-moulded little
head, and long, fair neck, which suited so well with the general
contour of her features, Edith felt that she had never looked upon
anything so lovely. Edward said but little; he was watching
with intense pleasure the effect of his wife's appearance and manner; and Edith, though she noticed his silence, was more at her
ease than she expected to have been, for his greeting had been
cordial and affectionate. The delight of the moment had made
him forget any causes of annoyance, if he felt them to exist. Mrs
Courtenay, afraid lest Laura should be suffering from cold or
fatigue, soon began to urge upon her, what, in a similar situation,
she would have thought absolutely necessary for herself,—a
speedy retirement to her own room.

'But,' said Laura, in the clear, joyous tone of one who had
never known care, 'you will make me think I am an invalid, and
I never was ill in my life. I am stronger than any one. I can
go to a ball, and dance all night, and get up just the same the

next morning ; and when we were in town in the spring, I was at the Opera regularly on a Saturday night, and yet, however late it was when I went to bed, I never missed being in time for the music at the Roman Catholic chapel on Sunday morning.'

Edith looked at her brother,—she thought he bit his lip, and a cloud passed over his face ; but he turned away ; and again, with a chilled, blank feeling, she gazed upon her beautiful sister-in-law.

' But, my dear,' said Mrs Courtenay, whose notions of right were more shocked by the idea of the Roman Catholic chapel than by the dissipation, and almost inevitable profanation of the Sunday, ' Edward never told me you were a Roman Catholic.'

' Oh no !' exclaimed Laura, laughing, ' I only went there for the music. In the country we always go to church once a day ; but in town there are so many engagements, it is not practicable.'

' Laura,' said her husband—and there was something in his tone, which, to Edith's ear, betokened anything but satisfaction —' you had better go to your room now, or you will be late for dinner. I suppose you had my letter,' he added, speaking to his mother ; ' we were not able to stop on the road, so I thought a late dinner would be the wisest arrangement.'

' I should like much to go all over the house first,' replied Laura. ' You promised me I should, and I have been dreaming about it all the way.'

' It is too late, my love ; you will see nothing to-night, and it will be a pity to lessen any pleasure you might have to-morrow. I should just like you, though, to come with me into the servants' hall, and speak to the housekeeper, and the other people about the place. I suspect they are all waiting there to see you.'

' It is too late, my love,' said Laura, with an arch smile. ' I don't fancy going into the servants' hall to-night. That pleasure shall be deferred till to-morrow too.'

' But if I wish it,' said Edward.

' But if I don't wish it,' continued Laura.

' You would not vex me, I am sure, my love. It is expected of you.'

' That is a pity,' said Laura, ' because you see there are such things as false expectations ; so now we will go up-stairs.' And, rising from her seat, she playfully put her arm within his to lead him from the room. Edith again glanced at her brother ; but the expression of dissatisfaction had passed away.

' You are a sadly spoiled child,' he said, only half reproachfully, as he watched his wife's graceful motions ; 'but you must have your own way, I suppose, to-night, at least as regards the servants.' And Laura's bewitching smile of gratitude completed her victory.

'It is not difficult to see who will rule at Allingham,' said Jane, when they were gone. 'How one is deceived in people ! I should have thought that Edward, of all persons, was the least likely to be governed by his wife.'

'Hush ! my dear Jane,' exclaimed Mrs Courtenay ; 'you speak so loudly. It is all very natural and right : you know they are but just married ; and she is very young.'

'Quite a child,' said Edith ; and the words spoke volumes of disappointment.

'And so beautiful !' continued Mrs Courtenay ; 'she must have been a most lovely baby.'

'I don't see that she is much more now,' observed Jane ; 'Charlotte said she did not look more than sixteen, but I must say I was not entirely prepared for such infantine ways.'

'My dear Jane, you are hard judging. Her manners suit her exactly.'

'That is just the objection to them. They suit her face and figure, but they do not suit her position. A playful kitten is all very well, but a playful bride is detestable. What do you say, Edith ?'

The question was either not heard, or not sufficiently agreeable to be attended to ; and, in a short time, the sound of the dinner-bell, and the re-entrance of Edward and Laura, put an end to any further observations.

'You are silent, my dear Edith,' said Edward, with a slight effort of manner, when the second course was removed, and the first *esprit* of the conversation had subsided ; 'I hope you are not ill ?'

'No, thank you, I never was better ;' and silence again ensued.

'You have been overworking yourself, I am afraid. I have told Laura what an indefatigable person you are, and that she must become your assistant.'

'But Laura did not agree to the proposal,' said his wife, with a smile which always had the effect of neutralising any unpleasant impression her words might occasion. 'I am rejoiced that there is some one to take the Lady Bountiful's burden from me ; it was always my horror in a country life ; besides, you know, it would be interfering.'

'She is only joking,' said Edward, observing the increased gloom on his sister's face. 'You will know her better by and by, and then you will not believe anything she says of herself.'

'No one was ever more in earnest, Edward—I don't understand such things, and never shall—so Edith shall be lady paramount over the Allingham charities, to her heart's content.'

'Thank you,' said Edith, gravely; 'but I have enough to do at Elsham.'

Laura looked at her sister-in-law as if rather astonished at her manner, and then sunk into an unusual fit of abstraction. Edward fidgeted, and began to be uncomfortable. He had that indescribable feeling of something being uncongenial in the elements of his family party, which perhaps is more painful than open difference of opinion.

'You have told me nothing about Gertrude,' he said, willing to change the conversation. 'What account does she give of my aunt?'

'Very much as usual,' replied Jane. 'Mrs Heathfield is always complaining; some people are.'

'I do so long to see Gertrude,' said Laura. 'She wrote me such a kind note just before we were married, as kind as any I had, even from my own relations; and I have a cousin who knows her, and says she is not at all like people in general.'

'I don't see that,' said Jane. 'She has eyes, nose, and mouth like the rest of the world; and eats, drinks, and sleeps, like a rational being. Then she is neither tall nor short, nor pretty nor ugly; neither a genius nor a dunce. In fact, I don't know where you would find a less singular person.'

'But her mind,' said Edward. 'We are scarcely judges, indeed, as to what she really is; but if her letters and general report speak truth, she is singularly good.'

'No, no, Edward,' exclaimed Laura; 'I am sure she is not like that. Singularly good people are always disagreeable. We had one staying with us once, and she did nothing but find fault from morning till night.'

'It is a melancholy truth though, with regard to Gertrude,' said Edward, smiling.

'Perfectly impossible,' continued Laura, 'or she would have sent me a sermon on my wedding-day, with a little book bound in silk and gold, as you put medicines for children into sugar, containing "Advice to a young wife." I had three given to me as it was, from three singularly good old aunts.'

'They meant kindly, my love,' said Edward, in the tone in which he would have gently reproved a forward child.

'Good intentions!' exclaimed Laura, laughing; 'I am tired of them. I had a fit of them once, and they made me uncomfortable, so I gave them up.'

'Certainly,' said Edith, 'they are of little use without good actions.'

'That is exactly what I feel; and as I am too humble to suppose I shall ever perform any good actions, I see no reason to trouble myself with the intentions.'

'You will frighten my mother if you talk so wildly, my love,' said Edward. 'She is not accustomed to such rhodomontade. Edith, I suspect, is alarmed already.'

'Not half so much as I am,' said Laura. 'Do you know, Edith, Edward has done nothing but describe your virtues all day.'

'I only told the truth,' replied Edward, in his natural kind manner. 'I hope she will not think it too much trouble to teach her own good ways to such an idle child as you are.'

Laura drew up her long neck, and appeared not quite pleased. Child though she was, she was fully aware of her position as a married woman, and did not desire the dictation of an unmarried sister-in-law; and Edward had no sooner spoken than he perceived his mistake.

'I have no ways to teach,' said Edith, coldly, her pleasure in the praise struggling with her disappointment; 'and if I had, I should rather have looked forward, Edward, to learning something from your wife.'

Edward looked ominously grave. He felt what was intended, and he also felt that it was neither the place nor the time for the observation to be made.

'All persons, I imagine,' he replied, in a tone as cold, 'have some points in which they may be useful to others. Laura has been accustomed to a London life; you to a country one. I suppose you may mutually benefit each other.'

'We will make a compact then,' said Laura, gaily; 'I will teach you the fashions, and you shall take charge of my duties.'

There was a smile from all but Edith, who was immovably rigid; and Laura, feeling provoked, proposed an adjournment to the drawing-room.

Edith's stiffness relaxed as they drew round the fire, and she tried to find a subject of conversation. 'Is this the last new reticule?' she said, taking up a large and very handsome carriage bag, which had been left on the sofa.

'No,' replied Laura. 'It was a wedding present; you shall guess from whom.'

'Gertrude,' said Jane; 'no one else would have thought of such a thing.'

'Because no one else is so much in the habit of consulting other persons' comfort,' observed Edith.

'The note I mentioned was sent with it,' said Laura; 'and she told me she preferred work to ornaments, because it was the association generally which made them valuable; and therefore she would rather wait till she could hope I really loved her, and in the meantime give me something useful. Just see how nicely the bag is fitted up.'

'Gertrude has a great idea of suitableness in presents,' said Edith. 'She always contrives to think upon the very thing one wants, even if it is a mere trifle.'

'She is rich,' remarked Jane; 'and can afford to give presents.'

'Not much richer than we are, now,' said Edith. 'And besides, she seldom does give what people call handsome presents.'

'Gertrude must be the hundred and first wonder of the world.' said Laura. 'I shall give up wishing to see her. I never met with agreeable perfection yet.'

'Her perfections are not dazzling ones,' said Edith, a little mollified by the appreciation of her sister's gift. 'You must know her intimately before you find out her superiority.'

'So much the worse,' observed Laura. 'Hidden goodness is the most alarming of all. One goes on blundering, and imagining one is doing and saying everything that is right; and, all at once, some unlucky look or word touches the vulnerable point, and a whole host of virtues stand up in battle array, and crush one before one is at all prepared.'

'Crush, my dear,' said Mrs Courtenay, who was just settling herself for her evening doze; 'don't talk of crushing—it is so cruel; put it out of the window carefully. I dare say it will recover.'

Laura laughed heartily; but it was not the Priory fashion to correct Mrs Courtenay's mistakes, and the conversation continued.

'One thing I really give Gertrude credit for,' said Jane, - 'consistency. If it were not for her, I should really think some-

times that all the world were hypocrites. They talk so well and
act so badly.'

'You learn to think them so, on the Continent,' said Laura,—
'at the Roman Catholic chapels. There can be no sincerity in
all the bowing, and ringing of bells, and walking about.'

'Were you there often?' asked Edith.

'No, we were only absent three weeks ; but the Sundays were
wet and dull, and I persuaded Edward to go, just for amusement.'

'People might say the same as you do of our forms,' observed
Edith, 'if they did not understand them.'

'Oh, no,' exclaimed Laura ; 'there is meaning in what we do,
but the Roman Catholic ceremonies are absurd. What is the
use of the little boys and the tapers?'

'I don't know,' said Edith ; 'I never was at a Roman Catholic
chapel.'

'Never!' repeated Laura, in astonishment. 'But it is a sight
to be seen, like any others ; and then the music is exquisite.'

'It can scarcely be right, though,' said Edith, 'to make anything solemn a matter of amusement. We should be shocked
to see the service of the Church represented in the theatre ; and
I can fancy good Roman Catholics feeling just the same when
their worship is considered a mere show.'

'As to the Church service in a theatre,' said Laura, 'I am no
judge, for I never saw it ; but I dare say I should not think it
wrong, if no one else did. You know in Masaniello they kneel
down on the stage, and chant, and very beautiful it is. It
makes one feel very religious at the time—so it must be good.'

'But do you think the people who sing are feeling the same?'
asked Edith.

'Oh no. They are mere actors—of course all that they care
for is singing in tune and putting themselves in proper atti-
tudes.'

'But the words,' said Edith, looking extremely grave,—'only
think of the words they use.'

'They don't mean them,' replied Laura. 'Greek and Latin,
or mere nonsense, would do just as well.'

'And the third commandment!' said Edith.

Laura seemed a little startled. 'We are running away from
our first subject,' she said. 'The chanting in "Masaniello" has
nothing to do with the Roman Catholic chapels. The people are
not acting there.'

'You said they were,' replied Edith. 'You called them **hypo-crites.**'

'I did not mean exactly that they were; only that they seemed so.'

'And when you go,' continued Edith, 'you of course put on an appearance of reverence, and yet all the time you are thinking of the service as an amusement. Who is acting then?'

There was a short pause, broken by Laura. 'You are hard upon me, Edith,' she said; 'I daresay you think me dreadfully wicked; but I was bred up with my notions, and you were bred up with yours; so we shall never agree; but I am sure you are a great deal better than I am.'

Edith felt this was true; and a certain consciousness of manner unfortunately showed it,—unfortunately, for it served to efface the impression her words had made. Laura would have been touched by humility and gentleness, in one whom she candidly acknowledged her superior; but Edith's smile of acquiescence irritated her. A little reflection indeed brought to Edith's mind follies, and worse than follies, both of thought and action, which sunk her infinitely low in her own esteem; but it was then too late to be humble. The conversation was interrupted by the entrance of her brother and the preparation for tea, and the opportunity was lost. So it is through life : we yield to the impulse of the moment, and utter a hasty word, or are silent when we should have spoken, or suffer a proud look to betray our evil feelings ; and then turn and repent, and bewail the infirmity of our nature ; and the sorrow, when it is the sorrow of a Christian, is seen and accepted, but the impression of our weakness is stamped upon another's heart, and its effect we may well dread to calculate. On this occasion it was plainly visible. Laura's constraint for the short remainder of the evening was the more perceptible, from the contrast it afforded to her general openness of manner; and when Edith, on her return home, thought over in solitude the occurrences of the evening, the remembrance of her sister's worldly notions and of Edward's inconsistency, was less painful than the consciousness of her own self-conceit and coldness of manner. And Edith was sincere in her self-accusation ; but the fault lay too deep to be easily corrected. Never-failing humility is the last acquired virtue of a Christian.

CHAPTER VIII.

'YOU are grave, my love,' said Edward, as he stood by the breakfast-room window on the following morning, pointing out the different objects of interest in the neighbourhood.

'Not exactly grave,' replied Laura, keeping her eyes still fixed upon the Priory, which Edward had been minutely describing—'I was only thinking.'

'Thinking of what?'

'Oh! nothing,—it is very pretty. That bow-window, you say, is the library?'

'"Nothing" will not do for me,' said Edward, as he drew her fondly towards him, and forced her to look in his face. 'Remember our agreement, Laura; we were to have no concealments of any kind,—whether in grief or joy, it was to be all the same.'

'So it shall be, when there is anything to be told; but it would be absurd to confess every foolish thought that passes through one's mind, and makes one look grave for the moment.'

'Not absurd, if I wish it,' replied Edward; 'so tell me what was it? Were you thinking of home?'

'Oh no,' exclaimed Laura, earnestly; 'why should I? You are my home now.'

'Then you are disappointed in the place: it is not so pretty as you expected.'

'Yes, it is a great deal prettier, larger and handsomer, and the view more extensive. I cannot tell you what it was, Edward, that came over me—it was a feeling more than a thought.'

'A feeling about the Priory,' said Edward.

Laura hesitated. 'I can hardly understand why I should have it; your mother is so kind; and Jane, too; and Edith'—

'Is what?'

'So—so good, I think: so much better than I am.'

'Time will prove that,' said Edward, as he imprinted a kiss on the fair, open forehead of his young wife. 'You are good in my eyes. Is not that sufficient?'

'But I am not good in Edith's,' continued Laura; 'I can see I am not—and I am frightened—I shall never feel at ease where she is.'

'Never is a very long day,' said Edward, smiling. 'It is only Edith's manner at first—she is so warm-hearted and sensible; you must be fond of her by and by.'

' That is not the question ; she will never be fond of me. She thinks I am not fitted for you. I am sure she does ; and you will find I was right about her not being my bridesmaid. She did not choose to be. and that was her only motive for declining.'

' Rather severe,' said Edward. ' You know I was vexed myself; but we agreed that we would not begin our home life with being annoyed. Her time is very much occupied, and I really think that nothing but necessity would have induced her to refuse. You must remember, too, that although we are all in all to each other, we cannot cut ourselves off from our relations.'

' Who would wish it ?' said Laura. ' I am sure I only want to be one of the family in everything ; but then I must be met half way.'

' And so you will be. In a week's time, Edith and you will be the dearest friends imaginable.'

Laura shook her head.

' I can never get on with any person I am afraid of ; and you know I am shy, though I do talk fast.'

' You were shy of the servants last night,' said Edward ; ' but you must conquer the feeling to-day. I want you to know them all—to take the management of affairs into your own hands ; and remember we are to be very economical.'

' Say it once more,' exclaimed Laura, laughing ; ' I have not heard it quite often enough yet. Economy is an admirable thing ; I like it extremely ; it means a handsome house and a fine park, and splendid furniture, and six thousand a-year. This room is a specimen of your economy ; it suits my taste exactly.'

' I am really in earnest, Laura,' replied her husband, more gravely than usual. ' It has been a great delight to procure everything that might make your new home pleasant ; but there is not the less occasion for care.'

' Of course you are right,' said Laura ; ' men always are. Papa recommends economy too, and with more reason : I know his property is encumbered.'

The colour mounted to Edward's cheek. ' I talked to your father,' he said, ' and he perfectly agreed with me ; and you must take advice upon our judgment. Ladies do not understand the details of business.'

' No, indeed,' exclaimed Laura ; ' I never wish to hear the word. Just tell me how much money I may spend, and I shall need nothing more.'

' Suppose I were to say that we ought not to exceed two

thousand a year?' and Edward looked earnestly in his wife's face.

'Then I should say you were speaking nonsense. With a fortune of six thousand, why should we confine ourselves to two? You must be growing miserly in your old age, Edward, or has the burden of a wife brought with it an overburden of prudence?'

'It has brought a burden of anxiety, lest my best earthly treasure should ever have a wish ungratified,' said Edward, affectionately.

'Then I may have my own way,' continued Laura, 'and we will hear nothing more about economy; it is such a very vulgar virtue.'

Edward felt ashamed of his own weakness, but had no strength to overcome it. He could not bear to cloud the brightness of Laura's prospects at the very opening of their married life, and contented himself with the knowledge that he had acted an honourable part by acquainting Mr Howard with the state of his property before he had made his proposal.

'You must learn to believe me serious, my dear Laura,' he replied. 'All comforts and luxuries that are suitable to your position in society I trust you will never want, but anything beyond we must both be contented without.'

'Thank you,' exclaimed Laura; 'I am perfectly satisfied. My position in society is a very desirable one—the mistress of Allingham, and the wife of one of the first persons in the county.'

'Not exactly one of the first; I could name six or seven at least whose fortune is more than double my own.'

'It is not fortune merely,' continued Laura; 'your family and connections must be considered; and, besides, you know, you will soon be a member of Parliament. Papa told me that.'

'It was more than I said,' replied Edward, hastily. 'I acknowledged that I might almost certainly be a county member if I wished it, because the seat has been held by the Allingham Courtenays for years and years; but I did not at all mean to imply that anything would induce me to stand.'

'But I should so like you to be in Parliament,' said Laura; 'you would speak so well. Papa said he was sure you would distinguish yourself.'

'Silly child,' replied Edward, in a tone of half earnestness; 'you must not talk of things you don't understand. Your father was fond of me, and saw everything I did or said in a favourable point of view; but if I had the united talents of all the first men of the age, I have not wealth to support a contested election. It would be ruin.'

Laura laughed gaily: ' They say that there is some point or other upon which every person is insane, and I do think this of economy is yours, Edward. If you practised it I should be frightened, and think you required a keeper ; but happily it all begins and ends in words.'

Unknowingly Laura had touched upon a discordant note. Edward could scarcely have told why the conversation was disagreeable; but he felt it to be so, and threw himself into a chair and took up a book.

' Not now,' said Laura, playfully, as she caught the volume from his hands. ' We are to go over the house together, and I am to look demure, and make speeches to Mrs Somebody the housekeeper, and Mr Somebody the house-steward, and beg them to keep all the other somebodies in order. You know I, who am nobody, cannot possibly talk to somebody, unless you are near to help me.'

' You who are everybody, you mean,' said Edward—' the pervading spirit of the establishment.'

' No, no !' exclaimed Laura ; ' I have warned you often before that I cannot be any such thing. You tell me that you have no intention of making laws for the nation, and I tell you that I have no intention of making laws for the household. They must take care of themselves.

' We shall see,' replied Edward. ' Some persons, you know, are born to greatness, some achieve greatness, and some have greatness thrust upon them. Now, as I conceive that a woman's greatness consists in the proper management of her husband's home, I must insist upon thrusting it on you ; and, as a preliminary step, we will go to the servants' hall.'

Laura made no further objection, and the remainder of the morning was spent in listening to domestic details—which she acknowledged could never be irksome while Edward was at her side—and in wandering from room to room, forming plans for the future, and talking of the friends who were to be invited to fill the house as soon as they were comfortably settled. Something also was said of the poor, and Mrs Dixon, the housekeeper, was strictly enjoined to have soup made three times a week, and allow nothing like waste amongst the servants—an injunction received with such low curtseys and fair promises, that Laura considered nothing more was required to be done.

'I have kept this for the last,' said Edward, as he threw open the folding doors that opened from the antechamber into Laura's morning-room. 'This is especially for yourself, dearest—a place of refuge when you are tired of me, or of your company. You see it is not finished yet, but I intend it to be perfect of its kind.'

Laura's delighted countenance spoke her full approbation, and she ran eagerly to the window to look at the view, but started back immediately. 'O Edward! that cottage—that frightful cottage!—it is precisely in the way.'

'What do you mean?' asked Edward; 'there is no cottage in the front.'

'No, but at the side. Just come where I am, and you will see. It hides the prettiest part of the village, and it is so detestably ugly—you will have it taken down.'

Edward looked considerably annoyed. 'I see how it is,' he said; 'I cut down one or two trees there just before I went away, and it made very little difference from below, but this new window has the full benefit. It was stupid of me not to think about it when I sent my orders. I am sure we might have managed the room differently.'

'But it will be easy enough now,' said Laura; 'you have only to order it to be taken down. The poor people will find plenty of other cottages to go to.'

'If it were a common labourer's cottage, it would not signify,' replied Edward; 'but, unfortunately, it is inhabited by my old nurse, who is fidgety and cross, and has met with many misfortunes; and when she went into it, I promised she should never be turned out again.'

'Shall I quote you a very, very old proverb about promises?' said Laura, as she looked very archly in his face. 'Don't be so solemn, Edward; I am not really advising you to break your word; but there are ways and means.'

'Fire, arsenic, and prussic acid, for instance,' said Edward.

'Oh fie! I never thought of anything half so wicked. What I meant were little, gentle, insinuating ways.'

'Such as the cuckoo uses when it turns its neighbour out of its nest, I suppose,' continued Edward. 'You must explain yourself more clearly.'

'Not yet, because I don't exactly know what I mean myself; but I am sure the thing is to be done, and well and graciously too ; and I shall never rest till it is.'

'Shall I tell you a better mode of satisfying yourself?' said

Edward. 'Make up your mind to bear it patiently, and not think about it. We should never forgive ourselves for making poor old Martha uncomfortable for the few remaining years of her life.'

'But she should not be uncomfortable,' persisted Laura. 'We could easily manage for her to have a cottage quite as good, and a great deal prettier. Besides, Edward, it is a question between your wife and your nurse—which do you love the best?'

'Which have I the greatest confidence in? you should ask. I think that my nurse is old, and ignorant, and fretful; but I think that my wife is sensible, and kind-hearted, and self-denying, and therefore I expect far more from one than I do from the other.'

'Very pretty,' said Laura, 'but not very true. Your wife never was self-denying in her life. It was not the Oakhampton fashion.'

'But it will be the Allingham fashion—and this shall be the first lesson.'

Laura looked disappointed, and there was a little petulancy in her manner as she moved from the window, and walked about the room examining the furniture.

'It is hopeless to think of planting it out,' she said, as she returned to the window; 'it would be years before any trees would grow high enough to hide it.'

'We might cover it with evergreens,' replied Edward; 'it will not be objectionable then. And it might be much worse; it is old and thatched.'

'But the time—just consider the amazing length of time before that hideous red wall can possibly be covered; and every person who comes into the room will see it and talk about it; and I shall have to repeat the story over and over again; and, after all, no one will understand why it is not taken away; for there is not one person in a hundred who would care like you for an old nurse.'

'Dear Laura!' said Edward; 'you cannot possibly be as vexed as I am.   I had set my heart upon your having everything to please you ; and if you only knew how I had planned the room for weeks and weeks, I think you would feel that it was not my fault.

'No,' exclaimed Laura, regaining in an instant her natural sweetness of temper, when she saw that her husband was annoyed; 'I know you could never do anything but what was kind and thoughtful. You will try, though,'—and she laid her hand upon his arm, and looked at him beseechingly.

'Why do you ask me? dearest! you know it is impossible;'—but the tone was less decided, and Laura saw her influence.

'Not quite impossible—only say you will think about it.'

'If it could do any good, I would : but where is the use of thinking, when it is out of one's power to act.'

'There can be no harm in it, and you may find some way of managing.'

Edward turned again to the window, and the cottage was more unsightly than before. He did not say that he would think; but he stood for some minutes in silence; and then, gazing intently on the lovely face at his side, proposed that they should go into the pleasure-ground.

CHAPTER IX.

THE dressing bell at the Priory was heard at the usual hour on that same evening ; and Mrs Courtenay and Jane retired to prepare for dinner ; but Edith still lingered by the drawing-room fire, her eyes fixed on the dreary scene without, but her thoughts wandering to other subjects. She had seen nothing of her brother and sister during the day, yet they had scarcely been absent from her mind for a single hour. They were now expected to dine, and she was to be ready to receive them ; and if they had been strangers, the task would have been easy ; but the recollection of the preceding evening's conversation was too vivid to allow of her feeling any pleasure in the prospect of a family party. She was uncomfortable in Edward's presence, from the doubt whether she had behaved kindly ; and Laura had scarcely uttered a sentence without paining her. To have seen her in society, and watched her graceful manners, and the varying expression of her features, and listened to her clear, silvery laugh, would have been agreeable and interesting ; but to hear her converse and be reminded every moment of Edward's weakness in suffering himself to be captivated by mere external attraction, was a trial of no ordinary nature. Such at least it seemed to Edith ; and as she recalled the different subjects introduced, and the opinions Laura had expressed, her vexation almost vented itself in tears. Instead of a friend and companion, she had found only an elegant, worldly-minded girl, with some natural cleverness, and a certain simplicity and warmth of manner, pleasing on a first acquaintance, but possessing no real charm apart from more valuable qualities. Whatever her disposition might be, it was evident that she had been spoiled by education; and the only hope for Edward's happiness was in his remaining blind to the follies of his wife. In a certain degree, this judgment was correct. Laura was as yet nothing more than an elegant, amiable, clever girl; but it is hard to say that the faults of eighteen are incurable; and whatever had been the defects of her education, the influence of her husband and his family might be all-powerful for good, if only it were exerted aright. In this, however, lay the difficulty. Edward's affection, and inherent weakness of character, caused him to be led, rather than to lead. His mother, and Jane, and Charlotte, possessed scarcely higher principles than his wife; Gertrude was absent; and Edith, the only person who could really be of use, was unconscious of the duty devolving upon her. Even now, as she pondered upon the deficiencies of Laura's character, it never occurred to her that she might be the instrument of effecting a change. Her own duties seemed evident; she was to pursue her usual path, attend to the schools, and visit in the parish and work for the poor, and Laura was to occupy herself as she chose. There was no probability that their tastes would harmonise; and, therefore, the more agreeable line of conduct would be not to interfere, but to wait patiently, in the hope that Edward's example might be of service in raising her tone of mind. And as the resolution was formed, Edith gathered up her work, and, startled by the sound of carriage wheels, went to dress for dinner. The second bell had rung before her toilette was completed, and she felt glad to be spared the irksomeness of the quarter of an hour's formal conversation in the drawing-room, since formal she had determined it must be, while there were so many topics on which there could be no sympathy. But Laura's merry laugh, and Edward's smile, as she seated herself at the table, and apologised for being late, gave no symptoms of formality; and in a few minutes Edith's restraint was subdued by the recital of some travelling adventures, and the grace and ease with which Laura took off the French manner, and mimicked the Normandy patois.

'It must be a delightful thing to have travelled,' said Jane, when they left the dining-room. 'It saves such an infinity of trouble in finding subjects of conversation; and really, with so many acquaintances, talking is the labour of one's life.'

'Not with you, Jane, I am sure,' said Edith; 'you seldom trouble yourself to entertain any one.'

'Nor with you, Edith; for you are never in the way when any one calls. My whole morning is often wasted by visitors.'

'It is not of so much consequence to you as it is to me,' replied Edith; 'for you have not as much to do.'

'There I must beg to differ,' said Jane, pettishly; 'my occupations are as numerous, although they are different from yours.'

'But you cannot mean to say they are equally important,' said Edith.

'Indeed I do. The cultivation of one's own mind is as important as the cultivation of other persons'.'

'Is this the best mode of cultivating one's mind?' asked Edith, ironically; and she took up the last volume of an inferior novel.

Jane made no reply, but her annoyance was evident in her countenance; and Laura, who had never been accustomed to anything like discordance between sisters, felt extremely uncomfortable, and endeavoured, if possible, to turn the conversation. Edith would indeed have been pained, if she had known the impression these few sentences produced. From long habit, she was not aware how perceptible the disagreement between herself and her sisters was to a stranger. She had been accustomed to speak openly—sometimes from an irritation of feeling, sometimes from a real, though mistaken, idea of doing good; and as the difference of opinion seldom went beyond a few passing expressions, or a satirical look, she had not supposed that it would be noticed. Neither was she in general sensible of the extent of the wrong she was committing. The error was so trifling in appearance, as frequently to be unthought of; but it is the constant repetition of a slight fault which effectually destroys the happiness of domestic life; and whether it be indolence, procrastination, carelessness, hastiness of temper, or any of the numerous other minor defects of character, it must always, in the end, mar the influence of the highest virtues. Edith was sincere, and generous, and self-denying; earnest in religion, and unwearied in exertion; and beyond the circle of her own family, was considered a pattern of all that is amiable in woman: but, in her home, she was at times irritable and forgetful, and pursued her notions of duty without sufficient consideration for the prejudices of others ; and her sisters acknowledged her goodness, but accused her of inconsistency, and felt little inclined to follow an example which produced so doubtful a result upon the general happiness.

'How often do you hear from Gertrude?' asked Laura, thinking the subject a safe one.

'Once a week, generally,' said Mrs Courtenay ; 'when her aunt is ill, she writes more frequently, or if she has anything to send. What was there in the packet that came this morning? I forget.'

'A new duet,' replied Edith. 'She fancied it would suit you, Laura, as Edward said you sang a great deal.'

'I used to do so at Oakhampton, for I had almost always a cousin or some one to practise with ; but I never sing anything alone.'

'You must practise a great deal now, my dear,' said Mrs Courtenay; 'you have such a beautiful instrument, and either Edith, or Jane, or Charlotte, when she is at home, will be delighted to sing with you.'

Laura looked at her sisters, expecting the proposal to be received with pleasure, but she was disappointed.

'I sing very little,' said Jane, 'only when no one is at hand to take my part. It is such a great exertion.'

'I don't care for the exertion,' observed Edith ; 'music is worth any trouble, but it takes up so much time.'

'But what is time given us for?' asked Laura, except to enjoy ourselves? I mean a lady's time. Gentlemen and poor people are different.'

'You shall come and stay here,' said Jane, 'and then you will discover. Edith intends giving lectures soon upon the useful expenditure of time, in contradistinction to the ornamental.'

'What do you consider useful, Edith?' asked Laura.

'Let me tell you,' said Jane, before her sister had time to reply. 'First and foremost, teaching reading, writing, and arithmetic, to the dirtiest children in the parish—the dirtier the better ; secondly, walking over ploughed fields and muddy lanes, to see poor creatures in infectious fevers, and returning home, to the serious alarm of your friends, so ill that you can neither speak nor eat ; and thirdly, spending every wet day in making flannel petticoats and smock frocks, and reading sermons.'

'That is an exaggeration, Jane,' said Edith ; 'but even if it were not, no one would deny that it would be a more profitable way of employing one's self than in music, and drawing, and worsted work.'

'And do you mean that you would never attend to such things?' asked Laura.

'Oh yes, occasionally, if I literally had nothing else to do; but that is never the case with me.

Laura was thoughtful for a moment. 'I cannot understand it,' she said. 'I hope Edward will never expect me to lead such a life.'

'What life?' inquired a voice behind her. 'I will answer at once that it can be none which you would dislike.'

'I don't know that, Edward; you have always told me that Edith was your pattern of goodness; and she thinks nothing right but teaching little children, and making poor people's clothes.

'And to a certain point I agree with her. In the primitive days women occupied themselves in necessary domestic duties, and works of charity; now, they fritter away their lives in drawing flowers, and working cross-stitch.'

'But these are not the primitive days,' said Laura; 'we are living in the nineteenth century, and you may as well tell us that we ought to dwell in huts, and live upon acorns. We cannot possibly follow the fashions of centuries ago.'

'It is a sad state of things,' replied Edward, as he seated himself in a luxurious easy chair by the fireside. 'The whole condition of society is corrupted; people seem to have forgotten the very meaning of self-denial, and start back when it is mentioned, as if its name only were a spell to conjure up the errors of Popery.'

'But what has that to do with drawing flowers, and working cross-stitch?' said Laura.

'I was merely thinking of the lives of the sisters of charity, and comparing them with our modern efforts of benevolence. I do most sincerely believe, that the nearest human approach to an angel's life upon earth has been made amongst them.'

'Very possibly,' said Laura; 'but again, will you tell me what has that to do with flowers and cross-stitch?'

Edward laughed. 'I want to hear you sing, my dear; I am sure your voice and Edith's will suit admirably; just try my favourite duet.'

'I will make you answer my question by and by,' said Laura; 'nothing is so unsatisfactory to me as hearing people talk so much of what used to be. What can it signify to us whether the sisters of charity were angels or not, if it is out of our power to be like them?'

'I never said that,' replied Edward; 'what I contend for is, that all ought to be like them. If there were any right feeling amongst us, we should see institutions of a similar kind introduced immediately.'

'But as there is not any right feeling, we may follow our own pleasure,' said Laura; 'I am glad at last to have arrived at a conclusion. So now, Edith, we will go and sing.'

Edward only smiled. As usual, he had theorised well; and with this he was contented, and spent the next hour in lounging in a comfortable posture, listening to the sweet voices of his wife and his sister, and forming Utopian schemes of possible perfection, which only served to impress upon his mind more fully the present evils of society, and the ignorance and folly of the world.

'To-morrow will be my last day of peace,' observed Laura, when the carriage was announced, and the evening closed. 'On Monday, I suppose, we shall be overwhelmed with visitors.'

'I depend upon you, Edith, to help Laura out of her difficulties,' said Edward, turning to his sister; 'you know every one so well, that it will be a real charity to introduce them and find subjects of conversation.'

'There can be no need of that,' replied Edith; 'your foreign tour will be sufficient.'

' But that will involve so much talking of one's self,' said Laura, 'and besides, it is tiresome to repeat the same things over and over again to twenty different persons; and if they happen to compare notes it becomes absurd.'

'You will be at Allingham, of course,' said Edward.

Edith hesitated. 'I would if I could see the use of it, and if Monday were not such a particularly busy day.'

'But is it impossible to obtain one morning's holiday? I should imagine even a secretary of state could do that.'

'A secretary of state is not half such an important person as Edith,' said Jane. 'I wonder you can compare them.'

'You may laugh if you will, Jane,' replied Edith; 'but it is very difficult to find a free day.'

Laura turned to Mrs Courtenay. 'I am sure,' she said, 'you would take compassion upon me if you could, but I was afraid it would be a tax upon you, and therefore I did not think of mentioning it.'

'Certainly, my dear, if I were but twenty years younger, I would do it directly; but either Jane or Edith will be delighted.'

'We did not reckon upon you, Jane,' said Edward, 'knowing you are so uncertain in your health.'

'You were quite right,' was the reply; 'I do not feel equal to support such a day's labour.'

'It will not be at all easy to manage,' said Edith, carelessly; 'but I will see what I can do.'

Laura looked and felt hurt. 'Oh! pray don't put yourself out of the way for me; I should be quite distressed if you were to do it.'

'My dear,' said Mrs Courtenay, 'Edith will like it. Nothing is so pleasant as to sit at home and see one's friends, and have a pleasant chat, when one is strong enough.'

Edith did not echo the sentiment; but merely repeated that 'she would see what could be done, only she could not promise;' and Laura, after again begging her not to inconvenience herself, wished them 'good night,' and returned to the Park.

CHAPTER X.

'I HAVE been looking forward to this introduction with so much pleasure,' said Miss Forester, as she glided into the drawing-room at Allingham, accompanied by Mr Dacre. Laura slightly bowed, and acknowledging the compliment, made the usual observations on the state of the weather.

'Yes, it is very gloomy without; but with so much comfort within, one easily forgets that the day is stormy. You don't venture out, I suppose, unless it is fine.'

'I have not done so yet; but Mr Courtenay laughs at my fears, and says that people who brave the weather seldom take cold.'

'That is so exactly a gentleman's speech. They never give ladies credit for anything but rude health; and I suppose Mr Courtenay is inclined to think lightly on the subject, from the example of his sister Edith: she goes out at all times.'

'A very good practice,' said Mr Dacre.

'Admirable. I have often envied Miss Courtenay's resolution, and lamented that my indifferent health prevents my following the example.'

There was a short pause, interrupted only by Mr Dacre's dry cough. 'Have you been much in this neighbourhood before?' he said, turning to Laura.

'No, never; and I am longing for the spring: they tell me that the scenery is beautiful.'

'Oh lovely, perfectly lovely,' echoed Miss Forester; 'but it may not please you as it does us, for you will find the most charming spots around your own door. We consider Allingham the gem of the county.'

Laura's good taste revolted against the flattery, and she took no notice of it.

'There is a pleasure in novelty,' continued Mr Dacre, 'which to some minds counterbalances everything.'

'I am not sure that it would to mine,' replied Laura. 'From having lived all my life in one home, I cannot fancy any place delightful without some association attached to it.'

'But it need not necessarily be a long one,' said Mr Dacre. 'There are feelings which can do the work of years, and we may hope,' he added, kindly and earnestly, 'that your first associations with Allingham will invest it with a charm beyond all other places.'

Laura felt that the wish was sincere, and her interest in her visitors was increased. 'I am fortunate in one respect,' she said, 'that my expectations were not too highly raised; Mr Courtenay was especially guarded in his descriptions.'

'That is so like him,' softly murmured Miss Forester: 'he is so very thoughtful upon all subjects.'

'Thank you,' said Laura, smiling; 'he ought to be here to thank you himself.'

'Mr Courtenay is coming towards the house now, is he not?' asked Mr Dacre, looking out of the window.

Miss Forester appeared surprised. 'I was not aware that you were acquainted, my dear sir.'

'We have met once before,' was the reply; 'but it is not very probable that Mr Courtenay will recollect me.' Edward, however, did recollect, and as he shook hands, made an allusion to their former acquaintance; yet there was a slight confusion in his manner, and an attentive observer might have discovered, that the circumstances recalled by the sight of Mr Dacre were not perfectly agreeable.

The awkwardness, however, soon wore off, and the conversation flowed rapidly and agreeably. The Continent, its scenery and customs, and the comparison with English habits, were discussed for at least the third time that morning ; but Mr Dacre's strong sense, and Edward's quickness of intellect, gave a superior tone to all that was said ; and Laura listened with delight, and felt annoyed when the entrance of a servant with a note and a parcel interrupted their remarks.

'These are a few lines from Edith,' she said, apologising for reading them ; 'she has sent me the duet we sang the other night, Edward, but she cannot come to us to-day, there is a school meeting in the way.' Edward looked very much disappointed.

'Miss Courtenay is so much occupied,' said Miss Forester, 'that she has but little time at her own disposal, I imagine.'

Edward was still grave and silent, and Laura felt uncomfortable. 'Do you know this duet ?' she said, taking up the music, and rejoiced at having found something to say.

'I have seen it, but I have only tried the second ; indeed, I never sing anything else—my voice is worth so little.'

'I don't know when I shall learn it properly, Edward,' said Laura, 'if Edith is so much engaged. It requires to be practised together.'

'She will not always be busy, my dear ; you must have patience.'

'It does require patience, certainly,' said Miss Forester, 'to wait for music ; one is always so anxious to hear it in perfection immediately—at least, if I may judge from myself. It is quite a passion with me.'

'I did not know that before,' observed Mr Dacre ; 'you have not opened the piano since I have been at the Grange.'

'Oh ! that was because I knew you to be such a judge, and I was shy.'

'I can scarcely understand how you could have known it. I have never mentioned music, and really can only tell what I like or dislike.'

'But that is everything with a correct taste ; it is far beyond mere scientific knowledge.'

'Experience must decide whether a taste is correct or not,' continued Mr Dacre ; 'you will be a better judge of mine when you have had a specimen of it. I like " Auld lang syne " much better than " Tu che accendi." '

' " Auld lang syne " is sweetly simple and touching, certainly ;
I have known some people quite overcome by it.'

' I never was overcome,' replied Mr Dacre ; ' if you mean
crying.

Laura laughed. ' At any rate,' she said, ' you would not confess it. I should like to try the experiment upon you some day.'

A melancholy expression passed over Mr Dacre's face. He
did not accept the challenge. Laura took up the duet, and
looked at it disconsolately. ' It is very tantalising,' she said,
' and I never sing solos.'

' Ah ! that is just like me,' observed Miss Forester ; ' perhaps
—I hope I am not intruding, but it would give me so much
pleasure if sometimes I could make myself useful, as a second,
when the Miss Courtenays are engaged.'

If Laura had watched her husband's countenance, she would
have discovered that the proposal did not meet his wishes ; but,
bred up in indulgence, and having never been taught to consult
any will but her own, she seldom considered it worth while to
inquire what was thought of her actions ; and Edward's fondness had hitherto caused him to see everything she either did **or**
said in so favourable a point of view, that it seemed impossible
he could object to anything which suited her inclinations. Miss
Forester's humble offer of making herself useful was therefore
accepted with pleasure ; and not without a feeling of satisfaction
in Laura's mind, from the consideration that there would be in
consequence less claim upon Edith's time. Since she had
proved herself either so unwilling or so unable to sacrifice her
usual occupations, it would be equally irksome to make a second
request, or provoking to be compelled to relinquish a favourite
amusement. Without hesitation, therefore, Laura fixed an early
day for a musical morning ; and Miss Forester and her uncle
took their leave.

' I wish you had consulted me before you made that arrangement, my dear Laura,' said Edward, when they were left alone,
' could you not see, by my manner, that I disapproved of it ?'

' Perhaps I might have seen it if I had watched ; but for such
a trifle it did not seem worth while to ask advice. It must be
entirely a matter of indifference to you.'

' The choice of your society, my love, can never be a matter of
indifference to me.'

' That is absurd, Edward. Singing a duet with Miss Forester
cannot be called choosing society.'

'It is the first step to it. Music encourages intimacy more than anything.'

'But supposing I am intimate with Miss Forester, why should you object ?'

'Ask yourself, my dear ; the question will be easily answered by your own good sense. What is the impression you have received from Miss Forester's manners and conversation ?'

'Oh ! that she is a very good-natured sort of person ; rather too soft and flattering to be perfectly lady-like ; but very well. More agreeable, at any rate, than half the people one meets with.'

'And these are sterling good qualities upon which it is safe to build a friendship ?'

'You are so extreme in your conclusions, Edward. If we are to wait till we meet with perfection before we form acquaintances, we may as well become hermits. We must take the world as we find it. Besides, if I don't practise with Miss Forester, I shall lose my music entirely.'

'You forget my sisters,' said Edward.

'No, indeed I don't ;—but what can I do? Charlotte takes the same part that I do, Jane is an invalid, and Edith is busy.'

'It is very provoking of Edith,' exclaimed Edward, hastily. 'But she would manage it, I am sure, if you were to ask it as a favour.'

Laura drew up her long, white neck, and looked very proud. 'I am not in the habit of asking favours of any one ; voluntary offers I am most grateful for, but a forced obligation is oppressive.

'But Edith cannot know how much pleasure she could give by a little arrangement of time.'

'Yes, indeed, she does. You were not in the room when we were talking about it the other night. Your mother made the offer for her, but she did not second it ; so I must entreat, Edward, that the subject is not mentioned to her again.'

'I have a peculiar aversion to Miss Forester,' said Edward, speaking his thoughts aloud ; 'almost a dread, she is so utterly insincere.'

'Well !' said Laura, with a disappointed air ; 'it is not worth while to vex you about it. I will give up the notion, though I can't in the least see why you should object to my making her useful.'

'Because usefulness between persons in the same rank of life implies familiarity. If we allow people to put themselves out of their way for us, we must do something for them in return. And this is all very well where there is real regard ; but, if not, there must be a pretence in the matter. Common civility will not satisfy a person who has been doing an uncommon kindness.

'You would do away with all the forms of society,' said Laura, 'if you would allow nothing but what is true. How many people are really dear to us, whom we call dear when we write to them.'

'Very few, probably ; but then every one understands that. Dear, in a note, only means that you have a kindly feeling towards them.'

'That you would not murder them,' said Laura, laughing. 'Well! perhaps you are right there. But about Miss Forester —I only want her to be dear in that sense.'

'Then treat her as you do the rest of the world—be civil to her, but nothing more. If you once allow her to advance one step towards you, you must advance one step towards her ; and if you don't, she will be offended ; and if you do, you will be untrue. There is no alternative, that I can see.'

'Poor Miss Forester !' said Laura ; 'there is little hope for her. She will never be admitted at Allingham.'

'Not on the footing on which your practising mornings would place her, certainly.'

'Then good-bye to my singing,' said Laura, casting a wistful glance at the splendid piano.

'That is exaggerating the case, is it not?' said Edward. 'You will soon learn to sing by yourself ; and my sisters, as I said before, will practise with you whenever they can.'

'Which will be never,' exclaimed Laura, petulantly. ' It is clear, Edward, you do not care to hear me sing.'

'O Laura ! how unkind ! If you only knew the delight it gives me.'

'Are you in earnest ?' she said, and a tear glistened in her bright eye. Edward was much pained ; it was the first tear he had seen since their marriage.

'I will not tell you how truly I am in earnest,' he replied ; 'you would think that I exaggerated. Yet you would not for that reason have me consent to what is wrong.'

'I do not wish you to consent to anything, Edward, for a continuance. I only wish to try just for two or three times, and then you shall see how well I can manage to be quite civil without being hypocritical.' Edward hesitated; and Laura's sweet smile showed that her hopes were raised. 'We will meet half way,' she said; 'you shall let me follow my own wishes for the next fortnight or three weeks, and then we will have another discussion.'

Still Edward hesitated. He knew that by yielding then, he was probably giving up the point entirely; but the compromise was all that was required at the moment; and too conscientious completely to sacrifice his judgment, too weak to say No, he laughingly observed that, 'All the world would say he was governed by his wife;' and Laura was triumphant.

CHAPTER XI.

MISS FORESTER'S proposal, as might easily be conjectured, was not entirely the result of disinterested kindness. It signified nothing to her whether the young bride were pleased or displeased, whether she sang or whether she were silent; but to be placed on an intimate footing at Allingham was an object of considerable importance. It involved amusement for her idle hours, of which she had very many; the enjoyment of luxuries without expense; and, most probably, influence over one who was likely to become the foremost in the society of the neighbourhood. Even in her childhood, Miss Forester had indulged in no dreams of ambition, for the success of which she was to depend on her own exertions. Her mind was of too low a stamp for the formation of those bright visions of fame, or rank, or magnificence, which, however delusive in themselves, imply a craving for enjoyments the world cannot give, and are often accompanied with an energy which may, when rightly directed, enable us to obtain them. She was not indeed insensible to their charms, but she sought them through the efforts of others, rather than through her own; and since the splendour of neither talent, rank, nor riches had been granted her in a degree equal to her wishes, she compensated for the deficiency by living as much as possible in the reflected light of those who were more fortunate than herself. She was mistaken, however, in supposing that Laura was entirely blinded by her flatteries, or willing to put faith in her sincerity. The real foundation of Laura's character was truth ; and however the false cold maxims of her home had corrupted her natural disposition, there still remained enough of simplicity and earnestness to render her easily alive to Miss Forester's artificial character. But beyond this she did not go. Knowledge and action had been so long disconnected in her mind, that the idea of checking an agreeable intimacy on account of its insincere foundation never suggested itself ; for *right* was not on the list of Laura's motives. Of what was pleasant, she thought constantly ; of what was necessary, she was forced to think occasionally ; but what was right she seldom took the trouble to consider, except when Edward endeavoured to imbue her with some of his own principles ; and then she listened, and smiled, and declared he was too good for the world—better than she ever imagined any one could be—so much better than herself that he quite frightened her ; and Edward praised her ingenuousness, and delighted in her humility ; and so the subject was dropped, and the good impression vanished as quickly as it had been made.

For some time, the resolution of holding Miss Forester at a distance, and only allowing her to be useful when the occasion offered, was carefully kept ; and Laura frequently appealed to her husband to acknowledge how well she had estimated her powers, and how exactly she meted out the due measure of civility. But, as Edward had foreseen, a change, gradual, yet not the less perceptible, was after a time produced in the intimacy between Allingham and the Grange. Miss Forester was so extremely good-natured, so easily pleased, so full of anecdotes of Elsham and its vicinity, that Laura's suspicions of her sincerity faded by degrees away. No exertion was needed for her entertainment, for she usually came stored with some family or village history, 'which must on no account be repeated, which she would not indeed have mentioned to any one except her dear Mrs Courtenay, on whose judgment and secrecy she placed such implicit reliance ;' and Laura, who, owing to Edward's engagements, passed many a solitary morning, was glad to escape from the irksomeness of worsted work, or the stupidity of a novel, or the fatigue of writing letters, to the excitement, false and petty though it was, of Miss Forester's tittle-tattle. The frequency of the visits at length, however, became so apparent, that Edward was obliged to enter his protest against them ; but he was met by the same pleading looks, the same earnest assurances that the acquaintance should never go beyond the bounds of ordinary civility, together with complaints of solitary hours, and comparisons between Miss Forester's attentions and Edith's neglect.

'It is useless to make excuses for her, Edward,' exclaimed Laura, at the termination of one of their frequent discussions upon her conduct. 'I know all that you would say, and I believe it to be true. Edith is a most superior person; but it is that very superiority which prevents us from assimilating, and makes her shun me.'

'My dear Laura, you are mistaken entirely; Edith does not shun you; but she is so engaged that she has very little time to bestow upon you.'

'Whatever the reason may be, the effects are the same. We never meet, or, at least, only just in the evening as a matter of propriety. As far as the Priory society goes, I might as well be living at Nova Scotia; and it really is hard, Edward, to be debarred from the company of the only person who is willing to take compassion upon my solitary mornings.'

'But such a person! I should have thought that the loneliness of a few hours would have been paradise compared to the prattle of so very ordinary a person as Miss Forester.'

'Perhaps it might be to a Latin and Greek scholar like yourself, or a saint like Edith; but I am neither the one nor the other; and you know, Edward, if you shut up a poor captive in a cell, he will create companionship for himself, even though it may be with flies and spiders.'

'Rather a spacious cell, though,' said Edward, as he looked round upon the handsome drawing-room, 'and containing considerable stores of amusement; but I am surprised, Laura, at your dislike of being alone: I had your morning room fitted up purposely, because I thought you would enjoy retirement.'

'I should be the first of my family who did, then,' replied Laura, laughing; 'and as to the morning room, it is perfect in its way—every one says so—but I cannot sit there till the cottage is gone. I feel like Aladdin in his fairy palace, only I have a roc's egg too much, instead of one too little.'

'I have thought about it often, my love, since you first mentioned it; but, indeed, I see no remedy except patience.'

'Which is the last remedy I am inclined to use. The wish is scarcely ever out of my mind.'

'But I am sure, dearest, you will not indulge it at the expense of another's comfort.'

'How can I help it? The thoughts come whether I will or not.'

'They may come, certainly, against your inclination; but it is at your own option whether they shall remain.'

'Oh no, Edward; I never can believe that. Actions may be ordered, but not thoughts.'

'My dear Laura,' exclaimed Edward, becoming graver than usual, 'you forget: if we were left to ourselves, you might be right; but you know there is a higher strength than our own, which will always be given us if we ask for it; and remember, in the Bible, evil thoughts are coupled with the greatest crimes.'

'How can that be? they seem sent to us.'

'So they may often be; but as we have it in our own power to cherish or reject them, we are responsible for them.'

'I never shall understand,' said Laura. 'Thoughts and feelings have been my puzzle from my childhood.'

'And, unhappily, they must be to the end of your life,' replied Edward, smiling. 'But we have proofs every day of our power over our own thoughts. If an idea is disagreeable, we turn from it.'

'Yes, but instinctively; we cannot help ourselves.'

'I beg your pardon; we merely obey our own will; and the same power which we exert then, is ours equally at all times. It is the will which is at fault; and one important reason for realising this truth is, that it enables us to study our own hearts so much more easily. Our feelings come and go, and we cannot recall them, but our thoughts are remembered without much difficulty, and by them we may try ourselves,—that is, we may judge whether we are improving, by seeing whether we encourage the good and reject the evil.'

'So I shall not be good, I suppose, till I leave off thinking about that hideous cottage,' said Laura, 'and that will be a very long time. Even you yourself, Edward, wish it away.'

'It is not the wish which is wrong, but the indulging it. You know that a wish is the germ of an action.'

'It cannot be in this case. I might try for ever, and I should not be able to turn that tiresome old woman out of her house. That must be your doing.'

'Yet, if you go on wishing, you will infallibly do all that you can. It is more dangerous for a man or a woman to play with wishes, than for a child to play with edged tools.'

'I should care less if there were any hope,' said Laura—'if I thought you would even hint at the subject.'

'There would be no use in it,' replied Edward; 'I know old Martha better than you do.'

Laura perceived symptoms of wavering in the tone in which this was spoken.

'A hint could not be wrong,' she said, 'and it would at least be satisfactory. It is so provoking to be obliged to sit down contentedly when no effort has been made to gain one's point.'

'But you would not be contented even then,' said Edward.

'That is prejudging; but I will not quarrel with you; though I own I am disappointed.'

The words jarred painfully upon Edward's feelings of affection, and Laura saw it.

'I ask only for hope,' she said, 'that you should promise to try, if you find a fitting opportunity.'

'Well, then, will you sit in your morning room, and like it?' he said, as he looked at her fondly.

Laura smiled, and was about to reply and thank him, when the sound of the hall bell interrupted the conversation; and a few moments afterwards Miss Forester's soft, sliding step, was heard in the passage. Edward seemed annoyed, and, taking up his hat, he opened the French window, and turning an angle of the house, was out of sight before Miss Forester entered.

'So very thoughtful! my dear Mrs Courtenay,' was the first exclamation. 'I am afraid I have intruded at a *mal-à-propos* moment.'

'No, not at all, my meditations were not peculiarly agreeable, since they were bordering upon impossibilities. I have been talking to Mr Courtenay upon the same subject which you and I discussed the other morning.'

'The cottage? But surely that is not an impossibility!'

'Perhaps not precisely; but there are great difficulties in the way; and I can only make Edward say that he will give hints; he will take no active measures.'

'Gentlemen are so tiresome,' said Miss Forester, who well knew that few things are more winning than sympathy in a supposed grievance: 'but he must own that it is frightful, and the view would be perfection without it.'

'Yes, Edward fully allows its ugliness, though he does not hate it as I do. If I were master, it should not remain where it is another day.'

'I suppose,' continued Miss Forester, 'that Mr Courtenay

would not object to anything being done if the old woman's consent were gained first?'

'No; but how is that to be accomplished? He does not say that he will not interfere, but I can see he is not inclined to do it.'

'Then, perhaps, he would prefer your saying something to sound the old woman. It would save his conscience, and might gain what he must desire nearly as much as yourself.'

'I don't think that is likely, because Martha is proverbial for obstinacy and ill-humour.'

'Then she certainly can have no claims upon your forbearance. Do you know her?'

'No; I have talked of going there several times, for Mr Courtenay has been rather anxious I should; but there are so many things to be done every day, and I am such a bad walker, that I have never yet been able to manage it.'

'It is not far,' said Miss Forester, 'and the morning is delightful; so very fresh and bracing.'

'I could not go without saying something to Edward first,' replied Laura.

'Mr Courtenay's horse was standing ready saddled as I passed the stables,' said Miss Forester, 'so I conjectured he was going out this morning.'

'Yes, he did intend it, but he can scarcely have set off yet; he was with me but a few minutes ago.'

'I heard the trampling of horses' feet just now,' continued Miss Forester. 'Does Mr Courtenay wish particularly to accompany you when you pay your first visit to this old favourite?'

'Not that I am aware of; but there would be no good in seeing her if we did not suggest something about the cottage, which I really should not like to do.'

'But it would not be necessary to speak openly; and, at any rate, a visit now would pave the way for future operations.'

'That is true,' replied Laura, thoughtfully. 'We might go and make friends, and by degrees prevail on her to yield; and, as you observed just now, Edward may prefer my taking the task off his hands, since he allows that it may be possible to give Martha a few hints, though he will have nothing done against her will.'

'Exactly so. Mr Courtenay would be pleased rather than otherwise, I should think, to find that you had taken so much trouble about the poor old woman.'

Laura's sincerity, at first, could not suffer an amiable motive

to be falsely imputed to her ; and she quickly disclaimed all idea
of goodness, though still agreeing that it would be worth while
to go, and that it might be of use in the end.   A slight misgiving
rested upon her mind as she went to prepare for her walk, and
once she recollected Edward's warnings against wishes ; but as
she was merely intending a kind, conciliatory visit, they did not
seem precisely applicable ; and when conscience again whispered that all was not right, she wilfully turned away from the
consideration of her real motives, and soon almost persuaded
herself that Miss Forester was correct, and that she really was
about to do what her husband would entirely approve.

CHAPTER XII.

THERE was something of timidity and hesitation in Laura's
gentle knock at old Martha's door ; partly caused by her
utter ignorance of the feelings and habits of the poor, and partly
by the secret self-distrust which yet lingered in her heart.   Miss
Forester, however, participated in neither feeling ; and finding
that no answer was given, lifted the latch, and without further
ceremony entered the cottage.

Martha was seated, in her usual position, on a low, half-broken
elbow chair, by the side of the open hearth.   A book was placed
on the little round table beside her, but she did not appear to
have been reading it ; and, bending over the smouldering fire,
she was busied only in watching the black pot suspended from
a stick that crossed the wide chimney, and from time to time
stretching out her withered hand to stir the burning logs, or to
add fresh fuel from the basket of chips in the corner.   An eye
accustomed to the sight of poverty, would have traced symptoms
of competence and comfort in the simple furniture of the room ;
in the short curtain hanging before the door, and the old-fashioned
handsome clock, and mahogany chest, and neat dresser, with its
range of pewter dishes and china cups and basins ; but Laura,
who from infancy had been carefully kept from all scenes but
those of opulence and luxury, thought only that the cottage was
low and dark ; that the walls were smoke-dried ; that the floor
was uneven ; and the furniture by no means sufficient for comfort.

' She must be glad to leave such a wretched hole,' whispered

Miss Forester, as she drew her dress closely around her, and bent her head in an assumed fear lest it should touch the dingy rafters.

Martha raised herself from her crouching posture, and gazed with surprise on the intruders. Her strongly marked features, and the cold, stern expression of her thin lips, and dim gray eyes, startled Laura so much, that she forgot, for an instant, the necessary apology ; and Miss Forester, feeling that the visit was not hers, was silent likewise ; but Martha was not in the humour to wait patiently for an introduction.

' Maybe you 'll be pleased to tell me what you 're come here for ? ' she said, in a harsh voice.

' We came to see you,' replied Laura, gently ; ' I am Mrs Courtenay, of Allingham.'

Martha's rigid features relaxed, and something which she intended to be a smile brightened her wrinkled face.—' Mrs Courtenay, are you ? Master Edward's fine lady. Well ! I 'm glad you 're here at last.'

' I am sure you must be extremely grateful to Mrs Courtenay for walking so far to see you,' suggested Miss Forester.

' Grateful ! yes, I 'm as grateful as most people where there 's anything to be grateful for ; I 'd be grateful to God first, and to Master Edward afterwards, and Miss Edith and the parson, but I don't know much about other folks.'

' You are an old servant of Mrs Courtenay's family, are you not ? ' said Miss Forester ; ' you seem very comfortably provided for.'

' Maybe I am,' exclaimed Martha, turning sharply round ; ' I lived twenty years up at the Priory there, and worked for them night and day ; so, 'twould have been hard if they had not done something for me.'

' I am sure Mr Courtenay would be very sorry if he thought you were in want of anything,' observed Laura, anxious to soothe her.

' 'Tisn't my way to doubt it,' said Martha, shortly.

' Mrs Courtenay will think you are not obliged for all that has been done for you, if you speak in that way,' said Miss Forester ; ' she is not used to it.'

' No ! I daresay not : Tom Slater says that down at their fine place no one is thought anything of that doesn't ride in a carriage.'

' Who is Tom Slater ? ' asked Laura ; wondering that any one at Elsham should profess an acquaintance with her home.

'Tom Slater is the head man who was at work up at the Hall there. Poor fellow: he and my Becky were to have made it up together, and then 'twould have been all very well; but the fever came, and Becky got ill, and when she was gone, 'twas all over with me in the way of being happy again! To have lived up at the Park would have been no pleasure then.' Tears filled the old woman's eyes, and Laura's naturally kind feelings were touched; yet she could not forego the occasion of introducing some allusion to the object of her visit.

'Then, I suppose,' she said, 'it does not signify to you where you live now; one place must be just like another.'

'Well! perhaps it is; but I never liked change; where I settled myself down, I chose always to stay.'

'Only, I suppose,' said Miss Forester, 'that when the trouble of moving was over, you would not care.'

Martha raised her head, and looked full in Miss Forester's face. 'Are ye driving at anything?' she said, her suspicions easily excited upon the subject which had lately been uppermost in her thoughts.

Laura felt a little abashed, but Miss Forester answered with *nonchalance*, 'We were only anxious to know if you were well off here, or would be more comfortable elsewhere. Mrs Courtenay is extremely desirous that you should have everything you may require.'

'Is she?' said Martha. 'I want nothing but to be left in peace where I am; and Mr Edward has promised me that.'

'I suppose,' said Miss Forester, 'he only promised it, in case he could not find any place better suited for you. He could not have thought this dark room as good as many others in the neighbourhood.'

'He never told me what he thought, but I told him what I thought; and if a dark room pleases me, 'tis no one's concern but my own.'

'You forget,' said Miss Forester, 'that there are many persons who wish to see you well provided for: Mrs Courtenay for one, besides your own family.'

'Who's the best judge of what's being well provided for?' said Martha. 'No one knows my own mind like myself. If Mr Edward would order a pint of porter sometimes for Willie's little girl, I'd thank him; and a shilling or two for the family, I shouldn't say "No" to; but I don't wish him to trouble about me.'

'Does your son live far off?' asked Laura.

'Something about half a mile; but he generally contrives to see me every day; or one of the children comes to me.'

'If you were close to them you would be more comfortable, surely,' said Miss Forester; 'you must spend so many hours alone.'

'It's best for an old woman like me: the children are noisy, and I can't bear them for long.'

Laura could scarcely help smiling at the pertinacity with which Martha refuted all the objections that could be made to her present situation; but the very difficulty of success served to increase her anxiety, and she sat for a few moments in silence, endeavouring to discover some new point of attack. Martha, finding that the conversation had dropped, turned again to the fire; and Miss Forester walked towards the door, unwilling to take any more trouble in a cause which did not materially affect her own personal comfort.

Martha was the first to break the silence, with a remark which plainly showed she desired the departure of her visitors. 'It's getting on late,' she said; 'my bit of meat will be ready by twelve o'clock; and I thought Miss Edith would have been here before,—she said she would.'

'Do you expect Miss Courtenay, then?' said Laura, half-alarmed at the prospect of a rencontre with her sister-in-law.

'It's her day for coming, and she most times keeps true to her word.'

'Don't you think we had better think of returning?' said Miss Forester, entirely participating in Mrs Courtenay's feelings.

Laura moved, with the intention of wishing good-bye. The few civil words at parting were quickly said: and she thought they were safe; but Edith, true to the appointment, approached the cottage just as they were leaving it; and the meeting was unavoidable. At another time, Laura might have felt indifferent to the smile on Edith's face, and to her expressions of pleasure that she should have taken the trouble to visit a poor person; but now, with the consciousness of a selfish motive, they sounded reproachfully, and the tone of her own reply was hurried, and to Edith's ear ungracious.

'It is the first day I have been able to walk so early,' she said, 'and I daresay I shall not do so again for some time.'

'Oh yes! I am sure you will, since you have once begun,' replied Edith, kindly; 'it is but the first effort that is difficult.'

'There is nothing very alluring in the occupation,' observed

Miss Forester, ' when only discontent and rudeness are to be met with.'

Edith almost started. In her surprise at meeting her sister-in-law, she had scarcely thought who was her companion ; but the well-known voice brought the fact forcibly before her ; and her satisfaction in the meeting was considerably damped.

' Martha is not very civil, certainly,' she said ; ' but there are great allowances to be made for her; she had no education, and was early soured by misfortunes; and her heart is much softer and more grateful than it appears.'

' It may be so,' said Laura, carelessly; ' but I wish you would give her a lesson in good manners. It will be long before I am tempted to come again.'

' But,' said Edith, ' when your motive is kindness, her civility cannot make any difference to you, except in the pleasure you receive. It is rather an additional reason, indeed, for seeing her often, and teaching her better.'

' Oh! I leave that to you; besides '—and Laura slightly coloured—' I don't wish you to think me better than I am, Edith ; my motive was not entirely kindness.'

Edith looked surprised, but did not know what reply to make ; and Miss Forester felt bewildered by a candour, to which there was no counterpart in her own breast.

' I should really feel obliged to you, Edith,' continued Laura, speaking very quickly, ' if you could find some means of persuading that tiresome old woman to move out of her cottage; she is beyond hints.'

' O Laura !' exclaimed Edith, indignantly, ' you have not been saying anything ! Remember Edward's promise. It would be so very wrong to urge the point.'

' Perhaps I am an equally good judge with yourself as to the right or wrong of the case,' replied Laura, in a cold, proud tone, —which proved that her transient fit of humility had vanished before her sister's reproach. ' I have given no hints that could be understood, or inflict the least pain, and you may be sure that Edward will be a very safe guardian of his own promise.'

' He will intend to be,' replied Edith; ' but you cannot be ignorant of your influence, Laura.'

' I think too highly of him to suppose I could make him do anything he considered wrong,' said Laura; ' but you seem to have a more unfavourable opinion.'

The assertion was provoking, from the mixture of unpleasant

truth it contained; for, doubtful as Edith had lately been of her
brother's firmness, she did not always acknowledge it to herself.

'Whether your power over Edward is great or small,' she
replied, 'it ought equally to be exerted rightly; and you cannot
really think it would be justifiable to ask any one to do a thing
they had promised not to do.'

'Really, Edith,' exclaimed Laura, 'I must discuss the subject
another time; it is too cold this morning to stand so long in the
open air—so good-bye.'

'Good-bye,' replied Edith, in a calm tone, which told little of
her real feelings; and with a distant bow to Miss Forester, she
walked towards the cottage.

'So you're come at last,' was Martha's salutation. 'If you'd
been here a minute before, you'd have seen Master Edward's
lady.'

'I have just seen her, nurse; we parted only ten yards from
your door.'

'Then maybe, Miss Edith, you can tell me what she came
for; it's more than I can.'

'Oh! it is not very difficult to imagine,' said Edith, striving
to evade the question. 'Being my brother's nurse, she must
naturally feel interested about you.'

'But it wasn't that,' said Martha, as she fixed her keen eye
upon Edith. 'She didn't come for nothing—I'm sure she didn't
—and her talk wasn't like it. Nothing of asking for the
rheumatism, or the pigs, or how I slept, and such like things,
—only speering to know if I shouldn't like to change house.
Maybe, Miss Edith, she means that I shall, whether I like it
or not.'

'You must not be fanciful, Martha,' said Edith; 'why don't
you think that I have some motive for coming here?'

'Because it wouldn't be like you,' said Martha, as she took
Edith's hand in hers: 'it wasn't like you when you was a child;
and I'm sure it isn't like you now, for all the village says there's
no one that thinks of them as you do—only the parson and his
lady.'

'But you must not praise me, and think unkindly of my sister,'
said Edith: 'she won't be willing to come here again, if you are
not more pleased to see her.'

'I shouldn't mind so much if she was to come alone,' said
Martha; 'but that Miss that was with her, no one ever found
any good where she was. All the people for twenty miles round

would tell you so; she is always prying and fault-finding, and doing some mischief.'

'Hush! hush! Martha,' said Edith; 'you know we are told not to speak evil of our neighbours.'

'It isn't evil,' said Martha; 'only what's true. They never give away to the value of a brass farthing up at the Grange.'

'But it may be evil though it is true,' replied Edith; 'and the less we speak of other people's faults the better.'

'Well, then, I won't say no more about her—only I never knew her to be seen anywhere but what mischief was sure to follow after; and so 'twill be now, as certain as I'm living.'

Martha's tones were so raised by the excitement into which she was working herself, that Edith did not hear the sound of approaching footsteps; and the first notice she received of the presence of a third person, was by a hand laid upon her shoulder, while Edward's voice asked 'how long she had been there.'

Edith's face brightened with pleasure. In his presence the charm of his society made her forget her doubts and disappointments, except when painfully reminded of them by Laura's conversation, or his own inconsistencies; and at that instant, when she thought that he was no partner in his wife's selfishness, the deep, pure love of her childhood, the love which years, and absence, and opposing interests may stifle, but can never extinguish, rose in its full force, and with a warmth which lately had been seldom shown, she expressed her delight at their meeting.

'One would think you'd been over the seas,' said old Martha, not entirely pleased at being made of secondary importance: 'I daresay now you was together all day yesterday.'

'No indeed,' said Edith; 'nor the day before, nor the day before that; we are becoming quite strangers to what we once were.'

'And whose fault is it, Edith?' said Edward, kindly, yet gravely. 'Not mine: you know the Hall is your home, at all seasons and all hours.'

'Nor mine,' replied Edith; 'circumstances cannot be avoided.'

'So we think when we do not make the effort: but we will talk of that by and by. I want to know how you are, Martha: how is the rheumatism? You must be feeling it again now, I should fear; the weather has been so damp till to-day.'

'Yes, it's bad enough sometimes,' said Martha, in a less sulky tone than usual; 'but it's not like last winter. The curtain up there keeps out a deal of air.'

' That was your thought, Edith,' said Edward ; ' it would never have entered my head ; but is the cottage comfortable, Martha? —you used to say it smoked.' ·

' So it does still with a north-easter, but somehow I 'm got used to it, and a little of it seems thick and snug.'

' That is a novel notion,' said Edward, laughing ; ' but you have turned over a new leaf since you came here, Martha, and are determined to make the best of everything.'

The old woman smiled grimly, as she answered—' No, no, Master Edward, that never was my way yet : but I don't care for things so much as I used, only for being quiet. A long life 's a long journey, and one is glad to sit down at the end of it.'

' Still I can't help wishing you had a more comfortable resting-place,' observed Edward. ' A little more light, for instance, would be an advantage.'

' So Tom Slater says, when he comes here and talks about the cottage at the end of the lane ; but I tells him to let me be quiet, for you 've promised I shan't move unless it pleases me, and I 'm sure it never will. As for the light, there 's a very good place for another window just behind the door, if so be as you 're inclined for it.'

This did not exactly meet Edward's wishes. During his solitary ride he had been pondering much upon his conversation with Laura, and longing to devise some plan for gratifying her ; and although without any intention of breaking his word, or forcing his old nurse to consent to what might be against her notions of comfort, the desire of pleasing his wife became, upon consideration, so strong, that after a little hesitation, he turned his horse's head in the direction of Martha's cottage, with the determination of sounding her upon the subject of the exchange. She seemed, however, more bent than ever upon being satisfied on this one point, though discontented on almost every other, and Edward felt irritated as the conversation proceeded, and as he found how insuperable a barrier lay between his inclination and his duty ; and breaking off abruptly in the middle of a sentence, he exclaimed, ' Well, Martha, I see you are resolved to live and die where you are ; but if you were nearer to us it would be better : Mrs Courtenay would be able to see you oftener then.'

' Laura has been here this morning,' said Edith : ' we parted just before you came.'

' Has she indeed ?' exclaimed Edward, with evident pleasure.

'That is so like her—doing the very things she knows I most wish, yet so secretly that I can never find them out till afterwards. You must go with her, Edith, now she has once begun seeing the poor people ; she will want some one to introduce her.'

Edith looked grave, and was silent.

'I don't think your young madam is much used to poor folks,' said Martha : 'she didn't seem to know what to do with herself when she came.'

'She was shy, I daresay, at a first visit,' replied Edward ; 'but she will be delighted to send anything for you that you may want from the Hall, and I am sure she will come and see you frequently.'

'Don't let her come with that Miss from the Grange, then,' said Martha : 'nobody wants her—there's always mischief at her heels.'

'Was Miss Forester here too?' asked Edward, turning to his sister, and speaking quickly. 'What could have induced Laura to bring her?'

'I only spoke to them for a minute,' replied Edith, 'and had no time to ask questions; but I wonder you are surprised : Miss Forester is always at the Hall.'

Edward frowned and bit his lip, scarcely knowing whether to be most provoked with Miss Forester's visits, or his sister's observations. 'Did the ladies stay with you long, Martha?' he said.

'Oh no; just while they were putting some questions about the cottage, and my liking it, as you might have been doing but now, Master Edward. They didn't seem to care for anything but that ; and if you please to ask them when you gets home, they'll be sure to tell you they was driving at something. They didn't come here for nothing, not they. That Miss never went nowhere for nothing.'

'What does she mean, Edith?' said Edward, taking his sister aside. 'What has Laura been doing?'

'Really I cannot say. As I told you, I only met her at the door, and then she seemed annoyed at Martha's manner, and asked me to find some way of making her consent to leave her cottage.'

Edward took up his hat as if to go away, but suddenly recollecting himself, exclaimed, 'I have no time to stay any longer, nurse,—I shall come another day, so good-bye now. Edith, you will walk home with me.' And they left the cottage together. Martha looked after them for a few moments in considerable surprise, and then, with a raised hand and a muttered ejaculation— 'Hugh! what's come over the young things? they're up and off like a windy day!'—she drew her chair nearer the hearth, and began her preparations for dinner.

CHAPTER XIII.

EDITH and her brother continued their walk for some little distance without speaking; but Edward's quick step and impatient flourish of his whip, as he demolished every thistle and bramble within his reach, showed that his feelings were not quite calm. 'What can be done?' he exclaimed at length, partly addressing himself to Edith, and partly giving utterance to his secret thoughts. 'She is the last person Laura ought to be with.'

'Who?' asked Edith, quietly.

'Why do you ask, Edith? There is but one person in the neighbourhood whom we really dislike, and it is so provoking that Laura should have taken such a fancy to her.'

'And still more provoking that she should be led by her,' observed Edith. 'I am certain Miss Forester was at the bottom of that visit to old Martha.'

'You must be mistaken there,' said Edward. 'Laura would not take any steps about the cottage without consulting me, and she knows my determination. I will never trust any one but myself to sound Martha upon the subject; she is so keen that she would see through it at once, and think I meant to break my word; and indeed it would be useless; I went as far as I dared just now, and it was evident that she will never willingly move.'

'Certainly,' replied Edith, 'nothing could be more clear; but I don't think I am mistaken in supposing that Laura wished to induce her to consent. In fact, she implied as much in the short conversation we had together, and I was longing to see you, Edward, to speak about it.'

'You don't mean,' exclaimed Edward, pausing abruptly in his walk, 'that you imagined for one instant that any persuasions could induce me to break my promise?'

'Not exactly,' replied Edith, hesitatingly, not choosing to inquire to what extent she had learned to distrust him; 'but the very idea would be painful to poor old Martha, and I don't think Laura perceives this; and she might wish you to propose, though not to urge it.'

'And you don't think I have firmness to refuse,' said Edward. 'That is not what I should have expected from you.'

The tears rose to Edith's eyes, and her voice slightly faltered, as she answered, hastily—'I don't know what you ought to expect now, Edward, it is all so changed.'

'What do you mean? who is changed?—not myself, I am sure. Tell me what you mean?'

'Nothing—nonsense. There is no good in talking of it: we cannot make things as they once were : and you would not wish it.'

'But you would,' said Edward, in a grave, reproachful tone.

Edith was silent.

'It is your own fault, Edith,' he continued. 'The change, if there is a change, is in yourself. The love which was yours before I married, is yours still. Allingham may be your home now, as it was then ; but you refuse it ; you estrange yourself from us, and then complain of alterations.'

'No, Edward!' exclaimed Edith; 'I do not complain—I never could—I have no right—your choice was your own, and no one can blame you for consulting your own happiness.'

'Then why is there this reserve between us ?' asked Edward. 'We have often talked of my marriage as a thing of course—no one could have entered more warmly into my feelings. Why should you shut yourself up from me now, and shun the society of the person I flattered myself would have been as dear to you as your own sisters ?'

'I do not shun any one,' replied Edith : 'but I have many occupations, and but little time to myself; and my society is not likely to give Laura any pleasure.'

'That will not deceive me,' said Edward; 'constrained humility never can.'

'I don't wish to deceive any one,' replied Edith, with something of haughtiness ; 'but if persons are unlike in taste and disposition, it is vain to hope they will ever assimilate.'

'Certainly not, if they resolutely determine that there shall be no neutral ground upon which to meet—and this seems to be your case.'

‘There can be no neutral ground formed, where none exists,’ said Edith ; ‘but we are talking foolishly, Edward ; you can never understand, and I can scarcely desire that you should.’

‘But, indeed, I do understand,’ replied Edward ; ‘you fancy that Laura, because she has been bred up with London notions, cannot enter into yours ; but she can into mine—and once, Edith, that would have been sufficient.’

‘Yes, once—once !’ exclaimed Edith, eagerly, ‘but !’—— and she paused.

‘Why should you hesitate ?’ continued her brother ; ‘my most earnest wish is, that you should speak to me without reserve.’

‘It is impossible !’ said Edith. ‘And I know I am wrong—I ought not to grieve over a disappointment which is a mere trifle, compared with what others suffer. If you are happy, Edward, I will be so too.’

‘You are unintelligible,’ replied Edward. ‘Where is the disappointment you speak of ? Is it in my affection ?’

‘Oh no—no !—but pray do not let us talk any more about it! it can only be painful to both.’

‘Nothing can be so painful as reserve between those who once shared every thought,’ said Edward ; ‘imagination always conjures up worse visions than reality.’

‘Not always ;’ and Edith sighed deeply.

‘I cannot bear this, Edith!’ exclaimed her brother, impatiently. ‘You know me too well to believe that I can. If you have any complaint to make of me or of Laura, I must entreat that you will speak openly.’

‘I have said before that I have nothing to complain of,’ replied Edith, with forced calmness ; ‘but, Edward, you are unreasonable to expect that I can tell you everything I think and feel, now, as I did before your marriage. Our positions are totally changed.’

‘They are, indeed !’ exclaimed Edward ; ‘more so than I could have imagined possible. I am only thankful there is still one person in the world who has no mysteries with me.’

Edith turned away in bitterness of heart, and then, giving way to the hasty feeling of the moment, ‘If you are satisfied with your wife, Edward,’ she said, ‘it is enough. Whatever I may think can be a matter of no consequence.’

‘But it is ; it must be a matter of consequence!’ he exclaimed. ‘How can I endure to see one who is dearer to me than my own

life, misunderstood and depreciated by those who ought to love
and delight in her?'

'Ought!' repeated Edith, ironically.

'Yes, ought!' continued Edward, 'if gentleness, and temper,
and grace, and all that can make a woman amiable, are to be
loved and admired, then Laura *ought* to have your warmest
affection.'

The irritable feelings working in Edith's mind were completely roused by what she saw to be the blindness and error
of the assertion; and forgetting the delicacy of her position,
and the respect due to her brother's feelings, she exclaimed:
'If gentleness consists in being led by no one but Miss Forester,
and amiability in wishing to turn old Martha out of her cottage,
few can give Laura more credit for both than myself.'

The words were no sooner uttered than they were repented
of; but the wish to efface their impression was as vain as the
endeavour to recall them.

Edward's face became very pale, and his brows were closely
knit. He did not trust himself with a reply; and making a
sudden leap over a stile near him, walked with rapid strides
across the adjoining field, and Edith was left alone to her
meditations.

CHAPTER XIV.

LAURA'S glance at her husband, as he entered the dressing-
room in which she was resting after the exertion of her
unusually long walk, convinced her that something had occurred
to annoy him; and her conscience reminded her instantly of
her offence, not indeed against his commands, but against his
wishes. In general, she would have risen with delight to meet
him, and her book would have been thrown aside without
regret; but now, with a faint smile, she merely observed that
he was quickly returned, and then, fixing her eye on the page
before her, appeared engrossed with its contents. She was
wrong, however, in imagining herself the sole or even the principal subject of his angry feelings. By far the larger share was
bestowed upon Edith; yet the truth contained in the observation that had so deeply excited him was too evident to be

entirely withstood; and although, while retracing his steps homeward, his quick and varying thoughts had found ample cause for indignation at his sister's unkindness, their bitterness was increased by the consciousness that her reproach was not without foundation.   Blindly and devotedly as he loved his wife, Edward was still, in some measure, alive to her faults; but there was a wide difference between an acknowledgment made in the secrecy of his own heart, and Edith's open accusation; and the faults which, from their apparently trifling character, were allowed, when observed only by himself, seemed unjustly magnified when they excited the attention of another.   Resentment against his sister, therefore, was the feeling uppermost in his mind; and it was one which he scarcely endeavoured to check, since it sprang from a sense of his wife's wrongs rather than his own; and the first glimpse of Laura's beautiful features tended considerably to increase his irritation against one who had proved insensible to her fascination.   For a short time he stood at the window, watching her in silence; and at last, annoyed at the change in her manner, said, with something of severity—

'Your book must be peculiarly interesting, Laura.'

'Yes! it is—very'—she replied, hastily, and not daring to lift her eyes to his.

'Are you tired, that you are lying down?'

'Tired? yes—no—not particularly—only I have been walking.'

'So I suppose: did you go far?'

'Yes—that is, not any great distance—I don't know exactly what you call far'—and Laura gazed again upon her book; but her natural ingenuousness overcame her timidity, and throwing down the volume, she rose from the sofa, and said, after some hesitation, 'I went with Miss Forester to see your old nurse.'

Edward's features did not relax, and his voice was even graver than before.

'If you had asked me,' he answered, 'there would have been no occasion for Miss Forester's services; it must have been a sudden freak.'

'You are vexed with me, Edward,' said Laura; 'I wish you would tell me so at once.'

'There can be no occasion for it, since it is so evident.   It cannot be a matter of surprise to you that I am annoyed at your preferring Miss Forester's society to mine.'

' O Edward! that is unjust—more than unjust—it is cruel; but you do not mean it.'

' I merely reason from facts. You knew that it was only necessary to express a wish, and I should have been delighted to go with you. I have been urging the visit for the last three weeks without success; but I must ask Miss Forester the secret of her eloquence, when I wish to gain my point another time.'

' This is nonsense, Edward,' replied Laura; ' you are not really jealous of Miss Forester's influence, or of any other person's. The idea is too absurd to make me angry. It would be much kinder to tell me plainly what is the matter.'

' I leave it to you to find out,' he said; ' if you are unconscious of having done anything against my wishes, of course I am mistaken.'

Laura became pale, and her voice was tremulous as she replied, ' I did not expect this from you, Edward. I thought our agreement was one of openness and sincerity on each side. But I will not be the one to forget it,' she continued, in a firmer tone; ' I have been wishing for something which you desired me not to think of; I have been longing to get rid of the cottage, and I have been sounding old Martha about it, but I have done nothing more; and I should not have ventured even upon that, if you had not almost promised me you would give her a hint yourself. If it is a fault, it is one easily repaired.'

' O Laura!' exclaimed her husband, his displeasure vanishing before the ingenuousness of the avowal; ' why will you not show yourself to every one such as you are to me? Why will you give rise to observations and misconstructions, and cause me the great pain I have experienced this morning? I felt Edith was harsh, and yet she said nothing but what was true.'

' Edith!' repeated Laura, in surprise; ' your sister! I knew she did not love me, yet she need not have spoken against me to my husband;' and Laura's tears flowed fast as she spoke.

' That need not be a cause of grief, dearest,' replied Edward; ' the whole world might speak against you, without causing the slightest shade of variation in my love; but there is something which ought to pain you, as it does me—that you should act in a way to give rise to any unkind observations.'

' But how—why—what have I done?' exclaimed Laura, raising her head; ' why should Edith interfere, and make remarks? I will confess to you, Edward, where I have gone contrary to your wishes; and I will bear anything and everything you may choose to say; but I will never submit to have my actions commented on by any other human being, much less one who has shown me so little kindness as Edith.'

'It is what we must all submit to,' replied Edward; 'the world, and our relations, and our friends, will comment upon our actions, whether we will submit to it or not; it is vain to hope that we can escape unnoticed; but nothing that is said against us can be of any consequence, unless it is well founded.'

'And what did Edith say?' asked Laura, eagerly.

'She implied that you suffered yourself to be led by Miss Forester; and she added something about your want of consideration for poor old Martha, which it was most painful to me to listen to.'

'And she heard it from myself,' exclaimed Laura; 'I said a little to her on the subject, merely because she should not give me credit for better motives than I deserved; and then she turned my own words against me, to injure me in my husband's estimation.   Is this your pattern sister, Edward?'

'Not to injure you in your husband's estimation,' replied Edward, fondly.   'No one can do that but yourself.'

'Yet you believed her, and felt angry with me.'

'I had reason to believe her.   Miss Forester's intimacy is daily before my eyes; and the motive of your visit to old Martha you had acknowledged yourself.'

'Miss Forester would never speak against me behind my back,' replied Laura.   'Whatever her faults may be, she will not endeavour to make mischief between us; and as to your old nurse, it is absurd to make a fuss about such a trifle.   I merely asked a few questions as to whether she was comfortable in her cottage, in order to find out whether she would be inclined to move; and she was extremely ungracious and disagreeable, and then I went away.'

'It would have been rather better to have waited, would it not?' asked Edward: 'I had not forgotten your wishes, and went myself for the same purpose; and I was much the most proper person to do it.'

'Perhaps you were,' said Laura; 'but you must own, Edward, that it was a very tiny fault, and extremely unkind of Edith to say anything to you about it.'

'I don't think you meant any great harm, certainly,' replied Edward, delighted to be relieved from the feeling of vexation against her; 'but you must be more careful another time.'

'Yes, believe me,' exclaimed Laura : 'I will never commit myself again. Since I know how my words are to be turned against me, I will be more sparing of them. Your sister shall not be troubled for the future with either my conversation or my society.'

'Hush ! my love,' replied Edward ; 'this is not kind to me. The first wish of my heart is that you should be loved and cherished by my own family.'

'Do not wish it,' said Laura, sadly ; 'it will never be.'

'It must be,' replied her husband. 'It is impossible they should be insensible to '——

'To what ?' asked Laura, archly ; 'I like of all things to hear my own praises.'

Edward only answered by a kiss ; and immediately afterwards left the room, with his feelings calmed, but with a bitter recollection of Edith's remarks, and a keener sense than ever of the neglect shown to his young wife.

CHAPTER XV.

IT is interesting and useful, though often very painful, to retire into ourselves, after the first tumult of excited feelings has subsided, and consider the probable consequences of our words and actions. We may indeed frequently be mistaken, and magnify or diminish the importance of what has occurred ; or look forward to events that may never happen ; but by endeavouring to connect the past and the future, we strengthen a habit of thoughtfulness, and are able to trace more easily the secret sources of the sufferings which so frequently arise, apparently from the ignorance or selfishness of our fellow-creatures, but in reality from some error in ourselves. The conversation between Edith and her brother was not of a nature to be speedily forgotten by either, but the pain it had occasioned was most acutely felt by the former ; and when she recurred to her unguarded expressions, and their probable effect upon Edward's mind, all feeling of displeasure against him or Laura gave way before her own self-reproach. She would willingly have made any sacrifice to efface the impression of those few hasty words—for it was easy to foresee that they would probably create a barrier which years even might not be able to remove ; and bitter was her regret for the weakness which had induced her to yield to an angry impulse. It was impossible to suppose that Edward would overlook and make allowances, for his feelings had been wounded in the tenderest point. If she attempted to be kinder than usual, he might think her insincere ; and if she were cold as before, the breach must effectually be widened. It was Edith's first lesson in the importance of words—in the fearful power which we possess of giving a body, as it were, to the thoughts within us, but a body which we are unable to destroy. Her repentance seemed as if it could be of no avail in preventing the natural consequences of her folly ; and she looked forward with shame and repugnance to the next meeting with her brother and sister. The awkwardness, which was equally felt by them, caused several days to elapse before it took place ; but having no excuse to offer for not going to the Priory, Edward at length prevailed on Laura to overcome her unwillingness and accompany him, with the secret hope that Edith might be absent. His wish, however, was not gratified. Luncheon was rather later than usual ; and the footman, ignorant of the effect produced by his words, informed them that Mrs Courtenay and the young ladies were in the dining-room.

'Just in time, my dear,' was Mrs Courtenay's salutation. 'We are so glad—I was only that instant saying what an age it was since you had been here.'

'It is rather long,' began Laura.

'Long, my love ! it seems a twelvemonth. But I won't complain. Now, do, Edith—no, not Edith, she has a toothache, poor child—Jane, you can ring the bell. Johnson never will bring up knives and forks enough.'

'I think there are some more on the side-table,' said Jane, languidly, turning her head. 'Isn't it bitterly cold to-day ?'

'Not bitterly,' replied Edward ; 'rather bracing it is, certainly ; I suppose, Edith, it is the cold which has given you the pain in your face.'

Edward tried to be unconstrained ; but Edith felt it was an effort, and her answer was given in the same tone—

'Perhaps it may be ; but it is not of any consequence.'

'Oh, my dear, don't say so !' exclaimed her mother ; 'nobody knows ; and it is so much better to take things in time : you know it may turn to tic-douloureux any day.'

'Is it very bad?' inquired Laura, feeling more grateful to a toothache than she had ever done before.

'Oh no; it is a mere nothing,' said Edith, in the same reserved tone as before ; and she rose as if to leave the room.

'You are not thinking of going out, of course, Edith,' said Charlotte ; 'it would be madness.'

'I don't know exactly : I ought to go if I could, and my face is better now.'

'A martyr, as usual,' exclaimed Charlotte ; 'what a pity it is that you had not lived in Queen Mary's reign ! I don't know any one who would have made a better figure at the stake.'

'You would not be so foolish, Edith,' said Edward : 'nothing is more likely to make you worse than this north-east wind. It is not fit for you to venture out.'

'That is right, my dear,' exclaimed Mrs Courtenay ; 'do try your influence ; nobody has so much : I often say that you have more power over Edith than all the world besides.'

'Had more power, you should say,' replied Edward, with a quiet emphasis, understood only by two of the party.

'I don't know why you should say that, my dear, except, perhaps, that now you are married, there are two persons for Edith to listen to, instead of one. Laura, I wish you would say something. Edith observed only the other day, that you never set your heart upon doing anything without accomplishing it.'

The colour mounted to Laura's cheek, and after a moment's pause, she said coldly—

'I could not be so presumptuous as to suppose '—— the end of the sentence was lost, for the speaker took up a glass of water, being apparently seized with a violent thirst.

'I don't know what you all mean,' said Jane, as she moved her chair from the fire to discover the cause of the silence ; 'but it seems to me that we are remarkably polite to each other ; so polite, that one could almost fancy we were on the point of being otherwise.'

'I am the cause, I am afraid,' said Edith ; 'but I very much wish no one would trouble themselves about me ; I shall do extremely well ; and really I must go.'

Mrs Courtenay sighed and looked resigned, and Charlotte coughed and looked provoked.

'You may take the club-book with you, if you will go,' she said ; 'we shall have to pay a fine as it is.'

'I have not finished it yet,' replied Edith; 'one day will not make much difference.'

'Why not stay at home, then, and do it now? It would be much better.'

'No, I don't feel that I could attend; and indeed I never can understand heavy books, except at night.'

'But you do not mean, my love,' said Mrs Courtenay, with a start of horror, 'that you ever sit up at night reading?'

'Oh yes, frequently,' replied Edith; 'but there is no fear, I assure you; I am extremely careful.'

'It is very well to talk,' exclaimed Mrs Courtenay, with a degree of energy unusual to her; 'we shall be burnt, I know we shall; it is in the family.'

There was a general laugh, in which Edith could not help joining. But Mrs Courtenay did not at all understand the cause of the amusement, and immediately began citing cases to prove the correctness of her assertion.

'My dear Edward, you must remember old Sir Lionel Courtenay in Henry VIII.'s time,—he was burnt at the stake. And there was his grandson in Queen Mary's; and your two little cousins, last year, in Kent. So, Edith, I must beg you won't read any more by candle-light. You know quite enough.'

'At all events,' said Edith, smiling, 'I don't think I can take the club-book; it is so large.'

'We might drive her to Elsham,' said Laura to her husband, in a low voice.

Edward hesitated. The tone of his family had seldom struck him so forcibly, and he was not inclined for Edith's company. Laura, however, repeated the suggestion, and finding that he did not object, followed Edith, to make her the offer.

It was decidedly refused; and Laura felt as if her overtures of peace had been rejected. Yet Edith's manner, cold and constrained as it seemed, was by no means an index to her heart. She was fully conscious of her own ungraciousness; and if Laura had been in the wrong, instead of herself, she would have been the first to make an advance towards reconciliation. But now, unable to conquer the feeling of shyness, arising from self-reproach, she hurried away to her own room, and the estrangement between the sisters-in-law was completed. Laura, piqued and disappointed, returned to the dining-room, resolving never again to attempt being on any terms with Edith but those of politeness—a resolution which her good-nature would, under

other circumstances, have made it rather difficult to keep. For
some time, indeed, she refrained from visiting the Priory more
frequently than was absolutely necessary ; and when in Edith's
company avoided any conversation with her. But the first irritation of feeling by degrees subsided ; and with a disposition
incapable of long retaining the sense of injury, she might easily
have been won over to cordiality, if Edith had only known how
to redeem her past mistakes. But of this, unfortunately, she
was ignorant. Though freely acknowledging her fault in the
one instance which had openly separated them, she was not
aware that a fundamental error lay at the root of all her actions
—the belief that family duties are of secondary importance ; and
the result was a continued series of petty neglects, which Laura's
quick perception, and hasty, though generous temper, could not
fail to resent. The breach, however, was not perceptible to the
world in general, and scarcely even at the Priory. Mrs Courtenay seldom noticed anything but the changes of the weather ;
Jane was engrossed with her maladies ; and Charlotte only
thought that Edith, as usual, made herself disagreeable, and
was not surprised that Laura cared so little for her society.

CHAPTER XVI.

THERE were, however, two persons whose interest in Allingham and the Priory rendered them fully alive to the clouds
which so frequently obscured the domestic sunshine—Miss Forester and Mr Dacre. The former, in pursuance of her object of
becoming useful and agreeable to Laura, was peculiarly observant
of the influence of others; and was not sorry to perceive the
numerous indications of indifference and reserve which every day
afforded, especially when it gave her an opportunity of civilly
making some remark to Edith's disadvantage, and thus venting
her spleen against the only person whom she considered likely to
rival herself in her uncle's regard. The sources of Mr Dacre's
interest were less simple. A worn out, solitary invalid—solitary,
not so much from the absence of outward friends, as from the
isolation of mind attendant upon a grief too sacred to be told to
any human ear, he had consented to remain at the Grange long
after the period fixed for the termination of his visit, not because

he was pleased with Miss Forester's flatteries, or gratified by the General's attentions, but from the powerful charm attached to the place where he had originally become acquainted with the wife he had so tenderly loved. It was at the Grange that they had first met—in its neighbourhood that they had enjoyed those opportunities of intimate acquaintance which first inspired a mutual regard, and then ripened it into love; and it was in the parish church of Elsham that they had knelt, side by side, before the altar, and in the presence of God exchanged those vows which death alone could sever.

Years passed away after that sunny time, and care, and sickness, and sorrow, and the deep yearning of the stranger's heart in a foreign land for its native home, were bitterly felt by both; but no circumstances, however untoward, could weaken an affection based upon principles of piety and mutual reverence; and when, after a union of thirty years, Mrs Dacre sank into her grave, under the influence of a lingering, painful disease, the stunning effects of the trial produced an effect upon her husband's health which his constitution never afterwards recovered. Had his two children lived, Mr Dacre's sufferings would, however, have been comparatively light; for a mind like his could not long permit sorrow to interfere with the duties of life, and the necessity of exerting himself for their sake would probably in time have diverted his thoughts from the one all-engrossing remembrance. But they also were taken from him. Within a few months of each other they were laid by their mother's side; and their father, his health completely shattered by this fresh blow, was compelled to return to England, as the last hope of preserving an existence which, at the first moment of his loss, seemed scarcely of consequence to any human being. But the sorrow of the Christian, though often great, can never be without alleviations; and Mr Dacre's heart had been too well practised in submission when all was prosperous around him, to sink under the burden of affliction. As his constitution became partially re-established by his native air, his energy of mind was again roused. The world had lost its charm, but it had not lost its duties; and projects of usefulness continually suggested themselves, to the accomplishment of which his uncertain health appeared the only obstacle. Day after day, and week after week, glided on, and still his plans were unsettled; but in that time his original attachment to the Grange and its neighbourhood had strengthened into a deeper home feeling; the result partly of habit, and partly of the interest excited by his acquaintance with Edward Courtenay. Edith, indeed, was the first to attract his regard, from a fancied resemblance to the daughter he had lost, and the charm of a simple, earnest, intelligent mind, bent upon the fulfilment of duty, at whatever sacrifice of personal enjoyment; but Edward's character, though in many respects strongly resembling his sister's, was as yet so imperfectly formed as to awaken a sympathy deeper, but far more painful, which the circumstances of their previous acquaintance tended considerably to increase. They had met at a lawyer's office in London, a short time before Edward's marriage, when Mr Dacre was endeavouring to arrange some business for a mutual friend ; and in the course of their transactions, the condition of the Allingham estate was, from necessity, made known to him, to a much greater extent than Edward desired. The information was not then of any importance, and would probably soon have been forgotten, but for his visit at the Grange, and the opinions expressed every day as to the value of Mr Courtenay's property, and the style in which he was expected to live. Even then, until he had gained a more intimate knowledge of Edward's disposition, he had thought but little upon the subject, considering the common belief merely the gossip of a country place ; but the observation of a few months made him fear the power of general opinion over an enthusiastic, unstable mind.

Edward was not accused of extravagance ; he indulged in no follies, and gave way to no expensive habits ; but he followed the customs of society, and complied with all that was considered requisite for his position ; and when that position was a false one the consequences were not difficult to foresee. The world said that Mr Courtenay's establishment ought to be on a certain scale ; Mr Courtenay himself knew that it was larger than his actual income would allow ; but it was expected of him—it would appear strange to live without it—economy might be practised in less obvious points ; and the butler, and coachman, and footmen, and grooms, lounged over their nominal duties, and injured themselves by idleness, and their master by waste, because it was necessary to keep up appearances. The world said that of course Mr Courtenay would not part with the splendid hunters, the pride of the Colonel's heart ; if he did not use them himself, there would be always some persons to appreciate them ; and Edward, though caring nothing for field sports, and even entertaining some doubts as to their being entirely allowable, kept hunters for his visitors, and grooms for his hunters, simply because he would not acknow-

ledge that he could not afford it.   The same principle ran through
everything — dinners, equipages, furniture, entertainments, all
were upon a like scale ; and daily and hourly the secret burden
of anxiety pressed more heavily upon Edward's heart.   But its
existence was scarcely acknowledged by himself, and perceived
only by Mr Dacre.   Similarity of taste, and, in a great measure,
of principle, had quickly softened the recollection of their previous
interview · and, after the bridal visit, Mr Dacre was a frequent
and welcome guest at Allingham : yet his desire of being really
Edward's friend was not completely gratified.   Friendship necessarily implies confidence, and while Edward was acting a part,
even though he persuaded himself it was a justifiable one, confidence was impossible.   The subject, too, was one of so delicate
and personal a nature as to forbid all interference, except from
relations or long-tried friends ; and Mr Dacre's only hope rested
upon Edith.   Laura, it was evident, either did not know the state
of her husband's affairs, or, if she did know, shared in his thoughtlessness ; but a few expressions dropped in the course of conversation with Edith, led Mr Dacre to imagine that she, like himself,
was acquainted with her brother's difficulties, and alive to his
yielding character, and the effects it must in time produce.   Here
again, however, he was disappointed.   From causes not confessed,
but easily to be conjectured by a mind of any penetration, a reserve had sprung up between Edith and Edward, which effectually excluded every hope of influence on her part ; and Mr
Dacre was forced to observe silently and thoughtfully the plan of
life pursued at Allingham, with the certainty that it must at last
end in suffering, but without the power of interposing a warning
voice against it.   Yet this very sense of inability served perhaps
to increase his interest.   It is with a kind of painful fascination
that a good mind notices the dawning of sorrow upon the young
and inexperienced.   There is the wish to save, and the consciousness of the vanity of human efforts ; the affection that would
prompt the breaking down of the barriers of custom, and the fear
lest a hasty action, or an ill-timed word, may defeat the purest
intentions.   To speak or to be silent seems equally dangerous ;
and the spirit thus endowed with the fatal gift of prophecy can
but watch anxiously, and pray earnestly, and strive to learn the
lesson of patient trust, which God would teach us all from the
miseries we see, but may not relieve.

So at least felt Mr Dacre, and his wish to remain at Elsham
became every day more fixed.   The world was before him, and

in his youth he would have delighted in travelling ; but even if
his health had permitted it, the knowledge that there was no one
now to share his pleasure would have effectually destroyed the
inclination. He had no near relations,—none who, from being
friendless and unprovided for, claimed his attention. Elsham had
been his home for the happiest period of his life,.and no other
place seemed so likely to soothe him in his present loneliness.
Miss Forester and her father, indeed, were not congenial, but in
his own house there would be no necessity for their constant
society ; while the footing of intimacy on which he was placed,
both at Allingham and the Priory, afforded him resources in his
solitary hours, which he could not be equally certain of finding
in any other situation, and might, if he remained in the neighbourhood, offer some occasion of guarding Edward against the
danger he was incurring.

So many considerations were not long in producing results.
As the Elsham world had long ago decided must be the case,
Mr Dacre determined upon taking a house ; but wonder and disappointment were in no small degree excited when his intended
residence was made known. The village doctor overlooked his
numerous engagements as he discussed the motives that could induce a man of Mr Dacre's wealth to be content with so humble
a dwelling. The lawyer rested his pen upon his desk, and philo-
sophised upon the falsity of common report, and the certainty
that Indian fortunes were always exaggerated. The coachmen
and grooms of the different establishments pronounced that Mr
Dacre could be no gentleman : a rich gentleman with only one
riding horse, was a thing never heard of. The elderly ladies
assembled round the whist-table forgot to mark tricks and count
honours, while comparing notes in loud whispers upon the fact of
their new neighbour being a shocking miser : and the ladies' maids
received but a gentle reprimand, although guilty of misplacing a
ringlet or producing a wrong dress, from the eagerness with
which they repeated to their young mistresses the innumerable
stories of the nabob's oddities. And during this time the object
of so much interest, the observed of all observers, with calm indifference pursued his own path—settled himself in his cottage—
furnished his little library with books—cared studiously for the
comfort of the friends who might visit him—and showed himself
fully sensible of the charms of order and even of elegance, when
it was to be enjoyed with others ; but made no preparations for
personal gratification beyond those which age and infirmity im-

peratively required. And why? Why, when the drawing-room and library were so stored with all that might minister to ease and innocent amusement, was Mr Dacre's private study so simple, even homely, in its appearance? Why were there no damask couches, no soft-cushioned chairs, none of the apparatus of luxury which are considered the necessary appendages of wealth? Why, when the only spare room the little cottage afforded was a model of refinement, was the chamber of its owner so perfectly unadorned? It was a question only to be answered by those who could have watched the secret principle of Mr Dacre's life,—who could have seen him in his hours of devotion, in his moments of suffering and trial, and heard the warning voice for ever sounding in his ears—'How hardly shall they that have riches enter into the kingdom of heaven!' From the period when prosperity first assailed him with its temptations, this difficulty was never absent from his mind. He noticed the progress of others from toil to ease; from ease to luxury; from luxury to selfishness and forgetfulness; and his knowledge of the human heart told him that such might too probably be his own course. The gradations were so gradual as not to be per-ceptible: the excuses so plausible as scarcely to be withstood. Society and friends; the noble and the mean; the prince and the beggar, alike have claims upon the expenditure of the rich man. To cut ourselves off from everything that may be deemed a superfluity, and rigorously to insist upon 'giving to nature no more than nature needs,' seems a disregard of the intentions of Providence, and a faithless fear lest evil should lurk under every occasion of enjoyment. Mr Dacre saw and felt this. He did not shut his eyes to the requirements of society and his family; but without any obtrusive singularity, he nevertheless persisted in the practice of strict self-denial, for the very reason which would have induced others to give way to self-indulgence. Because his means of gratification were ample, he guarded against yielding to his own inclinations; and while his house, and his table, and his equipage, were in accordance with his station in the world, he himself, even in India,—the land of indolence and ease, pursued in secret a course of life which by many would have been considered one of severe mortification. The apparent inconsistency might have surprised yet wiser persons than the gossips and newsmongers of Elsham; especially when it was known that Mr Dacre's charities, although extensive, were not such as obviously to demand any unusual economy. He subscribed freely to the schools, gave largely at the offertory, and was foremost in providing for the necessities of the poor, but he by no means relieved his neighbours from the obligation of contributing their share also. With benevolence which, after a short experience, no one could doubt, he still kept within such limits, that none could plead the munificence of the rich Indian as an excuse for their own selfishness. That there must be a considerable surplus, even after every possible expense had been taken into calculation, was decided ; and how was it appropriated? Was it stored up for his heir-at-law—a distant cousin —himself the owner of a considerable estate? It was possible, but not probable; and the idea, when suggested at a tea-party in Elsham, was almost immediately rejected. Was it to be an inheritance for Miss Forester? The notion was plausible, but the lady in question was not sufficiently a favourite in society for it to be generally received. All felt it was the last way in which they should dispose of their own money, and the natural supposition was, that Mr Dacre shared the same feeling. Some said he intended to found an hospital; others, that he was wishing to endow alms-houses; a few declared that plans were preparing for a new church ; and one or two, incapable of attributing liberality to their neighbours from being totally devoid of it themselves, hinted that the first idea was the true one, and that, with all his show of generosity, Mr Dacre's disposition was miserly. Time and observation threw no light upon the subject; at the end of six months the Elsham world was still in a state of uncertainty as to the private affairs of their wealthy acquaintance, and, after many discussions, finally arrived at the conclusion that he could not be as rich as had been reported. This, however, was a mistake; Mr Dacre's fortune was large, and the claims upon it, according to the usual standard of benevolence, were small; but the measure of the world's charity is very different from that of the Christian's; and while India, with its enormous heathen population, its fearful ignorance, and scantily endowed Church, stood before him as the land from whence his property was derived, there could be no limit to the demand upon his resources. English blindness and wickedness might be great, and the destitute state of the Church a never-failing source of regret, but Providence points out to all who wish to be so guided, the true objects for their grateful offerings; and even in those cases in which we are apparently most at liberty to follow our own will. a heart earnestly bent upon obedience will rather seek to discover the path indicated by circumstances, than to chalk out a line of action merely in accordance with inclination. India had been the source of Mr Dacre's wealth; and to India he desired it should return.

The great interest excited even by a rich widower in a country neighbourhood, cannot, however, continue undiminished. Mr Dacre's affairs were at length only occasionally canvassed, when some fresh eccentricity, as it was deemed, or some remarkable munificence, again attracted observation. His health, too, though a constant source of suffering to himself, did not as yet appear likely entirely to fail, and speculations as to the ultimate disposal of his fortune were forgotten in admiration of his winter charities, and his splendid presents to General Forester and his niece. Yet, in the monotony of everyday life, his vicinity was felt to be a considerable relief. There was always something to be told about him,—which road he had chosen for his walk, what visits he had paid, how he was looking, whether he wore a great-coat—or some wonder to be expressed as to why he had not thought proper to walk at all; and in the absence of cultivation of mind, or business of consequence, these topics formed the staple source of conversation with the unoccupied better class of Elsham; varied only by similar remarks upon their other neighbours, and especially by minute criticisms upon the dress, manners, and conduct of the beautiful Mrs Courtenay of Allingham.

Laura, in the meantime, unsuspicious of evil, and seeing no indications of any necessity for prudence, felt no scruple in urging upon her husband the gratification of each wish as it arose. Expensive ornaments, new carriages, costly furniture,—all were successively thought of; when thought of, desired; and when desired, considered indispensable; and Edward, driving from his mind every idea but that of giving her pleasure, persuaded himself that each separate expense was so trifling as to be of no consequence, and though often distrustful of his own conduct in secret, still laughed and talked, rode over his farms, inspected his improvements, and formed plans of benevolence far beyond his means, as energetically as if no causes of uneasiness lay beneath his outward prosperity. Edith looked on in sorrow; but her influence with her brother was gone. He was guided (though unknown to himself) solely by his wife; and she, in equal unconsciousness, was yielding day by day more completely to the soothing power of Miss Forester's flatteries; and was soon

persuaded by her that, as the wife of Mr Courtenay of Allingham, it was absolutely requisite she should be surrounded with
every luxury which selfishness and indolence could devise. And
to the outward eye there was no change for many months ; but
there is One who 'seeth not as man seeth,' and before whom
each day, as it passes, registers the growth either for good or
evil of the inner man ; and if Edward Courtenay had compared
the state of his mind half a year after his marriage, with that
which he had believed it to be when he made his offer to Laura,
he must have been aware of his own religious declension ; but
the variations from week to week were as unnoticed as from
hour to hour, and even the symptoms which might naturally
have awakened distrust were disregarded. Perhaps among the
chief of these, was the constant recurrence of one small wish,—
the same which he had once endeavoured to check in his wife.
Each morning, as Laura seated herself in the drawing-room,
Edward recollected the pleasure he had felt in preparing the
morning-room, and sighed over her disappointment. Sometimes
he accused Laura of fastidiousness, and sometimes quarrelled
with old Martha for pertinacity ; and the cottage at length became an eyesore to him, and he would go considerably out of
his way to avoid it, unless, as was frequently the case, he visited
it under the pretence of kindness, but with the real though secret
intention of making another effort to gain his point.

His frequent allusions to the possibility of a change did not
fail to excite old Martha's suspicions. She complained to Edith ;
but, believing it impossible that Edward could ever think of
breaking his word, and not daring to approach the subject with
him, Edith tried to persuade her that she was fanciful. The
impression, however, on the old woman's mind, weakened as
she was by age, was too strong to be overcome ; and it was not
without foundation. Edward did at length firmly resolve to
effect his purpose ; he determined to gratify both himself and
Laura by insisting upon Martha's agreeing to his wishes, in return for the many kindnesses she had so long been in the habit
of receiving. He even fixed upon the cottage to which she was
to remove, and planned the particular steps which it would be
necessary to take ; but the opportunity for effecting his object
was never afforded him. Some unguarded expressions used by
him so worked upon the poor old woman's enfeebled mind, and
so increased her dread of being forced into compliance, that her
strength and spirits gave way ; and when Edward went to her

with the intention of acting upon his selfish resolution, he found her incapable of listening to him. The cause of her illness he did not suspect; and without noticing the secret feeling of satisfaction which arose in his mind, he believed, as he gave orders for everything to be provided for her comfort, that he was obeying the dictates of a benevolent heart.

Apparently he was unpunished for his conduct, and so was Laura; but the consequences of our sins are not the less certain because they are long delayed, and in the blindness of our reason we cannot discover the connection between causes and effects. If Edward had strenuously resisted this temptation from the first moment when it assailed him,—if he had never given Laura reason to suppose that he would yield to her wishes, even against his own knowledge of right, the breach between himself and Edith, the source of so much unhappiness, and such future trials, might never have taken place; his moral principle would have been strengthened, and his conscience have become more sensitive to the approach of evil in any other shape. But his resistance had been only in words. Immediately after cautioning Laura against wishes, he had acted against his own convictions, and so he had continued; not, as in other instances, from impulse and weakness, but wilfully; and the injury to his moral character could only be estimated by future trials. It is a fearful mistake to believe, that because our wishes are not accomplished they can do no harm.

CHAPTER XVII.

' IS Edward at home, Laura?' asked Edith, as she walked into the drawing-room at Allingham, one morning soon after breakfast.

'At home? Yes, he is, but he is engaged: do you want to see him particularly?'

'He told me to let him know when anything was settled about a girl to wait upon old Martha; and Mr Dacre has been proposing a niece of his housekeeper's. He is coming here himself presently; I left him in the road talking to General Forester.'

'I don't think Edward can attend to you very well, just now, said Laura. 'He is busy making a plan for taking in the conservatory.'

Edith appeared distressed, though not surprised. She seldom came to Allingham without finding some alterations either proposed or commenced; and before she could reply, Edward entered the room.

'Will this do, Laura?' he said, after he had spoken a few words to his sister; 'it looks pretty well on paper, I think.'

'Oh! beautiful,' exclaimed Laura; 'and you will begin about it at once.'

'I don't know as to that; one must consider expense a little.'

'For such a trifle? why, it will not cost fifty pounds.'

'Nearer a hundred.'

'Or two,' said Edith, gravely; the next minute repenting of having interfered.—'Can you attend to me, Edward?'

'Wait one minute. You see, Laura, it will be very well if we can manage about the wall; but it won't do to endanger any other part of the house; so I should like to have a mason's opinion.'

There was a ring at the bell, and Mr Dacre was announced. Edward was going to put his drawing aside, but Laura took it.

'I must have Mr Dacre's opinion,' she said, as she advanced to shake hands. 'Won't this be an immense improvement to our room? We are thinking of opening it into the conservatory.'

'Extremely pretty, indeed,' said Mr Dacre; 'not quite equal to this though;' and he pointed to a splendid design for Torrington Church, which lay on the table.

'Oh, that!' replied Edward, hesitatingly—'it is only a plan: to realise it would require thousands; therefore it can be but a matter of amusement.'

'Even in that way it must be a great pleasure,' said Mr Dacre; 'but I doubt if it would be quite satisfactory.'

'Why not?'

'Merely because it is an amusement and unreal.'

'I don't see how it can be otherwise, when it is so much beyond my means.'

'The thing one feels in these cases,' said Mr Dacre, 'is a distrust of one's self; at least, I know I used to have it as a young man.'

'Were you given to day-dreams then?' said Edward.

'Yes, constantly; and I can remember now the pleasure of

putting by the first five pounds towards the fifteen hundred which I once wanted.'

'Oh! Mr Dacre,' exclaimed Laura, laughing; 'I see you are an enemy in disguise. If I let Edward talk to you much longer, I may say good-bye to the conservatory.'

'It is more a case of feeling than anything else,' said Edward, 'I should not suppose myself at all nearer my object because I had advanced a snail's step towards it.'

'Very likely,' replied Mr Dacre, in an indifferent tone; 'but sometimes one is glad of an earnest of one's own sincerity;' and turning from the subject, he began talking about old Martha. A few arrangements were to be made for the girl who was to live with her; and Edward entered into the most minute details, though Mr Dacre seemed to think it more a lady's province, and proposed that it should be left to Edith to settle. He did not know that Edward's present consideration was a salve to his conscience. Edith listened, but finding that she was not of much use, soon proposed going; and was just wishing Laura good-bye, when Mr Dacre stopped her. There was something pointed in the way in which he asked her to wait, and allow him to walk home with her; and she fancied, as she had done once or twice before in the course of the conversation, that he looked restless and disturbed, which for him was very unusual, and after a little more conversation he took his leave. Whatever his motive might have been for desiring Edith's society, he did not seem inclined to take advantage of it; and neither of them spoke till they had walked some little way. Edith was meditating upon the conversation, and at length uttering her thoughts aloud, said,—

'I can scarcely imagine my brother understood all you implied just now.'

'Perhaps I did not express myself clearly. It is such an awkward thing to give opinions which appear like advice.'

'You seemed afraid to press yours at least,' said Edith; 'but I am sure they were right.'

'So I am, as a general rule; but one does so much harm by being dogmatical, especially when it is not one's business. And after all, your brother may not have the same reasons to fear being visionary that I had when I was at his age.'

'That is not likely,' said Edith; 'no day-dreams can surpass his, I am sure; and he has no one to warn him against them.'

Mr Dacre thought for a few moments, and then said, rather

abruptly, 'Do you remember our conversation the first day we met in the Park, last autumn?'

'Yes,' replied Edith : 'it interested me too much to be easily forgotten.'

'We spoke of influence, I think,' continued Mr Dacre ; 'it is a subject often in my mind.'

'I have no influence with Edward,' said Edith, 'if that is what you would imply. Do you think I have?'

'If I answer your question,' he replied, 'I am afraid I shall be forced to obtrude some more opinions.'

'Not obtrude,' replied Edith, 'if you mean they would not be acceptable.'

'Will you then give me an old man's privilege, and forgive me if I say that you ought to have an influence, though it is not always evident that you have?'

'It never can be,' said Edith. 'Who could rival Laura?'

'Who would wish it? But I was wrong in saying that you had no influence, since no human being is without it. The difficulty is, to make the best use of it.'

'Mine is so slight now,' said Edith, 'it can be of no importance.'

'You hold a common opinion,' said Mr Dacre ; 'but have you ever considered what we should feel if we were suddenly made to see the effect of every careless word and action? I think we should scarcely say then that we had no influence.'

'It is a frightful thought,' said Edith. 'I don't think I could always bear it.'

'No,' replied Mr Dacre ; 'our eyes are blinded in mercy ; but it is well sometimes to realise the truth, though only for an instant. All that we have once said or done may fade from the memory, but it does not therefore die.'

A bitter recollection flashed upon Edith's mind, and she felt as if it would be impossible to speak.

'You must forgive me,' continued Mr Dacre ; 'I was accustomed to talk upon these subjects once with my own child, and the habit is renewed unconsciously.'

'Oh !' exclaimed Edith, 'if you would only look upon me in the same light, and tell me all you think I ought to do, I might be saved from many trials. I do wish,—yes, most earnestly wish to do right.'

'No one who is acquainted with you could for a moment doubt it,' said Mr Dacre, in a tone of deep interest. 'Unfortunately, I am so circumstanced as to deal only in generalities, and they are most frequently useless. I cannot tell you how you may influence your brother, but I know that a great power has been placed in your hands, as it has been in the hands of every human being, and that we shall have to render a most strict account for it; and I own I am very anxious to impress this truth upon you.'

'And why?' asked Edith.

Mr Dacre paused. 'Are you satisfied,' he said, 'that your brother's life is likely to be a happy one?'

'I don't know,' said Edith, hastily, surprised at the question; 'do you ask me because you are afraid for him?'

'If I were a member of your family'—— began Mr Dacre.

'But why should you not consider yourself such?' said Edith; 'I am sure we are not common friends.'

'No, I hope not. But I may be mistaken; and many persons would think me ridiculous in fancying that your brother is not quite alive to the expenses of his splendid establishment.'

Edith was silent from astonishment; the remark implied a knowledge of Edward's affairs which she could not account for.

'Pray don't think me impertinent,' continued Mr Dacre; 'indeed I have reasons for what I say.'

'I should scarcely have imagined,' replied Edith, 'that Edward's style of living would be thought beyond what six thousand a year permits.'

Mr Dacre felt puzzled. He had ventured as far as he dared, and began to think that, after all, his conjectures must be wrong, and that Edith knew no more of her brother's affairs than the rest of the world.

'A clear income of six thousand a year might possibly cover all expenses,' he said, pointedly.

Edith paused suddenly in her walk. 'A clear income!' she repeated, as she anxiously watched the expression of Mr Dacre's face. 'Then, do you know?—has Edward told'——

'He has not told me anything, my dear Miss Courtenay; but our acquaintance did not commence at Allingham. We met once, previously to his marriage, at a lawyer's office in London.'

'And it was there you learned all!' exclaimed Edith. 'Do you know how deeply'——

'I know but few particulars,' said Mr Dacre, interrupting her; 'but I certainly understood enough to convince me that the most prudent economy was required,—and to make me feel frightened this morning, when General Forester told me he was going to propose to your brother to stand for the county at the expected dissolution of Parliament.'

Poor Edith looked aghast at this announcement.

'I don't wish to alarm you,' he said. 'Very probably your brother may not even have the wish to be in Parliament.'

'But he has, I know!' exclaimed Edith : 'and Laura will urge it ; and Edward is so blinded by his affection for her, he will do anything to please her.'

'Then, perhaps,' said Mr Dacre, 'she is the most important person to influence. Of course she knows more of Mr Courtenay's affairs than any one.'

'I think not,' said Edith, trying to overcome her agitation. 'It may sound strange, but I am nearly certain she is as ignorant as every one else. Edward never told any one but me, and then it was with an implied promise that I was never to mention the subject.'

'It is very unfortunate,' said Mr Dacre, thoughtfully ; 'but at all events you can do something, and you are the only person. As to myself, I have taken now a step which many would consider an intolerable liberty.'

'Their feelings would be very different from mine,' said Edith ; and her sweet smile brought a fond remembrance to Mr Dacre's heart. 'But you don't know Laura. We are so unlike in taste and disposition ; and besides'—— She stopped, remembering that there were other causes why her sister-in-law was not likely to be guided by anything she might say.

'There must be some points on which you may meet, surely,' replied Mr Dacre.

'None !' exclaimed Edith, despairingly. 'Edward must take his own course, for I have no power to stop him.'

'Yet he is your brother.'

'Yes ; but natural ties are slight when circumstances combine to separate them.'

'Are they indeed slight ?' said Mr Dacre, very gravely. 'They are formed by God, and what He has joined together, who may dare to put asunder ?'

Edith looked bewildered and miserable. 'You talk to me as if all were in my power—as if Edward's safety or ruin depended upon my actions ; and you may be right,—but if I were to dwell upon the thought, I should be incapable of doing anything. Who will venture to walk in darkness, when one false step may do such incalculable mischief ?'

'May I answer you in very solemn words?' replied Mr Dacre. 'You must remember where it is said, "Who is among you that feareth the Lord, that obeyeth the voice of His servant, that walketh in darkness, and hath no light; let him trust in the name of the Lord, and stay upon his God." And is not life all darkness?'

'It is so now to me,' said Edith, with less of calmness than usual.

'It is so to us all; but perhaps you may have sometimes watched a lamp let down into one of those deep wells which, centuries ago, were cut out of the solid rock, and seen how, as it went down, it threw a clear light immediately around, though above and below all was dark as before. Did it ever strike you as a type of the principle of faith, which gives us just sufficient comfort for our hour of need, though the past and the future may still remain mysteries?'

'Oh!' exclaimed Edith, 'if I could only have some one with me always, to whom I could talk freely! but no person can enter into the difficulties of a family, except those who live with them; and if we are doing wrong, we can have no right to trust to the lamp of faith.'

'And have you really no one to sympathise with you?' said Mr Dacre. 'You will not think the question a curious one?'

'If Gertrude were at home,' said Edith, 'everything would be well. She understands so much better than I do what ought to be done, and she would never give offence.'

'I thought you knew but little of her. She is seldom at the Priory, I believe.'

'Yes,' replied Edith; 'but her letters, and the interest she takes in everything, make us feel as if she lived amongst us. Perhaps, though, she could not help me now, for she has never been made acquainted with Edward's affairs; and all my feelings about his marriage were so mixed up with anxiety upon this one subject, that I have scarcely ventured to allude to them, lest I should say something which might seem like a betrayal of his confidence. She thinks me reserved, I know; and I can never tell her,—I feel I must be left alone.'

'Yet I must again entreat you to do your utmost,' said Mr Dacre, 'if you should find your brother at all inclined to listen to General Forester. It may be a great temptation, and the consequences may be of such infinite importance to him.'

Edith sighed deeply; 'I don't think there is any cause to be afraid really,' she said, 'because the danger is so evident. A man cannot deceive himself about elections ; every one knows they are ruinous, unless there is a large fortune to support them ; but the notion frightened me very much at first.'

Mr Dacre's silence showed that he was less sanguine as to the power of Edward's common sense ; but he had said all that he considered necessary, and he felt that he was not called on to interfere farther. They parted at the gate leading to old Martha's cottage. A tear glistened in Edith's eye, and her voice trembled, as she bade Mr Dacre good-bye. The shadow of a coming sorrow was passing over her mind, and Mr Dacre saw and felt it ;—felt it the more, that he had been himself in some degree its cause.

' You will think of me as a friend who longs to be of service to you,' he said, as he warmly pressed her hand ; 'and may I also remind you, that if I am powerless, there is One who can guard you and all you love from harm.'

CHAPTER XVIII.

' JANE, my dear Jane, are you both going out this morning ? My knitting is so tangled, I shall never put it right again ;' and Mrs Courtenay's voice was rather more elevated than usual, and not entirely free from querulousness.

'Edith will be at home presently,' replied Jane, who was standing in the doorway, prepared for a morning visit, and not at all inclined to delay the gratification of exhibiting the new bonnet and scarf which had arrived from town only the previous evening.

' Just look, my dear,' continued her mother ; ' here are three stitches let down ; and my eyes are so bad I shall never take them up properly.'

Jane advanced slowly into the room, and carelessly surveying the work, declared it to be in such a state that it was better to begin it entirely afresh ; and as she knew very little of knitting, it would be foolish to undertake the task herself ; and, besides, they should be late for their visit, if they did not set off at once. ' Don't you agree with me, Charlotte ?' she exclaimed, as her sister entered.

'Oh! of course. I don't know at all what you are talking of; only I guess it is something about staying at home.'

'It was about my knitting,' said Mrs Courtenay: 'Jane tells me it must be begun again. I wish Gertrude, dear child, had thought upon something easier; but then she did not know how you were all occupied.'

'I suspect Gertrude knows very little of anything that any one else knows,' exclaimed Charlotte; 'she and Edith will do admirably to go through life together. My dear mamma, I quite agree with Jane, you had much better wait till Edith comes.'

'So provoking it is of Edith,' said Jane, pettishly; 'she is always out of the way. This is the fourth day we have seen nothing of her from breakfast to dinner.'

'She is gone to see old Martha to-day, my dear,' said Mrs Courtenay; 'so you must not complain of her.'

'I don't complain,' replied Charlotte; 'the business would be hopeless if one once began it. All I wish is, that we lived in a mud cottage, and went about without shoes and stockings, and then we might hope to have a little of Edith's attention.'

Mrs Courtenay raised her eyes from her work, and looked at her daughter in vacant astonishment. 'No shoes and stockings, my dear,—how very dreadful! Pray don't say so before Edward.'

'I would say so before the whole world,' said Charlotte, laughing: 'I don't mean to be hard upon Edith, but I must say she neglects home duties. Come, Jane, we have no time to spare.'

Jane quickly obeyed the summons; and Charlotte, having given her opinion upon Edith's faults, went for her walk with a contented conscience.

For the next quarter of an hour Mrs Courtenay meditated in silence and solitude upon the three delinquent stitches; and then, finding the occupation slightly wearisome, walked to the window, sighed and yawned, and at last crept up-stairs, to search in the right-hand corner of her oaken cabinet for a piece of silk to make a bag; the use of which was not yet decided upon, only bags were always useful. The sound of Edith's voice disturbed her, while yet undecided between the different claims of brown and purple; and with natural kindness of heart she hastened to inquire for old Martha. Edith was looking tired, harassed, and ill. She had unexpectedly again met with her brother on her way home, and while Mr Dacre's words yet weighed heavily upon her mind; and the conversation which had taken place between them, instead of affording any opening for attempting to warn him against his danger, had been short and unsatisfactory. Edward's thoughts were full of the splendid drawing-room which was to open upon the conservatory, and he paid but little attention to the few observations made by his sister; and Edith mused sadly upon the days that were gone by, and upon the barrier which a slight want of consideration, and a few hasty words, had raised between them. She longed to speak as she might once have done, freely and openly—to tell him of her fears—to entreat him to be on his guard : but it seemed impossible. At the period when their confidence was unbroken, the task would have been difficult; and with their present estrangement, she scarcely dared hope that he would listen to her, even if she had summoned up resolution to introduce the subject. Perhaps, if she had known all the weakness of Edward's heart, she might have been more inclined to excuse herself; but the only remark he made which at all interested her, showed thought and kindness for poor Martha; and Edith blamed herself more than usual for having ever said anything to vex him. They were together but a few minutes, for Edward pleaded Laura's solitude as an excuse for returning to the Park, and Edith assented directly, and, without any expression of regard beyond a careless shake of the hand, allowed him to depart. And yet, at that moment, she would have given up all that was most valuable upon earth—time, and comfort, and health, and affluence, and scarcely reckoned it a sacrifice—to save him from suffering.

With so much to depress her, the recollection of the absence of sympathy in her home was more painful than ever, and she felt relieved on hearing that her sisters were gone out; but Mrs Courtenay met her in the hall, and assailed her with a host of rapid, unimportant questions, to which, notwithstanding some newly-formed resolutions of respect, Edith found it difficult to reply with temper. There was, however, no escaping from them; and too weary to bear the exertion of standing, she proposed adjourning to the drawing-room, and was just entering, when the appearance of Miss Forester, stationed by the table, with a book in her hand, caused both herself and her mother to draw back in surprise.

'I am afraid I startled you, my dear Mrs Courtenay. The servant went to let you know I was here, and in the meantime I have been amusing myself with some of your enticing books. Is this interesting, Miss Courtenay?' and Miss Forester held out a volume of Jane's usual studies.

'Really I don't know, I never read novels.

'Indeed! but I was foolish to ask the question. I confess myself a mere ordinary mortal, so I am not ashamed of doing what every one else does. But you will have very little time for reading for several months to come; canvassing votes will be a sufficient occupation for all Mr Courtenay's family, since Parliament is to be dissolved immediately.'

Edith's countenance betrayed her uneasiness. Although professing in her own mind never to believe more than one-half, at least, of any news brought by Miss Forester, yet this decided assertion made her almost fancy that everything was settled.

'I am not surprised at your astonishment,' continued Miss Forester; 'it has astonished every one; but there was a long debate the night before last—ministers were beaten, and the consequence is a resignation, and, of course, a dissolution; so now I must congratulate you. My father says Mr Courtenay is certain of success.'

Mrs Courtenay was breathless from astonishment. Her eyes opened to their fullest extent, and, unable to speak, she turned to Edith for an explanation.

'This is the first intelligence my mother has received,' said Edith, recovering herself completely, and speaking in the calm, dignified tone with which she generally succeeded in checking Miss Forester's friendly impertinence; 'I heard the report of the dissolution from Mr Dacre just now.'

Miss Forester looked angry, as she always did when Edith mentioned her uncle's name. 'Indeed! I should have imagined him less communicative. The news has only just arrived. It was brought privately to my father, and he set off for Allingham instantly.'

'Then the congratulations are rather premature.'

'Oh no! there is not the slightest doubt of Mr Courtenay's being returned. The feeling of the whole county is in his favour. My father questions even whether Mr Vivian will oppose him.'

'But you seem to have forgotten the principal point,' said Edith; 'my brother must first consent to stand.'

'You do not mean to say he would refuse? But, no, I see you are only joking; no one could hesitate with such a prospect before him.'

'What is it, my dear?' said Mrs Courtenay, laying her hand

on Edith's arm. 'My dear Miss Forester, what is it? what are they going to do with Edward?'

'Nothing, I hope,' said Edith.

'Make him a member of Parliament,' replied Miss Forester.

'Well! yes, certainly,' said Mrs Courtenay; 'that will be quite right. The Allingham family always were members till the poor Colonel died; and then, you know, the little boy was too young.'

'There is very little use in thinking upon the subject,' said Edith, coldly, 'where the only foundation for the idea is report.'

'There I shall beg to differ from you. All that I say comes from the very highest authority;—and here are your sisters: I must see if they are equally unbelieving.'

'Unbelieving about what?' exclaimed Charlotte, as she shook hands; 'my creed is unbelief; so I can give you but little hope.'

'I merely wish you to believe in the fact, that Parliament is about to be dissolved immediately, and that, as a necessary consequence, your brother will be member for the county in the room of Mr Vivian.'

'The first proposition admits of no doubt, since you are the person to vouch for it; the second —— what do you say, Edith?'

'Your sister denies the possibility entirely,' said Miss Forester, 'though she has not informed me upon what grounds. But you do not seem at all surprised: had you heard the news before?'

'A rumour as to the resignation of ministers reached us when we were paying our last visit, but I did not give any particular attention to it: nothing was said about Edward.'

'But don't you agree with me?'

'Certainly, as to the fact that he will stand: it is just the foolish thing he would do. Success is another question.'

'Why should you say he will do it, if it is foolish, Charlotte?' said Edith, still unable to endure patiently any implication upon Edward's stability of character.

'Your sister is as strong a champion for her brother as ever, I see,' observed Miss Forester to Charlotte, with a soft bitterness of voice, peculiarly her own. 'I should have supposed that six months of matrimony—eight months, indeed—Mr Courtenay, I believe, was married in October—might have had some effect upon her zeal.'

Edith took no notice of the observation, though her heightened colour showed that it was understood.

'Our curiosity will soon be set at rest,' said Jane. 'If Edward has resolved upon standing, he will give us the earliest intelligence.'

'Or rather Laura will,' said Charlotte. 'In fact, my own opinion is, that if we wish to know Edward's determination, the most certain mode will be to ascertain hers.'

'Are you not a little severe?' said Miss Forester.

'Why should you think so? Laura merely exercises a wife's rightful influence.'

'All married women rule,' said Jane; 'only some have more tact than others in hiding it. A perfect stranger could discover it at Allingham.'

Edith longed to change the conversation, feeling that such a discussion of family affairs before a common acquaintance was not merely a breach of good taste, but implied a degree of intimacy which she was not at all inclined to acknowledge. As usual, however, her suggestion was of no avail, from the awkward manner in which it was made.

'There is nothing to be gained by knowing who rules, or who does not rule,' she said, shortly. 'Edward's affairs are his own, and he must be the best judge as to what most conduces to his happiness.'

'Can I do or say anything for any one at Allingham?' said Miss Forester. 'My time is precious, and I must go and congratulate Mrs Courtenay upon her husband's prospects.'

'And urge her not to allow him to neglect them,' said Charlotte.

'Yes, certainly, I shall make a point of doing it. As a matter of duty to my father, to further his wishes, I shall state all the advantages he foresees. Not that there can be any need of my arguments: Mr Courtenay is too sensible a person to resist the entreaties of his best friends ;' and Miss Forester, aware, from Edith's manner, that she disliked the idea of Edward's being in Parliament, trusted that she had inflicted some little pain.

'Well!' exclaimed Charlotte, 'I can only repeat what I said before—whoever wins Laura, wins Edward.'

'Then I am certain of success. Mrs Courtenay and I have often talked together upon the subject, and I know her wishes perfectly.'

Edith sighed, and so deeply as to attract general observation.

'Your sister seems to take a very gloomy view of the subject,' continued Miss Forester. 'I am afraid her influence will be exerted in the opposite scale to mine, so I had better take the field at once. There is generally great wisdom in being beforehand. Good morning to you. I will call on my return to let you know Mrs Courtenay's feelings.'

Even Jane was roused by this freedom, and observed sharply, that 'it would be an unnecessary trouble, for they should probably have heard everything long before ; but Edith, conscious of the power which Miss Forester exercised over Laura's mind, and with a vivid remembrance of Mr Dacre's warnings, sprang forward to stop her as she was about to leave the room.

'Pray, pray,' —— she began, and then paused.

Miss Forester gazed upon her with the same unpleasant smile she usually wore.

'Let me beg'—— Edith again commenced, and Miss Forester was still silent.

'Don't keep your friend in the draught. my dear,' said Mrs Courtenay : 'no one can stand it. My last cold was caught in that way.'

'What is the meaning of this nonsense?' exclaimed Charlotte. 'Really, Edith, you are too ridiculous.

'I am in no hurry,' said Miss Forester, keeping her sharp bright eyes fixed upon Edith, whose embarrassment was every moment increasing.

'Will you—will you ask Mr Dacre's opinion before you urge'——

For the third time the sentence remained unfinished. Edith felt that she could give no explanation of the request. Miss Forester's indignation, however, was sufficiently excited.

'There can be no occasion to apply to my uncle to learn his opinions upon any subject,' she exclaimed, in a tone of proud anger, very unlike her usual affected suavity. 'Your opinions. it is well known, are his ; where so much is to be gained by agreement you would not venture to differ.'

'I do not understand you,' said Edith, restored to self-possession by the sight of Miss Forester's irritation. 'All that I meant to say was, that Mr Dacre has had great experience, and I am certain has my brother's interest at heart, and I think he would say that it is unwise for any person to attempt to influence Edward's decision.'

'You are behaving in a most extraordinary manner, Edith,' said Charlotte. 'You seize upon Miss Forester, and begin speaking vehemently, and look most mysterious ; and when the explanation comes, it is merely that you think one person will consider it unwise for another person to try to influence Edward. If you are so uneasy lest he should be induced to stand (though why you should be no one can imagine), you had better go and advise him. A sister's opinion will surely be listened to.'

Edith scarcely waited for the concluding words before she had left the room, overcome by a painful sense of her own want of self-command and presence of mind, and keenly sensible of the ridicule she had incurred. Yet, as she ran up-stairs, she could not avoid hearing Miss Forester's words, spoken expressly in a loud tone :

'I may tell Mrs Courtenay, then, that you are rejoicing in the idea ?'

Charlotte's reply was not clear, but Miss Forester's laugh was ; and, as the climax of consolation, she departed with the assurance that, even if Mrs Courtenay disapproved, there were arguments to be brought forward which must be all-powerful with her husband.

CHAPTER XIX.

AN unusual excitement prevailed at Allingham on that day, not from the number of visitors, or the preparations for an entertainment, or the tumult of unexpected grief or joy, but simply from the great, almost magical effect of a few mysterious looks and words. General Forester called, and was told that Mr Courtenay was gone out. 'It was a most unfortunate event. Which way was he gone? How long was he likely to be absent? Had he said anything about his return? No message could be left, for a personal interview was absolutely necessary ;' and the obsequious footman suggesting the privacy and convenience of the library, the General, after ascertaining that Laura was not in the house, remained, as he thought, unobserved for the next quarter of an hour, whilst the unemployed domestics, making various excursions in front of the window, watched him carefully perusing papers and writing notes, and went back to their companions to conjecture and decide upon what was going to happen. Then came their master's return ; and a long conversation in the library with carefully-closed doors, through which, however, General Forester's pompous tones were occasionally caught, as he spoke of patriotism, and self-sacrifice, and family influence, and the necessity for exertion in such troubled times. Mr Courtenay's answers were at first low and short, indicating firm decision ; but the General was not easily to be repelled, and longer explanations, and greater energy, were soon brought into play. Still the exact purport of the interview was unknown; but a practised listener would have detected a certain softening of the pleader's voice, and an earnest deprecatory emphasis in the defendant's replies, which showed that the latter had begun to place more reliance upon the sound than upon the strength of his arguments. After two hours spent in this manner, the General took his leave, with a pleased, satisfied smile upon his lips, and an expression of conscious importance in his demeanour. Edward, on the contrary, was moody and restless. He inquired for his wife, and finding that she was not returned, paced the colonnade rapidly and steadily for a considerable time, and then suddenly walked away in the direction of Mr Dacre's cottage—and here the curiosity of the Allingham establishment was baffled; but neither, if it had been possible to gain an insight into Edward's mind, would it have been easy to discover the motives of his actions. He had, in fact, no determinate motive. General Forester's proposition, when first made, had been declined, gratefully, but decidedly ; then gratefully but thoughtfully ; and at last gratefully and waveringly ; and now, with an agitated, excited mind, Edward was about to apply to a human counsellor, disinterested indeed and high-principled, but still only human ; because he could not brave alone the struggle between duty and inclination, and dared not, in the secrecy of his own chamber, ask for that guidance from God which he was conscious of being but little inclined to follow. And in this, as in many other instances, Edward acted so as completely to deceive himself. He acknowledged the all-sufficient obstacles in the path of his ambition ; he believed he saw them in their strongest light ; and he felt that, in applying to Mr Dacre, he was consulting a person who would not for an instant allow his judgment to be blinded by sophistry ; but he did not see that, until these obstacles were removed, the opinion of a third person could not be required ; and that, in submitting the case to human judgment, he was, in fact, leaving himself free to decide according to his own will. A self-chosen authority may be self-deposed, and can never be of any avail, except in cases where the question of right and wrong is so nicely balanced as to be difficult of adjustment, or when we entirely distrust ourselves, and are willing to submit implicitly to another, whether for or against our inclinations. Edward's state of mind was the very reverse of this. Even in ordinary cases he piqued himself upon abiding by his own decision, unconscious that weakness of resolution was his prevailing defect; and when shown into Mr Dacre's study, he entered far more like a person who has performed a noble action, and is in expectation of well-merited praise, than one who is desirous of advice under trying circumstances.

'You are come, I suppose,' said Mr Dacre, 'to tell me something more about your old nurse and my little *protégée;* I am sorry you should have so much trouble.'

'That was all settled this morning with my sister," replied Edward; 'my business now is rather more important. You must have heard the news before this.'

'The resignation of ministers?' said Mr Dacre.

'Yes, and the consequent dissolution. The papers have not yet publicly confirmed the report, but General Forester has had private information, which puts it beyond doubt.'

'And are you come so early to canvass for Mr Vivian?' said Mr Dacre, with a considerable misgiving as to the answer he should receive.

'No, no,' exclaimed Edward, eagerly. 'You forget that we differ entirely.'

'Then for his intended opponent?'

'Wrong again;—but I am not come to canvass at all,—merely to ask advice.'

Mr Dacre's countenance resumed its usual expression of grave interest.

'That is to say,' continued Edward, 'not advice exactly; but I should be glad to know whether our opinions agree. What— what should you think if I were to stand myself?'

The very tone of his voice was an index to his wavering mind, and Mr Dacre's ordinary self-possession was rather shaken.

'The suggestion is startling to you, I see,' added Edward, who, though not in general vain, felt slightly annoyed at perceiving

that his friend did not consider him the fittest of all persons to
represent the county.

'It is natural to be surprised when such a notion is started for
the first time,' said Mr Dacre; 'but you surely cannot be
anxious for my advice on this point; you must know so much
better than I do the reasons for or against it.'

'As in most cases, there is much to be said on both sides,'
replied Edward. 'General Forester has been with me nearly
two hours this morning, setting forth in the strongest manner
the reasons which should induce me to come forward.'

'The General is a party man,' observed Mr Dacre.

'So he may be, but our principles entirely agree. He said
many things which were very striking;—and certainly these are
times when to be in Parliament is to obtain a vast influence.'

'Fearfully vast,' said Mr Dacre.

'But you would not on that account shrink from it, I suppose?'

'Not when a clear path of duty is pointed out; but the difficulty in these cases is to decide whether it is our path or some
other person's which we fancy ourselves called upon to enter.'

Edward was provoked at finding that his adviser's decision
was likely to be in favour of his conscience against his inclination; and a little reflection at this instant might have convinced
him that his judgment was not so irrevocably settled as he had
imagined.

'Then you think,' he said, endeavouring to conceal his pique,
'that the path of a member of Parliament is not mine?'

'Before I answer,' replied Mr Dacre, 'I must ask you to explain your meaning rather more clearly. Do you wish to know
whether I think you fitted for the office, or merely whether it
appears prudent in you to stand for it?'

'Both—both: I include everything,' said Edward, hastily.

Mr Dacre was considerably embarrassed. If Edward had
openly stated his difficulties, and then appealed to his judgment,
the case would have been easily decided; but now it was impossible to speak conscientiously, without alluding to those pecuniary
affairs which seemed, by a tacit agreement, to have been hitherto
forgotten by both. 'The question of personal fitness,' he said, at
length, 'must be left to every man's conscience. I should consider any person with a clear judgment, and strict, unbending
principles of duty, justified in obtaining, if possible, a seat in
Parliament, provided that his situation in life offered him the
means.'

'Yes,—certainly,—yes,'— said Edward, hesitatingly; 'but, in fact, General Forester assures me that the expenses of the election shall cost me nothing. The gentlemen of the county, he is certain, will guarantee them.'

'I would not distrust the gentlemen of this or any other county,' replied Mr Dacre; 'but experience is against the fact of any man's obtaining a seat in Parliament without expenses. And then the consequences, a frequent residence in town, and the perpetual claims, and the exertions to maintain popularity.'

'Ah! but I should make no exertions,' exclaimed Edward. 'No person can be less inclined than myself to pay court to that "many-headed monster-thing," the people.'

'So much the worse,' continued Mr Dacre, 'as far as your expenses are concerned. You may pay court to the little farmer and the petty tradesman with tobacco and small beer, but your supporters in the higher ranks will require ices and champagne.'

'No, no!' exclaimed Edward, impatiently, 'you do not understand my ideas. If I went into Parliament, it would be on a totally different footing. I could never lower myself by trying to conciliate any one; it would not be worth while. The seat itself is a mere nothing to me; it could neither add to nor diminish from my happiness, yet it might open a wide field of usefulness, and this is the only thing which makes me hesitate,—although,' he added, in a less determined manner, 'I have declined General Forester's proposals for the present; that is, I have told him he must not depend upon me.'

Mr Dacre seemed disinclined to speak, and Edward continued in a loud, eager tone :—'It is a most alarming responsibility, certainly, to take upon one's self—but something must be done. If men of property, and educated in good principles, do not sacrifice themselves, the country will infallibly be ruined. Just look at the manufacturing districts—the abject misery of the poor, and the enormous fortunes of the rich ;—look at the statistics of crime—at the rapidly increasing population, and the misery occasioned by the New Poor Law ; and then turn to the colonies —see the mass of vice which is daily accumulating in our convict settlements, with scarcely a hope of improvement, and almost destitute of a church ; and then consider for one instant the condition of that Church in England—deprived of all power by the state, forbidden to assemble in convocation, and illegally robbed of the means of providing for her children. The Church !' —and Edward became still more excited and enthusiastic—

'yes, if it were for the Church alone, I should long to be a member of Parliament.'

'It is an awful, a most awful picture,' said Mr Dacre, in a tone of solemnity which contrasted forcibly with Edward's energy; and then, resting his forehead upon the mantelpiece, he appeared for some minutes buried in thought. 'Yet,' he continued, rousing himself from his reverie, 'unless we are clearly pointed out by Providence as the instruments of so great a work as the salvation of our country, I think we ought to consider seriously before we undertake it.'

'Then who will dare to attempt it?' replied Edward. 'No one can look into his own heart, and say that he is qualified to judge correctly upon the least of those subjects upon which men are perpetually required to legislate.'

'It is not an inward, but an outward call which I should deem necessary,' said Mr Dacre; 'not merely a man's talent and principle, but the being provided with the means of exercising them.'

'Money!' exclaimed Edward, with a slight, a very slight, accent of sarcasm.

'Yes, money: you have expressed precisely what was in my mind.'

'But surely—surely,' continued Edward, 'you cannot see any connection between the possession of money and the making just laws.'

'There is no necessary connection, I own; but if a father, perfect in wisdom and goodness, were to place his child in sight of a battle, and, after enjoining upon him strict obedience to whatever line of conduct he might point out, were to fetter his hands and chain his feet, I think we should say that the duty of that child was patience and submission rather than active exertion.'

'It is an imaginary case,' said Edward, 'and it cannot be mine. If I were to stand, General Forester assures me I should be brought in free of all expenses. I am not blind enough to take such a phrase literally, but it must mean something.'

'Even then I confess I should have considerable scruples,' said Mr Dacre.

'Why, why?' asked Edward, impatiently.

'Because it would be engaging in a most important business without the authority to control it. Every one knows the mischiefs of an election,—the drunkenness, and falsehood, and deceit

—I will not say bribery and perjury—which are almost always its attendants.'

'But you cannot imagine I should allow such things,' exclaimed Edward, looking extremely hurt : 'then indeed you have mistaken me.'

'No, believe me ; I am certain you would not ; and it is for this very reason I am convinced that after consideration you could not allow yourself to be brought forward by others, instead of standing independently.   If they undertake your expenses, they must manage your affairs.   You will be a mere tool in their hands. Whatever they may do will have the sanction of your name, and yet you will not be able to raise a finger against it.   Can you trust yourself to this ?'

There was a silence of several minutes, whilst Edward communed with his own thoughts.   ' You are right,' he said, at length, turning to Mr Dacre ; ' I see it now even more clearly than before. It must not be ; and yet, do not consider it merely the vanity of a young man : I think I should have done my duty.'

' I am sure, quite sure, that no man would ever have entered upon the office with a more firm intention of doing it ; but I think you will agree with me, that when we place ourselves in any position which it is not clearly the intention of Providence we should occupy, we have great reason to doubt whether our best intentions may not fail. All situations of importance are situations of temptation likewise.'

' If we could shut our eyes to the miseries of the country,' replied Edward, ' it would be easy to submit to a life of seclusion and inactivity ; but it is impossible to look at what England is, and what she might be, and not long to exert oneself.'

'And are you sure that there may not be exertions for good made in private, as powerful as any which a public man may exercise—the influence of daily example, for instance ; meekness, and purity, and charity ?   If it is the will of God that England should be saved, is it not possible that the end may be attained by the constant prayers and efforts of good men whose names may never be heard beyond their own narrow circle ?'

' But to feel that we have a power, and to be forbidden to use it,' said Edward, 'that is the trial. To see other people acting on false, low principles, and know that our own education has been different, and therefore to hope that we should act from higher motives, and still to be patient !'

' The highest of all principles,' replied Mr Dacre, ' is surely obedience. If we are deficient in this,—if we have a wish to escape from it,—we cannot answer for any other.'

' I scarcely see the case in as strong a light as you do,' answered Edward ; ' but I suppose it is right to distrust oneself.'

' It is safest, at least,' replied Mr Dacre.

' Then it is decided,' said Edward ; ' that is to say, your opinion is merely a confirmation of my own ; but I am glad to have had it.

This speech, so evidently a salve to Edward's wounded pride, would have been amusing to almost any person except Mr Dacre ; but although, with his peculiarly clear insight into human nature, he detected instantly the feeling from which it arose, it only gave him a sense of insecurity and doubt as to Edward's ultimate conduct ; and with this he could not be amused. Yet there were many kind words at parting ; many expressions of gratitude and regard ; and a stranger would have supposed that Mr Courtenay's decision was immovably settled ; but Mr Dacre thought otherwise.

CHAPTER XX.

WHEN Miss Forester left the Priory, it was with the intention, as she had said, of calling at Allingham ; but the sight of Mrs Courtenay's low phaeton and gray ponies, in the road leading to Elsham, proved that her visit would be useless ; and not being able to satisfy her curiosity in the way she desired, her next step was to return home as quickly as possible, to obtain from her father all the further information he was able and willing to give. And as she walked, visions—bright, tempting visions—dreams of luxury and magnificence—of elegant dinners, and fashionable society—balls and soirées—Almacks and Buckingham Palace—filled Miss Forester's head ; and the stepping-stone to this grandeur was Edward Courtenay's seat in Parliament. Let this point once be gained, and everything else was easy. As his wife's intimate friend, but little management would be required to enable her to share her pleasures ; and Miss Forester, notwithstanding the five and thirty years which had passed over her head, dwelt upon the idea with the false excitement of a girl of eighteen. Laura, in the meantime, drove into Elsham ; paid her visits in proper form ; inquired after the

health of the various households ; discussed the weather, and
praised the children ; and then, that she might return home
with a conscience completely at ease, turned her ponies' heads
in the direction of the Priory. It was a duty-visit, such as she
now was in the habit of making at regular intervals, and which
was becoming daily more and more irksome. It was not merely
that Mrs Courtenay was weak-minded, and her sisters-in-law
either thoughtless and satirical, or cold and uncongenial ; but
there was something in the family circle, scarcely to be told in
words, but jarring even upon the least susceptible nerves, which
to Laura was peculiarly distressing. Almost every sentence,
and gesture, and action, betrayed the absence of harmony ; and
as Laura became, by observation, more alive to the distinctive
traits of character, she naturally felt more painfully the little
intonations of voice, and trifling marks of selfishness, which by
an ordinary acquaintance would probably have been unheeded.
And then she thought of Edith's sense, and decision, and energy,
and self-denial ; of her kindness to the poor ; her affection for
Edward, blended with her forgetfulness of her home and the
unkind words and great neglect of herself ; and the problem
became too difficult for Laura to solve ; only she felt that, if
Edith were good, goodness was disagreeable.

Jane and Charlotte, with their mother, were still in the drawing-room when Laura entered, and, imagining that she was come
to inform them of the expected event, addressed her with questions and congratulations, so rapidly as to give her no time to
inquire their meaning.

'Just think, my dear,' began Mrs Courtenay, 'what a change !
and you will be in London so much ; and poor Edward is not at
all strong ; we never thought he would live when he was two
months old.'

'Rather jumping to conclusions, without giving the premises,
mamma,' said Charlotte, observing her sister-in-law's bewildered
expression ; 'but really, Laura, we do want to know what Edward says to this business.'

'Yes, my dear,' interrupted Mrs Courtenay ; 'sit down here,
and tell us all about it ;—a little closer—you know I'm rather
deaf ; now then, when did he hear about it first ?'

'This morning, of course,' observed Jane. 'Miss Forester
said the General went off directly.'

'Went off where ? what do you mean ? what are you all talking about ?' exclaimed Laura.

'Oh! my love, you know,' said Mrs Courtenay; 'and we are so longing to hear—pray tell us quickly.'

'But what? tell what?' repeated Laura; 'I should be very much obliged if some one would explain.'

'There is no particular explanation needed, that I can see,' replied Jane; 'we only want to know if Edward intends standing.'

'Standing!' again repeated Laura.

'Yes, my dear,' said Mrs Courtenay; 'if you would only make haste, I should be so glad; I really am nervous from being kept so long in suspense.'

'And there can be no good in it,' continued Jane 'for we must know sooner or later.'

'Besides, I thought you disliked mysteries,' said Charlotte; 'and if you did not, elections are such public things, it is useless to attempt keeping them to one's self.'

'Then Parliament is dissolved!' exclaimed Laura, starting from her seat, in an excitement of surprise and pleasure; 'the very thing, of all others, I have been longing for.'

'So he will stand, my dear?' asked Mrs Courtenay, in a tremulous voice; and she laid her hand upon Laura's arm in order to be certain of detaining her till the question was answered.

Laura moved away; and, heedless of anything but her own gratification in the prospect suddenly opening before her, began, in her turn, to ask questions with such volubility that poor Mrs Courtenay, in silent despair, laid down her work, and sat, patient and resigned, with her head bent forward, endeavouring to extract an answer for herself, since it seemed in vain to expect one from others. A few words of explanation sufficed to prove that Laura was equally ignorant with themselves; but her wishes were so decidedly in favour of Edward's coming forward, that Charlotte, at least, felt little doubt as to his decision.

'He will have the cordial support of every one in the family except Edith,' said Jane · 'she sets her face decidedly against it —why, no one can tell.'

'And no one would wish to tell, I should think,' observed Charlotte; 'but you must not let her talk to Edward, Laura, if you wish to persuade him without trouble.'

'I have no fear of any persuasion,' began Laura, proudly; but her sentence was interrupted, for, at that instant, the door opened, and Edith appeared. 'Good-bye; I must go; the ponies will be very fidgety if I keep them so long: Edith, you must excuse my running away, but' ——

'But you cannot rest till you have secured Edward's promise to stand for the county,' said Charlotte, laughing. 'You see, Edith, whom you will have to fight against.'

Edith looked not merely vexed, but unhappy ; and seeing that she should probably have no other opportunity of gaining a patient hearing, determined upon following Mr Dacre's advice, and endeavouring, if possible, to accomplish the object upon the importance of which he had so strongly insisted.

'I would not willingly detain you, Laura,' she said ; 'but indeed it is of great consequence that I should say a few words to you alone.'

Laura slightly shuddered, and recurred involuntarily to her many offences. 'If it is of consequence,' she replied, 'I can say nothing ; but I assure you I have no time to spare ; would not to-morrow do ?'

'I am afraid not ; but really I will not keep you more than a few minutes ;' and with a countenance grave, almost to severity, Edith opened the folding doors, and ushered her sister-in-law into the library.

Laura sighed in submission to her fate, though at the same time feeling considerably irritated ; for it was Edith's misfortune frequently to wear the appearance of pride, when she was in reality humble ; and this was peculiarly the case in the present instance. The stiffness of manner, which to Laura appeared haughtiness and conceit, was in fact merely the effort to restrain deep and anxious feeling ; but its effects were painfully repelling, especially when heightened by the constrained tone in which she began : 'You must forgive me, Laura ; I know it is not my part to interfere ; but indeed it is only from a sense of duty.'

The words were humble, but the tone was not ; and Laura, from childhood unable to endure suspense, hastily interrupted her with —'I will forgive anything you wish, if you will only tell me at once what is the matter—what have I done ?'

'Nothing,' replied Edith ; 'it is not what you have done, but what you are going to do.'

'Me ! I am not going to do anything, except to drive back to Allingham.'

'But you are intending, at least you said you were—you want Edward to stand for the county.'

'Yes, certainly,' said Laura, looking extremely surprised ; 'and so do you, I suppose ; so do all his friends.'

'Not his real friends,' replied Edith ; 'those who sincerely value his happiness would most strongly urge upon him the folly of such a scheme. I am sure you would, Laura, if'——

'If what?' continued Laura ; 'am I not his sincere friend? Is not his happiness my happiness? Are not our interests one and the same? Why should you speak of ifs?'

'Because I don't think you have well considered the subject, and calculated the expenses. I think you are led away by excitement, and not likely to have an unbiased judgment.'

'Very possibly,' said Laura, in a tone of pique ; 'but pray, have you the same opinion of Edward? I thought he was your paragon of excellence.'

'My opinion of Edward has nothing to do with the case,' said Edith, coldly : for any allusion to what she had formerly felt for her brother was never patiently borne. 'It is you, Laura, of whom I am speaking now. Everything depends upon your influence ; and you cannot tell the importance of what you are going to urge Edward to do.'

'So I can well imagine. I dare say he will make a noise in the world, and be thought a great deal of.'

'But that is all nothing,' said Edith ; 'pray, pray, think of the expenses.'

'No, indeed,' exclaimed Laura ; 'that is not a wife's province. If Edward thinks he can afford it, I am sure I shall not be the person to say nay.'

'And you will not warn him?' said Edith.

'Why should I? What are your objections?'

'I can't explain them all,' replied Edith, looking embarrassed ; 'but some must be clear to every one.'

'And you wish me to follow your guidance against my own inclinations?'

'Because I have your truest interest at heart,' said Edith ; 'besides, it is impossible not to see the danger of extravagance.'

'Extravagance! nonsense,' repeated Laura ; 'if Edward cannot afford election expenses, I am certain he cannot afford to live in the style he does. He must have money at command, for I never ask for a thing which he does not give me.'

'And therefore you would ruin him,' said Edith, gravely. 'O Laura! listen to me but this once ; I only desire to save you from suffering.'

'I cannot understand you, Edith,' said Laura ; 'and I am in a hurry.'

'Only one moment!' exclaimed Edith, in a tone of deep

anxiety; 'I am sure you don't know all, or you never could persist.'

'I know that I am determined Edward shall be in Parliament.'

'But won't you believe me?' said Edith; 'I can have no object but your happiness.'

'Indeed!' answered Laura, ironically; 'I should scarcely have supposed that from past experience, considering that the only harsh words Edward ever spoke to me were caused by your remarks.'

Poor Edith's eyes filled with tears. She remembered Mr Dacre's words: the solemnity with which he had reminded her of the account to be rendered for influence, as for every other talent; and she felt that hers had been neglected. Now, when it was so much needed, it was gone. It was the first time that Laura had ever directly alluded to the chief cause of their estrangement. Yet Edith dared not explain or apologise: for the opinion she had incautiously expressed was still retained.

'Then you will not listen,' she said; 'and I must appeal to Edward.'

'No, no,' said Laura; 'that shall never be. I will trust nothing that concerns us in any hands but my own. Whatever I may be in your eyes I am dear and precious in my husband's; and I will never allow a cold, unsympathising perfection to come between me and him. Tell me what I am to say, and I will promise to deliver your message without variation.'

'There is no need,' replied Edith, as calmly as her agitation would allow. 'I had hoped that you would have consented to discuss the subject dispassionately; and then you might, perhaps, have been induced to view it in a different light. I know that Edward will be influenced, more than he will himself allow, by your wishes, and therefore I desired to enlist you on the side of prudence.'

'And why, if I may ask,' said Laura, drawing herself up, and speaking in a tone as calm though less gentle—'why are you alone to be the judge of what is prudent? Why may not Edward be considered the fit guardian of his own affairs? And why should you urge upon a wife to undertake the task of dissuading her husband from his public duty.'

'Because there is a private duty which is more imperative,' replied Edith; 'and Edward knows it. I cannot say more; but since you have promised, Laura, to deliver any message which I may send, let it be that,—it may be but casting words to the

wind,—yet it may also induce him to hesitate,—and to-morrow'
—— 'I will see him myself,' she was about to add, but something in the expression of Laura's countenance checked her.

'To-morrow,' said Laura, 'you will probably find that Edward has decided upon his duty without asking counsel of any one. If you have nothing to say upon any other subject, Edith, I had better go, for my time is valuable.'

Edith coldly held out her hand, which Laura as coldly took. A formal good-bye was spoken on both sides; and, without returning to the drawing-room, Laura seated herself in her pony-carriage, and drove from the Priory. Edith watched her as she left the room, and listened to the departing sounds; and then, unable to control her vexation, shed tears of regret and self-reproach.

CHAPTER XXI.

PROUDLY as Laura had behaved during the interview with her sister-in-law, she was not entirely untouched by what had passed. Edith's opposition, though unaccountable, was still too earnest not to awaken some idea that it might be well-founded; and when the first excitement of her feelings had subsided, Laura resolved upon repeating to her husband all that had been said, without offering any comment of her own, and then demanding an explanation; but unfortunately the resolution was made at the very moment of passing the Grange, and the sound of Miss Forester's siren voice, as she stood by the lodge-gate and entreated that her dear Mrs Courtenay would give her the pleasure of ten minutes' conversation, proved so soothing to Laura's temper, that she could not resist the temptation to alight. There was no difficulty in discovering that something had happened to disturb Laura's equanimity, and her openness of character quickly revealed the cause to one so keen in observation. Miss Forester's selfish tact had never, perhaps, been more carefully brought into play. She suggested a jealousy of Edith's influence over her brother, ridiculed the idea of prudence being necessary to a man of Edward's fortune, lauded his splendid talents, and repeated her father's opinion of his certain success; and then proceeded to describe in glowing colours the path that was open to his ambition—the position in which he would be placed—the popularity he would command—the gratification of being looked up to and courted; and Laura listened to the honeyed words, and yielded unresistingly to the temptation of dreams so alluring to a young mind, and, before she left the Grange, gave a promise that if Edward were inclined to hesitate, no argument which she could use should be spared in inducing him to consent. The conversation lasted so long, that, on reaching Allingham, Laura found that dinner had already been announced, and heard with pleasure that General Forester was to be her guest. It was evident that Edward had not yet decidedly refused; and much as she longed to be with him alone, she was willing to bear the delay of a few hours, in the hope that the General's arguments would render her own entreaties needless. The dinner was dull and uninteresting. The General, a shrewd, worldly politician, bent upon obtaining Edward's consent, because it was most likely to ensure success to his party and render himself a person of consequence, carefully abstained from all allusion to the subject uppermost in his thoughts, but could not prevent his attention from wandering from the trifling topics of conversation. Laura watched every change of her husband's countenance, in the hope of gaining some clue to his determination; and Edward sat silent, endeavouring to satisfy himself that, in inviting General Forester to dinner, he had merely performed the part of a friend, without any wish of swerving from the resolution of the morning. At length the dessert was placed upon the table, and the servants retired; but Laura listened in vain for the subject in which she was so deeply interested. Farming and manufactures, railway and mining companies, were successively introduced and languidly discussed—but then came a solemn pause; and having lingered as long as etiquette could possibly allow, she was obliged to retire. The solitary evening seemed as if it would never end. Hour after hour wore away, and still the gentlemen in the dining-room continued in earnest conversation. Laura ventured twice to summon them, but finding the message disregarded, gave up the attempt, and, after many endeavours to amuse herself, forgot her anxiety in sleep. She was awakened by the sound of voices in the hall. General Forester was taking his leave, thinking it too late again to intrude upon her. Edward's tones were so low as to be unintelligible, but the General's concluding words were perfectly audible,—'Then by eight to-morrow I shall hear from you ;' and the next minute his carriage drove off.

Unable to restrain her eagerness, Laura, after waiting a few moments, hastened into the hall to meet her husband, but he was not there. She knocked at the door of his study, but received no answer; and was going back to the drawing-room again, when, the hall door being opened, she caught sight of him in the colonnade. He was pacing it with rapid strides, his arms folded upon his breast ; and the cold light of the moon, as it fell upon his noble features, so deepened their expression of thought and anxiety, that Laura became alarmed.

'Are you ill, Edward?' she exclaimed, suddenly arresting his progress.

Edward started, as if recalled from a dream. 'Ill, my love? no ; why should you think so ?'

'But you are ill ; you look so—pray come in.'

'There is nothing for me to be afraid of on such a night as this,' he replied, and he pointed to the glittering heavens ; 'but it is too late for you to remain.'

'I could not rest even if I were to leave you ; besides, Edward, your thoughts concern us both.'

'Indirectly, perhaps ; but politics are not a woman's business. I merely wish to consider something General Forester has been saying.'

'And to decide that to-morrow you will consent to stand for the county,' added Laura.

'Where did you hear it?' he exclaimed ; 'I thought it was merely a question of private business between the General and myself.'

'It has long been considered a matter of course by every one ; and this you know quite well, Edward ; but my first intelligence of the dissolution was from the Priory.'

'And what did they say there?' inquired Edward, with eagerness.

'Approved entirely, of course—all, that is, but Edith.'

'Edith ! did she object? what reason did she give ?'

'None ; at least none that I could understand ; but she chilled me by her manner, and teased me with her words, and so I came away as soon as possible.'

'She must have said something, though. Did she think me unfitted ?'

'No, nothing of that kind. It appeared to be some notion of

the expense which she had in her head; and then she talked about private duties. Stop, I think I can recollect the whole sentence; it was a sort of message to you. I was to tell you that there was a private duty which was more imperative than a public one.'

The words were an abstract of Mr Dacre's arguments; and Edward, shrinking from their truth, turned away, unwilling to hear more. Laura watched him in silence, and then, fearful lest his determination should be about to fix in a direction contrary to her wishes, again ventured to interrupt him.

'You consider that women have no concern in politics,' she said, putting her arm within his; 'and yet you are anxious to know the opinion of your mother and sisters; and have you no thought also for your wife?'

'It is because I think of her too much, that I do not speak to her on the subject,' replied Edward, with a faint smile. 'Only . say that it is a matter of indifference to you, and I shall not be afraid to tell you what I have resolved upon.'

'Not to decline!' exclaimed Laura, in a tone of extreme disappointment: 'you could not have been so foolish.'

'So wise, rather;—so willing to sacrifice everything—ambition, and fame, and influence—for the interest of one who is dearer to me than my own life.'

'And do you think,' exclaimed Laura, pausing suddenly in her walk, 'that your wife would be unwilling to risk the same consequences as yourself for the sake of seeing you what you ought to be?' Would it not be worth any sacrifice to know that your talents were estimated,—to feel that you were honoured throughout the whole country? What can the consideration of a few paltry thousands be to such a prospect as yours if you only consent to come forward?'

Edward was silent; but he gazed with a feeling of love and admiration, mingled with something of compassion, upon Laura's young and lovely features, lighted up with an enthusiasm, which, though false in its origin, might be directed to so much good; and, drawing her towards him, said gently, 'Laura, you will not ask me to do wrong—your husband could refuse you nothing.'

'Then you will not refuse me this,' exclaimed Laura, eagerly seizing upon the weakness caused by her own fascination, whilst the recollection of Miss Forester's brilliant prophecies came vividly before her. 'It is the first, the sole object of my wishes; and it is not for myself alone,—it is for the good of thousands;

you have yourself said it. What is to become of your resolution, dearest Edward, if you shrink from the contest because you will not incur the expense?'

Edward pressed his hand upon his eyes, and sighed deeply; and little did Laura guess the bitterness of the struggle which was then passing in his breast—the last dying effort of duty to regain its power. 'Laura,' he said, at length, 'you are urging me to a step which, when once taken, cannot be retraced. Are you indeed sure that you will never be inclined to repent having done it?'

'Never!' answered Laura, earnestly. 'Whatever trouble or anxiety it may cause, I can never look back with regret upon having entreated you to place yourself in the position for which your fortune and talents have so evidently fitted you. But after all, Edward, why are you to be ruined by acting as thousands have done before you, who had not half your means?'

'It need not be ruin,' replied Edward, attempting to smile; 'certainly it would not be, if General Forester's offer were accepted.'

'What offer? What has he said? You can have no secrets now from me.'

'He proposes that the expenses should be borne by the gentlemen of the county, who are all willing to support me; and the plan is plausible, but Mr Dacre suggested objections.'

'And have you really been consulting Mr Dacre?' exclaimed Laura; and there was something of scorn in her light, silvery laugh. 'Have you determined upon making him your oracle in an affair which requires mere common sense and knowledge of the world?'

'I do not make him my oracle,' replied Edward, proudly; 'I would make no man such.'

'Then why attach such weight to his opinion? It is but the decision of one man, and there are hundreds who would be against him.'

Edward made no answer. The decision of that one man was, he well knew, the decision of an unbending, conscientious mind; and as the impression of the morning's conversation returned in full force, once more his wavering resolution might have been fixed, but for the jealousy of Mr Dacre, suggested by Laura's observation.

'It is not worthy of you, Edward,' she continued; 'and when you see what opportunities of good you have lost, it will not satisfy you to remember that you gave them up merely because you chose to follow Mr Dacre's dictation, rather than your own judgment.'

' But what will he think when he finds that I have so soon changed my determination ? '

' Rather, what will the world think when it is known that you have made it ? '

' The world,' repeated Edward, mournfully ; and, walking a few paces aside, he leant against one of the pillars of the colonnade. For some minutes he continued silent, listening to the plashing of the fountains in the garden, as their slender columns rose into the still air, and then fell sparkling in the moonlight into their marble basins, while his gaze was fixed intently on the deep blue sky, through which the moon was tranquilly sailing, undimmed by even a passing shadow. ' It is a glorious night,' he said, at length, as Laura drew near to him. ' Is it not strange that we, upon whom such beauty has been lavished, should be so insensible to it ? '

Laura looked at him in wonder. ' Do you mean,' she said, ' that because we have been speaking upon other subjects, we are therefore unable to feel how lovely it is ? '

' We do not feel it,' replied Edward ; ' it is too calm—too pure. What has the world to do with the moon and the stars, and the unutterable vastness of the heavens ? '

' I do not understand you,' said Laura. ' If it is wrong to think of the world, why should we have been sent to live in it ? '

' I did not say it was wrong,' replied Edward ; ' but it is so strange—so incomprehensible. Tell me, Laura,—is not the bustle of the election more important in your eyes than all the beauty of nature ? '

' Perhaps so, at this moment,' replied Laura ; ' but it is natural.'

' Yes, natural, perfectly natural ; but that itself is the cause of wonder.'

' It is not so to me,' replied Laura. ' The election is nothing, but you are everything.'

' Are you sure, dearest,' said Edward, ' that it is only for me you are anxious ? '

' Do not ask that question again,' replied Laura ; ' it implies distrust. If I have visions of distinction, they cannot be for myself ; I am but a woman, and fame can be nothing to me.'

' But we can be happy without fame,' said Edward, in a tone

which evidently showed his willingness that the assertion should
be contradicted.

'Yes,' exclaimed Laura ; and again her clear, sweet voice was
marred by an accent of sarcasm ; 'and we may be happy in a
hovel, labouring with our hands for our daily bread. Philo-
sophers tell us so—Mr Dacre is a philosopher.'

'If there were no obstacles'—— began Edward, pursuing his
own train of thought aloud, rather than replying to his wife's
observation.

'I do not see them,' interrupted Laura ; 'and surely I must
be a better judge than Mr Dacre ; he cannot be as intimately
acquainted with all that concerns you as I am.'

Edward's conscience painfully smote him. His first want of
moral courage in not acquainting Laura with the encumbered
state of his property was beginning to work its punishment ; for
the only reason which could satisfy her of the propriety of his
refusal was truth, and truth it seemed now impossible to tell. To
confess that he had deceived her would, he felt, be a degradation ;
yet her implicit reliance upon his sincerity was more galling than
the keenest reproach. Besides, he was becoming, every instant,
more and more convinced that the obstacles of which he spoke
were not insurmountable. At the distance of several hours Mr
Dacre's suggestions were seen through a dim, unsubstantial haze,
while General Forester's baits hung rich and glittering before
him. He had been promised the support of almost every man of
consequence in the county ; flattered with insidious praises of his
talents, bribed by the hope of lucrative and honourable appoint-
ments ; and now he required but one more inducement to determine the balance, and this was Laura's entreaty ; and Laura's
natural inclinations had been strengthened by Miss Forester's influence, and Miss Forester's influence was mainly to be attributed
to Edith's neglect. How little can we discover of the secret chain
of human events ! and how little did Edith imagine, as she sat
alone in her chamber, dwelling in wretchedness of heart upon the
fatal step her brother was meditating, that her own conduct was
one of the ultimate causes of the decision he was about to make !
Laura perceived the wavering of her husband's mind, and well
knew how to take advantage of it. It was not the first occasion
on which she had exerted her power over his affections to gain an
object desired ; and now, gently forcing him to re-enter the house,
she led him into the drawing-room, and seating herself by his
side, looked up into his face with a smile of such exquisite sweet-

ness, that a man of far greater strength of mind than Edward might easily have found his resolution shaken; and then she said—

'For your wife's sake, Edward; it is the first wish of her heart.'

Edward's countenance was grave, but his tones were yielding, as he replied: 'And when I am taxed with imprudence and ambition, will my wife uphold my cause? Or, if others undertake my expenses, will she answer that my affairs shall be conducted in an honourable manner?'

'This is beyond my comprehension,' exclaimed Laura, laughing. 'You have been talking to Mr Dacre, Edward, till you are become as visionary as himself. Do tell me all his objections in a few words.'

'He allows that there are but two—the expense being one; this would in a measure be done away by accepting General Forester's proposal: but the next difficulty seems to be, that, if the management of the affair is to be taken out of my hands, I shall not be able to put a stop to anything I may think wrong in the way in which it is carried on.'

'How extremely absurd!' exclaimed Laura: 'so like Mr Dacre's ultra-particularity; as if it were possible to have an election conducted without things being done to which one must shut one's eyes. And so, Edward, you will throw away your greatest chance of being really useful to your country upon a mere scruple of conscience, which common sense must at once condemn?'

Edward did not exactly see the truth of this observation, but it was given authoritatively, and sounded well; and he was not inclined to contradict it. 'I must own,' he replied, 'that Mr Dacre's arguments do not strike me as unanswerable. It would be at my option to retire if I saw things going on in a manner which I disapproved.'

'Certainly it would,' exclaimed Laura; 'and the example then would be more valuable than all which you do or say now.'

'I should retire undoubtedly,' repeated Edward; 'nothing would induce me to allow the horrid system of bribery and wickedness which generally accompanies an election; and I own I should be glad to show the world that a business of this nature may be carried on on high principles.'

Laura placed a sheet of paper before him, and put a pen into his hand. Edward still hesitated. 'Mr Dacre will think it very strange.'

'Still Mr Dacre!' exclaimed Laura, impatiently. 'I did not think you were to be governed so easily.'

The arrow was rightly aimed. Fear of being led was Edward's most vulnerable point; and, taking up the pen, he commenced a letter to General Forester. Laura leant over him as he proceeded, strengthening his resolution by insisting upon the benefit to be derived from such an example as his must necessarily be; and when the letter was concluded, Edward delivered it to his servant, with strict injunctions that it was to be sent to the Grange before eight o'clock the next morning, and retired to rest with scarcely a doubt that he had acted nobly and conscientiously.

CHAPTER XXII.

WHEN Edith met Mr Dacre after the first public announcement of Edward's intentions, it was in the drawing-room at the Priory, and in the company of strangers, where private conversation was impossible; and nothing but an earnest pressure of the hand showed that he understood and felt for her uneasiness. The chances of the election were then under discussion, and she was compelled to listen with apparent indifference to hopes, fears, and congratulations, which were all equally painful; until Mr Dacre, with a tact and delicacy peculiar to himself, led the conversation from the election in particular to elections in general, and from them to the political subjects of the day, and the customs and habits of foreign countries; and Edith was again at ease. One look, one more cordial shake of the hand, as they parted, told her gratitude; and then, as if by mutual consent, the subject was avoided during several succeeding interviews. Both felt that conversation was useless, and could not be entered into without throwing reproach upon Edward. But Mr Dacre, though a silent, was not an unobservant spectator of what was passing, and each day gave him more reason to apprehend the consequences of Edward's weakness. Allingham was now the centre of attraction to the whole neighbourhood; for Mr Courtenay, with lavish hospitality, opened his house, not only to his friends, but to his most distant acquaintances; and, casting aside his weekly bills, contented himself with the belief that it was absurd to think of expense at such a moment,—the election must cost him something, and it was better to let everything take its course, and do what was absolutely necessary, without making himself uneasy as to the result. And Laura entirely agreed. She was now in her element—admired, courted, flattered, caressed, by all who sought their own interest through Edward's advancement, and by many who, with greater disinterestedness, were captivated by her beauty, grace, and vivacity. Every day she was assured of the certainty of Edward's success, and that, when once in Parliament, he would necessarily be placed amongst the most distinguished men of the age ; and with her youthful ignorance, and warm affections, she implicitly believed all that was told her, and already began to contemplate the duties which must devolve on the wife of a Secretary of State, or, it might be, the First Lord of the Treasury. During this time, Edith withdrew herself more and more from her own family circle, and found her greatest relief in solitude at home, and active exertion abroad. She wrote also frequently to Gertrude ; for the advantages of the election were in themselves so doubtful, that she was able, without any breach of confidence, to express her disapprobation ; and Gertrude's letters in return were so considerate, so full of gentleness and sympathy, that, at times, Edith felt as if the diminution of her brother's regard was repaid by the increased affection between herself and her absent sister. But in that one word 'absent,' was contained the great obstacle to her comfort. No love, no interest, however sincere, could make amends for the want of daily intercourse ; and once Edith was on the point of writing to entreat that Gertrude would come to them, if it were only for a few weeks ; but the same day's post brought such painful accounts of Mrs Heathfield's debility and suffering, that she felt it would be selfish even to indulge the wish. Unfortunately it was on that morning also that the nomination day was publicly announced, and this alone would have been sufficient to depress her ; for while all others were in the highest spirits, delighting in the brightness of Edward's prospects, she believed that they were delusive. Miss Forester especially was full of flattering prophecies ; and feeling delighted at Mr Dacre's more frequent visits to the Grange, which she attributed entirely to his increasing regard for herself and her father, she rejoiced equally in the prospect of excitement and gaiety for the present, and the hope of a splendid legacy, if not a fortune, for the future ; while she flitted between Allingham, and the Grange, and the Priory, as unceasingly as if everything depended upon her gossiping information of what was going on. Edith spent a part of the morning alone, answering Gertrude's letter ; and then, carefully stealing into the dining-room, when she was sure that every one else had left it, ate her hasty and uncomfortable luncheon, and went out as usual to visit some poor people. Amongst them, old Martha had the chief claim upon her attention. The illness with which she had been attacked was rapidly gaining ground, and every day brought some fresh symptom of declining strength and powers. Edith willingly gave her all the time that could be spared from her other engagements, and was thankful to perceive that the secret feelings of gratitude and devotion which had occasionally been hidden by the old woman's roughness of manner, had now the effect of softening her natural infirmity of temper, and enabling her to bear her trials with patience. Yet there was an oppressive contrast between the careless merriment, the stir and interest, which surrounded Edith's domestic life, and the awful truths so clearly brought to view as she stood by the poor old woman's sick-bed. Even when repentance and faith gave an earnest of happiness to come, it was impossible to watch in silence the sinking struggles of a spirit about to appear before its Maker, and not to feel that death and eternity, and the inward preparation of the soul, were the realities of existence ; and fame and riches nothing but the delusions of a perishing world ; and though, happily for Edith's peace of mind, she did not understand the share which Edward had had in aggravating Martha's sufferings, it was with a feeling approaching to terror that, in the midst of light words, and gay smiles, she sometimes recalled the image of the dying woman, and involuntarily placed it in stern contrast with those about her, outwardly so different—but soon, it might be, to be brought into the same condition.

There were seasons when she could almost have envied them their thoughtlessness. Yet she had no cause. Edward himself, in the height of his popularity, and according to all human probability, about to attain his highest wishes, had moments, and even hours, of suffering to which Edith's anxieties were as nothing. He had plunged into the whirlpool, and he was carried on without his will, but not without his knowledge. Mr Dacre's words were realised ; and he was no longer master of his own actions. With a sense of honour almost fastidious, he was dragged into the trickery of an election ; forced, if not to say and do himself, yet to consent that others should say and do for him, things from which both his taste and his principles revolted. He had put himself into the hands of a party, without inquiring into their intentions, and his punishment was bitterly felt. The idea of drawing back,—that one point on which he had dwelt so much beforehand,—did at times cross his mind, but it was rejected. The interests of his friends, and his own honour, were at stake; for after the support that had been tendered and accepted, he felt bound to carry the contest to its conclusion. What the event would be, his supporters did not seem to doubt; but the possibility of sacrificing so much, and gaining nothing in return, sometimes crossed Edward's mind with a pang of dread; and then he exerted himself more, and gave way to whatever was proposed, and at last wrought himself up to a pitch of feverish excitement which carried him through any difficulties, but also made him sink under any temptations. And time fled swiftly on, affording but few and transient intervals for thought, till the night preceding the nomination day. The midnight clock had struck, and the household at Allingham were gone to rest. Silence, and the semblance of peace, reigned throughout the mansion; but a light still gleamed through the window of one room, where, seated at a table covered with papers, Edward was engaged in writing. It was but a calculation of votes which he was making, for the fifth time, on that day; but his thoughts were intently occupied, and without his notice the door of the apartment was softly opened, and Laura, gliding into the room, laid her hand upon his shoulder.

'Edward, this must not be; you will never be able to stand the fatigue of to-morrow. Why should you sit up longer?'

'Because I cannot sleep. When to-morrow is over'——

'And the polling days,' added Laura.

'To-morrow will perhaps decide. Mr Vivian is sure to resign if he sees the case is hopeless.'

'Then all anxiety may be at rest in a few hours,' exclaimed Laura, and her face brightened; 'and we shall be thankful and happy. You could not bear this life long.'

'Bear it! No, indeed; but Laura, there may be something worse, if I fail.'

'Impossible! you have reckoned every chance of disappointment.'

'But if I should?'

'Why mention it or think of it?' said Laura.

'Only tell me how you should feel; I shall be less uneasy if I know you are prepared for everything.'

'But I am not prepared; I never should be. After the trouble, and the exertion, and the'——

'What?'

'The misery, I was going to say; but it seems too strong a word.'

'It is misery!' exclaimed Edward. 'If I could have known one-half of what I have had to bear, I should never have ventured upon the undertaking.'

'And to fail after all,' said Laura; 'it could not be.

Edward rested his head upon his hand: it was one of his short intervals of repentance, and the errors which he had been striving to banish from his mind crowded before him. Laura leant over him, and kissed his forehead, and endeavoured to cheer him by repeating the almost certainty of success; but it was not the comfort which Edward needed.

'This is weakness in you,' she said, at length; 'who would imagine to see you as you have been,—as you will be again to-morrow, that fear could have such power over your mind.'

'Oh! Laura,' exclaimed Edward, 'how little you know! Who can judge except myself whether the prize is worth the sacrifice?'

'I can,' said Laura, firmly. 'When the day is gained, and you feel that you have the power of doing good to thousands, you will laugh at your own doubts.'

'Good,' repeated Edward, thoughtfully: 'if I could be sure of that'——

'I will not listen to you,' said Laura. 'This is but the distrust of a morbid mind. You shall not write any more,' and she took the paper from his hands.

'I must look over it once again,' said Edward, with a deep sigh. 'I am not satisfied. What did you do with the other corrected list?'

Laura began searching amongst a collection of books on a side table, and after some moments took up a long roll of papers. She brought it to the light, but it was not the list of voters,—it was the plan for Torrington church, and she was about to throw it aside when Edward unfolded it. The design was his own, and many were the hours of enjoyment it had afforded him. 'But now,'—Laura spoke his thoughts as she unrolled the list of voters, which she had just found, and placed it by the side of the church ;—'that is gone by,' she said: 'it can never be done.'

'Why should you say so?' inquired Edward, with something of irritation in his manner.

'Because it is impossible. Even I, with my careless notions, can see that: but, dearest Edward, you look really unhappy, as if you had done something wrong: and, after all, it is but exchanging one duty for another.'

For once, Edward was deaf to the flattering sweetness of his wife's accents. 'Leave me! leave me!' he exclaimed.

'Then you will not sit foreboding evil, Edward. Remember, you have intended only to do good.'

Edward's answer was a hasty motion of his hand, and Laura saw by his countenance that she must not urge him farther. She did leave him to the trial of his own thoughts: and it was not till morning dawned that Edward's mingled agitation and remorse were subdued, and he closed his eyes to gain a few hours' rest, before the coming fatigue of the day.

The election morning shone bright and beautiful—a dazzling sun and an unclouded sky—and Edward, forgetting the suffering of the previous night, felt the flush of exultation as he welcomed his friends at the breakfast-table, and listened to the confident assurances of success which reached him on all sides. The numbers had been calculated again and again; every doubtful vote had been set aside, and the lowest computation made, yet a large majority was fully anticipated on the first day's poll.

'And without doubt,' said General Forester, who had been talking in a mysterious undertone to Edward, in order to convince the rest of the party that he was the most important man amongst them; 'without doubt the affair will be ended to-day. Vivian will of a certainty withdraw. I heard it in a roundabout way, but from most excellent authority; and it will be just like him, exactly what a haughty fellow would do. He knows what a victory we shall gain if he persists in carrying matters to extremities. Your friends at Elsham are to have the earliest intelligence, that they may ring you a welcome on your return.'

Edward smiled incredulously, and could not promise himself so easy a victory; but his spirits were raised by the certainty of those on whom he most depended: and when the splendid procession, with its long train of carriages, and well-mounted horsemen, and waving banners, at length set forth, he could scarcely believe the possibility of a defeat.

The day was one of interest and excitement to the whole neighbourhood; all who could find means of conveyance, and rooms for their accommodation, whether feeling personally interested in the election or considering it merely an amusement for the passing hour, crowded to the county-town, which was distant about four miles, and amongst them the first, and the most anxious, were Mrs Courtenay and her two eldest daughters. But Edith was absent. Entreaties, and sarcasm, and ridicule had been used in vain. Her refusal was given decidedly, and not quite graciously; and when Mrs Courtenay and Jane had seated themselves in a comfortable lounging position, and were duly provided with salts and Eau de Cologne, and Charlotte had properly arranged the folds of her peach-blossomed silk dress, and given the final shake to the falling feather in her white bonnet, the carriage drove from the door; and Edith, taking up a book, resolved to occupy herself strenuously, and not to allow her mind to dwell upon a subject so entirely beyond her control. But she had miscalculated her powers. The words were before her eyes, but they were not regarded; and the sentences were in her thoughts, but they were not understood; and after half an hour's fruitless effort, she turned to another occupation. This soon proved wearisome; and at last, with a faint hope of relief from restlessness, she resolved upon a walk. It was a sultry, oppressive afternoon; a dim mist was floating in the horizon, and a few white clouds. rising against the wind, gave signs of an approaching thunderstorm. There was a deep stillness prevailing around; even the hum of the insects had ceased, and large flocks of birds, forewarned by instinct of coming danger, were swiftly wheeling their flight homewards. But Edith scarcely noticed these symptoms; her mind was wholly engrossed, although her ideas were wandering and unconnected, turning from the present to the future, and in a moment reverting to the past, often without any apparent chain of association. She thought of Edward, and his prospects; of the change which that day's success might make in his destiny for life; and of the pride which her father would have felt in seeing him occupy a position of such importance. And then she dwelt, almost with regret, upon the total extinction of the elder branch of her family; and the painful surprise which Colonel Courtenay would have experienced, if, before his death, he could have known how soon his name would be uncared for, when his place was filled by another. And again she recurred to the future—to the question how soon it might be the same with Edward: and in the uncertainty of even the longest life the delusion of earthly honours seemed more startling to her reason than it had ever done before; while at the very instant her heart beat quickly as in fancy she heard the sound of the Elsham bells, and remembered that a peal from them was to be the signal of Edward's triumph.

Finding her anxiety increase as the time drew near for the return of the election party, Edith continued her walk towards the village, with a secret hope of meeting some one who might voluntarily give her the information which she had not the courage to ask. Once she passed the turning to Martha's cottage, and felt partly inclined to go to her; but the hope that her mind might be more at ease in another quarter of an hour, induced her to follow her first intention; and it was not till she had nearly reached the beginning of the village, without meeting a single person, that she decided upon returning. On approaching the cottage, the young girl who had lately been Martha's attendant, came out of it, dressed as if going on an errand. Yet, natural as the circumstance was, a strange foreboding of something sad and unusual flashed in an instant upon Edith's mind. She quickened her steps, and when the girl drew near, asked eagerly, and as if certain of the answer, whether the poor old woman was much worse. 'They think she is dying, Miss Edith,' was the reply, ' and you said you would be told.'

'Dying!' repeated Edith, shocked at the suddenness of the intelligence, notwithstanding her previous impression. 'Why was I not sent for before?'

'The change was so quick, Miss,' answered the girl; 'only within this quarter of an hour, and the doctor was called, but he was out; and Mr Grantley is there, and one or two of the neighbours, and they are doing all they can; some of them thought you had better not know, but I was sure you would be angry if you didn't.'

Edith waited no longer, and without inquiring whether Martha was sufficiently sensible to derive any comfort from her presence, hastened forwards. But she was scarcely prepared for the scene which presented itself. The sick woman was stretched upon her low bed; her arms extended upon the dingy coverlid, and her hands feebly moving. The paleness of death was resting upon her wrinkled brow and hollow cheek, and her dim, half-closed eye, and distorted mouth, showed that the last struggle of mortality was at hand. Yet sense and consciousness still lingered, and with them the longing for that support in the hour of trial which prayer alone can obtain; and as Edith lifted the latch, and softly entered the cottage, the first sound that fell upon her ear, mingled with the moanings of the suffering woman, was the solemn entreaty to the ' Father of mercies, and God of all comfort, that He would look graciously upon His servant, and strengthen her with His Holy Spirit.'

Edith's natural impulse was to draw back, half in alarm, and half fearful of intrusion ; but the words of fervent intercession calmed her agitation, and after a few moments she also knelt to ask that the pardon of the immortal spirit might be ' sealed in heaven ' before it was summoned from the earth. Deep and earnest was the petition, and as it proceeded poor Martha's restless murmurings were stilled, and a fixed but tranquil expression settled upon her wasted features. Edith buried her face in her hands, and continued kneeling after the prayer was ended. There was an awful silence in the chamber, broken only by the quick, faint breathing of departing life ; and then, from without, was heard a distant heavy roll of thunder,—another, and another. One vivid lightning-flash lit up the rigid countenance of the dying woman ; and when it passed away, there came, blended with the peal of the advancing storm, a clear, joyous sound of village bells. Edith started. One glance she cast upon the bed, and it told that all was over. The tumult of life, and the fearful stillness of death, had met in that hour. One spirit had passed to the world where riches and honours are nothing, and another had entered with pride and hope upon a new era of mortal existence.—Edward Courtenay had gained the object of his ambition.

CHAPTER XXIII.

WE must pass over the space of four years before we again attempt to watch the progress of events at Allingham and the Priory. Time, which produces so great an effect upon all things gifted with life, had made but little alteration in the internal appearance of either place ; and the drawing-room at Allingham, on the morning on which we would resume our story, was, in its principal features, such as it had been when Laura was first introduced into it, save only that her husband's affection had induced him to gratify her wishes to the utmost, and open it, as she desired, upon the conservatory. Its in-mates, however, were not so entirely the same. Laura was seated at her work-table, with a form as elegant, and a face as lovely as ever; but the careless thoughtlessness of very early youth had faded from her open brow and brilliant eye; and except when she gazed, with a mother's fondness, upon the beautiful boy who was playing at her feet, it was easy to perceive that her heart was burdened with many a secret care. At a little distance from her stood Edward, his counte-nance expressive of a restless, dissatisfied mind, and by his side a plainly-dressed elderly man, who, with bent brows and a care-worn face, was turning over some folded papers which lay upon the table. Edward looked on without speaking, but a few heavy sighs involuntarily escaped him, as from time to time he pondered the titles of the different packets. There was an air of business and solicitude in the countenances of all; the only sound, except the rustling of the papers, which disturbed the solemnity of the little party, being the occasional laugh of the merry child, whose attention seemed fully engrossed by the presence of a young lady dressed in deep mourning, who was seated on a sofa at the farther end of the apartment, and beckoning him towards her. She had, apparently, but just entered the house, for she still wore her walking-dress, although her bonnet was thrown aside, as if to enable her more easily to amuse herself with her little playfellow. Her figure was slight and delicate, and her face chiefly remarkable for a high, thoughtful forehead, and a mouth which, although indicating great gentleness, betokened also a spirit of natural energy and decision. Her complexion was sallow, and her clear, dark gray eyes told rather of a sensible, meditative mind, than of any superior quickness of intellect. Yet Gertrude Courtenay was not a person to be seen and for-gotten. Even by the side of her beautiful sister-in-law, it might have been doubted which possessed the greatest power of awakening interest. At a first notice, it would have been said that hundreds in the world resembled her—that such features were to be met with continually; a second glance more firmly riveted attention, from the expression of inward peace which pervaded her countenance; a third established as a certainty that there must be something in her very different from the world; and when she moved and spoke the charm was completed. There was no resisting the winning tones of that low, clear voice, the softness and quietness of those gentle actions, the least of which seemed inspired by some consideration for another, some wish to give pleasure or comfort. Whether Gertrude's disposition was naturally lively, had often been a question with her friends ; and, on a slight acquaintance, it might perhaps have been supposed that some suffering in early childhood had subdued her spirit, and cast a shade over the light-heartedness of youth ; but it was an opinion contradicted by the mirth which so frequently lighted up her eye when her manner was the most self-possessed, and by the delight with which she was welcomed by the companions of her own age in their gayest and happiest hours. No one felt her presence a restraint, except in moments of heedless folly, and one look was sufficient. If she refused to smile, the thoughtless laugh was instantly checked ;—and yet Gertrude seldom ventured to find fault, and when she did, it was with such humility, such consciousness of her own deficiencies, that no offence could be taken. The magic of her influence was to be found, not in words—scarcely in actions—but in her inward, unceasing remembrance of the God in whose presence she lived. It was her earnest endeavour never to forget Him, and the recollection purified her heart, and hallowed her daily conduct, until the careless and worldly-minded felt that the atmosphere with which she was surrounded was one in which they could never venture to dwell.

Even now, as she sat with her eyes fixed upon the laughing child, who, after conquering his pretended shyness, ran eagerly towards her and jumped into her lap, there was something in her countenance which bespoke a mind that naturally turned to subjects beyond the amusement of the moment. It seemed to be the pressure of a first grief that checked the bright smile with which she gazed upon her little companion, for there were traces of sorrow in her voice and manner, as well as in her mourning dress ; but Gertrude's affliction was blended with so many thoughts of happiness, that it could only cast a temporary gloom over her feelings. She had lost her aunt about six weeks previously, and the separation from her best and earliest friend was, in itself, a bitter trial. But Mrs Heathfield's great age and weakness had prevented her for the last two years from being in any degree a companion to her niece ; and one who had watched her patient suffering, and perfect resignation, could scarcely lament when a spirit so purified by earthly trial was at length summoned to its rest. After the time spent in making some necessary arrangements, and paying a short visit to a friend in

the neighbourhood of Farleigh, Gertrude's natural wish was to
return to her mother's roof, for there was a pleasure expected in
the home of her childhood, and the society of her family, to which,
notwithstanding the remembrance of her former disappointment,
few could have been more alive.   The few days she had as yet
passed at the Priory had been so full of novelty and interest, as
often to divert her mind from thoughts of grief ; whilst, from the
same circumstances, she still remained in some degree ignorant of
the extent of those sources of annoyance which lay hidden under
an exterior at first sight so promising.   Gertrude's return had
been hailed with delight by all.   Mrs Courtenay received her
with the warmth and sincerity of a mother's affection, and Jane
forgot her illness, and Charlotte her sarcasm, in the pleasure of
welcoming her, whilst Edith's spirits rose to their former cheerfulness in the prospect of a companion who could understand her
feelings.   For the time, Gertrude was the one object of attraction
at the Priory, and hardly less so at Allingham, though Edward
was sometimes conscious of something uncongenial in the guileless openness of his sister's disposition, and Laura was not sure
that she enjoyed the presence of one whose actions were perpetually reminding her of her own deficiencies.   The little boy was
the great link between them, for grief can often find solace in
the simple innocence of childhood, and no mother can withstand
the most endearing of all attentions—that shown to an only
child.   Neither was Edward insensible to the interest taken by
his sister in the one object on which all his hopes and all his
ambition were centred ; and on this morning, as he stood by the
table, apparently intent only upon business, his eyes often wandered to the farther end of the room, and for a few moments he
forgot his cares whilst watching Gertrude's endeavours to retain
her restless charge.

  ' Hush, Charlie, hush !' she said, softly, as the spell of silence
was again broken by a joyous laugh.

  ' We must be quiet.   Hark ! listen to my watch.'

  The little fellow laid his head upon her shoulder, and seemed
wrapped in wonder at the hidden sound ; and Gertrude, bending
over him, parted his clustering ringlets, and kissed his fair, delicate forehead.   ' Charlie loves aunt Gertrude,' whispered the
child, as he threw his arms round her neck.   There was a slight
quivering in Gertrude's lip, a momentary glistening in her eye ;
perhaps the tone of innocent affection,—even the affection of
infancy,—came home to her the more forcibly from the remem-

brance of all that she had lately lost; and hastily lifting the little boy from her lap, she moved towards the distant window at which Laura was working.

'We ought to beg your pardon, dear Gertrude, for bringing business into the drawing-room,' said Edward; 'I did not intend troubling you or Laura so long when we began talking, or I should have gone to my study.'

'No one will complain of the trouble if you can be cheerful about it,' said Laura. 'But indeed, Mr Rivers, the sight of you will soon be associated with everything that is depressing. Edward is not like himself for two or three days after you have teased him with those horrid papers.'

'Nay, my dear Laura,' replied Edward, 'you must not say that Mr Rivers teases me; it is I who tease myself. He is always begging me to have nothing more to do with them.'

'Certainly,' said Mr Rivers, in a serious voice; 'if I might be allowed to say it without offending you, I must own that it would give me great satisfaction to feel that they were the last with which I should have any connection.'

'Then I will promise you,' said Edward, with a laugh which sounded hollow and unreal: 'since you have such an objection to them, you must not think it strange if I trouble others rather than yourself, the next time they are required.'

Mr Rivers took up his hat, bowed to Laura, and walked to the door, followed by Mr Courtenay.

'You understand me,' said Edward, in an undertone, as he held out his hand; 'I can quite appreciate your kindness, but if this sort of thing is painful, why should you be worried with it?'

'It is not painful for me, only for yourself,' replied Mr Rivers. 'You do not know the end, and I do. I have seen, I may almost say, hundreds running a similar course.'

Edward knit his brow, but in suffering, not in anger. 'What would you have me do? What can I do?'

'Retrench. It was my first, and it will be my last word. You must excuse my saying it; we are not acquaintances of yesterday.'

'Again I must ask, how is it to be managed?' replied Edward.

Mr Rivers smiled gravely. 'We have discussed the subject often,' he said; 'and I fear there is nothing new to be brought forward. I must wish you good morning now, for my time is precious.'

'Those dreadful lawyers!' exclaimed Laura, when Edward

returned to the table. 'Why should you have anything to do with them? with Mr Rivers in particular! he is a complete bird of ill-omen.'

'That may not be his fault,' replied Edward; 'but we will not trouble Gertrude with business; she is come to pass the day here, of course.'

'Not quite that,' said Gertrude; 'I expect Edith every minute, and then I have promised to go for a long walk with her to Torrington Heath; but she was engaged at home when I left her, and I thought it would be pleasant to spend my spare minutes here.'

Laura looked pleased; but Edward was recalled to the recollection of something disagreeable by his sister's words. 'Torrington,' he repeated, thoughtfully. 'Oh! I remember now. Those unhappy poachers were to be brought here at twelve, and it must be nearly that.'

'Five minutes after,' observed Laura, looking at her watch, and almost at the same instant a servant entered to summon his master away. Edward gave orders that the men should be taken to his study, but still lingered, as if unwilling to enter upon a painful office.

'If it were not Torrington you would not care,' exclaimed Laura, with a smile which had in it something of the arch brightness of former days. But the smile had lost its power. Edward's brow grew darker, and his manner sterner, and without noticing the observation he left the room.

When he was gone, Laura's countenance resumed its former expression of care, and turning to her sister, she said, 'You will have the thanks of the county if you will undertake to reform the Torrington people, Gertrude. That is your mission, I suppose.'

'Hardly,' replied Gertrude, smiling. 'I really don't know why we are going there to-day; only Edith wished it.'

'I beg Edward not to worry himself about them,' continued Laura; 'but he will do it. You know that the greater part of the hamlet belongs to him, and it is out of Mr Grantley's parish; and the rector is a very old man, who can do nothing himself, and cannot afford to keep a curate; and the nearest church is two miles distant; so the people are left to themselves, and certainly they are a set of desperate wretches, beggars, and thieves, and poachers, and even worse, some people say. But what good can it be to distress one's self about a case in which we can do nothing?'

'Yes, if we really can do nothing,' said Gertrude, in a tone so gentle, that it scarcely seemed to imply reproof.

'Is it not so?' inquired Laura. 'Think of the enormous claims Edward has upon him. The mere expense of his parliamentary dinners, and his house in town, is enough to ruin him. And he is not like a common person—people think so much of him for his talents; he is forced to be a great man, whether he will or not.'

Gertrude was not forced to give an opinion in answer, for the conversation was changed by Laura's exclamation that a carriage was coming down the road.

'It is my mother,' said Gertrude, going to the window; 'she and Jane proposed taking a drive this morning, but they did not say they were coming here.'

'They do not often favour me,' observed Laura; 'your mother is so nervous, and Jane such an invalid; that is, according to her own account.'

Mrs Courtenay appeared, wrapped in a silk cloak and furs, although the bright April morning would have rendered an ordinary spring dress oppressive to many; and Jane followed with languishing steps, and a countenance which evidently demanded sympathy.

'Ah! Gertrude, are you here?' was her mother's first exclamation. 'Why did you not wait for the carriage? it would have been much pleasanter. They persuaded me to go out to-day, my dear Laura, so I told the coachman to drive here; but I don't know—your road is very steep, it frightens me to death.'

'Then it would not probably have been agreeable to Gertrude,' said Jane, shortly, as she took possession of an easy chair.

'I am not sure of that,' replied Gertrude. 'Persons' nerves are very different when they are young, from what they are as they grow old. Let me take off your cloak, dear mamma, or you will find the change by and by.'

'Thank you, my love, perhaps it will be best. Now, Charlie, come and speak to grandmamma.' The child hesitated, from wilfulness and shyness.

'Don't be naughty, Charlie,' said Laura, in a voice of mild entreaty. Charlie moved a few steps forward, and then turning quickly round, ran and hid his face in Gertrude's lap. 'Never mind,' continued Laura, 'he will go presently; he is not accustomed to see so many people in a room, and I think he is cutting a tooth; he has been so fretful for the last few days.'

'What a blessing children's teeth are to them!' observed Jane; 'they bear the burden of every fault!'

The colour rose in Laura's cheek.

'Poor little darling!' said Mrs Courtenay. 'Have you tried the soothing syrup, my dear? I am certain it will do wonders. My grandmother constantly used it. She had seven children, and most of them had strong convulsions in cutting their teeth. It was a great trial to her, and only three lived beyond two years.'

'An additional reason for Laura's putting faith in it,' said Jane. 'Gertrude, you seem to be the favourite; why don't you attempt to rival our great grandmother's soothing syrup, and persuade Charlie to be a good boy?'

'Perhaps you had better let the matter rest,' said Gertrude. 'Laura thinks he is not well.'

The yielding tone of this reply had as great an effect upon Laura's irritated feelings as the celebrated syrup could possibly have had upon her little boy, and she immediately begged that Gertrude would make him do what was right; but whether the endeavour would have been successful was not destined to be known; for at that instant Edward reappeared, followed almost immediately by Edith.

'Have you been waiting for me long, Gertrude?' asked Edith, after she had coolly shaken hands with Laura and kissed the child. Gertrude's reply was attentive, as usual, though at the instant her thoughts were engrossed by the painful expression of her brother's face. His conversation with his mother was evidently constrained; and Laura, although lately accustomed to see him gloomy, could not avoid noticing his manner.

'What have you done about the poachers, Edward?' she inquired, in a tone of greater timidity than she would have used four years before.

'Nothing,' was the reply; 'it is a bad business. My keeper is much hurt, and the affair must be inquired into more.'

'Torrington people, I suppose,' said Jane. 'One never has a doubt upon that point.'

'Torrington is not in this parish, I believe, ' said Gertrude, who perceived directly that Edward was anxious to avoid the subject of the poachers, and hoped to turn the conversation unperceived.

'No, my dear,' exclaimed Mrs Courtenay; 'it is in the parish of Ringwood—old Mr North's. Your grandfather gave him the living—four hundred a year it used to be. Every one thought Mr North would have died ten years ago, but now no one seems to think about it.'

'Poor Torrington!' said Edith ; 'it is a miserable place ; no schools, no clergyman, no anything.'

'And they are such a bad, ungrateful set,' observed Mrs Courtenay. 'They abuse you so dreadfully, my dear Edward. Miss Forester was with me for a whole hour yesterday, telling me all about it. She says they grow worse and worse ; and '——

'Do you want your pony-carriage this afternoon, Laura ?' said Edward, contrary to his usual habit, interrupting his mother in the middle of a sentence.

'Not if you do. I have settled to take a drive.'

'I cannot want it,' replied Edward. 'I only thought it might as well be ordered in time, and perhaps Gertrude would like to go with you.'

Laura blushed, and hesitated ; and Gertrude began to decline, saying, 'that she had a prior engagement with Edith, but she should be very glad to take advantage of the offer another day.'

'Then to-morrow,' persisted Edward. Gertrude again glanced at her sister-in-law, and reading her wishes in her countenance, laughingly observed, that 'it would not do for such a busy person as herself to form plans beforehand. She had undertaken to make acquaintance with the whole neighbourhood, and she must not think of mere pleasure.'

'That is right, my dear,' said Mrs Courtenay ; 'I am so glad you like paying visits. Poor Jane never can, and Edith has no time ; and so Charlotte is left alone, and has to do it all, and I know we are sadly rude : but now you are come, Gertrude, there will be no difficulty. You can always go, since you enjoy it.'

'I don't know that I exactly enjoy it, dear mamma,' said Gertrude ; 'but I shall be very willing to take my share in the duty.'

'We are going into Elsham now,' said Jane ; 'but I suppose you won't give up your walk for the pleasure of accompanying us.'

'Impossible !' exclaimed Edith. 'It is the first walk Gertrude and I have promised ourselves. Indeed, Jane, you must not think of such a thing.'

'I never knew before there was any harm in thinking,' said Jane ; 'but you need not be frightened, Edith ; I am not going to run away with your new idol.'

'Not till the new idol runs away with you herself,' replied Gertrude. 'You know, Jane, I must pay visits by and by, and then I shall be most thankful to any one who will take the trouble to go with me.'

Jane was soothed by her sister's manner; and, in a more good-humoured tone than usual, proposed to her mother that the carriage should be ordered round. Mrs Courtenay made no objection; and after ten minutes spent in adjusting cloaks, saying good-bye, and bribing the little boy to good behaviour by the promise of sugar-plums, the formal morning visit was concluded. Gertrude followed her mother to the carriage, to see that she was comfortably settled, and to endeavour, if possible, to arrange Jane's cushion for the head in the way she deemed indispensable to her comfort, and then with a smile hoped they would enjoy their drive, and returned into the house to summon Edith.

CHAPTER XXIV.

'LAURA,' said Edward, when they were left alone, 'what was the cause of your repelling manner to Gertrude just now? No one but herself could have endured it.'

'Repelling!' exclaimed Laura; 'indeed I did not mean it to be so. It was not convenient for me to take her, that was all.'

'You mean,' said Edward, almost sternly, 'you are engaged with Miss Forester—why don't you tell me so at once?'

'Because '—— and Laura hesitated, and her eyes sank under her husband's gaze. 'You know it never pleases you to hear of her, and therefore I always think the less that is said the better.'

'The less that is done, I should say,' replied Edward. 'You have had a specimen this morning of her gossiping interference in public matters, and you will be grievously mistaken if you imagine it will be different in private.'

Laura's cheek became suddenly flushed, though for what cause it was difficult for Edward to understand.

'You must forgive me for speaking in this way, dearest,' he added, mildly; 'but you know the subject of complaint is an old one. Miss Forester never ought to have been your friend.'

'But if she is,' answered Laura, 'what is to be done? We

cannot draw back, after taking her to London and introducing her everywhere as our friend.'

Edward restlessly paced the room, and after a pause of some instants, exclaimed, 'And the General, too—how one is deceived! There is no truth—no sincerity'—— Again he paused.

'Yes,' replied Laura, desirous for private reasons to turn the current of censure in another direction, and not considering that it was impossible to separate the interests of the father and daughter,—'the General, I do believe, is false. He will support you, Edward, whilst you submit to him implicitly; but the very instant you propose to differ, he will cast you off.'

'Let him do it!' exclaimed Edward; 'let him turn against me if he will! I am not a person to submit implicitly to any man, far less to a pompous fool, whose only talent is intrigue. I will never be the slave of a party, and he knows it—they all know it, and that is the cause of offence.'

'It is so unfair, too,' said Laura, 'after your allowing them so much liberty at the time of the election, and doing so many disagreeable things merely to please them.'

'And what has been the consequence?' exclaimed Edward, indignantly; 'I acted against my own sense of honour, because I fancied they had more experience than myself; and now they complain of me, because they say I have disappointed their expectation. What reason had they to suppose that because I listened to them in one case I should do so in all?'

'Miss Forester says,' began Laura ——

'I wish never to hear the name again,' interrupted Edward. 'Forgive me, my dear Laura: you cannot know the family as I do; your nature is too open and guileless to understand them. They are false—false in word and in deed; and if it were possible to taint the simplicity of an angel's mind, they would make you false also.'

Laura's brilliant colour for an instant faded to a deadly hue, and then as suddenly returned, while with a hasty impulse she rose from her seat, and advanced towards her husband, as if about to speak, but the resolution, whatever it might have been, passed as rapidly as it had been formed; and without answering him, she occupied herself in collecting her work from the table. Edward's mind was too much absorbed to notice this sudden change; and recurring to his former subject of complaint, he repeated his indignant expression at General Forester's presumption, in supposing that he would consent to be an instrument in the hands of any man.

‘And what is the point of issue between you?’ inquired Laura ; ‘is it anything of importance?’

‘Of the utmost vital importance. But it is not one point— there are many ; questions which concern the Church, and the poor, and the manufacturing districts, and on which the whole prosperity of the nation depends ; and he and his party think that, because they supported me at the time I first came forward, I am now to agree to be led blindfold, and to vote just according to their will.’

‘There may come another election soon,’ said Laura ; ‘when you will be better able to stand alone.’

She stopped, expecting an answer ; but Edward did not give it. He leaned his head upon the mantelpiece, as if struck by some overpowering thoughts ; and at the same moment the sound of footsteps announced the approach of a visitor ; and Laura, with a conviction that it must be Miss Forester, hastened to prevent her from intruding herself upon Edward in his present mood of irritation. Left alone, Edward roused himself from his musing posture, but not for the purpose of exertion. He stood for some minutes, looking thoughtfully upon the splendid furniture of his drawingroom—the gilded couches and silk hangings, the marble vases and mosaic cabinets—the varied refinements of luxury with which taste and extravagance had filled it ; and then turned to gaze upon the beauty so profusely lavished upon the fair domain which owned him as its possessor. A brilliant sunlight was resting upon the foreground of the landscape, where the massive trunks of the splendid forest trees were marked with glittering lines, and the young leaves, just bursting into life, were sparkling with a golden hue. Deep shadows were cast upon the turf by the outstretched branches, beneath which the herded deer sought refuge from the noonday heat, and between the natural arches were caught occasional glimpses of the distant country, shrouded in the rich purple mist, which veils all that when clearly seen might mar the loveliness of nature. Edward gazed, but not in admiration. That which a stranger would have dwelt on with delight, to him brought no charm : for, written in legible characters on every tree and flower, traced even upon the cloudless heaven, he saw but one word— ruin ; how distant he could not tell—how near he dare not think. Yet, whether close at hand, or thrown far off into future years, equally in the end, ruin—and inevitable. Ingenuity and expedients might for a time ward off the evil day, but the follies of the past could never be retrieved. For one moment he ventured to contemplate the prospect, for he pictured only his own suffering; but the next brought before him the image of Laura, in her youthful grace and refinement, the spoiled child of luxury, and the remembrance of the innocent child, whose earthly fortunes would be sacrificed to a father's imprudence; and unable to endure the bitterness of his feelings, with a vigorous effort he turned from the idea, and left the room to seek, as he had often done before, a temporary forgetfulness in the claims of parliamentary business.

CHAPTER XXV.

'AND that is Torrington Heath,' said Gertrude, as she stood with her sister on the summit of a steep hill, from which was seen, at a short distance, a wild, open common, covered with furze and brambles, indented with cart ruts, and enlivened only by a long line of low, mud hovels, the broken windows and bent palings of which bore testimony to the poverty of the inhabitants.

'Yes,' replied Edith; 'and unfortunately you are looking at the best side of the picture. Those cottages are much worse in the inside than the outside.'

Gertrude forgot her usual habit of attention, whilst watching the groups of squalid children, who were playing in front of the cabins. 'And can Edward really do nothing for the people?' she said, at length.

'He has done something, replied Edith; 'that is, he has repaired the houses, and given the children clothes, and sometimes excused a few from paying rent; but they are such a wretched set; and the district is so large—it extends to the other side of the hill.'

'It is clear what they want,' said Gertrude; 'a church, and a resident clergyman.'

'Yes; no one doubts that: but I wish you would not talk of it.'

'Why not?'

'Because it recalls so many hopes and plans which have come to nothing; it was a grievous mistake, Edward's going into Parliament.'

' No, no,' exclaimed Gertrude ; ' I cannot agree with you there ; with his high talents and principles, what could he have done better ?'

' You don't know,' began Edith ; and then stopping suddenly, she added, ' can you bear a half-confidence, Gertrude ?'

' I hope I could, but I have never been tried ; perhaps it may be difficult from a sister.'

' Yes,' said Edith, thoughtfully ; ' sisters ought to be all in all to each other ; but no sisters are '——

' Few, rather,' said Gertrude ; ' we may be among the exceptions.'

' Not if you require unlimited confidence. You know I have told you in my letters that I could not explain everything I alluded to.'

' Your letters have been puzzles very often,' said Gertrude ; ' but with regard to confidence, I am very willing to take as much, or as little, as you may be able to give. Where we love, we must also trust.'

' But if there is some one else whom I can talk to with greater freedom than I can to you, what should you say then ?'

' Trust again,' replied Gertrude ; ' besides I really have no right to expect that you should be able to talk to me as if we had been together all our lives.'

' But I wish it, above all things,' said Edith ; ' if there were no obstacles. You will never guess the name of the only person who consoles me in all my troubles.'

' Mr Dacre,' said Gertrude ; ' I could have seen that he was not a common friend the first day he was with us, even if you had not spoken of him so often.'

' Miss Forester is jealous,' said Edith, laughing ; ' though I don't believe she has ever yet made up her mind whether I intend to be his wife, or his adopted daughter. But to return to matters of fact ; Mr Dacre is really my principal friend and guide in all cases of difficulty ; but why he is so must be one of the mysteries.'

' And are these mysteries of consequence ? ' inquired Gertrude.

' Really I can hardly tell ; once I thought they were of the greatest ; but lately, both Mr Dacre and myself have begun to doubt our own convictions. Edward's very extravagance makes me comparatively easy about him.'

' You forget,' said Gertrude, ' that I don't know the circumstances you refer to.'

'Some are easily told,' replied Edith : 'there are reasons which used to make me afraid that Edward was living greatly beyond his income ; but since he has been in Parliament he has been so separated from us, that we know much less of his affairs than we did ; and now there is a report that he is to have a government appointment whenever a change of ministry comes, which every one declares must be soon ; not that I believe reports in general, but there seems some foundation for this, because of Edward's style of living, which would be madness if he had not some prospects of the kind.'

'I can hardly fancy that,' said Gertrude ; 'he has a very good fortune.'

'Ah ! if you did but know all,' began Edith ; and then remembering her promise to Edward, she added, 'it seems so unkind, Gertrude, to be reserved with you.'

'You must let me be the judge of the unkindness, dearest,' said Gertrude, affectionately ; 'only tell me that you are not unhappy about anything.'

'No, I don't think I am—that is, not very—in fact, I don't let my mind dwell upon the future ; it can do no good. Edward must understand his own affairs, and if he is to have this appointment I hope it may all be right. But this would not have satisfied me some years ago, Gertrude. I should have been miserable then if he had not told me all.'

'Yes,' said Gertrude ; 'a wife makes an essential difference.'

'Yet I could have borne that ; I could have borne anything,' exclaimed Edith ; 'if—tell me, Gertrude, do you like Laura ?'

Gertrude smiled at the abruptness of the question. 'Like her, I do very much—more than I expected from your account. Love her I do not yet, but I am nearly certain I very soon shall.'

'Do you really think so ?' said Edith ; 'she is so unlike you ; she has no idea of acting from fixed motives—it is all from impulse.'

'An amiable impulse often, I should think,' said Gertrude.

'Perhaps so, but still it is only impulse, and that is not likely to suit either you or me ; at least I can answer for myself. Laura and I were not formed for the same hemisphere.'

'Except that you have been placed there,' said Gertrude in a careless tone, under which a grave meaning was only partially hidden.

'That is no reason for our suiting,' said Edith.

'No ! only for trying to suit.'

'But you would not have any one who is endeavouring to do right associate with a person whose principles are worldly, would you?' exclaimed Edith: 'the whole tone of the mind would be lowered by it.'

'Don't you think there is a difference between relations and other people?' said Gertrude.

'Not much; only that if they are disagreeable, they are ten times worse than they would be as strangers, because you can't escape from them.'

'Ah!' said Gertrude; 'that is the very point; I know we cannot escape from them, and so, I suppose, it was intended we should make the best of them.'

Edith sighed. 'I don't mean, of course,' she said, 'that I do not love my brother and sisters, or that I have no interest in my connections; but it would be impossible to dance attendance upon them all day without neglecting other duties.'

'I dare say it is difficult,' said Gertrude; 'and I know I am not a fair judge; but perhaps a little "dancing attendance," as you call it, might win their hearts, and induce them to help in the duties.'

'It might be so,' answered Edith, thoughtfully; 'but I don't think it likely at home.'

Gertrude did not urge the subject. She had given a hint, and she left it to work its own way. They walked on for several minutes in silence.

'You don't mean to say,' observed Edith, at length, 'that you would give up visiting poor people, and attending to schools?'

'No, no,' replied Gertrude; 'all that I mean is, that our duties are like the circles of a whirlpool, and that the innermost includes home; and the next, perhaps, the rich and poor immediately about us. The circumstances of our position in life, our fortune and talents, seem in fact to point out our business.'

'Rich people!' said Edith, in surprise.

'Yes,' replied Gertrude; 'do you not remember my showing you the other day that Bishop Andrewes mentions, amongst the persons to be interceded for, those who were entitled to his prayers by vicinity of situation; as if that were in itself a sufficient claim?'

'But surely we should feel so tied down,' said Edith, 'in being forced to think of and care for people, merely because they live near us.'

'I don't know that that is an objection; because, if we are

not tied down, there may be as much self-will in choosing duties
as pleasures.'

Still Edith was inclined to object, and Gertrude, disliking even
to appear dictatorial, made some common remark, so as to give
an opening for changing the conversation; but Edith could not
bear the thought of casting blame upon another when she had
been in fault herself; and again recurred to Laura.

'Can you understand, Gertrude,' she said, 'that when I complain of Laura, it is not because I feel innocent. She may be
wrong in some things, but I have been wrong too. You remember, perhaps, that I told you, a long time ago, we had had a sort
of quarrel about the removal of old Martha's cottage, because it
intercepted the view from the morning-room. It stood just
where the opening is now, which shows the spire of Elsham
church, and the top of the Roman hill. Laura urged that
Martha should remove in defiance of Edward's promise—and
Edward himself would have liked it, though I am certain nothing
would have induced him to break his word. I own I was very
angry, and said some unpardonable things, and Laura behaved
extremely well; but we never made it up. I was shy, and we
differed about the election; and, unfortunately, the day of the
nomination I was too unwell to go to Allingham in the evening,
which gave great offence. Stupidly enough, I sent a message
instead of a note, and the message was not given. I have learned
a lesson, however, from that for the rest of my life. I have never
trusted to messages since. Then, after Martha's death, they
pulled the cottage down, and Laura rejoiced. I can't say that I
sympathised, and I am not sure that Edward did either, for he
had it taken away during his absence, and never said anything
about the view. A few observations passed then between Laura
and me, which did not make us better friends;—I could not bear
to see her so cold-hearted. But the worst thing of all was, that
when they went to London, they took Miss Forester with them.
I hated the intimacy, and so did Edward, but it still goes on,
and it is considered a settled thing for her to go to town every
year with them.'

'I must say that is strange,' said Gertrude. 'Miss Forester
and Laura I should fancy differed in everything—that is, if
Laura's countenance tells truth. Independent of its beauty,
there is an openness and purity in its expression which charms
me; and Miss Forester's is so very unlike it.'

'So it is,' said Edith; 'and I really believe both faces speak the characters. Laura is very sincere, but Miss Forester has an immense power over her, notwithstanding : lately, indeed, there has been a change. Miss Forester still governs, but I think it is in a different way. Laura seems afraid of her, and I have seen her sometimes shrink away, as if she knew what Miss Forester was, and yet did not venture to cast her off. And besides this, Laura is grown so grave—melancholy I may say, at times ; and she and Edward don't seem so happy together as they used to be. Edward is irritable ; and Laura appears frightened at him. I have been at Allingham more the last few months, and have seen more of it. Generally Laura is in town at this season, but this year they hurried back unexpectedly, and gave no reasons for it. In fact, Gertrude, there is some mystery, but I have given up attempting to fathom it ; and we all do tolerably well together. Laura and I are very civil.'

'And Charlie,' said Gertrude ; 'does not he help you to be friends?'

'Oh no ; he is quite spoiled, and I can't bear to see it. If I were his godmother it would be different ; but a cousin of Laura's stood, because Jane refused, so I feel I have nothing to do with him. You must allow, now, that progressing at Allingham is out of my power ; I could never waste time in telling Charlie he is the sweetest little creature in the world, which is the only way to Laura's heart.'

Gertrude did not say that she agreed, and Edith pressed for an answer.

'I don't see things exactly in the same light you do,' replied Gertrude, after a short silence ; 'because, if Laura were a labourer's wife you would go and play with her child directly, for the very purpose of making her feel you took an interest in her.'

'But, if I do not take an interest,' said Edith ; 'you would not have me a hypocrite?'

They had reached the door of the cottage which Edith was wishing to visit, and Gertrude's reply was short : 'You are interested in poor people,' she said, 'because they are fellow-creatures, and want help, and have never perhaps been properly taught their duty ; and especially you are anxious to assist them, if they are members of the Church ; Laura has all these claims, and one besides—she is Edward's wife.'

Edith would willingly have continued the conversation, but the approach of the woman, to whom the house belonged, prevented her; and Gertrude was not sorry to defer a longer discussion until her sister had had more time for reflecting upon what had been said.

CHAPTER XXVI.

DAY after day glided on swiftly and silently, each bringing hopes and fears, pleasures and pains,—to the careless eye all light and momentary, and in such rapid succession as scarcely to lay claim to remembrance. Yet under the most unruffled surface of domestic life flows a deep under-current either of joy or sorrow, which, gathering strength from every trifling action and event, bursts at last suddenly, and often overwhelmingly, upon hearts that have not learned to watch the bubbles which indicate its existence. Perhaps it is well that it should be so. It may be in mercy to many that their eyes are blinded, and their ears closed, and, like the victim about to be sacrificed, they are able to advance gaily and unhesitatingly to the scene of their trial. If it were otherwise, might not existence to them be a burden wearisome and intolerable?—haunted by spectres of coming evils, the sight of which can only be braved by those who have learned at their first entrance into the world that lesson of unshrinking faith which the experience of a long life so frequently fails to impart? It was but a gradual change that was passing over the inmates of Allingham. No one could tell the exact moment when Edward's countenance grew more gloomy, and Laura's smiles were deepened into sighs. No one could look back to the precise time when care first invaded a happy home; but few could fail to perceive its withering effects, in the hasty word, and the moody reverie, and the silent and daily increasing reserve, which had sprung up where once there had been only open, unsuspicious confidence. The original fault lay with Edward—in the weakness which had induced him to conceal from his wife the encumbered state of his property. From that error followed, as a necessary consequence, innumerable others, and amongst them many in which Laura was by no means free from participation. Even had her husband's fortune been all that she imagined, it could not have sufficed for the gratification of every idle wish—still less for the fearful extravagances of London dissipation; and this she well knew:

but, unaccustomed to self-control, and led by Miss Forester's persuasive flatteries, she had set no bounds to her expenses; and whilst Edward brought himself into notice by making splendid speeches in public, followed up by splendid dinners in private, Laura gained equal notoriety by the magnificence of her frequent entertainments. Edward murmured, remonstrated, and paid his bills—the last being a conclusive evidence to Laura's mind that she had done no wrong. But the moment at length arrived when he was compelled to interpose his authority. At the commencement of a third season of thoughtless frivolity, a discussion, the first of an angry nature which had yet arisen, was ended by a peremptory enforcement of strict economy, and Laura soon afterwards returned to Allingham, in the beginning of the London season, with no hope of solace or amusement beyond the few hours which Edward was able occasionally to devote to her—the society of a country neighbourhood when half its members are absent—and the friendship of Miss Forester. But notwithstanding her life of indulgence, Laura bore the sacrifice with temper and patience.

The follies of fashionable life had not as yet weakened the force of that strong attachment to her husband upon which so many virtues might have been grafted. He was still the object of her love and reverence, and his will, when once openly expressed, was a law which, however she might dispute, she would not venture to disobey. It was not regret for the morning breakfasts and the evening *fêtes*, the gay acquaintances and insidious flatteries, from which she was thus suddenly snatched, that caused her melancholy. Past pleasures were remembered and longed for, but the loss of them would have had no lasting power to mar her happiness. If Allingham had been what it was in the first days of her married life; if Edward had been still the companion of her walks and drives, the promoter of her daily amusements, and the sharer of her every feeling; above all, if there had been no thought which she dared not communicate, no action which she dreaded to confess, a spring spent in the country might have proved a season of enjoyment rather than *ennui.*

But the case was far otherwise. Edward's engagements were numerous, his absence was frequent, and his attention pre-occupied. Affection, indeed, he still gave her, deep and sincere, but shown only in fleeting moments, and upon passing impulses. If Laura had her causes for reserve, he had his also; and more

painful, more enduring, since they involved not merely the prosperity of all he most loved, but the sacrifice of those firm principles of right upon which, in his parliamentary career, he had
hitherto constantly acted.   His talents were by this time known
and appreciated ; his character was respected ; his opinions were
received with deference : but for the purposes of a party he was
too independent ; and whilst he persisted in carrying out his own
views in opposition to his influential friends, there seemed no
prospect of his obtaining, under any circumstances, the position
of prominence for which so many had declared him calculated.
The knowledge of this fact had, at first, only stimulated Edward
more openly to prove himself free and unbiassed.   There was a
satisfaction in the consciousness of self-sacrifice which nerved
him against ridicule, and gave him something of a martyr's pride
in his devotion to the public good.   Every suggestion of flattery
was repelled ; every thought of a compromise rejected ; and, for
a time, the task was comparatively easy.   But when at length
there seemed a prospect of his own friends being in power, the
trial assumed a different shape.   In the excitement of public life
he felt equal to any resistance ; but then came quiet hours and
seasons of comparative retirement—moments when a present
pressure and a future dread weighed down his spirits and bewildered his judgment, and when the prospect of escape from
impending evil seemed a blessing to be purchased at any price.
The hope of bribing him to abandon his principles was one which
no person who knew him would have ventured to entertain ; but
there were other forms in which the proposal could more
delicately be made ; and when it was whispered in his ear that
some concession upon two or three important points might soon
be the means of placing him in a situation, which, by increasing his influence, would also increase his usefulness, it seemed
scarcely right at once to refuse the idea without consideration.
As on other occasions, Edward listened to the temptation, thought
upon it, and rejected it, and then carried its remembrance in
his heart, to be dwelt upon and coveted.   It was at this time that
a temporary cessation of parliamentary business allowed him to
return with Laura to Allingham ; and, with the growing conviction in his mind that on the success of his public career depended his prosperity or his ruin, the evident symptoms of
distrust which he discovered amongst his former supporters were
naturally regarded with considerable alarm.   Officious friends
were constantly on the watch to remind him of danger, and to

retail speeches and anecdotes, some half true, others wholly false, but all tending to show that unless he could consent to give up the opinions he had hitherto most strenuously asserted, his success, upon the event of a new election, would be most doubtful. General Forester, in particular, shook his head with looks of surprise and reproach, upon finding that the member he had himself proposed—the man for whom such sacrifices had been made—was resolved to follow the guidance of his own judgment, and steadfastly set his face against many of the most approved measures of the day.

It was a perversion of reason attributed to ignorance, and argued against accordingly; but as weeks went on, and no impression was made upon Edward's prejudices, the General's zeal in his behalf sensibly diminished; and nothing but respect for his talents, and the certainty that, if Mr Courtenay ceased to be member, he himself would cease to be a person of any importance, induced him still to range himself amongst the number of his political adherents. Since Edward's return to Allingham, however, General Forester's hopes of his conversion had considerably revived. With such a spy as his daughter upon the family secrets, he could not be entirely ignorant of the position of Mr Courtenay's affairs; and his own knowledge of Edward's character made him easily believe that no compromise need be despaired of whilst it was possible to hold out to him the prospect of relieving himself from his difficulties; and that this might be done, if he remained in Parliament, the General had good reason to imagine. He had indeed no idea to what extent Edward was embarrassed. It was a secret only in the possession of his lawyers; but Miss Forester had gained, by observation and questions, an insight into his hidden subjects of care, which years of intimacy would have failed to impart to Laura. And this knowledge she felt no scruple in imparting to her father.

And there was yet another person who watched the onward course of events with deep, untiring interest. The four years which had glided over Mr Dacre's head had been unmarked by any incidents of importance, but each as it passed had borne with it some portion of strength from the body, and added some impress of heaven to the soul. Calm he was still, and thoughtful, and dignified, and self-possessed; but it was the calmness rather of a spirit escaped from earthly cares than, as it once had been, of a heart too heavily oppressed to be conscious of them. None but himself knew the toil and watchfulness, the careful examination and earnest prayer, by which alone the last clinging to bygone recollections had been subdued ; and few could understand the fulness of peace, which seems granted as the foretaste of eternal rest, when the spirit, after its weary struggle with sin and sorrow, has at length been permitted to attain that high point of human excellence from which heaven in its purity is seen unclouded above, while the mists and shadows of the world float unheeded beneath. Yet it was this very elevation of character which caused Mr Dacre's unwearied care for the welfare of those whom he saw still battling with the trials of life. They who have escaped from danger can best understand the difficulties of others when plunged into it ; and although Edward's reserve and secrecy had latterly induced Mr Dacre to believe, as Edith had said, that he must be in expectation of some sources of affluence unknown to his friends, and thus in some degree diminished his anxiety, yet it was impossible to watch without deep regret the gradual deterioration of a naturally noble mind, gifted with a clear perception of the path of duty, but weakly turning aside at every step. He had failed, too, in obtaining that intimacy with Edward, of which he had once hoped to avail himself. Allingham was open to him at all hours, and his welcome gave him no cause to consider himself an intruder ; but the day of confidence was over ; for, having once rejected Mr Dacre's advice, Edward was unwilling to confess the consequences which his own wilfulness had brought upon him ; and guardedly abstained from all allusions to his personal feelings or his private affairs. And at the Priory it was equally hopeless to obtain any information as to his true position. Edith, who knew most, now daily lamented her estrangement and ignorance ; but there was a pleasure in feeling that it was in his power to be a comfort to her, which induced Mr Dacre to take frequent advantage of Mrs Courtenay's hearty assurances, that ' it was quite a relief to see him frequently, for really she began to think sometimes he would go out of his senses with melancholy if he kept so much to himself.' Perhaps, if he had known the effect of his visits, they might even have been more frequent ; but the most pure and holy are also the most humble-minded ; and Mr Dacre would have been the first to feel surprise at being told that his presence was a check upon Charlotte's satire and a stimulus to Jane's energy ; while Mrs Courtenay often wondered ' what there was in Mr Dacre which made things seem different when he was there :

everybody was so quiet, and all went on so much more smoothly; she thought it must be because he was such an invalid that people were afraid of talking out before him, for fear of distressing him.'

'Mr Dacre has forgotten us for three days,' said Charlotte, as she lingered one morning in the breakfast-room, a practice which, since Gertrude's return, had become more enticing than formerly.

'Not forgotten, my dear,' said Mrs Courtenay; 'but you all tire him out when he is here. I thought he never would have done walking up and down the terrace the last time. Poor man! and the night air is so bad for him.'

'He is rather a romantic person for an old one,' observed Jane: 'I am sure he likes moonlight a great deal better than I do.'

'We were matter-of-fact enough that evening,' said Edith. 'He was talking about the poor man who shot Edward's keeper, and settling what was to be done with the wife and children.'

'Ah, yes!' exclaimed Mrs Courtenay; 'to be sure that must be it. I dare say he is gone to see after them now. What a good thing it is to be so kind.'

'Yes,' said Jane, more earnestly than usual; 'if one were but to equal it. I can fancy a great deal of pleasure in being able to do what he does.'

'Mr Dacre is a miserable invalid,' said Edith, shortly. Jane's colour rose, and she was about to make an angry reply; when Gertrude, turning to her mother, inquired if she were not intending to go for a drive in the middle of the day.

'Why, yes, my dear, I did think of it, and Jane too; but why did you ask?'

'Because, if you were, I thought perhaps you would not mind going by Torrington Heath, and taking Susan Philips a little bundle of clothes we have been looking out for her—that is to say, if it is ready; but I must work hard to finish making up the baby's frock.'

'Leave it for to-day,' said Edith, 'and come with me to the school; we shall meet Mr Dacre there, perhaps, and then he will tell us what he has been doing, and you will be able to say anything you wish.'

The last words were spoken in a tone which implied that a conversation with Mr Dacre was an all-powerful temptation; but Gertrude resolutely resisted it.

'If you would wait till the afternoon,' she replied, ' it would be more convenient, because I really should be glad to finish my work, and I want rather to help Charlotte to put in her seeds.'

' But you don't mean to say you would stay at home for such a trifle as that?' exclaimed Edith; 'I thought you were very anxious about poor Philips, and I am nearly certain we shall hear something from Mrs Grantley, if we don't meet Mr Dacre.'

'We should not be delayed very long,' said Gertrude; 'and it is such an exquisite morning for gardening, and Charlotte and I have been looking forward to it. You must remember the work, too.'

'We would take it up ourselves to-morrow,' persisted Edith; ' and it would do just as well, and better, because we should be able to talk to Susan.'

'I thought,' said Gertrude, 'that if mamma took it, perhaps she would not mind telling Susan how to doctor her baby. I am sure she knows a great deal about it, and we could not help her at all in that way.'

'If mamma would,' said Edith; ' but she dislikes getting in and out of a carriage.'

'Perhaps Susan would be able to tell her about the child without giving her that trouble,' said Gertrude. ' Don't call me wilful, Edith; I really do hope to go out with you in the course of the day.'

'What is that you want me to do, my dear?' inquired Mrs Courtenay; 'you must not ask me to go amongst any of your people: it makes me so very nervous—it upsets me quite.'

' I did not mean you to be worried about it, dear mamma,' said Gertrude; 'but you know so much about children, that perhaps, if Susan Philips came to the carriage door you could just tell her something that might be good for her baby.'

Mrs Courtenay hesitated, thought, and at last acquiesced. Prescribing for babies was the point on which she peculiarly piqued herself, and this Gertrude had lately discovered.

' Well, then, it is settled, I suppose,' said Charlotte ; 'and we will go to our gardening, Gertrude, and leave the others to their own devices.'

' Only if you could spare me a little time to finish my work first,' said Gertrude, ' I should be very grateful.'

Charlotte looked disappointed ; and Jane, following the example set her of assisting others, offered to undertake the task.

Gertrude was obliged, but not too much so. She did not appear to consider that Jane had made an unusual effort, which would have implied that she was generally selfish; and thanked her more for the favour conferred on herself than for the kindness done to the poor woman. And Edith looked on in surprise: that her mother should take any trouble for a sick child, and Jane put herself out of the way to work for it, she would an hour before have considered perfectly unnatural. Now, both actions came as a matter of course, while Gertrude seemed to have cast aside her own duties, and to devote herself merely to a trifling amusement—why, Edith, notwithstanding her late conversation, had yet to learn.

The morning wore quickly away, and Gertrude talked, and laughed, and gardened, and discussed the merits of a new club book, and assisted her mother out of the intricacies of her knitting, as if her whole thoughts were devoted to the present hour. No one would have imagined that she had any one engrossing subject of thought, or that any other motive than mere curiosity caused her to listen so frequently to the hall bell, and wonder whether Mr Dacre would come to luncheon. Yet at that very time Gertrude was longing to indulge the day-dream, which for years had been floating before her, and which nothing but a firm habit of self-control had kept from occupying her mind, to the exclusion of her daily duties. It was a dream, not of fame and honour, not of luxury and earthly splendour, but of riches dedicated to the God who had conferred them. And at length the period seemed arrived when she might be permitted to realise it. Even before Gertrude had been made aware of her aunt's intentions in her favour, her naturally generous temper had led her to form plans for giving pleasure to others; and all that could be spared from her personal allowance was bestowed freely, sometimes even profusely and extravagantly. upon her friends. It was the family defect. The luxury of making presents was too great to be resisted, and poor Gertrude had often brought herself into difficulty by the thoughtless kindness which had induced her to lavish her last sovereign upon a knick-knack for a companion, when she was in want of absolute necessaries herself. But, with more steady principles came the corrective of this error. The first check which she received was from the knowledge that she could not throw her money away upon idle fancies, and also have enough to bestow upon the poor; and although it was not so agreeable, at first, to relinquish a purchase for which she was certain to receive warm thanks and caresses, in order to buy a hundred of coals, or a few yards of flannel, with scarcely any prospect of gratitude in return,—yet the lesson was learned at last ; and Gertrude was contented to be thought prudent and economical by the world, so that she could be generous in the eye of God. Her natural disposition, however, though diverted into another channel, still remained in full force. The visions of the future which came the most frequently, and were the most difficult to subdue, were of some time when she should be able to build churches, and found hospitals, and endow alms-houses, and give up everything to religion. They constituted to her the romance of life ; for they were associated with all those feelings of reverence, and self-devotion, and dedication to the service of another Being, which, even when turned upon earthly objects, are among the highest and purest of which our nature is capable. And since her return home, the occasion seemed afforded of gratifying her most cherished wish. She had wealth beyond any others of her family, since she shared her father's fortune equally with her sisters ; there were no pressing claims upon her charity, and if, with the sanction of her friends, she might take upon herself the duty which had been exclusively her brother's, and sacrifice her fortune for the church so much needed at Torrington, she could scarcely be accused of going beyond her appointed sphere of action. The first thought upon the subject was one of exquisite delight—the next of deep humiliation. In bygone ages there had been a monarch ' in whose heart it was to build a house of rest for the ark of the covenant of the Lord, and for the footstool of his God ; and who had made ready for the building. But God said unto him, Thou shall not build an house for my name.' And after the rejection of David, the man after God's own heart, Gertrude trembled, lest it might be presumptuous in one so young, and frail, and untried as herself, to venture upon a similar undertaking. Her spirit sank as she dwelt upon the greatness of the work, and her own weakness and sinfulness ; she longed to find some person who would enter into her feelings, and advise her rightly, whilst she shrank from confessing her secret wishes and hearing her ideas discussed and argued upon, and, it might be, ridiculed, by those who would consider it a deed of merit, rather than an infinite privilege, to make an offering of worldly wealth for the benefit of the Church of Christ. Delicacy naturally prevented her from speaking to Edward, and reserve formed an

equal barrier to applying to Mr Grantley, of whom she had seen
but little ; next to him her mind turned to Mr Dacre, whose intimacy with the family made him appear an old friend.   Once or
twice, in their late conversations, she had endeavoured to introduce subjects of the kind uppermost in her thoughts, in order to
gain an insight into his opinions, and discover whether she might
dare to acknowledge her wishes and her own self-distrust, without fear of being considered weak and enthusiastic; for Gertrude,
like all persons of a warm and earnest temperament, could better
have brooked open opposition, than a matter-of-fact, uninterested
inquiry into the reasonableness of her views.   Edith had, as yet,
been her only confidante ; and even she, though delighted at the
prospect, seemed to consider principally the sacrifice her sister
was about to make, and spoke of it as an act of munificence,
which she desired might be known to every one ; and poor Gertrude, humbled by praise more than by censure, dreaded lest
after all she should be mistaken in Mr Dacre's character, and
receive flattering commendations, where she desired only
sympathy and advice.   It was with a beating heart, therefore,
that on this morning, when she had resolved if possible to speak
to him unreservedly. she heard his now well-known ring, followed
by the inquiry for Mrs Courtenay and the young ladies.   Objections to her plan started up instantaneously.   Mr Dacre might
consider it premature—an infringement upon Edward's peculiar
province ; he might think it hasty, and counsel delay ; or he
might see other and less interesting claims upon her fortune ; or,
still worse, he might be preoccupied, and so might give her only
a half attention.   And at the instant Gertrude felt as if the least
check would throw her back upon herself, and make her bury
her wishes in her own bosom for ever.   Mr Dacre appeared in
due time, was chided for his long absence, invited to take
luncheon as usual, and then pressed to give every particular
about the unfortunate poacher and his family.   It was a hard
trial for Gertrude ; yet she forced herself to attention, by remembering how much of happiness or misery to a fellow-creature
was involved in the subject ; and no one, in listening to her considerate questions, would have imagined how great was the
effort of making them.   All was, however, at length told ; and
Gertrude waited for a pause, as an excuse for breaking up the
party ; but Mrs Courtenay was too delighted at finding a new
topic of conversation to relinquish it willingly, and continued
asking questions till the carriage had been twice announced ;

when, to Gertrude's disappointment, it was insisted that Mr Dacre should go for a drive with them. He was to return, however, to dinner ; and again Gertrude meekly submitted to the delay, and strove to turn her mind to other subjects.

CHAPTER XXVII.

'I CANNOT imagine, Gertrude, how you contrive to be so calm about everything,' said Edith, putting her arm within her sister's as they left the dining-room, and leading her into the garden ; 'I watched you during the whole of dinner, and never once saw you look absent.'

'I saw myself, though,' said Gertrude, smiling ; 'but indeed, Edith, you are enough to prevent any one from being calm—half my worries now are for you. I am sure you will be grievously vexed if objections are made.'

'Naturally enough,' said Edith ; 'and angry too, perhaps ; for, after all, who is to hinder you from doing as you like with your own money?'

'No one, legally,' replied Gertrude ; 'and if I were some twenty or thirty years older, and had experience and judgment, I don't think any one would ; but it is the old story of times and circumstances pointing out duty. I should feel I was presumptuous in determining upon it, if such a man as Mr Dacre seriously objected ; for I sometimes think, Edith,' and Gertrude's voice involuntarily assumed a deeper tone, 'that holy works should only be undertaken by holy persons.'

'And who is holy if you'——, began Edith, but the sentence was unfinished.

'Who is holy, indeed?' said Gertrude, not perceiving her sister's meaning—'holy as one should be who desires such a privilege as I am seeking. Does it never seem to you, Edith, when you look upon beautiful scenery, that nature is the only temple fit for the worship of God?'

'Yes,' replied Edith, 'and I suppose, if our minds were in a right state, devotion would be the natural result of all keen perception of beauty ; but, as it is, we can so seldom view it without some lower associations. It constantly appears to me like a stranger—as if I could see only the outward form, and the spirit was hidden.　I have looked upon this view, for instance, day after day, and gained no real pleasure or benefit from it.'

'I can understand that,' replied Gertrude, 'and it is humbling and disappointing to have nothing but mean or common ideas suggested by what we admire so much.　That is the reason, I suppose, why the solemnity of a church is generally necessary to raise our minds.　The natural temple is profaned.'

'Yes,' continued Edith, 'the earth may be a temple for angels, but it can never be for us.'

'Only as we become more like them,' replied Gertrude; 'and then,' she added, with greater earnestness, 'can you not fancy, Edith, the infinite charm of being able to read the spirit of nature truly; of being so thoroughly religious, as never to look coldly upon the meanest flower, because God made it, and really to feel that His voice was in the thunder, and His glory upon the seas?'

The tears were in Edith's eyes, and she paused before replying.　'O Gertrude!' she exclaimed, at length, 'if it were only possible to be what we know we ought to be!　But how is it possible?　If we lived alone in deserts there might be a hope: but there can be none for us, when we are constantly in contact with our fellow-creatures, and so have our worst feelings brought into play at every instant.'

'I have thought lately,' replied Gertrude, 'that the difficulty might be less, but for our way of looking at people, and thinking of them.　If we could constantly realise the fact that we are baptized members of the Church of Christ, to live with our fellow-creatures would be not merely an intercourse with human beings, but with souls training for eternity.'

'One is so apt to forget the very existence of a Church,' said Edith.

'Yes, and yet I am sure that no mind can be raised to its highest tone without a remembrance of it; because there is much involved in it: it tells in a wonderful way upon daily life.'

'I don't see that,' replied Edith; 'of course it is a truth, and a great one; but there seems nothing very practical in it.'

'So I should have said once,' replied Gertrude, 'but I think, when a person begins to act up to the rules of the Church, however imperfectly, they must be felt to be a great assistance in keeping the mind in a right state; even though their meaning and spirit are not thoroughly understood.'

'You are speaking of yourself, Gertrude,' said Edith. 'I always felt there was some great difference between us.'

'Yes,' replied Gertrude, 'I was speaking of myself, because we must be better judges of the effect of certain principles from our own experience than from hearsay. My notions about the Church began from practice. A friend talked to me of the duty of observing certain days, and attending daily services, which were just introduced at Farleigh; she was not at all a clever person, and understood nothing of controversy, but she was most entirely in earnest, and never, that I could find out, knowingly omitted a duty; and all her argument was, that fasts and festivals were ordered, and that there was a form of daily service in the Prayer-book, which the clergyman of the parish intended to use; and she asked me whether I thought we were at liberty to follow our notions of right, rather than obey the rules of the Church.'

'It is a strong way of putting the case,' said Edith: 'the reasoning I have generally heard has been upon a question of expediency.'

'Perhaps I might have been inclined to reason with any one else,' said Gertrude, 'but it was impossible in that instance. I do not think she would have understood it; and when she saw me pause and consider, she merely said, "Don't you think it would be safer to do what we are told?"'

'And did that convince you?' exclaimed Edith.

'Not as to the theory, but it did as to the practice.'

'Yet you must have felt yourself immensely superior to her all the time,' began Edith; but Gertrude stopped her before the completion of the sentence.

'O Edith!' she said, 'you do not know of whom you are speaking. Even then I felt she was meet for happiness, and three months afterwards she died. How could I be her superior?'

'In intellect, surely you were, from your own account,' said Edith.

'But what is intellect?' replied Gertrude. 'How can it weigh for one instant in the balance against an honest and good heart, which she possessed in a greater degree than any other person I ever knew?'

'I am afraid,' said Edith, with a sigh, 'that I should not feel as you do. I could scarcely have brought myself to listen to the suggestion of one whose judgment I thought lightly of.'

'I did not think lightly of it,' replied her sister. 'Consider,

Edith, from whom all good comes. Her knowledge of duty was clearly not the result of human reasoning, and therefore seemed to claim the more reverence.'

'But about the Church,' said Edith. 'I don't see how thinking of it will act upon daily conduct.'

'Try,' said Gertrude. 'The next time a morning visitor comes, and you are worried at being interrupted, just think of her as a member of the Church, and therefore as having the same blessings and the same prospects as yourself, and see whether you will not feel an interest in her, and be much more inclined to be kind and attentive to her.'

Edith laughed, in spite of the seriousness of the subject. 'Don't be shocked at me, Gertrude,' she said ; 'but you know morning visitors are allowed to be the greatest torments in life. Every one says it ; and it seems absurd to talk gravely about them.'

'That is rather what I said just now,' replied Gertrude : 'we create difficulties for ourselves. Look at a morning visitor merely as a morning visitor, and the tone of your mind is lowered directly ;—you cannot help it. She very frequently breaks in upon your time, and tries your temper, and you cannot help wishing to be alone again ; and when you once have this feeling, your style of conversation will be lowered too ; and as a mere mode of passing a few minutes, you will naturally speak of your neighbours.'

'Yes,' said Edith ; 'I have felt that many times. I don't think really I am fond of gossip, but persons would think I was who heard me talk, merely because, as you say, I want to pass away a few minutes.'

'And yet morning visits are not trifles,' said Gertrude. 'Even those which are most hurried and uninteresting must make some impression upon our minds—they must tell in some degree upon our destiny for eternity.'

'It is a fearful way of viewing things,' said Edith.

'But if it is true, dearest, why should we shrink from it ? Will it not be better to pass through life with awe and trembling, watching our every step, and so learning to lean the more steadfastly upon God, than to wake up, when it is too late, to the knowledge that what we called trifles were the only opportunities afforded us of fitting ourselves for heaven ?'

'There would be but little merriment on earth if all thought as you do, Gertrude,' said Edith.

'No,' replied Gertrude : ' there would be care, and prudence, and at times anxiety ; but when we once set ourselves earnestly to the work, we should be cheerful, as children are cheerful, who can play in the midst of danger, because they have faith in a father's power to protect them.'

There was a short pause, which Edith was the first to break. 'I can fancy,' she said, ' that dwelling much upon our position as belonging to the Church would make things appear more serious, if we could only remember it at the right time.'

' It would become a habit by degrees,' said Gertrude, ' and then it would influence every action ; and for this reason, that it is to the Christian what the consciousness of noble birth is to the man of the world. It gives a feeling of dignity and importance, though without any admixture of pride. When we know ourselves to be what the Bible says,—" heirs of God and joint-heirs with Christ,"—I think we shall hardly be tempted to act lightly, and the fear of falling away will be constantly before us, to make us watch against sin. Do, dear Edith, read over St Paul's Epistle to the Ephesians, carefully, and see whether the whole argument does not rest upon this foundation ; and then think what a calm, contented. humble tone of mind must be the result of it.'

' I am not sure that I do see it,' replied Edith.

'You will own,' replied Gertrude, ' that as members of the Church, there can be no rivalry, or selfishness, or wish to attract notice beyond others. Think of the feeling there is in a family when any one is distinguished beyond the rest. The gratification is felt by all, because the honour belongs to all ; and so it is in the Church.' Edith still looked doubtful, and Gertrude continued :—' What I mean,' she said, ' is, that if we labour for the prosperity of a body, not for our own benefit, we strike at the root of all selfishness ; and if we are poor, or have no talents, or no opportunity of exercising them, we shall still be satisfied, because the object we have at heart—the good of the Church of Christ—will surely be attained, though not through our means.'

'And would that satisfy you ?' said Edith. ' Could you, for instance, bear to be told that the church at Torrington was to be built by another person ?'

Gertrude was silent, and when her sister turned to look at her, the expression of her countenance showed that the question had excited some painful feeling.

'You have misunderstood me, dearest,' she said, at length, in her usual quiet manner; 'I could not dare to speak to you of myself, or of what I should feel under any circumstances. To see the height one longs to attain, is far different from setting out on the weary journey to reach it.'

'Yes,' said Edith, and she sighed deeply; 'it is a weary journey. And if you find it so, Gertrude, what must it be to me?'

Gertrude was about to answer, when the appearance of Mr Dacre at the farther end of the walk stopped her.

'The hour is come at last,' said Edith, with a smile, which was checked as she saw the colour fade from her sister's cheek, and felt her arm tremble.

'Who would think I could be so absurd?' said Gertrude: 'yet if he should bring forward any objections I have not seen, it would be such a bitter disappointment.'

Edith was inclined to remind her of her own principles, but she felt it would be almost a reproach. Gertrude, however, needed no suggestions. 'I know what you would say,' she continued, observing that Edith was going to speak; 'if it is not my duty, it will still be performed by the person whom God sees fitted for it ; and then, Edith, you must teach me to submit.'

Edith pressed her sister's hand, without venturing upon a reply ; and, turning into another path, left Gertrude to open the subject of her wishes to Mr Dacre.

CHAPTER XXVIII.

'WE thought you would have been tempted out before this,' was Gertrude's first observation, as she walked by Mr Dacre's side, not knowing how to introduce the desired topic.

'Ten years ago I should have been,' was the answer ; 'but illness makes an old man think more of the charms of repose than of a beautiful evening ; besides, you were so fully engaged, I should only have been an interruption.'

'Not that, indeed,' exclaimed Gertrude, in an eager, trembling voice : 'I was wishing for you so much—I thought—I wanted'——

'Anything that I can give?' said Mr Dacre, struck by the hesitation so foreign to her usual manner.

'I do not know,' replied Gertrude, struggling to regain self-possession; 'and yet I do know. If you would listen to me—I think that is what I want most.'

'You are looking upon me as a stranger,' said Mr Dacre, in a tone of gentle reproof, 'and it does me injustice. I was a father once, and I have not forgotten a father's feelings.'

Gertrude tried to answer, but her words came with difficulty. 'I will tell you,' she said, at length, 'but, indeed, I do not think of you as a stranger; if I did, I could not let you know what is in my thoughts.' She stopped again; and Mr Dacre looked at her inquiringly.

'Do not keep me in suspense,' he said; 'if I can be of any service, you have only to name it.'

'I don't know why I should trouble you,' replied Gertrude; and then, unheeding the appearance of abruptness, she continued, rapidly, 'I have a wish—a great wish: it has been in my mind for years—and I think it is right, but I am not sure. It is such an important thing; so very serious; it does not seem as if it could be intended for me to do it;—only I have the means. I—I wish,—I should like,'—and with evident effort the words at last were spoken,—'I should be so glad to build a church at Torrington.' She paused, and finding that Mr Dacre did not immediately answer, continued, as if anxious to relieve herself of a burden weighing upon her heart,—'You must know, I think, that I am richer than my sisters. My aunt's fortune is mine now; I have five hundred a year at my own disposal, and there are no claims upon me yet; and if there were, this would seem almost the greatest, because the place belongs to Edward, and he cannot do anything for it himself,—he has said so several times. If it were a common thing, I should not hesitate; but I think you will understand; it would give me such pleasure, I am afraid I may not see whether it is my duty; and if I am presumptuous, and do not undertake it rightly, God's blessing may not go with it; and I think about it sometimes till I am frightened, and fancy that perhaps I ought to give away my money differently now, upon things which would be greater sacrifices, and wait for this till I have lived longer, and suffered more, and learned to be better, only the case seems so urgent; but then again I long to be able to do it so much that perhaps I am not a good judge. It may not be my duty, though I fancy it is—if you would only give me your opinion.'

Mr Dacre still hesitated, and Gertrude, looking at him anxiously, said, 'I have tried to prepare myself for objections and disappointment.'

'Needlessly, I hope,' said Mr Dacre, recovering from the feeling of surprise at a request for advice so different from any he could have expected ; 'I will tell you first, that I fully understand your feelings. An offering of this kind is a most solemn duty, and must not be undertaken lightly. It may be that the spirit in which it is commenced will prove a blessing or a curse upon generations to come.'

'Thank you,' exclaimed Gertrude ; 'I thought you would understand me. It has always appeared to me very sad that worldly motives should be mixed with works of religion ; and occasionally, when I have seen the ruins of old churches and abbeys, I have thought that there might have been something wanting in the spirit in which they were begun, and therefore they were suffered to decay ; and it seemed impossible then that it could ever be my duty to attempt such things.'

'Yet,' replied Mr Dacre, 'we must be careful that self-distrust does not lead us into a morbid fear of being presumptuous. The most fervent piety could not prevent our offerings from being marred by some earthly alloy ; and it would be rather a doubt of God's mercy than of our own worthiness, which would lead us to fold our hands and do nothing, because what we did was not perfect.'

'Then you think that I might—you do not see any objections?' inquired Gertrude.

'Not at this moment,' was the reply; but Mr Dacre's tone was less certain than Gertrude had expected. 'Can you bear to hear the subject discussed in a cool, dispassionate, perhaps you would call it a worldly, manner, now that you know how entirely I feel with you ?'

'Why should it be worldly ?' said Gertrude.

'The word sounds out of place, I own; but when I say worldly, I do not for an instant mean to imply that we must lower our principles, but merely that we must not let zeal, however pure, warp our sober judgment.'

Gertrude's countenance expressed disappointment. 'It frightens me to hear zeal condemned,' she said ; 'these are not days when it is too abundant.'

'It is not the virtue, but the manner of exercising it, which we must guard against,' replied Mr Dacre. 'I have often found it advisable, when my heart has been very much set on any object, to endeavour to view it in the same light in which it would be regarded by men of the world; and I hope, by that means, I may have avoided giving unnecessary offence.'

'And what do you think a man of the world would say to my project?' inquired Gertrude.

'The first question he would be likely to ask,' replied Mr Dacre, 'would be as to any other claims upon your fortune; but this you tell me has been already considered.'

'I think so,' said Gertrude; 'there are no family claims, certainly.'

Mr Dacre hesitated a little before proceeding. He was doubtful how far his suggestions might be considered intrusive. 'Perhaps,' he said, 'there are no claims which are absolutely pressing; but is it not as well to guard against any appearance of injustice? I mean, that when you are calculating how much you may expend, you should take into consideration, that other persons may have naturally and fairly looked forward to some increase of their own comforts when you came into possession of your property.'

'I understand you now,' exclaimed Gertrude. 'I know that I cannot live at home upon the same footing with my sisters, though we have all an equal share in the family property. I ought to add something to it.'

'Yes,' he replied, 'I think you should; and this might be first cared for. It will not prevent your following out your own wishes afterwards; but it will prevent any one from blaming you for doing it. It will be avoiding the appearance of evil.'

'And my sisters,' said Gertrude. 'I have thought of them also. Edith agrees so entirely with me, that she will not hear of my reserving any portion for her; but I should be sorry for the others to be disappointed.'

'And most probably,' observed Mr Dacre, 'the very care you show for them will induce them to enter more fully into your plans, and be anxious to share them. It is a great thing to put it into a person's power to act rightly.'

'One so longs to do everything,' said Gertrude, 'but I suppose in all these cases there must be some self-denial.'

'Yes, and where there is not, any virtue must be doubtful

generosity, for instance—which is a mere luxury, unless it is founded upon the restriction of personal indulgence.'

'And justice,' added Gertrude, smiling, 'which you have been so carefully inculcating upon me.'

'Not because I thought you had quite forgotten it, but because it is a grave, shy virtue, very fond of keeping in the background —hidden like the stars by the sunlight of generosity—though without it the most munificent actions may be, and generally are, condemned, and by none more than by keen-sighted, cold-hearted men of the world ; and so we return to the point from which we set out,—that it is well to look at our actions in the way in which they look at them, that we may not give unnecessary offence, and repel instead of attract them.'

'I am afraid,' said Gertrude, 'these necessary provisions will principally interfere with the endowment. The church need not be large for such a small district, and I could manage it without the least difficulty. What I should have wished certainly would have been to have done all that might be required—schoolrooms, and things of that kind ; but I suppose it would be better not to attempt too much, the endowment is of so much more importance.'

'Yes,' said Mr Dacre ; 'once provide a good clergyman, and as far as human calculation goes, you need have no fear of the result being what you wish.'

'It will be but a small income,' replied Gertrude ; 'five thousand pounds, or even six or seven, will not go very far in these days.'

'If it is all that is allowed you to give, there can be no cause for regret. The blessing rests not upon the little or the much, but upon the spirit in which it is offered.'

Gertrude sighed. 'And that,' she said, after a short silence, 'we forget. Things become so low and earthly when we descend to details.'

'Yes,' replied Mr Dacre ; 'they are the body of dust in which the spirit is enshrined ; and I fear you are scarcely aware of the trouble and even pain you are bringing upon yourself by engaging in them. But it is a great victory when we have learned to infuse a holy principle into the minutest concerns of life— money matters especially.'

'Edward must be spoken to,' said Gertrude, 'and mamma, and my sisters ; but I wish there was no occasion for it.'

'Your brother of course has the first claim to be consulted.

I should be glad to spare you the effort of mentioning it, but it is impossible.'

'It will be the hardest task of all,' said Gertrude. 'And I seem to know so little of him. I shall be sadly afraid of jarring upon him.'

Mr Dacre smiled, but it was not cheerfully. 'You must jar upon him,' he replied ; 'for many reasons you must. Principally, because the duty is one which was once his own ; and scarcely any person can bear to see another fulfil his office. And now I must give you one piece of advice, which I am afraid will sound cold and prudent beyond what is necessary. If, at the end of six months, you see no reason to alter your plans, then I hope you will be able to begin immediately ; but I think you will be doing right to wait, and well consider every objection,—to " count the cost," in fact, before you undertake so great a work.'

Gertrude was scarcely disappointed by this suggestion, for she had not believed it possible to follow out her plans immediately. All that she desired was the permission to think upon them. Mr Dacre did not press the point. He seemed wearied, and Gertrude proposed they should return to the house. He stopped, however, before entering, and in a voice almost tremulous from repressed feeling, said, 'The first wish of my heart would have been gratified, if it had been permitted me to have had such a conversation with my own child as I have now held with you. Will you let me consider it a bond of union between us, and allow me to help you, if possible, under all circumstances, as I would have helped her ?'

Gertrude's answer was a warm pressure of the hand, which said all that Mr Dacre required. Edith met them at the door, and read in her sister's calm, sweet smile that all her doubts were at rest ; but there was something of disturbance in Mr Dacre's countenance, which, now that Edith's thoughts were less occupied by Gertrude, she could not avoid noticing. It was remarked, however, only by herself. The evening passed as usual ; if any secret care was preying upon his mind, it was diverted by music and conversation ; and when the little party broke up, the observation made was, that Mr Dacre had seldom appeared so comfortable. And Gertrude retired to her room, to indulge for the first time without fear the dream that had haunted her from childhood. She knelt in her accustomed place to repeat her accustomed prayers ; but as she closed her eyes to shut out all earthly objects, tall, clustering pillars, and carving, and fret-work, arose before her, and in imagination she felt herself worshipping in the temple of holiness which she was about to raise to her Maker's honour ; and when her head was laid upon her pillow, the same visions floated before her in dim and shadowy beauty ; while tones of solemn music seemed borne upon the soft night breeze to soothe her sinking fancy, with the prophecy of what might **so** soon be reality.

CHAPTER XXIX.

IT was late on the following morning that Laura, after a *tête-à-tête* breakfast with her husband, of more than usual length and silence, wandered into her morning-room, to endeavour, if possible, to find some occupation that might pleasantly engage her thoughts, and prevent her from dwelling upon the contrast between Edward's present gloom and reserve, and the light-hearted cheerfulness of former days. It was useless to account for the change by attributing it to a passing annoyance. Certainly he had pronounced the coffee insipid and badly made, the eggs not sufficiently boiled, the marmalade inferior, the cutlets uneat able ; but Laura felt too truly that the real grievance lay in the secrecy of his own heart. It might perhaps have been increased by some information in the letters, which so deeply absorbed his attention as to cause him entirely to forget his wife's presence ; or it might be attributed to the last night's interview with Mr Rivers, which had occasioned her a dreary, solitary evening ; or it might be the result of General Forester's visits, which had latterly become very frequent, and never failed to put him out of humour ; but after long consideration, it still remained a mystery, known only by its fatal effect upon her domestic happiness. From her husband, Laura turned for comfort to her child, but the nurse had taken him out, and he was nowhere to be found ; and in his absence she would willingly have had recourse to a friend ; but at the thought of Miss Forester, Laura's countenance assumed a deeper gravity, and something like a tear dimmed her bright eye. There was but one person whom at that moment she could have seen with pleasure, though why, she could not have told. Gertrude's features were plain, her manners were simple, her talents were not brilliant ; she never was known to flatter—she did not appear anxious to please ; and Laura had been idolised from her cradle, and taught to consider elegance, beauty, and vivacity essential to an agreeable person, and their deficiency only to be atoned for by the homage shown to her own superiority. There could not have been two characters more unlike—and Edith would have said, that, as a necessary consequence, it would have been useless to attempt creating any mutual interest between them. And yet, in Laura's present state of depression, the thought of Gertrude's gentle smile, and the recollection of her soothing voice, was like the oasis in the wilderness—the one green spot on which alone she could bear to dwell. For Gertrude had gradually and unobtrusively connected herself with Laura's best and happiest feelings. In many a morning conversation and evening walk she had given her that which we are accustomed to consider a trifle, to be bestowed according to the humour of the moment—sincere, unaffected attention. Laura spoke of her childhood, and Gertrude's questions led her to enter into details of her home ; she mentioned her first acquaintance with Edward, and Gertrude, instead of bringing forward other instances of happy marriages after a short acquaintance, made her relate the little details which were fondly treasured in her memory. She told of her foreign tour, and Gertrude, though she had never travelled herself, entered fully into her pleasures and disappointments ; and, above all, when, with a mother's doting partiality, Laura praised her darling child, Gertrude showed no symptoms of weariness, but listened to the little incidents of his daily life, and deduced from them his future character, with as much earnestness as if their positions had been reversed : and this without effort or insincerity, but because she had taught herself to look upon all connected with her, or related to her, as portions of one great family, into which she had been born at her baptism. It is a habit of immense importance— that quiet attention of which we think so little : we speak of sympathy, and commend it, and wonder that it is so rare and so difficult of attainment ; and the next minute lose ourselves in a dream of business or enjoyment, and repel with a short answer or an abstracted look the very persons who most require our friendship ; and when once repelled we may regret, but we can scarcely hope to retrieve, our error. The regard and confidence, however, which Gertrude had thus awakened in Laura's mind, were as yet shown only in trifles. Laura had not become sufficiently unreserved to speak to her of her hidden causes of anxiety. All that she felt was a sense of protection in Gertrude's presence ; and when oppressed by care, something of refreshment and repose in the tones of kindness, which expressed sympathy without asking why it was needed. But on this morning Laura was not destined to receive any such comfort. A short time only elapsed after she had left the breakfast-table, and she was still standing sadly at the window of her morning-room, when a gentle, a very gentle tap was heard at the door, and with an involuntary shrinking she gave permission for Miss Forester to enter.

'Alone as usual,' was the first observation that greeted Laura's ear, recalling in insinuating accents her now frequent subjects of complaint against Edward ; 'I thought it would be so.'

'We have just finished breakfast,' replied Laura, impatient at any imputation upon her husband from another person, however she might be inclined to find fault with him herself.

'Ah ! you are late at night, I know ; and my father says Mr Courtenay looks dreadfully harassed just now. This prospect of a change of ministers, and another election, must give him a great deal to think of.'

'So soon ? it is impossible. He has said nothing to me.'

'Very likely ; the thing is not certain ; and gentlemen seldom think it worth while to converse with ladies about politics—my father excepted. He tells me everything. But I did not intend to talk to you about elections ; my business is a little private affair of our own.' And Miss Forester drew her chair near to Laura, and lowered her voice to the strictly intimate mysterious tone, while she took from her reticule a packet of papers and letters. Laura with difficulty suppressed a heavy sigh, and looked uneasily at the door. 'You need have no fear,' continued Miss Forester ; 'if any person should come in, they would not understand anything. In fact, there is little to understand ; it is a mere trifle ; and I should not have reminded you of the affair, but that Hanson's bill came by this day's post. and I thought you would be glad to see it.'

'And know the worst,' murmured Laura.

'No, no ; you must not call it the worst,—a few hundreds can be nothing to you. It is absurd to look at this splendid room, and then think of your being distressed at a jeweller's account.'

'You forget Waterloo House, and Madame Larue, and yourself.'

'Myself! that really is not worth mentioning; merely a question of five hundred pounds to you who have thousands. Waterloo House, too, is nothing; and as to Madame Larue, she is a perfect impostor. Hanson is the most provoking of them all; and of course impertinent dunning from him comes home to me, because the last purchases were made in my name.' This was said with a martyr-like air, which was both painful and irritating to poor Laura; but without trusting herself to notice it, she said, hesitatingly—

'I thought—but I must have been mistaken,—only I understood that you could arrange these things, without trouble, for me.'

It was now Miss Forester's turn to be confused; but she had studied her part beforehand, and knew well how she was to act. Her eyes were bent on the ground, and her fingers busy with the silk tassel of her parasol, while, with an effort more evident than was necessary, she said—

'Certainly I had thought so; nothing could have given me greater pleasure; but you know,—I can scarcely bring myself to say it,—these are not times when it is in one's power to do all that one wishes. With Mr Courtenay's guarantee there would be no difficulty; but without it, however my own inclinations might prompt me to make sacrifices for one so dear, I do not think my father would approve.'

'But you said—you told me'— began Laura, and her voice trembled as she spoke.

'And at the time,' interrupted Miss Forester, 'I fully believed that I could have accommodated you without difficulty; but the last few days have forced me most unwillingly to alter my views. My father so highly disapproves'——

'General Forester!' exclaimed Laura, starting from her seat and drawing up her slender figure to its full height, while the flush of indignation crimsoned her face and neck. 'How could he know? how could he venture to offer an opinion upon the subject?'

'You forget,' replied Miss Forester, coolly, and a sarcastic smile curled the corner of her thin lips, 'the business is mine! and the interests of a father and a daughter are inseparable. Laura reseated herself, despairingly, and the expression of sarcasm on Miss Forester's countenance became more marked as she proceeded: ' It was a disagreeable task, but my father is not a man to be trifled with.   The money which I had advanced was indeed my own, but the authority of a parent is too sacred to be disputed; and when he insisted, a few days since, upon receiving some account of my little pittance, that he might be better able to settle a business matter of his own, it was impossible for me to refuse.'

' Your promise !' murmured Laura.

' Yes, I own it was broken in the letter, but not in the spirit. Your affairs are as safe with my father as with me.   The only misfortune now is, that I no longer feel my own mistress.   I cannot do what I would.   It is so distressing, so very distressing to confess it.'

Laura shrank from the touch of the hand which was placed caressingly on her shoulder.   The plausible excuse for the moment silenced her; but the feeling of distrust which had long been gathering in her mind was increased to aversion.

' The affair itself is a trifle,' continued Miss Forester ; ' but just now, when Mr Courtenay is likely to be much worried, it is a most unfortunate moment to be obliged to call upon him for money ; and gentlemen never make allowances for a little im‑prudence in ladies.   These tradespeople, too, are so very pressing. One thing is, that the difficulty will soon be over; it is but the momentary effort of mentioning what has been done.'

Laura raised her head, but the expression of her countenance was beyond Miss Forester's comprehension.   She would have ridiculed as impossible the idea that any person in Mrs Cour‑tenay's position could be more grieved at the recollection of having been guilty of deceit, than at the prospect of confessing folly and extravagance.

' I am afraid,' added Miss Forester, ' that my father will not endure the subject to be mentioned again, unless indeed,—but I need not tease you about politics, I know you dislike them.'

Laura made a gesture of impatience: ' Why keep me in suspense about anything?' she exclaimed; ' nothing can tease me.'

' But it is such an intricate business, and unless you give your mind to it you won't understand it: and if you do, you may not view the case as we do.'

' Why?   What are you speaking of ?' inquired Laura; and she rose from her seat, and stood before her tormentor with a coun‑tenance so beautiful even in its suppressed suffering, that Miss

Forester's selfishness was for the moment overpowered by regret for the pain she was inflicting.

'My father says,' she replied, 'and I think he must know, that after Mr Courtenay's heavy expenses since the last election, he should be wrong in permitting me to involve myself in any way without security being given; and he implies—(you must not think I believe it though)—that just now this would be a difficult matter; that,—in short, you know what I mean,—all gentlemen are distressed at some time or other, and if it were to come to the worst, a few years abroad would set everything to rights.'

A glimmering of the truth flashed upon Laura's mind. Edward's gloom, and impatience, and reserve; the long visits from Mr Rivers; the restless irritation with which, day after day, he had opened his letters, all tended to confirm it; but the effect of the idea was not what Miss Forester had imagined. Laura neither shed tears, nor fainted, nor burst into exclamations of distress; but a red spot burned upon her colourless cheek, and her pale lips were scarcely seen to move, as in a nearly inaudible voice she replied—

'Tell me why you say this?'

'Perhaps it will be best to be candid at once,' said Miss Forester, soothingly; 'and when I have put the case before you, you will see there need be no cause for uneasiness, if Mr Courtenay can be persuaded to be reasonable. You must know that he has peculiar opinions of his own, and will go against the wishes of his party. My father has often talked to him, but he can make no impression; and if he persists there really is very little chance of his re-election, at least, so my father says. There is no doubt, indeed, that instead of walking over the ground without a rival, some one else will be brought forward by many of his former friends to oppose him.'

'And what has this to do with me?' exclaimed Laura, impatiently.

'You will see in one moment,' replied Miss Forester, in the same unruffled tone as before. 'The being re-elected would not in itself, perhaps, be of so much importance to Mr Courtenay. I dare say he could be very happy in private life, though certainly he would be casting away most brilliant prospects; but a letter my father had yesterday from a very influential quarter, says, that Mr Courtenay would certainly be appointed to a very high office under the new ministry if it were not for his obstinacy—

(excuse the word)—upon two or three points; the same, in fact, which his friends in the country are so anxious about. From this you will understand how much depends upon his being re-elected.'

Poor Laura had but a faint perception of Miss Forester's words. They appeared spoken without any object; and again, though more mildly, she entreated to be told what connection there could be between Edward's being in Parliament, and her debts.

' I think you will understand upon consideration,' said Miss Forester, coolly. ' A child could see the difference between entering into a money engagement for the wife of a member of Parliament, holding a government office, and the wife of a private gentleman, reported to have considerably outrun his fortune.'

' It is false! it must be false!' exclaimed Laura, driving from her mind the doubt which had a few minutes before possessed it. ' How can General Forester lend himself to such gossip?'

' It may be false or not,' replied Miss Forester; ' but one thing is quite true,—that my father will not consent to allow my affairs to remain in their present state without interfering, unless he finds Mr Courtenay's prospects assume a different shape from their present one. A fourth part of the legacy left by my grand-mother is already risked.'

Laura's crushed spirit was roused by the threat implied in this speech. ' I will not give General Forester or any other person the trouble of mixing himself up with my affairs,' she replied. ' By to-morrow all shall be settled;' and she moved, in order to suggest to her visitor to leave her. But this was far from Miss Forester's idea. She had no intention of bringing matters to a crisis, and separating herself from Laura entirely. Her wish was rather to draw her more completely into her power. Notwith-standing the opinion she had given as to the state of Mr Cour-tenay's affairs, neither she nor her father believed him to be suffering from more than a temporary embarrassment; but the opportunity of forcing Laura to use her influence over her hus-band, was one of which both, from different motives, were most desirous to take advantage. Since another election had been considered probable, General Forester had been endeavouring by every argument in his power to bring Edward to his views, and induce him to pledge himself to his party upon the points at issue between them, and Edward had continually refused. If this refusal were persisted in, his former friends were certain to forsake him, and bring forward another candidate : there would then be a division of interests, and the cause which General Forester fancied he had at heart would most probably be lost ; or perhaps, as the truer motive, General Forester's lately acquired importance as Mr Courtenay's adviser and oldest friend would be at an end ; and he would return to his former insignificance. Miss Forester's reasons for wishing Laura's position to remain unchanged were very much the same with those which had first caused her to thrust herself upon her friendship. She liked to be on terms of intimacy with a person of fortune and fashion, and felt herself raised in dignity, both in town and in the country, by being known as the chosen companion of the beautiful Mrs Courtenay. And within the last year she had experienced the satisfaction of ruling one whom all others were willing to obey. She had fostered Laura's extravagance, assisting her originally by trifling loans, but afterwards by sums which she had no power to repay; and at length, by inducing her to keep her affairs a secret, from the dread of her husband's displeasure, she had bound her to her, as she hoped for ever. Her will was now the law whenever they were together, except when Edward occasionally objected ; and even then there had been but few instances in which she had not been in the end victorious, by insisting upon Laura's urging in private what she could not venture to mention in public. Laura felt the tyranny, and struggled to escape from it ; but every day's delay in confessing her folly to her husband, rendered her more completely Miss Forester's slave. The very ingenuousness of her disposition made her shrink from acknowledging deceit ; and though she had often been goaded by the misery of her feelings to the point of owning all, she had never yet summoned resolution even to allude to it. Miss Forester knew well the person she had to govern, and felt but little afraid of any sudden fit of heroism.

'You understand your own affairs, no doubt,' she said, in answer to Laura's proud speech. 'If you think it well to trouble Mr Courtenay with money matters at this time, I have nothing to say. I should dislike the task myself, because there is no doubt of his being very much pressed ; and with the prospect of a new election before him, he will certainly be extremely angry now, though by and by he might not care about it.'

'I thought,' said Laura, indignantly, 'that it was only a question between General Forester's interference and my own."

'Oh no ; you mistake entirely. My father would not think of such a thing, if he were not obliged to do so from consideration to me. He and I have been talking a great deal about the affair since yesterday, and he really has but one wish—to do what is best.'

'Best !' repeated Laura, scornfully.

'Yes, best. It must be for Mr Courtenay's advantage to give up these foolish scruples, and secure his seat and his appointment ; and it certainly must be for yours, because, in that case, nothing would be told to Mr Courtenay at present, and I should no longer be forbidden to help you, as I have been able to do before. My father would be satisfied with your promise to use your influence. However, since you are willing to take the matter into your own hands, I may as well leave Hanson's bill with you, and go.'

She held out the paper, but Laura did not take it. She stood for a moment as if stunned ; and then her head grew dizzy, and her knees trembled, and, sinking into a chair, she burst into tears. At that instant the door opened, and a servant entered the room with a note, which he was going to give to his mistress, but seeing her incapable of attending to it, he laid it on the table and withdrew,—sufficiently observing what was going on, to enable him to report in the servants' hall that something was very much amiss, for Mrs Courtenay was in violent hysterics. But Laura was not in hysterics, nor anything approaching to them. For a few minutes her tears fell fast ; but they were quiet and unobtrusive, requiring no aid from the Eau de Cologne which Miss Forester was offering, as she stood over her, with a patronising air, smoothing her shoulder, and begging her to be composed. She was also quite aware that the note had been brought, and fully equal to the exertion of reading it, though Miss Forester entreated her not to trouble herself about it, and proposed to open it instead, and see whether it required an answer. Taking it from her hand, Laura hastily read it ; but something there was in its contents which evidently took her by surprise. A second time she perused the few pencil lines, and turned the paper in every direction, to extract some further information ; and at last, folding it together, she said, coldly—

'I have been wrong in allowing myself to give way ; but I am not equal to discussing these things further. They must be delayed till I have had time for consideration, and then I will write.'

Miss Forester was frightened, for Laura had seldom appeared so determined. She would willingly have pressed the subject, but finding that Laura would not listen, she pushed the papers towards her, saying—

'Then I may suppose you are decided. You will find the accounts correct. The old ones and Hanson's bill together make up more than six hundred pounds.'

Laura mechanically laid her hand upon the papers, and then, scarcely waiting for Miss Forester to leave the room, threw herself upon the sofa in an agony of distress.

CHAPTER XXX.

THAT little note—how much pain had it caused! Edward had left her for London;—left her, without even returning from Elsham, where he had gone to speak with Mr Rivers, to give her one parting kiss, one word of explanation. Yet his expressions were more than usually affectionate, as if purposely meant to soften the annoying intelligence. He entreated her to forgive him for what might appear unkindness in his sudden departure, which was caused by important business, and begged her on no account to make any change in their plans for the week. The archery party which had been invited for the next day but one was still to be received, for he had little doubt that he should be with her before their arrival. If anything occurred to vex her, he should recommend her applying to Mr Dacre. And this was all; and again and again Laura read the note, and again and again pondered its contents, but without gaining any insight into its meaning, beyond the certainty that something was amiss. Yet, although in most cases the first thrilling apprehension of impending evil is worse than the fatal reality, to Laura, the hints she had received from Miss Forester, even when coupled with Edward's absence, brought ideas so vague as to make but a faint impression upon her mind. Her own cares were more pressing than her apprehensions for the future. A dark cloud was hanging over it, but what might be behind she did not attempt to conjecture. It was sufficient suffering to know that Edward had gone away from her, depressed and harassed, and that when he returned she must either brave his displeasure, and add to his heavy anxieties, by confessing her past folly, or persist in a course of deceit, and put herself completely in Miss Forester's power. She thought long and deeply, but, although shrinking from the prospect of a life of wretchedness such as she had lately endured, she still felt herself unequal to the task of increasing Edward's uneasiness at such a time. Delay seemed everything, and the hope of relief which had been held out was too tempting to be rejected. At what sacrifice it was to be obtained she did not fully comprehend, for she had never inquired particularly into Edward's views, and cared so little for politics, as to consider it generally a matter of indifference which side he supported, so long as he distinguished himself. Besides, General Forester was a man of honour, and Edward's friend, and she had no just reason to doubt the kindness of his intentions; and influenced, partly by the hope of saving her husband, and partly by the wish of saving herself, Laura smothered her pride, though not without considerable difficulty. and endeavoured to believe that by giving the promise to do her utmost in furtherance of General Forester's wishes, the threatened storm would be dispelled, and all be bright as before.

The morning, however, passed slowly; work was irksome, reading was impossible; even little Charlie's gentle tap was answered by an order to run away then, and come again by and by; for Laura's mind was dissatisfied. Her thoughts would revert to the past; the events of her married life came before her, one after the other, and still with each was associated some remembrance of Edward's trust in all she had done or said; while the words which he had used in the conversation held the day after their first arrival at Allingham haunted her incessantly: 'We were to have no concealment of any kind.' This had been their agreement, and how had it been kept? If she followed General Forester's advice, how must it be kept? Sincerity was still the foundation of Laura's character,—hidden, but never destroyed, by the false principles of her education, and the follies of her life; and, miserable at the idea of continued deception, she longed for some friend in whom she might confide without fear; and the wish was no sooner felt than the image of Gertrude rose before her. But how would it be possible to apply to her? Could one so free from weakness, so superior to herself, sympathise with her anxieties? Would she not turn away in disgust from the thoughtlessness which she could not understand, and reproach instead of advising her? If it had been Edith, Laura

felt that she could have endured any pain rather than confess to
her the smallest fault; but Gertrude's winning gentleness and
sympathy had so softened the effect of her strict principles that
Laura's awe of her superiority was forgotten in the recollection
of her humility ; and before the afternoon was over she had
ordered her pony carriage, and was on her way to the Priory,
with the purpose of acknowledging to her sister-in-law the errors
which had produced such bitter consequences. And Gertrude,
in happy ignorance of the gathering storm at Allingham, had
spent the morning in writing for Mr Dacre a detail of all the
plans respecting the church, and in trying to amuse her mother.
Mrs Courtenay's usual habit was to retire to her own little
sitting-room soon after breakfast, from which she was seldom
known to emerge till nearly luncheon-time. How she occupied
herself in the intermediate time was a mystery, which none of
her family had hitherto thought it necessary to penetrate. Sometimes, indeed, a letter was produced for the post—the result of a
morning's thought ; and occasionally she was heard to inquire
for a club-book ; but these were the exceptions: as a rule, she
was never actually discovered to have done anything ; but the
general belief was that she principally employed herself in
putting drawers in order, and looking over old papers ; and with
this idea, Jane, Charlotte, and Edith felt perfectly at liberty to
follow their own inclinations. Mrs Courtenay never complained,
so of course she was happy. Gertrude, however, thought differently, and constantly endeavoured to persuade her mother to
join them in the drawing-room ; but it was not Mrs Courtenay's
way, and even if she consented, it was evident that she was out
of her element, and preferred her own apartment, though she
confessed that sometimes it was rather lonely. 'Don't trouble
yourself about me, my dear,' she said, as Gertrude made a last
effort to persuade her to remain with them, by proposing to
assist her in her difficult knitting. 'You know I never knit in
the morning: I am a great deal too busy; though, to be sure,
the day before yesterday, you all laughed so, I had rather a wish
to come down.'

'I don't think you would have entered into what we were
laughing about, mamma,' said Charlotte ; 'it was a book Gertrude
was reading out.'

'Very probably, my dear ; I dare say I should not ; but you
all seemed very merry, and I liked to hear you. I hope you will
do the same to-day.' And with this wish Mrs Courtenay

gathered up her keys, her spectacles, and her knitting, and left the room. Her departure was succeeded by the beginning of an entreaty that Gertrude would enable them to follow the advice which had been given ; but Gertrude had disappeared ; and Mrs Courtenay had only just reached her room, when a soft voice asked for admittance. 'Your room is so quiet and sunny, dear mamma, and mine is not in order yet,—would it worry you very much if I were to sit here for a quarter of an hour and read?'

Mrs Courtenay's face brightened with pleasure. She insisted upon Gertrude's occupying her favourite seat, and moved away everything she thought might be in her way ; and Gertrude thanked her with a kiss, and opened her book.

'That is so like your dear father, my dear ; so fond of reading he always was. I have seen him sit for hours together, and not open his lips, when he had a book he liked.'

Gertrude smiled, and said that she had learned to prefer quiet employment from being so much with an invalid, and the conversation dropped; but after a short pause it was again resumed by Mrs Courtenay.

'Is it a very interesting book you have there, Gertrude, my dear?'

'I don't know that you would exactly call it interesting,' replied Gertrude. 'It is a volume of sermons, which has just been lent to me. There is one not unlike part of Mr Grantley's last Sunday: I think you will remember it.' And she read out a few lines.

'That is not all, my dear, is it?' said Mrs Courtenay, her ear caught by the beauty of the language and the melody of Gertrude's voice.

'Not all,' replied Gertrude ; 'but I thought perhaps you would not like me to go on.'

'Ah! you are tired, my love, I dare say ; but I don't very often have any one to read to me.'

'No, indeed, I am not tired,' exclaimed Gertrude. 'I used to read to my aunt for more than an hour at a time. Should you mind my finishing the sermon aloud?'

'Oh no, my dear, I should be glad. It is not very long, I suppose?'

Gertrude relieved her mother's apprehension as to the length, and began to read. As she proceeded, Mrs Courtenay laid down the papers which at first she had rustled incessantly, took off her spectacles, and drawing her chair close to Gertrude's, listened as she would have done to the tone of a familiar air sung in a voice she loved.

'That sounds better than when Mr Grantley preaches,' she said, as Gertrude paused, fearing that her mother's attention might be wearied. 'Your voice is so clear I can tell every word, though I am a little deaf. But why don't you go on? isn't there some more?'

Gertrude accordingly continued; and, as she closed the volume, ventured to say, 'If you would like it, dear mamma, I can read another day to you anything that you like.'

'Well, that would be very nice,' replied Mrs Courtenay; 'but are you going away now?'

'Not if you like me to stay,' said Gertrude; 'I was wishing to write something, and I can do it as well here as down-stairs; but I must go and fetch my desk first.'

The desk was in the drawing-room; and Gertrude no sooner appeared, than she was assailed by half laughing, half serious reproaches for running away.

'There,' said Charlotte, drawing a chair to the table, and almost forcing her sister into it, 'you must stay, Gertrude. Here is the book open at the very place; now begin. You have no excuse, for the gardening was all done yesterday; and Jane and I have a good fit on us, and are going to work, so you are bound to encourage us. That is so like you charitable people,' she continued, observing that her sister looked rather puzzled; 'you never will believe that any one out of your own set can do a virtuous action.'

'Some day or other, Charlotte,' said Gertrude, smiling, 'you shall tell me what you mean by a set; but now I must go back to mamma, for I promised I would.'

'Mamma!' exclaimed Jane; 'what business can you have with her? You don't mean that she has admitted you into her cabinet of antiquities.'

'Admitted and begged me to remain,' said Gertrude.

'What have you been doing there? Why are you going back again?' And at the idea of Gertrude and Mrs Courtenay's spending a morning together, even Edith's attention was roused.

'I will tell you,' said Charlotte; 'mamma is going to publish a treatise on the art of knitting, and Gertrude intends to edit it.' Three of the party laughed, but not Gertrude.

'Mamma was busy when I went in,' she said; 'but I did no

observe particularly what she was doing.　And when she saw I had a book, she wished me to read out.'

'Read out what?' inquired Charlotte; 'Smith's "Wealth of Nations," or "Jack the Giant Killer?"'

Gertrude held up the book which she had in her hand, and showed the title.　Charlotte looked slightly abashed; and Edith observed that her mamma had been better employed than she had been.

'Thanks to Gertrude,' said Jane.　'What an immense pity it is that you are not a man, Gertrude.'

'Why! what do you mean?'

'Only that you would have made such a first-rate missionary. I don't think any one could have resisted you.'

Gertrude looked grave, and closed the conversation.　'When I have finished what I have to do in mamma's room,' she said, ' I dare say there will be time for a little reading before luncheon, and I will come back again.'

Edith sighed as her sister left the room, and the sigh was echoed by Charlotte; and then struck with a sense of absurdity, both involuntarily laughed.

'Now, for confession,' said Jane; 'what was your sigh for, Edith?'

'Charlotte is the elder,' said Edith; ' you should apply to her first.'

'Mine!' exclaimed Charlotte; ' I don't know that I can tell. It had something to do with Gertrude, but I am not clear what.'

'And yours, Edith!　Such a lucid explanation is quite an example.'

'I have no doubt what mine was for,' said Edith; 'but I am not so certain that I shall be disposed to own.'

'Envy,' exclaimed Jane; 'that must have been it.　You are envious because Gertrude has such a peculiar knack of making herself agreeable.'

'The strange thing to me,' said Charlotte, 'is, that Gertrude finds time for Edith's duties and her own too.　She takes immense care of her district, and works, and has her days at the school, but she manages her time so well.　I do wish you would take a lesson from her, Edith.'

At another time Edith might have been angry, but Gertrude's humility was infectious.　' I mean to do it,' she said; ' I should be more glad than I can tell to be like Gertrude.　It would be so pleasant to feel that one's presence was like oil upon the troubled waves, and that is always the effect being with her has upon me.'

'A very old simile, very well applied,' said Charlotte. 'I must own that sometimes I am guilty of the weakness of believing that if Gertrude were to set up a convent and turn lady abbess, I should choose to be one of her nuns.'

'It would be a peaceful household, if it had no other recommendation,' said Jane ; 'and that is a rare thing to find in these days.'

'I don't know that,' observed Edith ; 'there are the Grantleys, and their seven children.'

'Peace and seven children ! did they ever dwell together for five minutes?'

'They would if Gertrude was at the head of affairs,' said Charlotte.

'Mrs Grantley is too indulgent ; she is as bad as Laura ; and there is a peaceful household,' exclaimed Jane, sarcastically ; 'Charlie !—to live in the same village with him shakes one's nerves out of all order, and to be in the same house would shatter them to pieces.'

'Allingham is a mystery to me,' said Charlotte ; 'and it has been ever since Edward married. I don't know why, but I never go there without feeling as if I were treading upon a volcano that was going to burst.'

'I can tell you why,' said Jane ; 'it is because of that careworn, abstracted look of Edward's.'

'And Laura's too,' said Edith ; 'I never saw any one so changed as she is lately. One would think sometimes she was brooding over a great crime.'

'To be committed?' exclaimed Charlotte, laughing ; 'Laura is very much indebted to you, Edith, for your good opinion.'

'No,' said Edith ; 'whatever sins Laura may commit, they will never be premeditated. But let the cause be what it will, I am sure she is very unhappy.'

'And Miss Forester is at the bottom of it,' said Charlotte ; 'that I have discovered. Just notice, the next time you have an opportunity, how Laura changes colour when her dear friend comes into the room.'

'Friend !' repeated Jane, with emphasis, 'I could as soon have petted a toad.'

'A viper,' said Charlotte ; 'toads have no sting.'

'A gift peculiarly reserved for human beings, some people

think,' said a gay, gentle voice ; and Gertrude's arm was thrown round her sister's waste, while she looked laughingly in her face.

'Now, Gertrude, that was a speech not intended for your ears, so you have no right to find fault. Besides, I protest against any one taking Miss Forester's part ; and moreover, you look satirical ; and I thought satire was your peculiar horror.'

'Always excepting on certain occasions,' continued Gertrude, in the same light tone, 'self-defence, *et cetera.*'

'Then this is not one—no one is accusing you of being a viper.'

'Only one of my acquaintances—I cannot say friend.'

'No, that would be too absurd. You Miss Forester's friend ! The poles are not more widely separated.'

'Yet friend, too,' said Gertrude, 'inasmuch as she is not my enemy.'

'I would not answer for her not being the enemy of every member of the family,' said Charlotte ; 'Edith's I am certain she is.'

'So much the more reason for taking her part,' replied Gertrude, rather more seriously than before. Charlotte looked at her sister, in the belief that she was in jest : but Gertrude's smile had nearly vanished, and Charlotte saw directly what was in her mind.

'No lecturing ! Gertrude,' she exclaimed. 'I will not bear it, even from you.'

'If one could only conceal one's thoughts better,' said Gertrude ; 'but when grave notions are in the mind, they will show themselves in the face,—in mine at least ; so please not to quarrel with me, Charlotte. Lecturing, as you call it, is my misfortune, not my fault.'

'Well, then, let me hear. I know you won't be happy till you have delivered your testimony.'

'It would be a very long testimony, if I were to begin,' said Gertrude, gaily ; 'and I don't at all think you are in the humour to hear it.'

'Never more so; I made some resolutions upon humility only this morning. Or, stay, I can give a lecture myself just as well. Listen ; I will divide my discourse into three parts : first, the characteristics of Miss Forester ; secondly, those of the venomous reptiles called vipers ; thirdly, the utter dissimilarity between the two ; to be concluded with some practical reflections upon the pernicious habit of evil-speaking. And first for the characteristics of Miss Forester '——

'Which shall be reserved till another day, to please me,' said Gertrude, playfully; 'because if we go on talking now, there will be no time for reading.'

'But I thought you were going to mamma,' said Edith.

'Yes, and I did go, but I happened to mention Susan Philips's name, and then she remembered having promised to mix some medicine for the child, and went to do it ; and I thought I would come down to you in the meantime.'

'We shall be a reformed household in time,' said Charlotte. 'If mamma takes to mixing medicines, and Jane and I to poor work, there will be no calculating upon anything. We may all end our days as Sisters of Charity.'

Gertrude smiled ; and, taking up her book, she begun to read, and so the morning passed ; and to many it might have seemed unprofitable, for Gertrude had nothing to show as the fruit of two hours' labour ; but one glance at the temper of mind culti- vated in her sisters by the sacrifice of her own occupations, might have induced a different opinion. Edith especially felt the difference caused by Gertrude's attention and tact, and stopping her as they were going into luncheon, said—

'I must say one word to you ; really I won't keep you five minutes, but I want you to tell me something. Why do you think Jane and Charlotte find so much fault with me ?'

'What a question, dearest !' exclaimed Gertrude. 'How is it possible that I should tell ?'

'But you must have some notion. Do I ever do disagreeable things ?'

'We all do occasionally,' said Gertrude.

'But I in particular. They are always complaining of me. I know I am untidy, and not at all punctual; but have you ever remarked anything else ?' Gertrude hesitated to reply.

'I should be very glad if you would tell me,' continued Edith ; 'because I often wonder why you suit them so much better than I do, when your notions are quite as different; and I am sure the fault must be in myself.'

'There are some little trifles,' said Gertrude; 'but they are merely trifles. One thing I thought I would tell you of : the other day, do you remember, when you were making breakfast, you had finished before any one, and you went away, and left us all to pour out the tea for ourselves ?'

'But what was the use of remaining? I had a great many things to do.'

'Merely that it was uncomfortable: it disarranged us, and broke up the party, and made us feel as if we ought all to be in a bustle too. And for the time being, you know, you were the lady of the house.'

Edith thought for a minute, and then said, 'Go on quickly, or they will wonder what has become of us.'

Gertrude smiled. 'I really can't remember in such a hurry; especially when they are not such very great offences. I think, perhaps sometimes you irritate Charlotte by your manner of saying you can't do as she wishes, or that you do not like things. You put the objection first, and the desire to oblige afterwards, and then it does not tell.'

'I don't quite know what you mean,' said Edith.

'It is only the turn of a sentence,' replied Gertrude; 'as I heard some one call it once, putting the negative before the affirmative in life.'

'Indeed, that is such a mere nothing,' said Edith.

'So it is; but the impression of the two sentences will be as different as possible ; and I am sure you will find it so if you observe.'

'The objections always come to my mind first,' said Edith.

'They do to most persons ; but if they are spoken they give the idea that you are not pleased, or that you do not wish to oblige, which is the last thing any one has a right to say of you.'

'And is that all?' said Edith; 'I should like to know every-thing.'

'Those are all the great faults I can remember to-day,' said Gertrude, laughingly, 'except, perhaps, such trifles as putting the chair you are sitting in in an awkward place, so as to make the room look uncomfortable; and running away in the middle of a conversation in which we are all interested, as if you did not care about it.'

'If I were not so busy,' said Edith.

'But it is easy to make a little excuse, and then no one would mind. I very often feel a blank when you are gone, as if the subjects we liked were of no consequence to you.'

'No, indeed, Gertrude ; whatever pleases you I am sure pleases me.'

'I know it does in reality; but at the moment I can hardly believe it.'

'One thing I must say,' replied Edith, 'that if we are to be so very particular, you do away with all the liberty of home.'

'Only in little trifles and courtesies,' said Gertrude; 'and I don't see how it can be otherwise, when a number of grown-up people have to live together. If they are not under some restraint they must quarrel. And certainly one's first object—earthly object, I mean—should be to make one's home comfortable.'

'I don't think Jane and Charlotte care much about it,' said Edith.

'Perhaps they have not quite the same principles to act from as you have; but when all are on an equality, some one must yield; and I think those who are most anxious to do right should set the example.'

Edith sighed and exclaimed sadly, 'I am always doing wrong, I know. I make all sorts of good resolutions in general, but I never know how to put them in practice.'

'You will if you study character more,' said Gertrude; 'and consider in the morning what is likely to happen in the day, and what you will be called on to do. It is the being busy and abstracted which makes it so difficult, and the business, I know, you cannot well avoid; though it might worry my sisters less if you could go out when they do, and stay at home oftener in the morning, to practice and read with them.'

'Such a waste of time all that seems,' exclaimed Edith; 'and accomplishments lead to so much vanity.'

'But not if they are cultivated from high motives,' said Gertrude. 'There is a difference between wishing to please and wishing to give pleasure.'

Edith seemed inclined to agree, and to continue the conversation further; but Gertrude was afraid of annoying her mother, and hastened her into the dining-room, where Mrs Courtenay was already beginning to be uncomfortable at her non-appearance.

There were many rumours afloat at Allingham on that day, as to the cause of Mr Courtenay's sudden journey: and the spirit of curiosity was not quelled by the sight of Laura's pale, tearful countenance, as she stepped into her pony carriage, with the intention of driving to the Priory. So visible, indeed, were the effects of her sorrow, that the old butler, who met her as she alighted, was tempted to inquire whether anything was the matter with Master Charlie; but hastily turning from him, she begged to see Gertrude alone, and walked into the library to wait for her. The few minutes of delay were an age ; and Laura stood before the pictures, and looked out of the window, and drew patterns on the carpet with her parasol, whilst her courage sank to its lowest ebb, and she almost resolved to go back as speedily as she had come. There were voices in the lobby and a message was given to a servant, and then a light footstep was heard on the stairs ; and Laura, conquering a strong impulse to run away, moved to the door, and met,—not Gertrude, but Edith. Her disappointment was evident, and Edith, too, did not appear pleased at the meeting. She was dressed for walking, and to be stopped was very provoking.

'You here, Laura !' she began ; 'how strange ! No one said anything about it ; but you are looking so ill,—what is the matter? where is Edward?'

'Nothing is the matter,' replied Laura, quickly ; 'nothing, that is, in which you can help me. I wanted to see Gertrude.'

'She is gone out, but I expect her home every minute. There is something the matter, Laura ; I am sure there is.'

'My head aches,' said Laura ; 'I think I have been walking too much lately.'

'But that is not all,' exclaimed Edith, beginning to be alarmed. 'Won't you tell me where Edward is ?'

'In London, I believe, or at least on his way there. He left me this morning.'

'In London !' repeated Edith ; 'but what took him there ?'

'I don't know,' said Laura, coldly ; 'he did not tell me.'

'And when will he return ?'

'I don't know—possibly the day after to-morrow.'

'O Laura ! this is cruel,' exclaimed Edith. 'I am sure something is the matter.'

'Not particularly with Edward,' said Laura ; 'but I suppose all persons have reasons for looking grave at times.'

'It is not merely being grave,—you are so pale. Can't I get you anything ? a glass of wine or some water only ?' And Edith's manner softened at the sight of her sister's uneasiness, till it became almost affectionate.

'Thank you,' answered Laura, with a faint smile ; 'but you can't do me any good. If I could only see Gertrude.'

'She must be back in a few minutes,' said Edith. 'Are you sure I can't help you ?'

'Quite sure.'

Laura's tone was decided, and Edith felt annoyed.

'I don't wish to intrude upon you, Laura,' she said: 'but it is natural to be anxious about one's own family concerns.'

'Yes, very natural,' replied Laura. 'How long has Gertrude been out?'

'More than half an hour; and she only went to speak to a person about some work. She must be here directly. Are you sure that Edward is well?

'So far as I can be sure from having seen him in perfect health this morning. Indeed, Edith, you need not worry yourself; my concerns are my own.'

'If I could be quite certain about Edward,' said Edith, half speaking to herself; and then she added, in a louder tone, ' He has looked so harassed of late. You say he has gone to London upon business?'

'Yes, private business. Why should you cross-question me in this way, Edith?'

'I did not mean to do it,' said Edith; 'but you make me so anxious by your manner. I only wish to be treated as a common friend,—as Miss Forester.'

Unknowingly, Edith had touched upon a most vulnerable point. Laura's cold dignity gave way under a torrent of bitter recollections, and she exclaimed, ' I have never had a friend. Those whom I looked to for affection neglected me.'

'Do you mean Miss Forester?' said Edith. 'You must indeed have been blind if you expected anything lasting from her.'

'No, no—not Miss Forester,' said Laura, striving to hide her tears; and as the wretchedness of her feelings became more overpowering, she added, in a tone of the deepest dejection, 'If Gertrude had been here, I should never have been left to her.'

Edith had no words to reply. That one sentence was the key to many a misgiving which had lately arisen in her thoughts as to the conduct she had pursued; and as a vivid consciousness of unnumbered neglects flashed like lightning upon her mind, Laura had no cause to dread the confession of her own follies: the heart just awakened to the sense of a hidden fault would have been the last to condemn another. For several minutes both remained in silence, Laura leaning her head upon her hand, and Edith standing by her side, longing, yet not venturing, to offer her sympathy.

Perhaps the delicacy of Gertrude's tact would have suggested, that, under such circumstances, solitude would be the most effectual relief; but Edith had never thought it worth while to observe the effects of her words and actions, and, as a consequence, she had no tact; and would probably even then have forced upon Laura the avowal of her own self-reproach, if Gertrude's entrance had not prevented it. Edith no sooner saw her, than she exclaimed, 'How long you have been, Gertrude! Laura has been waiting for you till she is tired.'

'Not quite that, I hope,' said Gertrude, glancing at her sister-in-law; and untying her bonnet, she placed it on the table, and then made Edith assist in arranging her dress. 'I really could not help myself, though I was uncomfortable all the time, knowing you would wonder where I was. Anne Downer would tell me a long story about one of her children being in disgrace at school. I said I could not understand it, because this was not my week; but she would persist, and at last I told her she should come and speak to you, and she is waiting for you in the hall. Won't you see her?'

Edith left the room, and Gertrude, going up to Laura, who had not till then summoned resolution to look up, placed her hand gently upon hers, and said, as she kissed her forehead, 'I should have been more vexed if I had thought I had vexed you.'

Laura again covered her face with her hands, and tears streamed through her slender fingers. For some minutes Gertrude did not attempt to stop the course of her grief, but at length she said, 'It would be such a pleasure to be a comfort to you.'

'To me!' exclaimed Laura, forcing herself to be calm. 'Gertrude, you do not know me.'

'I know myself, though,' replied Gertrude; 'I know that I cannot bear to see you unhappy.'

'But I deserve it,' exclaimed Laura; 'I have done wrong—worse than you would have imagined. Do not despise me, Gertrude.'

Gertrude shrank from the word. 'It would be sad indeed,' she said, 'for me to dare to despise any one,—most of all my sister.'

'And will you indeed think of me kindly?' said Laura. 'Will you listen to me? I have so much to tell, and I am so miserable —so very miserable.'

'Say to me anything—everything—dearest,' replied Gertrude;

'let it be much or little as you please; only give me the opportunity of helping you.'

Laura heaved a deep sigh: 'That cannot be,' she said; 'even you cannot undo the past.'

'But perhaps I can be of use to you for the future.'

'I have no hope,' replied Laura, mournfully; 'I do not come to you for that; but Edward is gone, and I am alone; and I am so wretched that I cannot bear myself.'

'Edward gone!' exclaimed Gertrude,—'so suddenly! You cannot be in earnest.'

'He is in London: he was called there on business; but he is to be back again the day after to-morrow.'

'And then you will be happier,' said Gertrude, gently.

'No, no,' exclaimed Laura; 'his coming can never make me happier. Not that I do not love him,' she added, eagerly;—love him?—none—none on earth can tell how well; but —— Gertrude, I cannot say it; you must despise me.'

'You will not repeat that again, I am sure,' said Gertrude: 'it pains me very much.'

'But I have deceived,' exclaimed Laura,—'deceived Edward, when he loved and trusted me. Yet, indeed, Gertrude, I did not know what I was doing when I began. Miss Forester urged me to do it. She told me that things were necessary, and I bought them; and wherever she went she was always admiring and wishing for what she saw, and I could not help giving it to her; and there were my own relations, who thought me rich, and looked to me for so much. I was obliged to spend money upon them too, and at last it all came to such a sum, that I was desperate, and was going at once to tell Edward—but she—Miss Forester, I mean—persuaded me not; she said he would be angry, and I knew that was true, for he was in a dreadful state whenever he was asked for money; and then she offered to lend me some, and from that time she used to tease me into doing whatever she wished, and so I could not go on better. She was always alluding to what she had done for me, and if she saw I was inclined to do what she did not like, she used to hint that she should be obliged to tell everything to Edward. I have many times made up my mind that I would confess it all, and rid myself of her, but, when it came to the point, my courage always failed. If I could only have avoided taking her to London, it would have been so much better; but I did not dare; and I was forced sometimes to make Edward angry, by persuading him to allow it, all the time hating it myself. And now, Gertrude, after all this, she has told her father, and I have had such a visit from her this morning. General Forester has said such strange things of Edward. He thinks, I believe, that he is going to be ruined, and that the only hope is for him to give some pledge which way he will vote, and then he will have a government office; and if I were to try and persuade him, General Forester would not mind his daughter's helping me even more than she has done; but if I don't, everything must be told to Edward at once. I thought at the time anything would be better than leading such a miserable life as I have done lately; but afterwards—Gertrude, it would kill me if Edward were to love me less. Even when he looks grave I am wretched; and how could I endure it if he were to change entirely?'

Gertrude's heart sank within her. Laura's statement, rapid, and even incoherent though it was, opened before her a vague but fearful prospect of trial for Edward and every one connected with him; yet even then her ready sympathy did not forsake her. She saw that Laura dwelt far less upon Edward's danger than upon her own fault; and setting aside her impatient desire to hear all that Miss Forester had said, she answered—'Are you not distrusting Edward, by imagining that he could change? Could you do so in his place?'

'I cannot tell,' replied Laura, sadly; 'but he would never have acted as I have done. Yes, he must change when he hears it. He can never think of me as he did.'

'He may not think you faultless, but he will surely forgive one whom he has promised before God to love and comfort.'

'And honour,' exclaimed Laura; 'you forget that, Gertrude. He can never honour me.'

'Not when he sees that you prefer the pain of owning all that has passed to continuing in what is wrong? Dearest Laura, indeed you do him a grievous injustice.'

'If I could only think so,' said Laura. 'Perhaps I might be able to tell all if he were here now; but my courage will never last till he returns.' And after a few minutes' pause, she continued: 'It is easy for you to talk, Gertrude, but you cannot know a wife's feelings. It would be such bitter degradation to confess.'

'But still more bitter to deceive,' said Gertrude. And then, fearing lest the words should have been too strong, she added, 'I know that I cannot tell all a wife's feelings, and I know too that it is easy to give advice which perhaps the person who gives it would be the last to follow ; but, dearest, have you not said yourself that any suffering would be endurable rather than that you have borne lately ?'

' It would only be delay,' said Laura ; ' and if Edward were to follow General Forester's advice he would not be worried about money, and then he would not care half as much when he heard what I had done.'

' And if he does not follow it ?' said Gertrude.

' But he must—there is no help for him. He will not be re-elected if he does not ; and I know he would make any sacrifice rather than fail in that.'

' Not the sacrifice of honour,' said Gertrude ; ' and you would be the last person to wish him to do it.'

' Honour !' exclaimed Laura, with a bewildered look : ' it is no question of honour ; it is merely a political affair, which ladies have nothing to do with.'

' So it is said,' replied Gertrude, ' and so I agree in most cases ; —but has General Forester spoken to Edward himself?'

' Yes, I believe so, a good many times ; but he says Edward will not listen to him ; and I suppose he thinks he will to me. Gertrude, why do you look so pale and shocked ?'

' And Edward is in London, you say?' continued Gertrude.

' Yes, he went away this morning, quite unexpectedly ; he did not even stop to say good-bye. Stay, here is a little note he wrote just before he started.'

Gertrude took the note, and read it hastily.

' He was so grave at breakfast,' continued Laura—' more so than usual ; and Mr Rivers was with him till twelve o'clock last night, and I am nearly sure Edward went to him again this morning. Gertrude, you would not have me make him more anxious than he is !'

' Dear, dear Laura !' exclaimed Gertrude, earnestly, ' do not ask me for advice ! I cannot give you what you will like,—and it is hard to feel that I am disappointing you.'

' Not disappointing,' replied Laura. ' I thought what you would say ; but it cannot be. It has gone with me through my whole life—that power to see the right. But, Gertrude, I am not like you—I have never yet been able to do it. The beginning of my life was weak and sinful, and the end must be so too.' And she burst into tears.

The faint colour on Gertrude's cheek went and came as her sister spoke; and as she watched the expression of despairing suffering which rested upon her young, fair features, a pang of bitterness shot through her heart at the thought of all that she might yet be destined to endure. 'Laura,' she said—and she knelt by her side, and looked fondly in her face—'when you promise your child that you will give him all that he may need, could you bear him to doubt your word?'

'He is too young to do it,' said Laura, in a tone of surprise.

'But if he were older,' said Gertrude, 'would it not vex and pain you?'

'Yes,' said Laura; 'but'——

'But are we not all children?' continued Gertrude; 'and is it not distrust to think that we shall be permitted to remain weak and sinful when we have but to ask for strength and receive it?'

'Do not talk of those things,' exclaimed Laura; 'I cannot listen to them; they have no power to comfort me.'

'Then there is indeed no hope for me,' said Gertrude, sadly; 'I have nothing else to say that can give you relief.'

'And will you leave me?' exclaimed Laura, bitterly,—'leave me to my misery?'

Gertrude's answer was in action more than in words. With the tenderness of a mother for a petted child, she threw her arm round her sister's neck, and, gently unloosening her bonnet, said, as she laid her head upon her shoulder, 'How could I leave you when you have confided in me?'

'And you will still love me,' murmured Laura, 'though I cannot feel as you do?'

'I must love you through everything,' said Gertrude; 'but it is a love which will but give me pain, if I may not talk to you upon the only subject which can be a blessing to you.'

'A blessing to the good, you mean, not to me,' replied Laura. 'There is no blessing for me, Gertrude; I am not worthy of it.'

'And who may expect it, if worthiness is needed?' said Gertrude. 'You may have done wrong, very wrong; but if there is no help for you, there can be none for the best of human beings. Will you not think of this, and pray?'

'It will not make me happy,' said Laura, in a faint voice.

'Yes, in time it will, it must,' replied Gertrude. 'If at this moment you could be assured of Edward's pardon, it could not be sufficient for your happiness without the pardon and the assistance of God; but if you have that you need not fear anything.'

'My life has been so different from yours, Gertrude. I cannot think about it at all now. When I have nothing else upon my mind I will try to be better.'

'And if that time should never come—if you were never to find courage to speak to Edward, and were to go on for years with this secret preying upon you?'

Laura shuddered.

'It is the power to do right which you want,' continued Gertrude; 'and that power cannot be obtained by your own efforts, and therefore you cannot look forward to any time when you will be able to amend. I know that you are miserable, dearest; and perhaps it seems idle to talk so generally, when you are thinking only upon one subject; but I cannot offer you comfort, which I feel to be false. I may tell you that Edward will forgive, and I am sure he will; but I am sure also that his forgiveness is not all you require, and that if you trust to yourself you will not have courage to ask it. You would not bear to believe that your future life was to be like the past.'

'No, no!' exclaimed Laura, vehemently.

'And you have owned to me that you are wretched, and that you are most grieved for having acted wrongly; and you wish me to help you. O Laura! why will you not confess this to One who can?'

'But,' exclaimed Laura, 'it is no use to be sorry, and pray to God to forgive me, whilst I am deceiving Edward.'

'No,' replied Gertrude; 'and if you feel this, there can be no doubt of your duty.'

Laura was silent.

'For Edward's sake, for your own sake, for all our sakes, do not delay!' continued Gertrude, in a deep, earnest tone. 'Only say that you will not—only ask that your courage may not fail!'

Still Laura was silent. The agitation of her mind was fully visible in her countenance, and twice she strove in vain to answer. At length, rising from her seat, she said, with a forced effort, 'I shall see you, Gertrude, to-morrow. I cannot talk of other things now.'

'To-morrow, if you will,' replied Gertrude; 'and shall it be at Allingham?'

Laura busied herself with her dress, and appeared not to hear; and Gertrude added,—'If I might, I should ask to be with you this evening. I should only be unhappy here in thinking you were alone.'

The manner in which this was said completely overcame Laura's effort at self-command. 'Why are you not with me always!' she exclaimed. 'Then I might be different; but now'——

'Now you will think of all we have been saying,' replied Gertrude, affectionately, 'and resolve, but not in your own strength, and then promise that you will act.'

'Yes,' began Laura, earnestly, 'I will promise you;' but Gertrude stopped her—'Stay, dearest,' she said; 'a promise is too sacred to be given in haste. When we meet this evening you will have had more time for consideration.'

'And you—will you not go back with me?' said Laura, imploringly. 'I have many things to say besides this one. If Edward should not return in time, what shall I do on Thursday? I am feeling so ill and tired, as if I could not possibly receive all those people alone.'

'You must trust that Edward will keep his word,' said Gertrude, encouragingly; but Laura's sigh reminded her that both his absence and his presence would be equally painful. 'At any rate, we can talk over your difficulties to-night,' she added; 'which will be more convenient to me than going back with you at once; and with so many sisters, it will be strange if you are left without some help.'

Laura tried to smile, but her heart was too heavy, and her manner alone showed her consciousness of Gertrude's affection.

CHAPTER XXXI.

IF Laura had need of solitude, it was not less required by Gertrude; and, dreading interruption, she shut herself up in her own room to think at leisure upon what she had heard. The interest of the conversation had prevented her thoughts from dwelling upon the fears which had been awakened for Edward, but when Laura was gone they returned in full force. She was too keen-sighted not to have perceived that something had been preying upon her brother's spirits ever since her return to the Priory; but it was the fashion to attribute it to parliamentary worries, and the style of living at Allingham forbade any one to think that economy was at all requisite. Even the conversation which she had held with her sister on Torrington Heath had only made her uncomfortable for the moment; as Edith herself seemed then to think that her former apprehensions were groundless, and it was difficult for Gertrude's charity to believe that one so perfect as Edward in word and feeling, could be so faulty in practice. And now, it was not that she at all surmised the true state of the case, but she was oppressed by that dark, fearful apprehension of coming evil, which is often experienced by persons whose early lives have been free from trial, and who know that, in the course of God's providence, affliction must sooner or later be at hand. Sad visions of care passed before her as she thought upon Edward, but there was something worse than care, which she scarcely dared to dwell upon. If he were embarrassed, who could tell how strong might be the temptation to free himself at any sacrifice ; and little as Gertrude had hitherto known of political affairs, she felt that the pledge proposed by General Forester could scarcely be consistent with strict honour. She tried to persuade herself that she had mistaken Laura's words, but the impression of them still remained. She reasoned, but reason was useless. It seemed impossible that Edward could act so dishonourably, but the firmest characters had failed in less trying circumstances. It was unlikely that the proposal had been made, but certainly Laura had mentioned it. General Forester was not a man of any weight, and Edward would not listen to him ; but he had lately been his chief guide in his election affairs. Gertrude's clear intellect was bewildered with fear. She closed her eyes, striving to shut out all that might distract her, that so she might more clearly see whether anything could be done to guard her brother from the temptation. Money seemed the one thing required ; and as she felt this, a doubt, painful almost to agony, crossed her mind. With an involuntary effort she resisted it, but again it came. Gertrude's conscience was not one to be trifled with. Once more she turned from it, but only for an instant ; and when still, through every other consideration, the question forced itself upon her, she knelt to pray that if the sacrifice of her long-cherished wishes were required, it might be made without repining. The words had scarcely been uttered, when a knock was heard at her door, and a servant begged that she would go and speak to Mrs Courtenay. Gertrude's first impulse was to send an excuse. It seemed impossible at that moment to give attention to any one ; but respect for her mother conquered her reluctance. and without delay she went to her room. Mrs Courtenay was resting after a drive to the county town, but seemed full of business and excitement.

'Ah! my dear,' she exclaimed, 'you have not been out. That is very wrong; you will never be well if you shut yourself up so. And what have you been doing? We have had such a nice drive. I saw the child, and she is a great deal better,—quite a different creature,—that medicine is so remarkably good; though, by the by, they have made it up very badly. But, do you know, we were intending to call at Allingham, and they told us at the lodge that Edward was gone to town; and Johnson says that Laura has been here, and that she was looking ill, and it put me in such a fright that I sent for you directly.'

'Laura has been here,' replied Gertrude, in a tone which, to any other ear than her mother's, would have betrayed a painful effort; 'I don't think she was looking particularly well, but I shall hear more about her this evening, for, if you have no objection, I am going to drink tea with her.'

'Objection, my dear! no, what objection could I have? but you had better order the carriage directly—Foster is not half as punctual as he used to be.'

'Laura will be alone,' said Gertrude, 'for Edward is gone to town.'

'But what for? He said nothing about it yesterday; and why doesn't Laura come and drink tea here, instead of taking you away. It would be much more sociable; just let me send and say so. Edward can't really be gone, though,—there is the party on Thursday; he must be at home then.'

'Laura hopes he will,' said Gertrude; 'but if he should not, she must do as she can without him; so I had better go to her this evening, because she wants to talk over some arrangements, and they would only be tiresome to you.'

'Oh no, my love! not at all tiresome. There is nothing I like better than arrangements. But it is best to let young people please themselves, so if you like to go, do; only don't let Laura think we should not have been glad to see her. I must give you some sugar-plums for Charlie, which he was to have had this afternoon, but we did not go in.' Mrs Courtenay dived into the depth of a most capacious reticule, and drew out one by one its various contents, commenting upon each as she laid it on the table. 'That—no, that is not it; it was a little square box; there are some lozenges for you in it too, my dear. I heard you cough last night several times. Wait one minute, I must take out the parcels first, and then I shall find it. The ribbon is for my morning cap; and the gloves I bought at Earl's—Sadler's gloves are so bad, they don't wear any time. So provoking it is! what is wanted first, is always sure to be last. Dear me! Jane forgot her letter for the post.'

'Can I help you, dear mamma?' said Gertrude, in consternation at the sight of a little packet of bills, two more boxes, and a thimble.

'No, my dear; no, thank you. I shall find it presently; it is one of these, but they are so much alike.'

'There is the first dinner bell,' said Gertrude, mildly.

'Never mind, my dear; it won't signify about your dress, we are only ourselves. So tiresome this is! I do think I must have left the box at Earl's.'

'Perhaps some one will be going to the town to-morrow,' said Gertrude, 'and then it can be asked for.'

'Well! that would be a good plan; but—now I recollect—I left the sugar-plums on the drawing-room mantelpiece, just by the middle vase; you had better go and fetch them, my dear, or somebody will be sure to take them.'

Poor Gertrude! what would she not have given for those few minutes alone;—but it was not to be. The sugar-plums were found, and brought back; and then, considering that Gertrude was in the room, and her maid not, Mrs Courtenay thought it better to trouble one than the other, and suggested that her bonnet should be put in the wardrobe, and her shawl in the drawer, and all the other *et ceteras* of her walking dress properly provided for, till the second bell rang before all her wants were attended to, and Gertrude had only time to make a hasty toilette, and descend to the dining-room with an apology for being late. The dinner appeared interminable; and, with all her endeavours, Gertrude could not prevent herself from occasionally beginning to weigh the conflicting claims of Edward and the church. Charlotte addressed her twice without being answered, and Jane several times begged for the salt in vain; and then both began to rally her upon her unusual abstraction, till the tears rushed to Gertrude's eyes, and a choking sensation was felt in her throat; and, as a last resource against observation, she pleaded—what was indeed the case—a bad headache. Edith watched her with the greatest uneasiness, and followed her to her room when dinner was over, to seek an explanation, but Gertrude could not feel at liberty to give it. All that she owned was that Laura was unhappy about some personal affairs, and had come to consult her; and this, with the headache, was the best information Edith could obtain.   She was silenced, but not convinced, and was just beginning an account of her own interview with Laura, when the carriage was announced, and the few minutes, which Gertrude had calculated upon having to herself, were gone. Yet there was no impatience in her replies, no annoyance in her countenance, not even a symptom of irritation in her manner, when Mrs Courtenay stopped her in the hall, to entreat that she would send an excuse to Laura, and go to bed, or (if that were impossible) take a dose of sal-volatile before she set off.   She did, what the most obedient of daughters would scarcely have thought necessary; and Mrs Courtenay returned to the drawing-room, to spend a comfortable evening, satisfied that poor, dear Gertrude's headache was nervous,—she could tell it from the way in which her hand trembled when she held the glass,— and nothing could be so good for nervous headache as sal volatile.   Charlotte resisted the notion of Gertrude's having any nerves; declaring that, in nine cases out of ten, they were only an excuse for ill-temper.   Jane complained very much of her going away; and Edith strongly took her part; and, in the olden time, such a source of disagreement might have brought on a skirmish of words for at least half an hour; but Edith had not passed several months under the same roof with Gertrude without learning something of her way of preserving family harmony; and the proposal of a few turns upon the terrace with Charlotte, followed by a little music, was successful in restoring unanimity of feeling.

It was late when Gertrude returned.   The drawing-room was empty, and the lamp extinguished, and with silent steps she stole up the stairs to avoid disturbing any one.   But Edith's quick ear had caught the sound of footsteps, and gently unfastening her door, she beckoned her sister to her room.

'They are all gone to bed, except me,' she said, as Gertrude entered; 'but I could not make up my mind to go till I had seen you, you looked so miserably ill when you went away.'

'Did I?' said Gertrude, with a faint smile.

'Yes; and you are not much better now.   There must be something very much the matter.   Why won't you tell me?'

'Perhaps I might tell you part,' replied Gertrude, 'though of course not what concerns Laura personally.   Do you remember something you said to me a few months ago when we were walking on Torrington Heath—it was about Edward?'

'And my fears?' said Edith, 'and Mr Dacre's? Yes, I remember it perfectly.'

'If they should come true?' continued Gertrude, in a calm voice.

Edith started. 'O Gertrude! tell me; pray tell me! What do you know?'

'Hush! dearest,' replied Gertrude; 'we must not frighten mamma; and I do not exactly know anything.'

'But you suspect something.'

'I suspect—indeed, I am nearly sure he is in very great difficulties. I guessed it from some facts Laura told me this afternoon, and I have been talking to her since; and though she will not face the possibility of the case being a bad one, she allows there is something amiss.'

'Then it has really happened as Mr Dacre and I imagined,' exclaimed Edith, bitterly; 'and Edward has been wilfully blind. What fortune of two thousand a year could stand the expenses of six.'

'How?' said Gertrude, and her tone of surprise awakened Edith to the consciousness of having betrayed her brother's secret.

'It is scarcely a thing to be kept private, now,' she replied; 'at least from his own family. When Colonel Courtenay died, the Allingham property was worth only two thousand a year; but no one knew it except Edward and his lawyers, and the one or two persons who learned it from him. My mother was never told, nor Jane, nor Charlotte; but at that time he kept nothing from me.'

'And Laura?' said Gertrude.

'I cannot tell. I have often tried to find out; but we have known so little of each other intimately, that it was impossible to do it; and after Edward married he threw such a veil of mystery over all his affairs, that I could not ask him anything about them.'

'Laura does not know, I am nearly certain,' said Gertrude. 'I have been talking to her a great deal this evening, and she has given me an account of their London life. Even with six thousand a year they would have been dreadfully extravagant.'

'Yes,' said Edith, 'I know they must have been. Charlotte spent one spring with them, and gave us details of enormous expenses; but it was just then that every one was praising Edward's talents and prophesying that he would be a great man, and I thought less about it.'

'And do you really mean,' said Gertrude, 'that Edward's income has never been more than what you say?'

'Never; and it was the knowledge of this which made me tremble at the election.'

Gertrude almost shuddered at the very name of the election. 'Tell me, Edith,' she said, after a short pause, 'if Edward's affairs are really in the state which we fear, how will he be able to bear it? Will he have courage to face the evil?'

'No,' said Edith, sadly, but decidedly. 'He will drive it from his thoughts till it is forced upon him without the possibility of escape. And then,—I cannot tell'——　And poor Edith turned away to hide, even from her sister, the bitterness of her feelings. 'You have never loved him as I have loved,' she said, when Gertrude strove to comfort her. 'You cannot know how all my purest enjoyments have been blended with him. If I have ever had a good thought, or been able to conquer a bad feeling, it was because of the principles he taught me; and he is good— he must be good now; others have been extravagant, too—it is not a sin. Gertrude, dearest—only say so; say you do not think the worse of him.'

It was a painful appeal for Gertrude's sincerity. Wilful extravagance involves so much of self-indulgence, and thoughtlessness, and neglect of solemn duties, that she could not bring herself to answer.

'You may condemn him,' continued Edith, eagerly; 'but if you had but known him as he once was—so noble, and kind, and careful for every one, and thinking so little of his talents, and only wishing to do good! Gertrude, he was perfect; yes, indeed, he was perfect; and oh! how I loved him.'

'And we all love him now, dearest,' said Gertrude; 'and must try to help him. And it was this which I wished to speak to you about.'

'And can you help him?' exclaimed Edith, a gleam of hope lighting up her countenance.

'Not permanently, but I might do something for the present; only then'——, the sentence was unfinished, but Edith understood it.

'No!' she exclaimed, 'that cannot be. After all your wishes —your plans—and it would not be right.'

'I cannot say,' replied Gertrude, quietly. 'There may be duties even greater than the building of a church. If it were to save him from a great temptation, Edith—from the sacrifice of his highest principles?'

'But is it so?' said Edith, in alarm; and, after a minute's consideration, she added, 'and if it were so, your fortune is so small.'

'It would be something; it might stay the evil, though not prevent it.'

'But you could not,' exclaimed Edith. 'The church has been your dream for years; you said so only the other day.'

'Yes,' replied Gertrude: 'yet that may be the very reason why it may be necessary I should relinquish it.'

Poor Edith felt confused by the conflicting ideas which presented themselves to her mind, and could not realise the danger to Edward's principles to which Gertrude had alluded. 'Have you really determined upon giving up the church?' she said, at length.

'No; I have not had time for considering the subject, and as yet everything is uncertain. But merely upon the supposition, I like to think how I should be bound to act. How could we endure any person's assisting him upon terms which are not honourable?'

'How could we endure any person's assisting him upon any terms?' interrupted Edith, proudly. 'Do not mention it again, Gertrude. A Courtenay submit to an obligation! Even Jane would sacrifice her last farthing to prevent it.'

'The Courtenays may be doomed to greater trials than that,' said Gertrude, mournfully. 'Dishonour is more galling than obligation. I would give—but it is not right to distrust—only it seems as if there would be less cause to fear if Edward were not gone.'

For some minutes Edith stood mechanically playing with the candle, and gazing upon its light; at length she said, 'Can you not fancy, Gertrude, what it would be to be borne along by the eddies of a whirlpool—to see before you the gulf in which you must sink, and to feel yourself at every instant approaching it with greater velocity?'

'Yes,' said Gertrude: 'life has its whirlpools, and this may be one; but we need not be afraid of sinking without the power of rising again; it would be a want of faith. Hark, Edith! the clock is striking twelve. How frightened mamma would be if she were to hear us!'

'Never mind,' replied Edith; 'we shall neither of us sleep very much, if we do go to bed.'

'But I have so much to think of,' said Gertrude: 'indeed I must not stay.'

'I would rather not go to sleep,' replied Edith; 'there will be the waking to-morrow with that vague, horrible feeling of some unknown evil hanging over one.'

'And the gradual dawning of the truth, and the wretchedness of the full reality,' added Gertrude, attempting to smile, as she took up her candle to go; 'but we will not fear; it is wrong.'

Edith's reply was a whispered 'God bless you, dear, dear Gertrude;' and the sisters separated, Edith remaining to meditate upon the long-dreaded events which seemed now approaching, and Gertrude stealthily treading the carpeted floors, to avoid disturbing the household, before she reached her room. And with what different feelings did she now enter it from those which had so filled her heart on the previous evening! There were the same walls, the same furniture, the same books. There was the table piled with drawings of churches, which it had been her pleasure to collect from her friends. There was the desk, on which lay the letter which she had finished for Mr Dacre. There were papers scattered about, on which she had even proceeded to make calculations of different items of expense. But the charm of all was gone. Scarcely allowing herself a glance, she replaced the drawings in her portfolio, and the letter and papers in her desk; and, forgetting the lateness of the hour, and the mental fatigue she had undergone, once more knelt to ask for strength, both in judgment and in action, and then set herself seriously to consider what ought to be her conduct under the circumstances which Laura had more clearly explained in their evening conversation.

CHAPTER XXXII.

THE breakfast party at the Priory was not now what it had been, when, more than four years before, Edith had so sighed over the absence of family union. Mrs Courtenay still complained of sleepless nights, and Jane lamented her habitual ill health; Edith also took as great an interest in the parish school, and Charlotte talked as lightly, and cut bread as diligently as before. But the sharp edges of character had been much worn away by the influence of tact and example ; and, notwithstanding their serious causes of uneasiness, Edith would have hesitated to exchange her present feelings, had they not been mixed with self-reproach, for the loneliness and discomfort which she had experienced on the morning when she received from Miss Forester the first hint of Edward's intended marriage. All trials are comparatively light whilst the sanctuary of home is untouched ; and Edith, though burdened with regret for the past and forebodings for the future, could still be thankful for the mercy which was sparing her the additional pain of domestic discord. Gertrude, however, was not so fully alive to the effects of her own conduct, and still saw much which she longed to alter ; but every other feeling was now engrossed in anxiety for Edward.

A sleepless night had brought its natural consequences—a continued headache ; and Mrs Courtenay's faith in sal-volatile was rather shaken, when she observed Gertrude's heavy eyes and pale lips.

'You were so late last night, my love,' she said ; 'Mitchell told me that you were not back till after eleven, and I am sure I heard you moving about after twelve.'

Gertrude pleaded guilty to being late, but said 'that Laura never went to bed early herself, and so persuaded her to stay.'

'And talk over to-morrow, I suppose,' said Jane. 'What does she intend to do, all by herself?'

'She depends upon Edward's returning,' said Gertrude ; 'but I tried to persuade her not to do it. It seems very uncertain.' .

'If it is uncertain,' observed Charlotte, 'you may be quite sure what will happen. Gentlemen only say they are uncertain when they have fully made up their minds, and have not courage to confess it ; and Edward hates archery parties.'

'Yet they are better than anything else,' said Edith—'less formal, and not so expensive.'

'Who cares for expense at Allingham ?' exclaimed Charlotte. 'Besides, from what I have heard Laura say, I suspect this will be anything but an economical affair.'

'A splendid imitation of the Vivian parties last year, I suppose,' said Jane.

'It will be an extremely pretty thing, if it is well managed,' said Gertrude. 'They are going to light up the conservatory in the evening, and give up the drawing-room for dancing, and the library is to be used for the reception-room, and the dining-room for the *déjeûner* and the refreshments.'

Edith sighed audibly, and Gertrude, fearful of her attracting observation, hastily continued—

'Laura will have so many things to do to-day that I have promised to help her. She is not at all equal to any exertion.'

'I don't think I shall go,' said Jane : 'it is a very agreeable thing to talk about ; but one pays a dreadful penalty afterwards for being amused.'

'Laura said she hoped we should all go,' observed Gertrude ; 'and, if Edward is not there, we might be extremely useful.'

'Yes,' said Charlotte ; 'she might station us at different places, with certain divisions to look after. Remember, I put in my claim for the dining-room. I venture to say I shall be more popular than any one of you.'

'The reception is the awkward part of the business,' said Gertrude ; 'half the persons invited are election acquaintances, and Laura has never seen them above once or twice, and some not at all.'

'I am not sure that I like these huge omnibus parties,' observed Charlotte ; 'one gathers up such a quantity of scum with them.'

'It is better than having the scum alone,' said Jane. 'If you must invite disagreeable people to your house, it is far better to swallow them whole, with something to make them palatable, than to have a separate dose of each individual.'

Gertrude felt distressed at the turn the conversation was taking, and quietly made an effort to divert it. 'Laura and I were wondering last night,' she said, 'whether Mr Dacre would go. He had a most pressing invitation, and says he will if he feels equal to it, but I suspect that is more than half an excuse.'

'I don't want to see him there,' said Charlotte ; 'he would be out of his element.'

'How unkind, my dear !' exclaimed Mrs Courtenay ; 'and we all make so much of him when he comes here.'

'The very reason why I hope he will keep away from Alling-ham,' replied Charlotte ; 'I respect him too much to wish to see him in a false position.'

Mrs Courtenay adjusted her spectacles, and looked at her daughter for a minute, but, reading no explanation of her words in her countenance, returned to the newspaper ; and Edith, weary of a trifling conversation, when her thoughts were engrossed with more important subjects, took the opportunity of a pause to rise from the table, and beg Gertrude to go with her into the garden.

'How can you talk with such indifference, Gertrude,' she exclaimed, when they were alone; 'and about things which come home to one so painfully? I thought I must have left the room when they were discussing the archery party.'

'I thought so too, at first,' replied Gertrude. 'Certainly nothing could be more contrary to one's inclinations than talking about it, except, perhaps, joining it: and poor Laura is so sadly worried, she says that if Edward does not come home, she shall never be able to go through with it. That is one reason why I suggested our all going; for really, if she is as unwell to-morrow as she was yesterday, we might be of the greatest use to her.'

'Not you, I am sure,' said Edith; 'you are more fit now to be in your bed than anywhere else.'

'To make up for want of sleep last night,' replied Gertrude, with a sad smile; 'but I am more comfortable upon one point. I have determined upon consulting Mr Dacre as to what should and might be done; and I have written to him to ask him to come to me this morning.'

Edith's face brightened with greater satisfaction than she had yet experienced. 'Yes,' she said, 'there is no one else to help us: and, Gertrude, I told you; he knows all. He learned it from some business transactions which he had with Edward's lawyer —that is, he guesses it, for I suppose he could not have been told details. But it is so strange. I cannot realise that there is any reason for great alarm, as I did last night. Then I was utterly miserable, now I think I am only irritable and impatient.'

'It is because everything about us is just the same; and besides, sunshine and beautiful scenery help persons through so much, when they are not absolutely overwhelmed.'

'And another feeling I have,' said Edith, 'is, that if anything is going to happen, I long that it should come at once. I think I could make up my mind to bear a great calamity, but it is the sitting still and watching for it which tires me.'

'Suspense is a great temptation to impatience, certainly; but the calamity will come soon enough, I suspect. There was something in the tone of the little note Edward wrote to Laura yesterday which makes me think he must be prepared for some shock, and that he is wishing to prepare her too.'

'Any change would be bad for her,' said Edith. 'To be obliged to reduce, with her habits, would half kill her.'

'I think you do her injustice,' replied Gertrude; 'she has one point of character, which is everything as a foundation.'

'Truth; yes, I acknowledge that.'

'And take her from Miss Forester, and place her in situations of trial, in which others are dependent upon her, and I am nearly sure you would find her very superior. Trial would strengthen her religious principles.'

'Religious principles!' exclaimed Edith; 'she has none;' and then, shocked at her own words, she began to qualify them: 'I mean, that she has never acted upon any.'

'It is hard to say that, when we cannot look into the heart,' said Gertrude; 'and Laura's candour, and good temper, and love for Edward are, it may be almost said, germs of religion;—very weak, indeed, and in themselves nothing, but showing that there is a good disposition to work upon.'

Edith walked on for several minutes in deep thought. 'Gertrude,' she said, at length, in a very serious tone, 'I felt yesterday, when Laura was miserable, as if I was the cause of it, and I was miserable too. I could almost wish that the feeling would continue.'

'Not exaggerated,' said Gertrude; 'there can be no good in that.'

'But,' said Edith, 'perhaps it is not exaggerated. Perhaps I might really have worked upon all the good which you say is in her character; and if she had been a different person, Edward might have been so too. I can speak about it calmly now, but I could not have done it last night, when I lay awake thinking upon it.'

'I am afraid,' said Gertrude; 'even the best of us would have something to regret, if we were to compare what we have done with what we ought to have done.'

'But what should you say,' continued Edith; 'do you think I have been very much to blame?'

'You must remember that I was away from you; how can I judge?'

'You can form some idea; you know something of what passed from what I have told you. I am sure you think I have done very wrong, and you are afraid to say it.'

'I am not afraid, if you are not afraid to hear it,' replied Gertrude.

Edith stopped suddenly, and her countenance changed; 'I did not believe,' she said, in a voice of mingled agitation and displeasure, 'that I was likely to be of any use. And there were other duties which I had been accustomed to, and I did not like to neglect them.'

'It seems cruel in me to say anything at this moment,' replied Gertrude.

'No one can think it is cruel to receive an opinion which has been asked for,' said Edith, with a little pique in her manner.

'But, perhaps, I implied more than I ought; there is such a difference between an error of judgment and a wilful fault; and, after all, it is impossible I should be able to decide how far you were right in acting as you did.'

'You need not retract,' said Edith, in the same proud tone; 'your first words were sufficiently plain.'

'Plainer than I meant them to be; and I am vexed with myself for using them, because they have given you a false impression.'

Edith bit her lip, without answering, and moved a few steps towards the house, and then, as quickly returning, she exclaimed, while tears rushed to her eyes,—'Gertrude, I am very wrong, but you have made me really wretched.'

'If I might only tell you, dearest, what I meant,' replied Gertrude.

'But I know it,' said Edith. 'You mean that I have been the cause of it all; that I might have prevented it.'

'No,' replied Gertrude; 'not *the* cause, as if there were only one. Edward's own weakness has been the cause, and his hasty marriage, and his ambition. There have been many causes.'

'But I have been one,' persisted Edith. Gertrude could not deny it, and Edith was not in a state to listen to any extenuations that might be offered.

'Yes!' she exclaimed, 'if I had been at Allingham oftener, and tried to please Laura more, perhaps I might have been to her what you are now; but she says that I neglected her, and she is right. And now the time is gone, and I can never make amends.'

'Do not say that.' said Gertrude; but Edith interrupted her.

'I must say it, for it is true. How can I make amends now ? Who can recall the years that are passed, and how can I save Edward and Laura from misery ? And when the worst is come, and they are ruined—ruined for their whole lives—how shall I feel, when they look back and say I was the cause of it ?'

'They cannot say so,' replied Gertrude, gently ; 'if they blame you, they must blame themselves far more.'

'It is no comfort,' said Edith ; 'do not think of it, Gertrude. Words are useless.'

Gertrude felt that at such a moment it was too true ; words were useless. And when Edith again walked away, though not proudly, as before, she did not attempt to follow her; but leaving the torrent of excited feeling to exhaust itself, before attempting to offer advice or consolation, she re-entered the house to find her mother, and occupy herself with her till the arrival of Mr Dacre. And now, as often before, Gertrude experienced the benefit of that self-control which she habitually practised. With her attention absorbed by one subject of anxiety, she was yet mindful of the duty she had imposed on herself the previous day ; and Mrs Courtenay's smile of pleasure, as she opened the door and told her she had been expecting her, would alone have been a sufficient recompense. But the effort, though painful at first, served to divert and relieve her mind ; and when before she had ended, the sound of a bell announced, as she believed, Mr Dacre's arrival, she scarcely dreaded the interview. It was not, however, Mr Dacre. It was a note, saying that he should not be able to call at the Priory till the afternoon ; and at the same time came a few hasty lines from Laura, begging that Gertrude would on no account delay going to her, adding, as a postscript, that the pony carriage had been sent, in order that there might be no excuse.

'I am so sorry for it, my dear,' said Mrs Courtenay; 'but it is all right, of course ; and do tell poor Laura to send here for any thing she may want for to-morrow ; plates, or glasses, or knives and forks.'

Gertrude could scarcely forbear smiling at the notion of Laura's knowing anything about the importance of providing such humble necessaries ; but she did not enlighten her mother's mind as to the extent of her daughter-in-law's ignorance of domestic affairs, and only assured her that there was no doubt the housekeeper would ask for all that was required.

'And Foster shall go for you earlier to-night, my dear,' added

Mrs Courtenay. ' It is bad for you to sit up late, and Laura, too, will have enough to fatigue her to-morrow. So mind you don't consent to stay longer than ten o'clock.'

Gertrude promised to attend to her wishes, and set off; leaving, however, a note to be sent to Mr Dacre, with a request that he would, if possible, see her at Allingham in the course of the day.

' My mistress is in her bedroom, ma'am,' was the information Gertrude received upon alighting ; and, to judge from the appearance of the lower part of the house, a bedroom seemed likely to be the only safe refuge from carpenters, housemaids, and footmen, who were rushing to and fro with chairs, and tables, carpets, benches, and lamps, all in preparation for the next day. But Gertrude moved on through the confused mass of furniture, without overturning more than one chair, or entangling herself more than twice with balls of packthread ; whilst she felt a little amused at the sudden transformation of the elegant, orderly house and establishment, though distressed at what must be an additional expense, at the very moment when economy was above all things needed.

CHAPTER XXXIII.

' YOU see what a state we are in,' exclaimed Laura, with a forced laugh, as she opened her door, just in time to save Gertrude from being struck by a long ladder which two men were carrying along the gallery : ' I have scarcely ventured out of the room the whole morning, and it has been so lonely.'

' Has it, indeed?' said Gertrude, kindly ; ' I thought you would be too busy to want me.'

' It would be absurd for me to interfere much,' said Laura ; ' my housekeeper understands everything; so I give the orders occasionally, and leave her to see them executed. But you must not think that I can never bear solitude. It is only rather bad just now.'

Gertrude was beginning to express regret for not having been with her sooner, but Laura stopped her : ' I cannot bear excuses from you,' she replied, sadly ; ' I have no claim upon you, or upon any one. It is very kind in you to come at all, and perhaps

you will read this, and help me to decide what is to be done;'
and she took up a letter which lay on the table.

Gertrude looked at her sister, as she spoke, with deep compassion. Her brilliant complexion was faded, and almost sallow;
her eyes were heavy and sunken; her lips parched; and even her
dress, so generally admired for its neatness and elegance, seemed
carelessly thrown on without any attempt at arrangement. 'You
know the handwriting,' continued Laura.

'From Miss Forester?'

'Yes, but I do not understand much more of all she refers to
than I did yesterday.'

Gertrude received the letter, and began to read, but found herself by no means as much perplexed as Laura. It commenced
with protestations of the strongest affection, which no circumstances, however trying, could weaken; it then went on to recall
the proofs that had been given of sincerity, hinting at enormous
sacrifices made, with no hope of an adequate return; and declaring that all which had been done was as nothing compared with
the happiness of being of service to one so dear. Then followed
mysterious allusions to impending dangers, from which there
could be no escape except by Mr Courtenay's following General
Forester's advice; and at last came vehement entreaties that, in
order to save herself and all around her from misery, Laura would
undertake to persuade her husband to yield his opinion upon
points of no importance. The letter ended with renewed protestations of affection, and as a postscript were these words:—'I
have said nothing about our own private affairs; delicacy forbids
me to enter upon them in detail; but you will yourself be the
best judge how far you can venture to explain all that has passed
to Mr Courtenay, at a moment when my father knows him to
be harassed almost to desperation. Delay I fear is impossible,
as my father will no longer allow matters to remain in their present state. I need scarcely say how sincerely I desire that you
should promise to use your influence in bringing Mr Courtenay
round. If his pledge were once given, my father's natural fears
on my account would be at rest, and I should be able fully to
indulge my own wishes.'

'What does it mean, Gertrude?' said Laura, as her sister
laid the letter upon the table with a disgust which she scarcely
endeavoured to suppress; 'is there really any harm in it?'

'Can you doubt it?' replied Gertrude, who, with all her
knowledge of human nature, scarcely understood, as yet, to what

extent a person of Laura's character would be influenced by a wish; 'I do not, of course, know all that General Forester requires, but there can be no question of its involving a sacrifice of some honourable principles.'

'I don't see that,' said Laura, musingly; 'and Edward would be happy again if he were out of his difficulties.'

'But, my dear Laura, is it a case which concerns General Forester, or anything he has said or done?   If he were to offer to settle everything, without any conditions, could you consent?'

Laura's lip quivered, and she could scarcely restrain her tears. 'I thought of it all last night, when you were gone,' she answered, in a half-frightened tone; 'and I said over to myself all that Edward would say, and fancied him just opposite to me, listening; and afterwards I went to bed, and then it came to me again, —the same scene I had been picturing: but he was changed. He looked at me as he had never done before, and he said that his love was gone; and I threw myself before him, and clung to him, and prayed him to forgive, and he spurned me.   Yes, Gertrude, he spurned me; and I know it must be so.'   And Laura leaned her head upon the table in agony.

'And will this save you, dearest?' said Gertrude, quietly. 'When you have gained your point, and Edward is in possession of all you expect, must not the confession be made?'

'But the time is distant,' replied Laura; 'he will be happy, and he will not care.'

'Happy that he has been mistaken in his wife?—that she talked to him, and persuaded him, apparently for his own good, when in reality she had secret motives of her own?   O Laura! concealment between any friends is dangerous—between a husband and wife it is certain misery.'

'I would only delay,' said Laura, faintly.

'And if delay could save you from suffering, without being wrong, can you think that a sister would not be more willing to help you than Miss Forester?'   Laura seemed unable to reply; and Gertrude, placing a sheet of paper before her, and a pen in her hand, said, 'It is but the work of a few moments, and it may be for your happiness for years; only say that you have resolved to speak to Edward.'

Laura took up the pen almost unconsciously; it seemed as if the burden upon her mind had destroyed her power of self-guidance; and trusting instinctively to Gertrude, she wrote the words which were dictated. But they were no sooner ended, than she drew her pen across the paper, and casting it aside, rose hastily from her seat, and walked the room.

'Go, Gertrude,' she said; 'you have done all that was in your power, and it is vain. Why should you distress yourself more?'

'No,' replied Gertrude, firmly; 'it cannot, and it must not be in vain. The decision is to be made now, and if you will not follow me, you must follow Miss Forester. Will you write and tell her so?'

Laura looked hopelessly around, as if seeking some means of escape.

'Will you bind yourself to her,' continued Gertrude, 'to be her friend and companion,—to have her with you always,—to risk even Edward's annoyance, rather than her anger? And will you consent to feel that General Forester knows more of your private affairs than your husband, and that at any moment he may betray you?'

'And can you be cruel, too, Gertrude?' exclaimed Laura; 'then my last hope is gone.'

'Not cruel, dearest,' replied Gertrude, earnestly, 'but merciful —most merciful; for I would save you from years of suffering.'

'And at what price?' continued Laura. 'You talk to me in ignorance, for you cannot understand my feelings.'

'And do you really think I cannot?' replied Gertrude. 'Do you think I cannot tell what you will feel when you have placed yourself in Miss Forester's power, and how you will shrink from Edward's love and confidence, and how bitterly you will repent having yielded to the temptation of this moment?'

Laura heaved a deep sigh, and again took a sheet of paper from her desk, and recommenced her note; but she had only written the first words when it was once more put aside. 'It is useless to write,' she said; 'I know she will call by and by, and I will see her.'

'The note may prevent her calling,' said Gertrude: 'Laura, why will you delay? If you are grieved at having deceived him, why will you not take the first step towards truth?'

Laura shook her head, but made no attempt to write : and Gertrude, vexed and disappointed, moved away from the table, when a sound of footsteps on the stairs caught her ears.

'She is coming,' exclaimed Laura, in a feeble voice of terror, and she sank into a chair. Gertrude ran to the door and locked it ; then, returning, said in a low voice, as she seated herself by Laura's side, while her whole frame trembled with agitation—

'You said to me yesterday that you would promise ; and I would not take your promise ; but now, if you have ever loved me, you will give it.'

Laura raised herself in her chair, and with a look of anguish her eye rested upon her husband's picture.

'Remember,' said Gertrude, as she watched the expression of her countenance : 'there is but one moment ; it is a decision between confidence in him whose every thought, whose whole heart is yours, or in Miss Forester. Laura, you must promise.'

Laura threw herself upon her sister's neck, and whispered, ' I will promise, but I cannot see her.'

'It shall be my duty,' said Gertrude, rising. 'Go into the dressing-room, and trust in me to say and do all that is necessary.'

Laura left the room ; and Gertrude, unlocking the door, admitted Miss Forester. There was a start of surprise at the meeting, followed by an expression of pleasure ; for Miss Forester, on the same principle which induces a child to stroke a mastiff, was always lavish of her civilities in proportion to her awe : and she had long since discovered that Gertrude was not to be dealt with as an ordinary person.

'I am afraid I am intruding,' she said, as she looked in vain for Laura : 'I was told I should find Mrs Courtenay here.'

'My sister has been here,' said Gertrude, with an emphasis upon the word *sister*, which served to remind her visitor that in Laura's house she had more right than a friend to feel at home : ' but she is not able to see any person just now, and I must ask you to excuse her coming to you.'

'Oh certainly, if it is necessary. I should have supposed, though, that Mrs Courtenay would have made an exception in my favour. Is she so very busy ? '

'Not busy,' replied Gertrude, 'but she is desirous of being alone. Can I be of any service in taking a message to her ? '

'I think she would admit me, if she knew I was here,' replied Miss Forester, stealing on tip-toe to the dressing-room door ; but Gertrude dexterously placed herself before it.

'I am sorry to prevent you,' she said ; 'but quiet is so essential to my sister, that I cannot allow her to be disturbed.'

A frown gathered on Miss Forester's brow, but her tones increased in gentleness, as she replied, ' Indeed ! I am so grieved to hear it.   How long has she been so unwell?   It must be quite a sudden seizure.'

'It is no seizure,' said Gertrude, coolly ; 'but she has had a good deal to think of this morning.'

'Ah, yes ! all the arrangements for this grand party ; but she is so energetic about everything.   I am afraid she has worried herself, without waiting for me to come and help her, as I promised.   Between ourselves, my dear Miss Courtenay, she is like many other lovely young creatures of her age,—not at all prudent.   I saw a great deal of it when we were in town lately : and when we go up again, I intend to keep a strict watch upon her.'

'Thank you,' said Gertrude, politely ; 'but with regard to her occupations to-day, the housekeeper manages everything so well, there is scarcely any necessity for Laura's interference.   She has been engaged this morning upon rather a different subject—this letter'—and she pointed to the lengthy epistle which lay upon the table.   Miss Forester glanced at it, and turned pale ; and then glanced a second time, and coloured; and stretching out her hand to take it, said, with a faint laugh—

'Oh ! that—it is not a matter of any consequence; to-morrow will do just as well.'

'I beg your pardon,' said Gertrude, 'but my sister is of opinion that no day can be like the present for business of this kind ; and being unable to undertake it herself, she has begged me to arrange it for her.'

'Certainly—if you will—no one more competent '—— began Miss Forester, and then stopped in confusion.

' She would be sorry,' continued Gertrude, 'for either General Forester or yourself to be misled as to her intentions.'

'My father would be unwilling to hurry Mrs Courtenay,' said Miss Forester, 'but—I may speak plainly, I see, to you, my dear Miss Courtenay ; it is a very awkward business.'

'Particularly so,' replied Gertrude, in a tone which Miss Forester did not entirely like or understand.   'If you will do me the favour to listen for a few minutes,' continued Gertrude, 'I think we shall be able to put things on a better footing.   With regard to my brother's opinions, General Forester must judge for himself how far it is right to urge any gentleman under any circumstances to profess a change without conviction.   It is a political affair with which my sister has no desire to intermeddle.'

'Oh yes, very right, quite natural ; but my father is so devoted to Mr Courtenay's interests—so anxious for his welfare,—Mrs

Courtenay may safely trust him,' said Miss Forester, evidently much piqued.

'Possibly,' said Gertrude, quietly; 'but in the present instance there is no necessity for trusting to any one. Laura would have spoken to my brother this morning if he had been at home, as she is desirous that you should no longer be inconvenienced by the assistance you have been kind enough to give her. In my brother's absence, perhaps my cheque will be equally satisfactory.' And without waiting for a reply, Gertrude seated herself at the table, wrote an order for six hundred pounds, and put it into Miss Forester's hands. It was received mechanically. For the first time for many years Miss Forester was sensible of shame;—she felt that Gertrude knew her.

'It is correct, I believe,' said Gertrude, rising. 'Perhaps you will do my sister the favour also to return the different bills of her London trades-people, which you have had the goodness to keep.'

'I really—I did not wish—I scarcely expected'—stammered Miss Forester. 'I should be so sorry to give Mrs Courtenay any additional trouble just now.'

'Pray do not distress yourself,' said Gertrude. 'It will involve no trouble to my sister; she merely wishes my brother to see them when he returns.' Miss Forester's keen face expressed incredulous surprise, but Gertrude did not choose to explain farther than was necessary. 'Perhaps,' she said, in a tone which, notwithstanding her native humility, was tinged with hauteur, 'you will also be kind enough to say to General Forester, that my sister prefers leaving to him the task of persuading her husband to profess a change of principles. She has neither the inclination nor the power to attempt it herself.'

Miss Forester looked things unutterable; but as she attempted to speak them, her spirit quailed before the calm, pure dignity of Gertrude's manner. Something she murmured of interests, and wilfulness, and regret, but the sentence was lost in confusion, as her eye met Gertrude's searching glance, fixed as if she could read her inmost thoughts; and, thrusting the cheque into her reticule, she turned away and glided from the room, without appearing to notice Gertrude's civility, when she hastened to open the door, and politely wished her good morning. Gertrude listened to her retreating footsteps, and when the hall door was closed against her, drew a long breath, as if relieved from a great oppression. The first act of the sacrifice she

expected would be required had been made, but she did not for
an instant regret it. Laura was saved from temptation; and if
Edward's affairs were prosperous, the obligation would soon be
repaid; if not, the experience of that morning had left but little
doubt upon her mind as to the course to be pursued. And
now, her first impulse was to go instantly to Laura, and tell her
she was free from Miss Forester's snares; but a little consideration checked her. When she had once owned what had
been done, it would be difficult to insist upon Laura's keeping
her promise, since it might appear that she had a personal
interest for urging it; and though Laura's word had been given,
Gertrude still felt doubtful whether, when the moment for confession came, she would not make some excuse for putting it
off. Yet it was a difficult resolution to keep, when, as she
entered the dressing-room, Laura sprang from the sofa, and
entreated to be told all that had passed. Gertrude gazed with
pity upon the countenance once so full of happiness, now so
marked by sorrow, and longed, as she had seldom longed before,
to act against her knowledge of what was right. One smile,
such as Laura had given in brighter hours, would have repaid
and satisfied her; but the time was not arrived; and Gertrude,
though with an effort known only to herself, could be as firm in
inflicting pain, as she was gentle in soothing suffering. A few
words of explanation were soon given. Gertrude merely thought
it necessary to say that she had told Miss Forester that Laura
declined interfering in political affairs, and intended upon
Edward's return to take some steps for the immediate settlement
of her affairs; and Laura, although she felt frightened at being
thus bound to her promise, without the possibility of delay,
seemed in a degree more satisfied. Edward's displeasure was
indeed inevitable, but she was no longer called upon to struggle
against her own failing resolution; and Gertrude, trusting that
she would now be able to take a little rest, persuaded her to lie
down, and left her.

CHAPTER XXXIV.

AND rest Gertrude required herself, but more for the mind
than the body; and hoping to find refreshment in solitude
and the open air, she wandered into the Park. On other occa-

sions, the beauty of nature had never failed to soothe her in her greatest uneasiness; but on this day its influence was gone. There were dark shadows passing over the distant hills, and thin lines of blue smoke curling upwards from cottages half hidden by trees; and the sunlight rested upon the tall spire of Elsham church, as it stood with its 'silent finger' pointing to the sky; and before her spread the green sward sprinkled with wild-flowers, and parted into dells and glades by the inequality of the ground, and the varied masses of oaks and beeches, the growth of years gone by. But Gertrude looked at all with a saddened heart. She seated herself on the trunk of a splendid tree, which had been one of the finest in her brother's possession, but which now lay leafless and prostrate, and closed her eyes, striving to forget, if possible, a beauty associated with so much earthly care. But care still haunted her—thoughts of Edward, and his talents, and his influence and station, and the account which must one day be required of him; and, shrinking from the prospect, she raised her head, and, turning involuntarily from the lovely land-scape before her, looked up into the clear, blue sky. It was the faint image of heaven,—taintless and unchangeable; and Ger-trude dwelt upon its purity, and strove to pierce into its depths, as if seeking to reach that home of peace, where her spirit longed to be. For she felt that the struggle of life was beginning. Hitherto the current of her existence had flowed smoothly and tranquilly, unmarked by sorrow except in the one first grief, which had left little but peace behind it. But those unruffled days were now vanishing. She was to feel, and act, and judge; to bear with others' sufferings,—to stand prepared for any duty; and though she had long looked forward to the day of trial, there was a natural failing of the heart at the first perception that it was near. And it is a bitter consciousness—(none can tell how bitter but those to whom it has been given)—when we are wakened from our youthful dream of happiness by some stern reality, and know that from henceforth it may never be indulged again—when an all-powerful though an all-merciful hand has passed over the beautiful vision we so fondly cherished, and its dazzling colours have faded beneath the touch, and we see that the form is the same, but the lustre can never be recalled. We may have thought that our minds are ready for the change,—we may have pictured it to ourselves, and sorrowed for the inevi-table hour, and even prayed for strength to bear it,—but the experience of one real grief will teach us what no preparation will impart. It will show us our own weakness, and the vastness of that mercy which stooped to share a nature endowed with such capacities for suffering. It will force us to look upon the unknown future with a chastened and a thoughtful eye; and whilst it bids us bear thankfully in our hearts the remembrance of our early joy, as the type granted us by God of the blessings reserved for us in heaven, it will tell us that from henceforth the warfare of human life must be ours; and that, till the grave has closed upon our heads, we may hope but for intervals of rest.

And so it was with Gertrude. Till within the last two days she had never known the value of the unanxious life which she had hitherto led. Not that a mind like hers could be insensible to mercies, or blind to the possibility of losing them; but her anticipations of the future had been vague and unreal, and from principle she had never suffered herself to dwell upon them. And now, almost without warning, trial seemed near at hand, and in the form most at variance with her own disposition. She could think, and repent, and amend for herself; but Edward was beyond her reach, except through that privilege of intercession, the power of which we so little understand; and to some minds the sufferings of others are far more dreadful than any personal sorrow. Sad, however, as Gertrude's meditations were, she felt that as yet she did not comprehend all that it might be required of her to bear. There was still much cause to hope that her fears might be unfounded; and in a calmer frame of mind she would have reproached herself for giving way to what might be a causeless dread; but in her present excited state—feverish from wearying thought, and want of sleep, and the agitation of the morning—it seemed that the worst reality would be preferable to the wretchedness of apprehension. It was a morbid state of mind—most unusual and painful; and Gertrude had indulged it only for a few minutes when she was conscious that it was wrong. She tried to bring her mind to the right temper of unhesitating faith, and was striving to collect her thoughts to pray for a spirit more in accordance with the will of God, when an approaching footstep startled her; and she turned and saw Mr Dacre coming towards her. Gertrude rose, and was about to utter an exclamation of pleasure; but the words died upon her lips as she saw the expression of his countenance. It was grave and sad—far more than usual; the lines of care more rigidly marked, and the anxiety of his mind revealed by the frown upon his forehead, and the compression of his lips.

'I have frightened you,' he said, in a deep tone, observing that Gertrude did not speak: 'I was told you were walking in this direction, and I knew you were wishing to see me.'

'Thank you, yes,' replied Gertrude ; and she reseated herself on the fallen tree, for her knees trembled so that she was unable to stand.

Mr Dacre looked at her with compassion. 'You have been exerting yourself too much,' he said, 'and you are ill.'

Gertrude shook her head, and, endeavouring to recover herself, said faintly, 'It was very kind in you to come so far.'

Only a morning's walk,' replied Mr Dacre ; 'and perhaps our meeting will be better here than elsewhere ; it will be less liable to interruption.'

Gertrude raised her eyes to his, and as they met, unable longer to endure suspense, she exclaimed, 'If you have anything to tell me, I would hear it now, at once—only speak.'

'And might I not say the same ?' he replied : 'I came at your request.'

'My request !' exclaimed Gertrude : for in the confusion of her feelings she felt a difficulty in recalling all that had been in her mind.'

'Yes ; and I hoped you were going to mention some way in which I might be of service to you.'

'Edward' —— began Gertrude, and then paused, scarcely knowing how to introduce the subject of her fears.

'Mr Courtenay is absent, I know,' continued Mr Dacre. 'He is in London on business.'

'But is he well ? have you heard anything ? will he return to-morrow ?'

'I have heard nothing of his movements,' was the reply ; 'but the dissolution of Parliament is hourly expected : will not that account for his sudden journey ?' His voice was steady, but his manner was agitated ; and Gertrude said, firmly—

'It is useless to attempt reserve ; there can be but one cause of uneasiness where Edward is concerned. You have heard, I am sure, the reports that are abroad, and you know that they are well founded.'

'I have just left Mr Rivers,' replied Mr Dacre, very gravely ; 'and therefore I cannot be totally ignorant.'

'And you can tell me,' exclaimed Gertrude, while the colour rushed to her pale cheek; 'is it what they say ? Has Edward indeed been acting so blindly ?'

'I will tell you all that I know,' replied Mr Dacre ; 'it is right you, at least, should be prepared for what must in all probability soon come.'

'At least,' thought Gertrude ; and she mechanically repeated the words to herself.

'Mr Courtenay has acted blindly indeed,' pursued Mr Dacre ; 'but we must be careful in our condemnation. He has done but what thousands have done before him, and perhaps with less excuse. The chief object now must be to prevent him from engaging in another election. It would be madness.'

'But is there nothing to rest on ?—no hope of retrieving ?' exclaimed Gertrude. 'If I could but know the worst !'

'It is soon told ; and I see that it will be no kindness to keep it from you. If anything could have been done to stay the evil, I hope I need not say to you who would have been most anxious to assist ; but in the present condition of your brother's property, his best friends cannot aid him.'

'But not for the present,' exclaimed Gertrude, eagerly,—'not to save him from a great temptation ?'

Mr Dacre looked at her in astonishment.

'I forgot,' she continued, and she bent her eyes upon the ground, for she was about to speak against those who were among his nearest connections : 'I fear that what I say may displease you ; but surely Edward's friends are guilty of a grievous error in urging him to pledge himself to them against his own convictions, and offering to reward him by an appointment.'

'Indeed I do not understand you,' said Mr Dacre. 'I have heard nothing of this,—who is your authority ?'

'Laura, and General Forester,' replied Gertrude, hesitating, as she pronounced the last name.

Mr Dacre started,—every muscle of his countenance seemed working with repressed indignation, and broken exclamations of 'base !' 'mean !' 'dishonourable !' escaped him, notwithstanding his utmost efforts to be calm. At length he said, as he leaned for support against a neighbouring tree, 'You may tell me all. General Forester's opinions and mine, I know, are very different.'

'It is but little that I have to tell,' replied Gertrude. 'The offer has been made, and General Forester has been strenuous in urging it, and hitherto Edward has refused it. I have known this only within the last two days ; but when I was told of it, I was told also of his embarrassments, and then it was that I became alarmed lest he should yield.'

'And do they really think,' exclaimed Mr Dacre, vehemently, 'that any cause will prosper when such means are used to promote it ? And if they were to bind your brother to them as they desire, what recompense could they offer him in return ?'

'They would save him from——ruin,' said Gertrude, and her voice trembled as she spoke.

'Do not believe it,' replied Mr Dacre, gently, but very gravely, as he seated himself by her side. 'It is better that such a delusion should be taken from you at once. Your brother may think—possibly he does think—that there is hope ; but there is none. If now the whole of his property were sold, he might be freed from his difficulties, but he would be left——without resource.'

Gertrude felt paralysed. Miserable as her suspicions had been, they yet fell short of the reality.

'If you knew—if you could imagine,' continued Mr Dacre, 'the bitter pain of being the first to open your eyes—but it may save you all from worse suffering. Let him pause now, and no one will dare to lift up a finger of reproach against him. Another year, spent as the preceding ones have been, and his loss may involve the sufferings of many others.'

'And does he know this ?' said Gertrude.

'Yes,' replied Mr Dacre, 'he knows it as far as words can make him acquainted with it ; but I am afraid he does not realise it. This morning I went to Mr Rivers, in consequence of the report which had reached me, for I hoped it might have been in my power to do some good ; and he then told me that for many months he had been endeavouring to force the truth upon him, especially since the election had been thought probable. Yesterday morning, when the dissolution was announced as certain, your brother went to make some inquiries, preparatory to coming forward a second time ; and when the hopeless condition of his affairs was at last put beyond doubt, he gave no hint of his intentions, but started immediately for London.'

'Then it is done,' exclaimed Gertrude, clasping her hands in agony ; 'oh that he had been spared the trial !'

Mr Dacre scarcely knew how to reply.

'You believe it is so,' continued Gertrude, raising her eyes to his face, with an expression of calm wretchedness which was more touching than any words ; 'or perhaps,' she added, in a voice so faint that it almost died into a whisper,—'perhaps you are certain of it.'

'No, no, indeed,' exclaimed Mr Dacre, eagerly, 'I am not certain of it. I am totally ignorant of the cause of his sudden journey.'

'But can you not follow him? Can you not save him? Can no one warn him?'

'It is too late,—he is to return to-morrow.'

'Dishonour!' murmured Gertrude to herself, in a low, bitter tone.

'There is hope,' said Mr Dacre; 'we must think of that. The temptation is less than you imagine—at least if he should allow himself to reason. It may be delay, but it cannot be escape.'

'God grant that he may see it,' said Gertrude, with a sigh of relief; 'it may all be borne but that : and when he had done it he would never know happiness again.'

'No ; and it is the knowledge of this which may give us hope that he will pause. His high sense of honour is not often to be met with.'

'And if he is firm,' said Gertrude, 'the alternative is ruin.'

'The world would call it so, but you will not.'

'You are right,' exclaimed Gertrude, eagerly ; 'there can be no ruin where there is no dishonour. If I could know that Edward were saved from that snare, I think I could see Allingham a desert, and scarcely consider it a trial.'

Mr Dacre gazed on her with sorrow, for he knew that she was little aware of her own feelings ; and the next moment Gertrude's mind had turned from herself to one who would be a far greater sufferer. 'Laura!' she exclaimed, in a tone of anguish, and unbidden tears rushed to her eyes.

'Do not think,' said Mr Dacre,—'if it is possible, do not think. There must soon be trial on every side of you ; but if you dwell upon it you may be prevented from alleviating it.'

'And can it be alleviated?' exclaimed Gertrude. 'Is it in my power? Tell me quickly, for it will be my only comfort.'

Mr Dacre looked towards the hamlet on the heath, the dark cottages of which were at that moment touched by the lustre of the mid-day sun ; and Gertrude felt the direction of his eyes, though she had not followed it.

'Do not fear to speak,' she said, gently ; 'I have already thought of it. It was a bright dream, but I was not worthy of it ; and it is over.'

'And can you indeed relinquish it?' said Mr Dacre, with

mingled pity and reverence: 'shall you have no regrets—no doubts?'

'Regrets!' exclaimed Gertrude, mournfully. 'It was the vision of my happiest days—the charm of my solitary hours. It has kept me from so many vain and evil thoughts, that it has seemed as a guardian angel sent to chase from my heart every earthly feeling; and I thought that it was blest by God; but His ways are best, and I must learn to think so.'

'You will think so,' said Mr Dacre; and he took her hand affectionately. 'The bitterness of this moment will pass—not it may be soon—not entirely for years; but it will pass; and when you look back upon it, you will own how great has been the mercy which has taught you, in your youth, to sacrifice your purest wishes without murmuring.'

'And now,' said Gertrude, 'tell me what I must do. You say that I cannot save Edward.'

'No,' replied Mr Dacre. 'His only safety will be in giving up Allingham immediately.'

Poor Gertrude shrank from a truth which she had not ventured before to utter, even to herself. 'His home!' she said, and her eyes wandered over the beautiful park, and rested upon the splendid colonnade, which was seen as the termination of a long vista of trees.

'It will be a heavy trial,' said Mr Dacre, 'but who would not rather leave his home with honour than live in it with self-reproach?'

'And where will he go?' exclaimed Gertrude, overwhelmed by the prospect which was opening before her—'how will he support himself? He will never consent to be dependent upon us.'

'The usual resource is a residence in a foreign country.'

'Oh no!' exclaimed Gertrude, 'he cannot do that. His life would be without object—he would be miserable, and his talents would be wasted.'

'I am glad you think as I do. There are indeed grave reasons against leaving our natural duties, though there may be cases in which it is necessary; but I do not see that your brother's is one. His profession is still open to him.'

'If he would return to it!' exclaimed Gertrude, while a feeling of hope lighted up her countenance; but it died as quickly as it had been excited. 'Who will persuade him to do it?' she added.

'That must be your duty. He will not bear the idea at first, for he will feel that he is exposing himself to public observation; but if he should consent, you' ——

'Yes,' said Gertrude, interrupting him; 'I see it now. If my fortune were Edward's, he would begin life a second time with comfort. But you do not know him—he will never listen to the offer.'

'I do not know him as you do, yet I think if it is in the power of any human being to induce him, it will be in yours.'

'He is proud,' said Gertrude; 'he will shrink from the very idea of obligation.'

'Not so much to a member of his own family—and you must remember the proposal may be made as a loan, not as a gift.'

Gertrude thought for a moment. 'Yes,' she said; 'it may be a loan now, and a gift in years to come.'

'That may not be necessary,' said Mr Dacre. 'If your brother should prosper in his profession, he may be able to repay the obligation, and you will be once more free to follow your own wishes.'

But Gertrude shrank from the words, as if struck by a sudden pain. 'Talk to me of Edward and his plans,' she said—'not of that;' and she turned away her head to conceal her tears.

'Forgive me,' said Mr Dacre; 'I thought it might have given you comfort.'

'No, no,' she replied, eagerly. 'Years must pass before I could venture to hope it; and I feel, now that it has been denied me, as if it would still be wrong to cherish the wish. But,' she continued, with greater unreserve, 'it could not have been presumptuous; the property was Edward's, and the people were so miserable; and lately I have been amongst them very often, and fancied them peculiarly my own charge, because I had been told by the rector that I might have a school at one of the cottages, and Edith and I had planned it, and next week we were to have talked to Edward about it, and to have made Laura take an interest in it; but it must all go now.'

Mr Dacre did not try to comfort her; he felt that it would do no good.

'It may be superstitious,' she continued, 'but I have sometimes had a horrid feeling in returning from the heath, as if there was a curse on the rest of Edward's property because of it;' and forgetting her resolution of forcing her thoughts from the subject, she fixed a long and earnest gaze upon the little hamlet.

Mr Dacre was still silent.

'If we could only look upon our fellow-creatures as we did in childhood,' added Gertrude, 'when they seemed but moving machines, and we lived with them, day by day, and had no consciousness that they were immortal.'

'You would not wish it,' said Mr Dacre.

'No; I would realise truth at whatever sacrifice of happiness: but there are moments when it is almost more than one can bear.' And rising, she walked a few paces apart; and, as Mr Dacre followed her with his eye, the remembrance of one, who, like her, had given up the best years of a young and happy life to the service of her God, and who was, he trusted, then reaping a glorious reward, rose before him. If Edith resembled his child in features, Gertrude was even more like her in character, and it was with a father's pity that he felt for her grief, and longed to inquire whether the idea, which, during the conversation, had been gradually strengthening in his mind, could ease the burden upon hers. After a few moments, Gertrude returned, saying that she wished to go back to Laura; but Mr Dacre observed that the cloud still rested upon her spirits. She spoke but little, and walked slowly and thoughtfully. There was no opening for what he wished to say, yet he could not leave her in such a state of depression; and as they approached nearer to the house, he became nervously anxious for some occasion of renewing the conversation, though conscious that his intended plan might to some minds give pain rather than satisfaction.

As they stopped at the shrubbery gate, Mr Dacre saw that Gertrude expected they should separate. 'My road lies in a different direction from yours,' he said, 'but you must let me go with you a few steps farther. I had one thing more to say to you.'

'I had many to say to you,' replied Gertrude; 'but I am afraid to leave Laura alone when she is ill. Perhaps we shall be better able to tell what is to be done after Edward's return.'

'I was not going to speak of him, but of yourself.'

'You would teach me to be satisfied,' said Gertrude, with a melancholy smile.

'I was going, not to teach you,' he replied, 'but to suggest a notion of my own, which might possibly—I do not know—but it might accord with yours; and if it did, it would give me greater satisfaction than I have felt for some years.'

'Is it what I can do?' asked Gertrude.

'Not what you can do, but what you would have done.'

Gertrude looked bewildered, and Mr Dacre was vexed. He had hoped that she would have guessed his meaning. 'I am a solitary man,' he said, 'with few claims in England, though many in a distant land; and perhaps the best offering I could make for the benefit of a place which is associated with so much of early happiness, would be the church in which we are both so interested.'

Before the sentence was concluded, its meaning had flashed upon Gertrude's mind. Respect and gratitude struggled fearfully with the keenness of a disappointment which till that instant she had never fully realised; and, yielding to a sudden impulse, she turned away without one word of reply. When she again looked for Mr Dacre, he was gone.

Poor Gertrude! it was a bitter moment—one that in after years was never remembered but with penitence and shame. She, who had believed that her will was subdued, even as her reason was convinced, had been betrayed into coldness and un-thankfulness towards the person whom of all others she most reverenced. With a heavy, aching feeling of regret, which none can understand but those who have suddenly failed when they surely trusted that they stood firm, she entered the house; wretched at the recollection of her proud, rebellious spirit, and doubtful whether it would ever be possible to re-establish herself in Mr Dacre's regard. After some thought, she determined upon writing to him at once, confessing her weakness, and begging him to return as early as possible, to assure her of his pardon. 'I cannot attempt excuses,' were the concluding words of her note; 'they will not raise me in your estimation, or render me less unworthy in my own; but as you once re-minded me that you could enter into a father's feelings, so, as an erring child, I would entreat you to forget, if possible, my apparent ingratitude. I believe I was disappointed at not being permitted to follow my own will; and the only evidence that will really convince me I am forgiven, is such as I scarcely dare to ask; but if I might be allowed to assist you in any way, it would prove to me (what now it is difficult to hope), that you will still give me the blessing of your friendship.'

CHAPTER XXXV.

WHEN this note was despatched, Gertrude's mind was comparatively relieved. She had done her utmost to atone for her fault in human eyes, but the fault was not therefore forgotten. It still remained, to increase the burden upon her spirits; and her manner was so altered, when she went to her sister's room, as to excite Laura's observation.

'I was going to ask you, Gertrude,' she said, 'to go downstairs and see what the people are about, but really you look so fagged, I don't think you ought to do it. Where have you been walking to?'

'Only into the Park. What shall I do for you below?'

'Anything you please. They have been to my room for orders half a dozen times already; and at last I said no one should come again on any pretence whatever; for my head aches so dreadfully, I cannot bear it.'

'Lie down again,' said Gertrude, 'and let me place the cushions for you, and then you shall send me about just as you please.'

'That is what I don't want; I had rather it should be as you please. There is some fuss about the conservatory; it must be lighted at night, and yet we want it to look pretty in the day, and they can't exactly tell how to manage it.'

'I will do my best,' said Gertrude; 'but you must remember it is not much in my way.'

'Quite as much as it is in mine,' said Laura, sighing. 'Edward had planned it all, and we talked it over one night; but I don't know exactly what he decided on. Is it not strange, Gertrude, how differently one feels now about things from what one did a few years ago?'

'Or a few months ago,' thought Gertrude, but she did not say it; though it seemed almost wrong, knowing what she did, to allow Laura to remain in ignorance of the whole truth.

'I think so much about to-morrow,' continued Laura; 'and ever since you have been away, I have been startled when I have been trying to go to sleep, by some sudden noise, which made me fancy Edward was here; and once I thought I heard Miss Forester's step; but you don't think she will come again, do you?'

'No,' replied Gertrude, 'you are safe from her at any rate; and as for Edward, we may hope that after to-morrow'——

'To-morrow!' interrupted Laura, in a tone strangely different from usual ;—'I feel as if to-morrow would be the end of one life, and the beginning of another. I have feared many days in my life, but none like it. Gertrude, what will come after to-morrow ?'

There was a wild sadness in the expression of her sparkling eyes, which chilled and startled Gertrude. She trembled, lest excitement and agitation should be about to produce fever ; and again entreating Laura to lie down and rest, she left her, and went down-stairs. Here she found everything in very much the same state of confusion as she had left it. In the absence of a presiding head, there had naturally arisen a conflict of public opinion ; and carpenters, gardeners, footmen, and housemaids, had all considered it incumbent on them to leave their several stations, in order to give their ideas for the general good. There was an assembly of the lower house in the entrance hall ; and the housekeeper, who justly considered herself entitled to at least the casting vote, was declaiming vehemently in favour of silver sconces, instead of oil lamps, when Gertrude appeared on the staircase. 'Hush! hush! here is the young lady—here is Miss Gertrude!' was murmured around ; but the full tide of Mrs Dickson's eloquence was not to be stopped by either mistress or master. 'How should they know?' she said ; 'which one of them was there that could tell a silver candlestick from a tin one, till she taught them the difference ; and now, for them to sit up and judge ! But it was the way of the world. She'd seen enough of it, and all she longed for was a quiet life, only she would see justice done. While she lived at Allingham, there wasn't one that should say that things weren't handsome : and silver sconces and wax candles there should be, if she bought them, and paid for them herself.'—'But 'tis what we all wants, that things should be handsome,' interrupted the butler ; and he was proceeding to expatiate in his turn upon the opposite side of the question, when Gertrude, stepping in amongst the group, caused a sudden dispersion. The carpenters took up their hammers, the housemaids their brushes and dusters, the footmen returned to their occupations ; even Mrs Dickson vanished, though not before Gertrude had overheard her issuing strict orders to one of the men, to run down to Elsham and tell them to send all the wax candles in Johnson's shop—there wouldn't be one more than was wanted, and if there was they could easily be returned. Gertrude could not smile. The thing might be a trifle—an accident—but it was a sympton of a most dangerous disease.

'Perhaps, ma'am, you'd be so good as to show us how we are to go on here,' said one of the workmen, accosting her respectfully; 'they've brought up the evergreens, but we don't know how Mrs Courtenay chooses to have them put; and Mrs Dickson says there's to be some flowers stuck up somewhere.'

Gertrude followed, rather as if about to superintend the preparations for a funeral than a *fête*. Her head swam, her eyes were dizzy, and the complete transformation of the house made her feel as if in a painful dream. The drawing-room was empty and uncarpeted, and strewn with branches of laurel, laurustinus, and evergreen oaks, some of which were carelessly piled against the delicate paper on the walls, and others struck against the splendid glasses, without taste or design. Gertrude sighed at the task before her, and, as a preliminary step, was going to propose that the room should be half cleared, when a merry voice exclaimed—

'*Chacun à son goût*, Gertrude. I should not have said this was yours.'

'Necessity,' said Gertrude, with a faint laugh; 'but what brings you here, Charlotte?'

'That which takes all women everywhere—at least, so say all men—curiosity. Where is Laura?'

'Up-stairs, very unwell.'

'That means I am not to see her; but I shan't break my heart. Mr Dacre, you may venture in—there is no one here.'

Mr Dacre appeared in the door-way, but was evidently shy of coming forward.

'What was your correspondence about?' whispered Charlotte to her sister. Gertrude's reply was a deep blush, and Charlotte looked very malicious. 'I shall leave you to your *tête-à-tête*,' she said, 'and when you have finished, you may send for me.'

'My errand is soon done,' said Mr Dacre, turning to Gertrude; 'I received your note just as I was talking to your sister, and I walked back with her to say, that if you had any plans or drawings you can let me see, I shall be very much obliged. Good-bye to you; I won't keep you when you are so busy.'

'Good-bye,' said Gertrude, and her voice shook; 'you shall have the drawings this evening.' And as she held out her hand, there was a long, warm pressure, which told that all was forgiven. Gertrude felt very foolish, almost as if she could have cried, but

Charlotte's eye was upon her, and she exerted herself to be composed.

'A strange person that,' said Charlotte, musingly, when Mr Dacre was gone ; 'but one can't think about him now. What are you doing here, Gertrude ?'

'Nothing.'

'What have you done ?'

'Nothing ;—and what am I going to do ?—nothing. So do, Charlotte, take the affair off my hands.'

'It looks inviting, certainly ; but may I have my own way ?'

'Yes, anything and everything you please. Laura can't work, and I won't.'

'Won't ! that is very unlike you. I thought you would do all things.'

'Would, if I could,' said Gertrude, with an unconscious emphasis upon the words.

'Well ! I like to see great geniuses baulked occasionally. So you leave the reins of government in my hands ?'

'Yes, if you will let me retire ;' and without listening for an answer, Gertrude ran out of the room ; for her heart was full, and she could not trust herself to another sentence. Charlotte thought her manner peculiar, but did not trouble herself to ask questions. The bell was rung ; the housekeeper summoned, and when Gertrude returned, she found her sister in full consultation with Mrs Dickson, as to what was going on, and giving rapid orders to the work-people for the decorations. The first sentence which she heard made her repent having yielded her authority.

'Mrs Dickson, these hangings look awkward ; I think if some one were to go down to Elsham, they might find some silk to match them, and we might have festoons between the windows.'

'Yes, ma'am ; yes, certainly. One of the housemaids shall go directly.'

'She can take a tassel to get a good match : and stop,' continued Charlotte ; 'let her tell Miss Harvey to send up all her artificial flowers. She had a great box from town, I know, only the other day.'

'And some more twine and tin-tacks, Mrs Dickson,' said one of the men.

Poor Gertrude listened in extreme discomposure,—the twine and tin-tacks seemed the climax of extravagance. 'You can't have used all I saw here this morning,' she said, as she picked up half-a-dozen from the floor ; and then went searching about for more. Charlotte burst into a fit of laughter, and begged to know what tin-tacks were a hundred.

'I don't know,' replied Gertrude, gravely; 'but it is as well to be careful.'

'Quite as well: mind they match the silk properly, Mrs Dickson.'

'O Charlotte! you are not in earnest,' exclaimed Gertrude; 'there is not the least occasion for it.'

'I thought I was to have my own way,' replied Charlotte.

'Yes, as long as it is a rational one.'

'That was not an article in our agreement.'

Gertrude could not dispute the point while the servants were present, and before she had time to speak to Charlotte alone, a summons was sent her from Laura. 'Promise me you will not send for anything till I return,' said Gertrude; but Charlotte was resolved, and although Gertrude was only wanted to report progress, the interruption was fatal to her economical wishes. Laura kept her in her room talking for a considerable time; and when she again went to the drawing-room, a shopman was measuring out lengths of pale blue silk, and Charlotte was kneeling by a bench picking out the handsomest artificial flowers from a heap which lay beside her, to form wreaths for the sconces and the glasses. The whole of that evening was as a miserable mockery to Gertrude. Charlotte stayed to dinner at her own request; and Laura appeared, and exerted herself to seem cheerful, and light conversation was held, and all the ordinary courtesies of life went on, as if no secret spring of grief was working beneath. Yet to Gertrude almost every word and look was burdened with a double meaning. The furniture of the room, and the elegancies of the table, were no longer Edward's. The deference of the servants was an outward show. She felt herself only acting a part in the general deception; and the dark eyes and stern countenances of the old family portraits seemed to reproach her with the ruin about to be associated with their name. Ruin—and it might be, dishonour; and as the possibility crossed her mind, she longed to shut her eyes to the light, and close her ears to the sound of human voices, and banish the very name of her family from the world's remembrance. Charlotte was too busied with her new office to notice very minutely what was passing; and dinner was no sooner ended, than she again adjourned to the drawing-room to put the finishing stroke to her work. The room was cleared, and the benches were put in order; and then some candles were lighted, and a few lamps placed in the conservatory, to give an idea of what the general effect would be the next evening.

'It is beautiful, you must own,' exclaimed Charlotte, when all was completed, and Laura was ushered into the room in state; 'and just fancy how it will look to-morrow night, filled with people. I am sure Edward will be pleased.'

A smile of gratification lighted up Laura's pallid features; but as it died away, a hectic flush crimsoned her cheek, and she put her hand to her forehead to still its painful throbbing. 'Why does she speak of him, Gertrude?' she said, in a faint voice, while the same wandering expression gleamed in her eyes, which Gertrude had noticed once before.

'She hopes he will come,' was the reply; 'and so we all do.'

'Come! yes, there is no doubt of it. Who says there is?'

'Now, Laura, look this way; at the effect through the pier glass,' interrupted Charlotte, beckoning her to the lower end of the room.

Laura went, and as she caught sight of her own figure in front of the brilliant reflection, she stopped, and a ghastly smile passed over her countenance. 'How will it be to-morrow?' she said, turning to Gertrude, who stood by her side, with her arm encircling her waist, from a vague fear lest she should be seized with a sudden giddiness or faintness. 'Edward will be here; and Miss Forester—what will they say?'

'Edward would say now, that you are tired, and ought not to be here,' replied Gertrude: 'will you not go with me to your own room?'

Laura took no notice of her sister's words. She stood for several minutes as if fascinated by her own exquisite beauty, and then, in a sad voice, murmured, 'He said that his love was gone;' and seating herself upon one of the benches, she burst into tears.

'I cannot leave her in this state,' said Gertrude, drawing her sister aside; 'mamma will not care. Tell her that Laura is not well, and that I shall sleep here.'

'She frightens me,' said Charlotte; 'what is the matter?'

'Don't ask,' replied Gertrude; 'only say what I tell you, and don't let mamma be anxious.'

'But what shall you do if she is not better to-morrow? how shall you manage?'

'I don't know—I can't think. To-morrow will be sufficient

for itself; let us do what is best to-night.' And Gertrude again began to entreat Laura to go to her own room.

'I cannot, indeed, I cannot,' she replied; 'I shall be alone. Hark! did you not hear a carriage?'

Gertrude listened anxiously, but caught no sound: 'It is but the wind,' she said, 'and your fancy.'

Laura dragged herself, rather than walked, to the door, to be quite certain; and Gertrude followed, assuring her that if she would only consent to go to bed, she would herself remain with her.

'But he may come; it is not too late,' persisted Laura; 'and he did not say he would not be here to-night.'

'And if he should come, will he be pleased to see you ill?'

'Pleased!' repeated Laura; 'pleased with me!'

Gertrude saw that it was in vain to reason, and assuming a different manner, she said, 'Laura, you must go. I will stay with you, and do everything you may require if you do; but if you do not, I will leave you directly.'

'Alone!' again muttered Laura; but her voice was faint, and when Gertrude gently led her from the room she no longer resisted.

The scene which she had just witnessed had convinced Gertrude that it would be right at any risk to calm Laura's mind as much as possible; and they were no sooner left by themselves than she told her in few words of all that had passed with Miss Forester. But the effect of the communication did not answer her expectations. Laura's gratitude and affection were excited to the utmost, but Gertrude saw that she had not understood her character. She no longer spoke of delay, but seemed rather to think that there was a greater necessity than before of confessing everything to Edward in order that Gertrude might not be inconvenienced. And the pressure of this idea still weighed upon her mind so painfully, that Gertrude did not venture to continue the conversation. Every mention of Miss Forester's name recalled some cause of repentance or regret; and Gertrude, feeling that her only hope of giving comfort was at an end, was obliged to confine her observation to common subjects.

CHAPTER XXXVI.

I T was late that night before Gertrude retired to rest. Laura's nervous agitation was so great that she could not bear a moment's solitude ; and after assisting her to undress, Gertrude sat by the bedside, watching her breathing, with the intention of sending for medical advice, if she saw any indications of increasing fever. The symptoms which had alarmed her seemed, however, more the result of anxiety of mind than natural illness ; for after some hours' restlessness, Laura's uneven pulse grew calmer, and her countenance more composed, and at length sleep gradually stole over her. It was then midnight ; but Gertrude felt no weariness ; she almost dreaded to lie down, from the knowledge of what her waking would bring. It was the first night, too, that she had passed at Allingham ; and the strangeness of the apartment, its size and furniture, so different from her own little room at the Priory, contributed not a little to the unnatural excitement of her feelings. A sensation of awe came over her, as she looked at the large bed and massive cabinets, and tried to find out what was hidden in the dark corners ; and then caught the still almost inaudible sound, which reminded her she was not alone ; and when she placed herself at the dressing-room door, which had been left open, and looked down the long gallery, listening to the dull, regular ticking of the timepiece in the hall, and feeling herself the only waking being in the house,—a chill fear, such as she remembered to have been the torment of her childhood, came over her, while shadowy forms seemed to be gliding near, and the rustling of her own dress, and the touch of her own hand startled her. Gertrude was not timid, but she was worn with harass of mind. She did not reason with herself, or even ridicule the absurdity of her own fancies ; but she quietly closed the door, and kneeling down, buried her face in her hands, and brought herself at once into the real presence of that unseen world, the shadows of which had caused her to tremble. God was guarding, and her Saviour was watching over her, and the Spirit of Holiness was strengthening her feeble heart, and angels of peace were waiting to minister to her comfort ; and when, with solemn reverence, the humble confession, and the earnest thanksgiving, the entreaty and the intercession, had been made, Gertrude rose from her knees tranquil and trusting, and when she lay down, slept as a child would sleep beneath a parent's eye.

With the first dawn of morning she awoke, but not with the wretchedness which she had anticipated. The light was indeed blue and cheerless, very different from the rich, fading glow of sunset; and the flickering of the expiring lamp reminded her that the rest of night was over; but Gertrude's last thoughts had been of peace, and peace had not deserted her. After a glance at Laura, which satisfied her that there was no particular reason to be uneasy, she went to the window, though with no wish to see if the weather was likely to be propitious for an archery party. She had almost forgotten that it was of importance, but the vain longing to know what 'the day might bring forth,' made her look upon its first opening with something of a superstitious eye. There was little comfort, however, to be gained from the outward world, for dimness covered the distant country, and the trees in the Park were still in comparative darkness. Only the white road gleamed in the twilight, and a thin column of smoke arose from one solitary cottage; while, far away in the east, a bright crimson streak was gradually extending itself and dispersing the masses of gray clouds which had gathered to greet the rising sun. For a long time Gertrude remained at the window, watching till the crimson streak had spread into a broad belt, and the gray clouds had separated into light flakes; and then the glorious orb of fire stole upwards between the shadowy hills, marking their smooth outlines, and brightening their glassy slopes; while still as it ascended, the mist floated from before it, and the radiant sky melted into a clear, pale blue; and silently and swiftly the gladdening rays travelled onwards, till hill and valleys, streamlet and trees, tall spires and clustering cottages, had felt their magic power, and started into life beneath their touch. Alas for Gertrude! That dazzling scene was not for her; those brilliant rays had no charm to cheer her burdened spirit. She was in Edward's home, looking upon Edward's property; and the next few months might see him banished from both by his own errors. With an aching heart she turned away, for the sunlight had brought with it visions of earth, and earth has no spell to soothe the troubled breast. Yet she was not condemned to inaction, that most painful of all trials when sorrow is at hand. The comfort of many might be promoted by her exertions; and it was with this thought that she steeled herself to bear, not only patiently but cheerfully, whatever might be in store for her.

By the time Laura awoke she was dressed, and ready to

attend upon, or talk to her, or do whatever might be needed; and Laura, refreshed by her night's rest, and ignorant of the chief sources of uneasiness, was less insensible to the influence of a brilliant summer morning, though something unnatural still lurked in her smile, when she spoke of all that was to be done during the day.

'I am so much better this morning,' she said, in answer to Gertrude's inquiries; 'and I must get up and see what they have been doing.'

Gertrude entreated her to remain quiet, and to think as little as possible, for that everything had been prepared the day before. 'If you will promise me not to worry yourself,' she added, 'I will leave you after breakfast, for they will be anxious for me at home.'

'I will be quiet if I can,' said Laura; 'but you will not be gone long?'

'Not longer than I can help, and I can bring my dress with me for the afternoon.'

'Ah! that reminds me,' exclaimed Laura, starting up in bed. 'Just look in my wardrobe, there is a dress there. I don't know how it is'—— and she sank back on her pillow; 'my head is very troublesome when I move.'

'Then do not move, dearest; stay where you are till after breakfast.'

'But the dress—Watson knows about it. It is that very pale, violet-figured silk, Edward's favourite. I shall wear it, I think.'

'And why am I to take it down?'

'I must look at it, and the white bonnet too—the new one with the wreath, and the lace mantilla. I should like to see them all.'

'But what is to be done with them?' inquired Gertrude.

'Nothing; but Edward asked me what I should wear, and I wish to be in time. He will be pleased to see me dressed; don't you think he will?'

Gertrude's fears of the previous night returned as Laura spoke; but after a few minutes she mentioned a few alterations which were to be made in the arrangements, with so much clearness that Gertrude could scarcely help accusing herself of being fanciful in feeling uneasy. 'Remember your promise,' she said, at parting; 'you are not to ask any questions, or trouble yourself about anything, and trust to my being back in time to see that all is ready.'

Laura agreed, and Gertrude set off for the Priory. There was but one person whom she dreaded to see. It would be easy to satisfy her mother and Jane, whatever inquiries they might make; and Charlotte, too, was not likely to suspect anything wrong, except Laura's illness; but Edith had a right to know everything; and after leaving her in such a state of distress the previous day, Gertrude really feared what the consequence might be when she was told the truth. She was not in the drawing-room, however; and Gertrude had only at first to reply to a string of questions from Mrs Courtenay, and assure Charlotte that Laura was not dangerously ill, and that no one had presumed to interfere with her decorations.

'Well, my dear, I am so glad!' exclaimed Mrs Courtenay; 'I did not know what was going to happen last night, when Charlotte came back without you; something terrible, I was sure. Edward's going up to town in that strange way seemed so odd, and then Laura's crying, as Charlotte said, and your looking so ill. But it is very natural after all. I know what it is to have a large party. Have as many servants as you may, they must be looked after.'

'Laura has not been well for two days,' said Gertrude.

'Poor child! it is a very nervous business, and Edward was very thoughtless in running away from her just now; but men always are so; your poor, dear father was exactly the same.'

'But about to-day,' said Jane; 'do you think Laura really expects us all?'

'She expects me,' observed Charlotte. 'I consider it my party, since I had the dressing up of the room.'

'It is very troublesome,' said Jane; 'one doesn't know what to put on. It is neither an out-of-door, nor an in-door affair. What shall you wear, Gertrude?'

'I don't know; I have two or three dresses that will do.'

'Now, is not that like Edith?' exclaimed Charlotte. 'Actually this party has been talked of for the last fortnight, and at last the day is come, and Gertrude has not made up her mind what dress she shall appear in.'

'But I have made up my mind,' said Gertrude, endeavouring to appear interested; 'at least, so far as to settle that it shall be one of three.'

'And you did really think about it?' said Charlotte, doubtfully. 'And you do consider it a matter of consequence whether you are dressed in brown holland or silk? Then you shall come

and choose for me. Miss Harvey has sent home my peach
coloured satinet such a figure that it is not fit to be seen. A
desperate scolding she shall have to-morrow, but that won't help
me in my difficulties to-day.'

Gertrude was dragged away to Charlotte's room, and soon
employed in deciding whether blue silk or white muslin would
be the more becoming; and comparing flowers and ribbons,
scarfs, mantillas, and gloves, in order to find out which would
suit best. Then came Mrs Courtenay, with an earnest request
that dear Gertrude would just try and alter the folds of her
black satin dress; she was sure no one could do it as well.
And she should like to know, too, whether Miss Harvey had not
put too many flowers in her bonnet. 'There are no lady's maids
in the house,' whispered Charlotte, satirically; but Gertrude did
not reply in the same tone. She did all that was required—
took out the flowers, and put them in again differently, sewed
some edging to a pair of cuffs, and then, when the clock had
struck one, petitioned to be allowed to return to Allingham.
And all this time she had not seen Edith. She had asked for
her several times, but no one knew anything about her, except
that at breakfast she had scarcely spoken; to which Charlotte
added, that she was pale, and did not eat; but since then she
had not been seen.

'You will find her at the school, I have no doubt, my dear,'
said Mrs Courtenay; 'I saw her go out with her bonnet on.'

'And did she say nothing about me?' inquired Gertrude.
'She must have thought I should be here.'

'No, nothing at all; but you are not going to run away, my
dear. Now I have settled my dress, I want you to tell me something more about Laura, and what time we are to go, and
whether you think the archery ground will be damp, because, if
so, I shall send my galoshes; and about Edward—when does
Laura expect him? Just sit down quietly, and tell me.'

Gertrude sighed inwardly but patiently. The pettiness of
trifling duties at such a moment was irksome almost beyond
endurance. Once or twice she felt an impulse to own everything.
The sorrow must come sooner or later, and deception seemed
wrong; but then she checked herself with the remembrance that
it was not her part to tell what Edward had concealed. The
trial ended at last. Mrs Courtenay repeated several times that
the carriage should be at the door exactly at half-past two, and
that she would put some cloaks and galoshes in, for fear they

should all take cold : and after desiring Gertrude to send word if Edward was arrived, and if she met Edith to be sure and tell her to be in time, she allowed her to depart.

'I am half inclined to go with you,' said Charlotte, as they met on the hall steps ; 'only there is the trouble of returning.'

Gertrude did not press the matter, for she longed to be alone. 'You will have fatigue enough,' she said, 'before the day is over ; and if you are not here, no one will be ready to start before three o'clock.'

' But that will be time enough ; we shall have plenty of archery between that and half-past four.'

'Yes, but mamma wishes it. She wants to be at Allingham before any one comes, because she dislikes going into a crowd. Besides, if you stay, you can attend to some little matters for me. I have looked out all the things I want and ordered them to be sent after me directly ; but I dare say the servants will forget, or send them wrong, if they are not watched.'

' That is the good of having so many idle people about,' said Charlotte. ' However, we are better than at Allingham. I tried to count the servants there one day, and actually I could not do it, there were such shadowy groups of kitchen maids and under-gardeners in the background. Rather expensive, I should think ; but Edward knows best.'

They were Charlotte's last words : and poor Gertrude, as she walked along, repeated them over and over again to herself, though not always attaching any meaning to them. She wandered through the Park, turning from time to time, as she fancied she heard the wheels of a carriage, or the trampling of horses. It was scarcely possible that Edward should have arrived ; but Gertrude was not in a mood to calculate pro-babilities ; and when she distinguished two figures, a gentleman and lady, at a little distance, the fancy crossed her that they might be Edward and Laura. A second thought made her smile at the folly of the supposition, and as she drew nearer she had no difficulty in recognising Edith and Mr Dacre. Edith was standing under the shade of the large beach, from which the full front of Allingham could be seen. Her face was not directed to Mr Dacre, and she did not appear engaged in con-versation ; but as she leaned against the huge trunk, her eyes seemed bent upon the ground, and when occasionally she raised her head it was but for a moment, and immediately she resumed her former dejected attitude. Gertrude hesitated whether it would be well to interrupt them ; but there was no time to spare, and she knew that Edith would naturally be desirous of seeing her : and, whilst she still doubted, Mr Dacre perceived and came up to her. Gertrude held out her hand rather in confusion ; for Mr Dacre might have forgotten, but she had not. It was taken exactly as usual, and as she looked towards Edith, he said in a tone of compassion—

‘I am glad you are come. Your sister has been forcing me to talk to her.’

‘Has she, indeed ?’ exclaimed Gertrude, and she sprang forwards.

‘Don't startle her,’ said Mr Dacre, ‘she is sadly upset.’

Gertrude's step was stilled in an instant. ‘I knew she must feel it,’ she said, ‘for many reasons—every reason.’

‘And you,’—he replied.

‘Do not think of me, but teach me how I may help others to bear it. Does Edith know all ? ’

‘All without reserve. One secret has been hers and mine for very long ’

‘Yes, *the* secret—the foundation of everything ; but it is use-less to look back. Oh ! if Edward would come and satisfy the one horrible doubt remaining.’

Mr Dacre said nothing till they drew near to Edith, when he stopped. ‘You will remember,’ he said, ‘that you were to allow me to be of use to you under all circumstances. I shall wait anxiously to know if there is anything I can do. And now good-bye : I do not think we shall meet again to-day.’

Gertrude did not press him to remain, for she felt that his presence might be a restraint ; and after watching him for a few moments, as he crossed the Park in the direction of his own cot-tage, she walked on. Edith was still standing motionless, with her head averted ; and her name was twice repeated before she recognised Gertrude's voice, and turned towards her. A look from each told what words could never have expressed of sorrow, and sympathy, and self-reproach ; and Edith, throwing herself into her sister's arms, wept long and bitterly. ‘Can you love me, Gertrude ?’ were the first words she spoke. ‘It is my doing —misery—misery for us all.’

‘Edith, dearest, you must not think so. Who could bear it ?’

‘And I cannot bear it ; but it is true—even you can do no good—no one can.’

‘That is despair,’ said Gertrude.

'Is there hope, then ?   Can anything save Edward ?'

'Not from earthly trial; but, Edith, you know that his present suffering may be his greatest good.'

'And I !' exclaimed Edith ; 'he will never look upon me with kindness ; and if he does, I shall not be able to endure it.   Gertrude, no one can tell how wrong I have been.   The world will blame him when it is my doing.   I was everything to him once, and I did not act by him as I ought.'   And she again burst into tears.

'I cannot leave you whilst you are so unhappy,' said Gertrude, kissing her; 'but I do not think you will care to hear what I could say.'

'I would rather be wretched,' replied Edith—'but must you go ?'

'Laura is expecting me, and it is late.'

'Then go, go,— do not delay an instant.   Yet there is no fear —you will not neglect her as I have done.'

'We shall see each other again to-day,' said Gertrude.

'Not at Allingham—it is impossible.'

'But it is Laura's wish that you should be there ; and for my sake I hope you will come.   Remember there is no one who can feel with me as you do ; and if Edward returns I may sadly want some one.'

'Yes, yes,' sighed Edith.   'But I am not afraid as you are. He could never be tempted to dishonour.'

'Perhaps not,' said Gertrude, doubtfully ; 'yet, at any rate, I shall long for you so much.'

'Am I fit for it ?' said Edith.   'I shall never bear to see Laura ; and to hear her laugh would be worse than any other suffering.'

'She will not laugh much,' said Gertrude.   'There are things upon her mind, as well as upon ours.'

'What things ?—what do you mean ?'

'I cannot explain now, but you need not fear her cheerfulness ; only come—it will be such a comfort to feel you are there.'

'Who could deny you anything, Gertrude ?' said Edith, earnestly ; 'but you would not ask me if you knew the effort it will be.'

'The long afternoon, alone,' said Gertrude, 'will be very bad. If we are together we can at least feel that we understand each other

'And you will be lonely in a crowd,' said Edith—'lonely and wretched from my doing. Gertrude, there is one thing you can never forgive me—the church.'

Gertrude tried to conceal the exquisite pain which the allusion gave her, yet she was not able. 'It is not your doing,' she said, but her voice was choked.

'Yes, yes, it is, it is all my doing. I blamed Edward once, and thought he had much to answer for, because Torrington was left without a church ; and now there might be one, if I had acted differently.'

'There is to be one,' said Gertrude.

'Is ?—impossible ! How can you do everything ?'

'I am not going to do it,—Mr Dacre is.'

There was no symptom of agitation in Gertrude's manner, and Edith looked at her in astonishment, and after a minute's silence, exclaimed, 'Is it really true ? And can you say it so calmly ? O Gertrude ! I shall never be like you.'

'Hush ! hush ! Edith. If you love me, never speak such words again. Will you come with me now ?' And with a rapid step Gertrude walked towards the house.

'Not now,' said Edith, following her ; 'but I have vexed you.'

Gertrude's lip quivered, and her voice was tremulous. 'No, you never vex me ; but I am so—I have been so wrong—I will tell you another time. Say you will come by and by.'

The sight of Gertrude's distress was decisive. Edith con-sented, and the sisters parted.

CHAPTER XXXVII.

WHO has not experienced the weight which presses upon the spirits, as the hour draws near for the arrival of a large party when but one wish is uppermost in the mind—the longing for solitude and silence ? Gertrude felt it intensely, as she approached the house, and saw the marquee erected on the archery ground, and heard the distant sound of the instru-ments which the musicians were setting in order for the *fête.* During her absence all the preparations had been completed ; the hall was dressed with flowers, the dining-room glittered with glass and plate, and the dancing-room, with its smooth floor and ornamented walls, looked inviting even in the daylight. Gertrude glanced into the different rooms, but had no time to inquire into the *minutiæ* of the arrangements. It was already a quarter-past two, and some punctual people would be sure to arrive by half-past ; and almost dreading reproaches for her delay, she hastened to Laura's room. She was standing by the window, her eyes directed to the road by which Edward must arrive. Gertrude entered unperceived, and when she gently said, ' Did you think I should never come ?' Laura started, and in a frightened voice exclaimed, ' You, Gertrude ! I fancied it was Edward.'

' He may be here soon,' said Gertrude.

' Have you heard? Is he come ?' exclaimed Laura, hurriedly.

' No, no one is come ; and I have heard nothing : but I am so late—I must go and dress quickly. I came though, to know if you wanted anything first.'

' Thank you ; but I think I am ready ; just look at me and see.'

Gertrude gazed with a criticising eye, but the most fastidious taste could scarcely have found anything to amend in the simple, elegant dress, which displayed Laura's slight figure and delicate features to the fullest advantage. She was less pale than she had been in the morning, for the flush of excitement was tinging her cheek, and the restlessness of her deep, hazel eye had ceased, though in its stead there remained an unnatural brilliancy, which Gertrude remarked with disquietude.

' You will find me in the marquee,' said Laura. ' I suppose I must go, and I believe I am longing for the fresh air.'

' Mamma and my sisters will be here presently,' said Gertrude, ' so they will help you ; but I can dress very quickly when I try ; and as I am not lady of the house, it won't so much signify if I am not perfect.'

' Perfect in mind,' said Laura, earnestly; but Gertrude did not wait to hear the compliment. She was gone to her own room to complete a more hasty toilette than she had imagined possible ; but with all her speed the rumble of carriages was heard in the Park before she could go down-stairs.

' The company are all in the marquee, ma'am,' said the butler: ' Mrs Courtenay, and the young ladies, and Lady Stapleton, and Sir Henry Colburn, and Mrs Ringwood, and Captain Stuart, and' ——

'Poor Laura,' thought Gertrude, not anxious to hear any more arrivals, and leaving the butler in the middle of his sentence, she hastened into the garden. It was even then a brilliant scene, filled with people, some clustered in groups and engaged in conversation,—others wandering leisurely through the walks,—and a few, just arrived, lounging at the entrance of the marquee. There were bright dresses, and young, happy faces, and the music was sounding joyously, and laughter and light words were passing on all sides ; and rich flowers—geraniums, fuchsias, heliotropes, and verbenas, and every choice treasure of the greenhouse,—were scattered in profusion amid the green lawns, and the unclouded splendour of a summer sun shed a dazzling lustre over all ; but the envied master of the *fête*, the possessor of so much beauty, was—where? Few cared, though many asked ;—only Gertrude, as she heard the whispered inquiries and civil regrets, felt that each word was torture, and watched the expression of the speakers' countenances, and weighed the accent of every sentence, to discover whether any but herself surmised the reason of his absence. It was some time before she could make her way to Laura, who was seated in the marquee, with little Charlie by her side. She was surrounded by a large party, and talked quickly and gaily. Her eyes sparkled, her mouth was brightened with smiles, and occasionally the sound of her silvery laugh was heard, as she replied to some witty remark or satirical observation. Was there indeed anything hidden beneath? Was it Gertrude's fancy that the brilliant flash of the eyes was unnatural,—that a convulsive movement as of great pain made her suddenly raise her hand to her head? and in that clear, sweet voice, could it be true that there was discoverable a secret tone of anguish? If it were so, none perceived it but Gertrude. Lovely and fascinating as Laura had always been considered, on that day she was thought to surpass even her former self. Praises of her dress and manner, and beauty, were circulated on all sides ; and even in the midst of her anxiety, Gertrude could not help feeling pleasure as she looked at her. But the pleasure was momentary,—the pain that followed lasting. As the music ceased for a few minutes, the rumble of a carriage was heard, and Laura's eye was in an instant directed to the turn of the winding road through the Park. Some one spoke to her, and she laughed ; but the remark that was made could not have been the cause, for she blushed, and apologised, and again gazed into the distance.

'Laura, my dear, Mrs Ferrers is waiting to introduce her daughter,' whispered Mrs Courtenay.

'Yes, certainly, most happy;' but Laura's head was fixed in the opposite direction, and Mrs Ferrers looked haughty and annoyed, while her timid daughter seemed ready to hide herself in the farthest corner to escape observation.

'Laura, my dear Laura,'—and Mrs Courtenay touched her arm.

'It is not Edward,' said Gertrude, in a low voice.

Laura breathed more freely; and without attempting an excuse, received the introduction as if nothing had been amiss. Mrs Ferrers was stiff and cool, but her annoyance was thrown away. Gertrude felt vexed, and moving from her seat, offered it as a little atoning civility. It was accepted, and conversation followed as a matter of course. Mrs Ferrers had never been at Allingham since it came into Mr Courtenay's possession, except at a morning visit; she had no idea of the beauty of the grounds —they were so extensive—Mr Courtenay must have such good taste, they were so well laid out. She remembered them in Colonel Courtenay's time, but now they were completely altered. The observations were very natural and civil; but to Gertrude they were fretting, so that she could scarcely listen to them with patience. From the mamma she turned to the young lady, but it was the same thing. What else could they say upon such a short acquaintance? Gertrude felt herself unjust, and started another topic. The charms of archery—the difficulty of practising —the good excuse it formed for bringing people together. She knew exactly what to say, for everybody makes the same observations at archery meetings, and she could almost have repeated the words in her sleep; and whilst she was able to keep to this subject, there was no difficulty in watching Laura, thinking of Edward, and noticing every one who passed, to endeavour to find out if Miss Forester had made her appearance. But Mrs Ferrers grew tired of her secluded position, and proposed to walk, and Gertrude had no excuse for not accompanying her. Miss Ferrers did not shoot, and took no particular interest in the amusement; and she thought it would be extremely pleasant to stroll through the gardens; and then Gertrude's penance again began. She was stopped every five minutes with admiration, inquiries, and regrets,—forced to explain where Edward was,— when he was expected,—condoled with upon the prospect of a new election, but congratulated that Mr Courtenay's success was certain. Even Mrs Ferrers laughed at hearing the same things repeated from all quarters.

'A tax for being related to a distinguished person,' she said. 'One is so thankful for one's insignificance on these occasions. However, it is better than being distinguished in any other way. It would be dreadful to go through the world with a story attached to one's name.'

Gertrude assented heartily. She felt as if the story of her name had already begun. 'Will you rest here?' she said, pointing to a bench upon a high, green bank, which commanded a view of the gardens and archery ground. It was the favourite point, and several parties had already collected there; and Gertrude hoped that amongst so many she might be spared the exertion of entertaining, at least for a few minutes. She began to be seriously uncomfortable at the effect which Edward's non-arrival might have upon Laura, and vexed with herself for having left her; and she dreaded also the appearance of Miss Forester, and the first meeting in her absence, which would bring back so much that was painful, and might even induce Laura to give some open expression of her feelings. But it was useless to gaze upon the marquee, and try to find out what was going on, for Gertrude was still kept a prisoner. Kind friends crowded round her, and Miss Ferrers, frightened at so many strangers, suggested that, instead of remaining where they were, they should walk up and down the pathway below, whilst her mamma rested. Gertrude's consideration made her fully alive to the poor girl's embarrassment; but just as they were leaving the little hill she caught sight of a bonnet with a profusion of feathers, and a rich satin dress, glancing in the sunshine. It was the glitter of a snake in Gertrude's eyes, but she did her utmost to feel charitable. Miss Forester was accompanied by her father and advancing to the marquee; and Gertrude as she watched her, and thought of Laura, forgot that she might appear rude, and making a sudden apology, committed Miss Ferrers to the charge of an elderly lady who was standing near, and quickly retraced her steps. Miss Forester saw and came towards her—a smile full of contemptuous meaning was on her lips. They met in silence, and bowed; General Forester bowed too. Gertrude could not understand the expression of his face; it was not contemptuous, but triumphant. They pressed on to the marquee, Gertrude longing to give Laura warning; but she was just then engaged in showing the prizes which were to be distributed, and the people were standing round and admiring them. Jane, wrapped in an Indian shawl, was seated by her; and Mrs Courtenay, in a state of nervous bustle, was insisting that no one could see either the ring or the pencil-case in such a bad light; but Edith and Charlotte were nowhere to be seen. Gertrude narrowly observed Laura's countenance, and as she did so, felt thankful for the crowd which kept Miss Forester from her view. Her face was flushed, the blue veins in her transparent forehead was swollen with agitation, her hands trembled, and from time to time, she cast a quick glance behind, and then with a slight shudder began talking rapidly. Charlie still stood by her side, amused and wondering, and sometimes as Laura looked at his innocent face, and heard him admired and petted, she smiled with a natural and happy smile; but in another moment the smile was gone, and in its stead came a forced, hollow laugh.

It is a miserable thing to see too deeply behind the exterior of any scene of earthly enjoyment. Gertrude marvelled as she saw the gaiety, and listened to the mirth around her. It seemed impossible that all should be deceived; there must be some who felt with her—who knew that Laura was wretched, and Edward ruined. They were but acting a part, and in a few minutes the veil would be cast aside, and the name of Courtenay would be a mark for their ridicule and contempt. The thought was in her heart, and she turned and saw Miss Forester's eye fixed upon her, and at the same instant a voice whispered in her ear—

'I was anxious to tell you a friend of mine saw Mr Courtenay yesterday, in London. He was at one of the Treasury offices. I knew you would like to hear of him.'

If Miss Forester desired revenge, she had it to the utmost of her wishes. Gertrude's face became deadly pale, but the tone in which she said, 'Who saw him?' was calm, from the very excess of her anxiety. Before she could receive an answer, there was a movement in the party, and Mrs Courtenay's hand was stretched out to greet Miss Forester.

'I am so sorry I did not see you before. Have you looked at the prizes yet? I suppose you have, though: Laura told me they were your ordering.'

Laura turned at the sound of her own name. Miss Forester approached sweetly and courteously as usual, but Laura seemed spell-bound. Miss Forester was resolved that there should be

no appearance of a diminution of intimacy ; and unheeding Mrs
Courtenay, who held up the prizes before her, she bent forward,
and taking Laura's unresisting hand, said—

'I am afraid you must have thought me very remiss in not
being with you the last two days, but I assure you it was not my
own doing.'

'Laura,' interrupted Gertrude, who, forgetting everything but
her dread lest her sister might betray her feelings too strongly,
had pressed forward behind Miss Forester, 'I think you are
wanted in front; there are many persons wishing to see you, and
you are quite hidden here.'

Poor Laura gazed upon Gertrude as upon a guardian angel.
She put her arm within hers, as if for support ; and Gertrude
passed her hand caressingly over her trembling fingers, and led
her from the marquee.

'Gertrude, my dear,' exclaimed Mrs Courtenay, 'if you are
going to walk, do see if you can meet Charlotte and Edith.
They were to have come with us, but Edith was not ready, and
so I sent the carriage back. But they ought to have been here
long ago, and they will miss the best part of the day.'

'Shall I look for them ?' said Miss Forester, following, and
though slightly abashed at her reception, determined to be one
of the family. Laura looked beseechingly at her sister.

'Take me away, Gertrude,' said she, in a faint voice ; 'I am
so ill ; I cannot bear it. If they would only go, all of them.'

'Perhaps, mamma,' said Gertrude, 'you would like to walk
round with Miss Forester. It is not far, and you will be amused
to see what is going on.'

'Oh ! yes, my dear, the very thing ; and Charlie, little darling,
shall come too. Jane, you can take care of him.'

Jane consented, though unwillingly ; and Miss Forester, having no objection ready, was obliged to set off with Mrs Courtenay
by her side. Gertrude felt that she had secured their absence at
least for half an hour, and seeing that Laura looked relieved and
tranquil, persuaded her to stay and watch the archery, and pay a
few necessary attentions to her guests ; but she soon repented
having done so. The last round was shot, and the marks were
counted ; and when this business was transacted, the prizes were
brought to Laura to be presented. All who had not seen them
came to look at them, and amongst them Mrs Ferrers and her
daughter. Mrs Ferrers was a connoisseur in jewellery, and admired in the warmest terms. She had never seen anything so

perfect as the workmanship of the ring; she remembered to have seen one like it in some great shop in town.

'Hanson's, I think, mamma,' said Miss Ferrers.

'Hanson's, was it? Yes, I think you are right. Every one deals with Hanson: the taste of his things is so perfect. Don't you think so, Mrs Courtenay?'

Laura's reply was indistinct, and Gertrude felt extremely uncomfortable.

'Tremendously expensive Hanson is,' said an officer, taking up the ring.

'And so enticing,' observed Mrs Ferrers. You can never escape from him. He has such a way of recommending things.'

'There will be a law against ladies entering his shop by and by,' said Captain Stuart; 'at least I am inclined to think I shall make one when I have a wife.'

'She will rebel.'

'Very possibly, but I suspect I should prove the conqueror.'

'He has never tried, Mrs Courtenay,' said Mrs Ferrers, laughing; 'and I don't think either you or I should advise him to make the experiment.'

Laura clung to her sister's arm, and trembled violently; and Gertrude looked round for some opening to escape, or change the conversation, but in vain.

'It is very well for ladies to talk,' continued Captain Stuart; 'but there are occasions on which a man must have his own way. A friend of mine was ruined the other day by his wife, and I am afraid it is a case beyond forgiveness.'

Laura uttered a faint exclamation, which to Gertrude's ear was agony.

'Hark! there is a flourish!' exclaimed Captain Stuart; 'now we shall hear who has been the winner. Mrs Courtenay, allow me to give you the prizes.'

Gertrude took them, for Laura's hand was powerless.

'Only for one moment exert yourself,' she whispered: 'it must soon be over; you can sit down for a minute.'

There was a little bustle of preparation, and an opening was made for the successful archeress. She was young, interesting, and happy looking; and as she came forward, Gertrude felt painfully the contrast between Laura's expression of misery and the brightness of one who appeared never to have known care. Laura rose; and Gertrude once more whispered to her to be calm. Again, for the last time, the bugle sounded. Was it the rattle of a carriage which jarred with the lingering notes? A thick shrubbery divided the archery ground from the road; and no one could see. Laura held the brooch in her hand, but her lips were parched, her voice was choked. Every one listened instinctively. The carriage rolled on, but stopped before it could have reached the house, and the attention of all was directed to the path leading into the Park. It must be Edward. Gertrude's countenance showed that she had little doubt, and Laura's face became crimson and pale at each instant. Some few advanced beyond the rest, and Mr Courtenay's name was repeated on all sides. Laura caught the sound, and the ring dropped from her hand. She withdrew herself from Gertrude's grasp, and rushed forward; but as she came in sight of her husband, a miserable fear overpowered her, and she stood motionless. Gertrude watched her with mingled interest and alarm, and would have followed, but Edward was close at hand. His step was firm, his manner collected, and his countenance—what would not Gertrude have given to read it? He came near to Laura, but she did not move; he held out his hand, but her eyes were bent upon the ground. Gertrude feared that she would faint, but in another moment the charm of his voice had broken the spell; she started, and raised her head; and when the crowd, which at this moment pressed in front, again separated, Gertrude saw her advancing towards her, leaning upon Edward's arm.

Could it be pleasure that made Gertrude smile, and step forward and speak words of congratulation? She did not know. All that she did or said was mechanical. She saw that Laura was composed, but in exterior only; that her manner to Edward was restrained, and that he was noticing and suffering from it. He turned to her perpetually, and seemed with difficulty to show the proper courtesies to his friends; but Gertrude could discover nothing of that which she so longed to be told : only once, when General Forester was seen at a little distance, Edward's brow darkened, and his voice grew louder, as he asked a few rapid questions of a gentleman who was near him. Laura noticed him too, and trembled, but Gertrude was prevented from observing anything further. There was a general movement towards the house, and in the crush she was separated from her own party. With her usual thought she looked round for her mother, and seeing her with no one but little Charlie at some distance, was hurrying towards her, when she was stopped in one of the walks by the sudden appearance of Edith and Charlotte.

'Gertrude running so fast!—what a dignified proceeding!' began Charlotte, in a laughing tone.

'Hush! hush!' exclaimed Edith; 'something is going on. Edward is come, I am sure.'

'Well, suppose he is, what does it signify! A very pleasant surprise it will be. Why should you all look like frightened hares?'

'Charlotte, Charlotte, pray don't talk so. Is he come, Gertrude?'

'Yes, don't keep me. I am going to mamma.'

'But have you seen him—what does he say?'

'Never mind,' interrupted Charlotte. 'Don't you see that Gertrude is in an agony at being kept? You are so tiresome, Edith!'

'Only one word.'

'I have scarcely spoken to him,' replied Gertrude; and without waiting for another question, she went on.

'Mystery!' exclaimed Charlotte. 'You do delight in it, Edith; and Gertrude too—I really am angry with her.'

'Gertrude!' exclaimed Edith; 'she is an angel, if you did but know it.'

Charlotte laughed, and Edith suddenly stopped. 'I cannot go with you,' she said; 'I told you I should be much better at home.'

'This is mere folly,' said Charlotte; 'after I have wasted the whole afternoon for you, and taken the trouble to dress you, and make you look respectable (for you were anything but that before), why should you be so tormenting? I can't go on the ground alone.'

'Stay, there is the bell,' said Edith; 'dinner will be ready in a few minutes: let us wait here till afterwards.'

'Thank you, what good will that do to either of us?'

'I cannot see Edward,' exclaimed Edith: 'it will drive me wild.'

'You will drive me wild, Edith, and I will not put up with it. I am your sister, and I have a right to know things as well as you.'

'A right?—yes: but if it is to make you wretched?'

'Then let me be wretched: it is not my fashion; but I suppose I shall survive it.'

Edith hesitated, and longed for Gertrude to decide whether she should tell. Charlotte held her firmly: 'I am resolved,' she said, 'we will neither of us go till I have learned all.'

'Then have your will—Edward is a ruined man.'

The words were just uttered, when the band struck up a joyous air, and the larger portion of the company crowded into the walk. Charlotte stood aside to allow them to pass ; and before she could reply to Edith, Gertrude and her mother came up.

'Take care of mamma, Charlotte,' said Gertrude. 'Jane is behind somewhere, and I must carry Charlie to his nurse.'

Charlotte felt it was no moment for explanations, but she caught Gertrude's arm, and said hurriedly, 'Is it true ? Is Edith dreaming ?'

'I don't know—who told ?—ask nothing now,' exclaimed Gertrude : and taking the child by the hand, she led him away.

'Charlotte, my dear, don't you see you are in the way?' said Mrs Courtenay. 'Move, my love, move.'

Charlotte looked round—Edith was gone, and Gertrude ; before her were passing groups of the gay, the beautiful, and the wealthy, and on all sides were sounds of mirth and light-hearted enjoyment. How could the words she had heard be true ?

'Charlotte, my dear, you have lost your senses ; pray, come on, we shall be very late.' Mrs Courtenay spoke in a tone which for her expressed great irritation. You know there will be such a crush presently. I wish I had not been so foolish as to send General Forester away ; but I wanted him to speak to Edward. I was just going after him to shake hands with Edward myself, when Gertrude came, and I meant to have got into the house before any one to avoid the bustle, but it has all gone wrong together.'

Charlotte silently offered her arm, and Mrs Courtenay's mind was in a few minutes relieved by the approach of a gentleman who proffered his services. They passed on to the house. Charlotte's eye sought her brother as she seated herself at the dinner-table, but his place was empty, and some minutes elapsed before he appeared.

'Mr Courtenay is looking remarkably well—don't you think so ?' observed Charlotte's right-hand neighbour.

'Yes, very.'

'And such an unexpected pleasure it is, his having arrived in time. Every one had given him up.'

'Yes, every one.'

'His stay in town must have been extremely short ; but railroads make travelling a mere farce compared with what it used to be.'

' Certainly—it is very different.'

There was a silence. Charlotte Courtenay was generally considered a lively, agreeable person, but at her brother's table on that day she did not shine.

' My master begs you will drink wine with him, ma'am,' said the butler to Mrs Courtenay.

Edward looked down the table. ' My dear mother, you will excuse me ; it is very old-fashioned, but we have not met before to-day.'

Mrs Courtenay was proud and pleased. Her son never forgot her, and she murmured her satisfaction to Charlotte. ' Dear Edward ! he is so unlike other people,—so very considerate, and it is such a pleasure to have him here. The party would have been nothing without him. And did you ever see a table so beautifully laid out ? Just look at the flowers in the vases, and all those curious pastry and sugar figures, and the cut glass and plate : how well it is all arranged ! Dickson is a very clever person, certainly. I suppose she managed it all.'

' I don't know ; I suppose so.'

' Courtenay,' exclaimed Charlotte's discomfited neighbour, ' you cut me dead, yesterday.'

' Yesterday ! '—Edward stopped, as he was about to address an observation to the lady on his right hand—' I was not here.'

' No, nor I neither. We passed each other as you were coming out of one of the Treasury offices. If you were not near-sighted I should have thought they had been making a great man of you, and given you a fit of pride.'

' Ah ! indeed !—Stupid fellow ! don't you see what you have done ? '

A plate of blanc-mange fell from the hands of one of the servants ; Edward bent his head, and trusted that Lady Paulett's dress was not hurt, and then turned angrily to the man. A little confusion followed. Lady Paulett's dress was very much spotted, and Edward was still more provoked. The servant apologised humbly, and retired as quickly as possible to complain to his companions that Mr Courtenay caused the accident himself, and afterwards laid the blame upon him. Charlotte watched the scene, but discovered in it nothing unusual, and Edith from the opposite side of the table watched too, and perhaps saw deeper into his meaning. And Gertrude—in a distant corner of the room, at a side-table, she was engaged in making herself agreeable to a little knot of young boys, invited out of mere compliment, who, from shyness and awkwardness had been the stragglers of the party, and suffered the usual fate of boys in a large party—no seats, and very indifferent attendance. Whether she noticed much beyond what was passing immediately around her, none but a very keen observer would have perceived. Several times, indeed, she moved her seat so as to obtain a view of Laura, and once she forgot to answer a question; but beyond this her whole mind seemed given to the task of entertainment. Enjoyment was the ostensible object of the meeting, and enjoyment all seemed determined to have, Laura not excepted. Gertrude distinguished her laugh, and saw that she was eager in conversation; and her mind rested contented, for she had lately learned to feel that, under some circumstances, 'sufficient' unto the hour, as well as unto the day, 'is the evil thereof.' Yet the ordeal was a trying one. The highest principle will scarcely stand the wearying exertion of appearing gay when the heart is sad, for any length of time; and Gertrude's spirits nearly failed her before the ladies rose from the table. The change was a relief, but only a temporary one. Laura's face told a tale of hidden suffering, which Gertrude trembled to see; and her first entreaty was, that she would leave the party, and go to her room. 'For an hour—only for an hour, dearest,' she said; 'we will do everything that is wanted, and you shall appear again when the dancing begins.'

Laura shook her head: 'You don't know what you are advising, Gertrude. Feel.' And she put her hand within Gertrude's. It was burning with fever. 'I must stay,' she said: 'an hour's rest would be no rest,—only do not leave me: my head is giddy—I cannot trust myself; and I might be obliged to talk—Miss Forester might come: I know her eyes are fixed on me now; I feel them wherever I move; but she shall not see. Gertrude, she sat near me at dinner. Did you hear me laugh?'

'Ah! my dear,' exclaimed Mrs Courtenay, who had overheard the last words, 'I wanted to know what you were so merry about. It did one's heart good to hear you. I must tell you,' she added, lowering her voice, 'everything was so very nice; I was charmed that it went off well—all but poor Lady Paulett's gown—dear me! there she is sitting alone; I must really go and ask her whether anything can be done about it.'

Laura followed, glad to have some excuse for moving; and Gertrude, rousing herself to exertion, did her best to make the next hour pass agreeably. She was left almost alone to the task, for Jane was tired, and Charlotte and Edith were gone. Gertrude from the window perceived them once at the farther end of the colonnade. They were talking earnestly; but as they turned the angle of the house she lost sight of them. Their conversation was no mystery—nothing was a mystery now but Edward's journey, and Miss Forester's meaning smile.

<hr>

CHAPTER XXXVIII.

'THE dancing is just going to begin, my dear; where are your sisters?'

Mrs Courtenay's voice awoke Jane from a reverie. 'Gertrude, mamma, do you mean? There she is, talking to that young lady in blue,'

'No, not Gertrude, but the others.'

'Oh! never mind, they can take care of themselves. Look, mamma, that really is perfect.'

The folding doors were thrown open, and a sudden blaze burst upon the spectators. The splendid drawing-room, apparently forming but the anteroom to the illuminated conservatory, glittered as if by magic lights, sparkling amid dark leaves and gay wreaths, and reflected, again and again, from opposite glasses.

'Charlotte's work,—how beautiful!' exclaimed Jane: 'what pleasure she will have in seeing it!'

A heavy sigh, so close as to be heard even amongst the murmurs of admiration, was the answer. Charlotte was standing near them in the doorway.

'My dear,' exclaimed Mrs Courtenay, going up to her, 'I have been looking for you so long. Captain Stuart has been asking for you; he wants you to dance the first quadrille.'

'Me? I can't dance; don't let him ask me.'

'My dear Charlotte, you are foolish. What did you come here for but to dance? Do persuade her, Jane. Where is Gertrude? I do hope some one will make her do it.'

Mrs Courtenay became agitated, as she often did when other persons would have been out of temper.

' Yes, where is Gertrude ?' exclaimed Charlotte ; and without attending to her mother, she moved away.

The music sounded, and dancing commenced ; but Gertrude was not seen. Standing in a corner of the library by the entrance of the drawing-room, she was watching with breathless interest the progress of a conversation between Edward and General Forester, who, taking advantage of the noise and gaiety, were evidently engaged in a discussion of no light moment. General Forester's manner was eager and authoritative ; his arm was occasionally stretched out, as if forgetting the attention he might attract in the importance of the question ; and once his hand was placed upon Mr Courtenay's shoulder, with the familiarity of an old, long-tried friend. And Gertrude's longing desire to discover as much, at least, as Edward's countenance could reveal, was granted. Pride was stamped upon his noble brow, and bitter thoughts of scorn curled his lip. He leaned against the doorway, and his foot moved with restless impatience, but his eyes were fastened upon the ground, and when from time to time he raised them, there was that in their expression from which Gertrude shrank. Was it her brother?—was it Edward? with his high principles, and splendid talents, and strong resolution. Could he be reckless and despairing? Oh ! who shall smile at weakness and think lightly at vacillation, when they may be the first steps on the downward road to ruin ?

The music ceased, and the hum of merry voices rose around. Gertrude heard her name repeated, and ventured forth. It was only her mother inquiring where she had been hiding herself ; but when she had once appeared there was no retiring again. To dance was not necessary, but to assist Laura was. Yet, was the exertion possible ? She stood by Laura's side, but her gaze was fixed upon Edward ; she moved, but her attention was still directed to him ; she knew the precise moment when he ceased speaking to General Forester ; she saw the effort with which he engaged in conversation ; she noticed every person whom he addressed, and heard his hollow laugh through the din of light-hearted merriment. And the moments fled away, and the countenances around her grew more joyous, and the music more exhilarating, and the brightness of the scene more dazzling. How was it that in Gertrude's ear a solemn under-tone blended with every note ; that when her thoughts wandered for an instant from the one engrossing subject, the glittering ball-room, its lights and decorations, passed from before her, and in their stead arose the dim, narrow aisles, and arches, and windows of a simple village church ? Was it strange that, when she looked at Edward, a feeling more bitter than regret crossed her mind ? There was indeed much to struggle against. The vision she had so long dwelt upon with delight, and which for the last two days she had so earnestly striven to forget, was recurring with painful distinctness. The remembrance of what might have been her duty, and of Edward's folly—worse than folly, his selfishness, pressed upon her mind. The sacrifice seemed so great ; would it indeed be necessary ? As she asked herself the question, a well-known voice whispered in her ear—

'Will you allow me a few minutes' conversation ?'

Mr Dacre was standing beside her. Gertrude coloured with surprise, and perhaps with the consciousness of her own thoughts. She felt that they were wrong, for she would have been ashamed to confess them.

'Did you speak to me ?' she exclaimed. 'I did not know you were here.'

'I am but just come,' he replied.

'So late ?' and Gertrude looked and felt alarmed. 'There must be a cause.'

'Yes ; can you grant my request ?'

'A crowd is the best solitude,' said Gertrude.

'But can you trust yourself ?'

'I don't know. I can bear anything but suspense.'

'Only for a few minutes. I am come because there is no one but yourself who can act in this case, and no one who will understand that it is necessary. Have you spoken to your brother ?'

'Yes, but not alone. There has been no opportunity.'

They were standing at the lower end of the dancing-room, and a quadrille having just finished, several parties came up to them. Mr Dacre seemed hurried and uncomfortable.

'It will not do here,' he said. 'We shall be interrupted. Is there no other place ?'

Gertrude led the way into the conservatory, and, seating herself on a bench by the door which led into the garden, said—

'We shall be private here for a few minutes at least ; and now tell me—I am prepared for everything.'

'Even for the fulfilment of your worst fears ?'

Gertrude grasped Mr Dacre's arm, and looked wildly in his face.

T

'I am torturing you,' he said; 'but I cannot help it. I know nothing for certain, but to-morrow (I heard it about half an hour ago from Mr Rivers) there is to be a meeting held previous to the announcement of the candidates for the next election. If your brother intends coming forward, he must declare himself immediately.'

'Intends!' said Gertrude, faintly. 'I have tried to think there could be no doubt of his refusal.'

Mr Dacre gazed upon her with an expression of the deepest commiseration.

'You are pitying me,' she exclaimed. 'Why? What have you kept back?'

'Nothing but '——

'But what? If you can feel for me, you will hide nothing. It is misery.'

Mr Dacre took her cold hand in his, and said in a tone of affection—

'I have not concealed anything, but I have a dread, it may be a fancy, that all is not right—that Mr Courtenay's journey to London may have determined him. He may be already pledged.'

Gertrude clasped her hands despairingly.

'To-night there is hope,' he continued. 'General Forester is here; with what intention we can both guess. Before he is gone your brother's resolution must be taken; and before this time to-morrow it must be known by many, and with it his change of principles; for he will be forced openly to declare which side he will support in every question of importance. If he does not, he will be forsaken by more than half his party. Will you save him? Will you go to him and urge him to pause?'

Gertrude closed her eyes, and her breathing was quick and irregular, but she made an effort to reply;—'Now he will not listen. He will feel that it is not for me to interfere.'

'Now or never. Who can say anything if you do not?'

'No one. I see it must be so; but I am ignorant. I have no arguments to use.'

'It is not a case for arguments. It is the heart, not the reason, which requires to be convinced; and I need not remind you, that if words are powerless, prayer is not.'

Gertrude sighed deeply.

'This is not the scene for such an undertaking,' she said; 'but if it is right'——

'Your brother is not here,' interrupted Mr Dacre; 'he left the dancing-room with General Forester at the moment we did.'

Gertrude started from her seat. 'If he is pledged!' she exclaimed.

'Still go to him,—pray him,—force him to retract. Tell him he cannot save himself. If you have ever loved him, do not let him sell his honour for a hope that must be vain.'

'Found at last,' exclaimed a bland voice.

Mr Dacre withdrew himself from the touch of Miss Forester's hand.

'I heard you were here, and I have been looking for you so long.'

'I thank you. You have given yourself too much trouble.'

'Oh no, none at all; but I was so anxious. Some one told me you had passed down this way, and I was sure you would take cold.'

Mr Dacre looked at Gertrude entreatingly.

'You have nothing more to say?' she inquired, in a low voice; 'no arguments?'

'Nothing. Only go to him immediately.'

'Perhaps you will tell my father where I am to be found, if you see him,' said Miss Forester, as Gertrude turned away: 'I suspect he is closeted with Mr Courtenay. They have been looking very business-like the whole evening.'

Gertrude did not see the look which accompanied the words: she was gone before the sentence was concluded.

'Where did you say your father was?' inquired Mr Dacre, coldly.

'I don't know exactly, but he told me he had a good deal to say to Mr Courtenay. In fact, I suspect they are just determining what the address is to be. My father wishes to carry it away with him. But, my dear sir, you do distress me so by staying here. Fancy what it would be if you were to be taken ill.'

'Very unpleasant,' said Mr Dacre.

'Now you will go back with me; I am really frightened about you. Remember I shall have to nurse you.'

'Thank you, but my housekeeper generally takes that trouble.'

'So obstinate, so very obstinate,' said Miss Forester, sweetly. 'You will at least let us take you home in the carriage. It is very late.'

'I am obliged, but I have no intention of going yet. Do you know where I shall find Mrs Courtenay?' And Mr Dacre walked hastily away.

Miss Forester's face was anything but amiable as she followed. The Courtenays, in some shape or other, seemed destined to come between her and every endeavour she could make to win Mr Dacre's favour.

The room was gradually thinning, and the spirit of the evening seemed evaporating. The dancing still continued, but many of the party were gathered together in little knots, talking with more than usual earnestness, and glancing occasionally at a group formed at the upper part of the room, of which Mr Dacre saw with uneasiness that Gertrude was one. She was bending over Laura, who was seated upon a sofa, talking quickly. The burning crimson of fever was on her cheek, and her eyes rolled vacantly but incessantly round the room. Edith and Charlotte were with her, and there was an evident desire to conceal what was passing. Gertrude looked at Mr Dacre, as if to ask his forgiveness for delay; but as he approached Miss Forester came up also.

'Stand near,' whispered Gertrude to Edith; 'she must not see her.'

Laura turned hastily.

'Go,' she said, wildly. 'You crowd me. Give me air. Gertrude—where is Gertrude?'

'Close to you, dearest,' said Gertrude, gently ; and she placed herself directly in front.

Mr Dacre held back, but Miss Forester pressed on. Several other persons came up at the same time, and Laura's voice was again raised, begging that they would leave her.

'She is not well; there are too many about her,' said Gertrude ; 'I must beg you not to come so near.'

The words were addressed to Miss Forester, but she did not or would not hear.

'Oh, it is the excitement! I knew she would do too much. I must offer her these salts.'

Her hand was stretched out, but Gertrude thrust it aside with a civil apology.—

'Excuse me; I must insist.'.

She looked round for Mr Dacre.

'Have you forgotten everything?' he said, as he came close to her.

'It is impossible to go,' replied Gertrude; 'Laura is ill.'

'It must be possible. Another quarter of an hour may be too late.'

'But Laura'——

'Leave her, leave her. There are others to care for her.'

'Let me come for one minute,' said Miss Forester, pushing herself before Charlotte. 'Dearest Mrs Courtenay, only try this. You used to be very fond of it.'

Laura had sunk back upon the sofa, and her head was averted; but the smooth accents fell upon her ear, with all their miserable associations, and with a scream of anguish she started up. The music suddenly ceased, and there was a general rush of inquiry.

'Go,' said Mr Dacre to Gertrude, almost sternly.

Gertrude cast one lingering look upon Laura.

'Remember, you are to see him, whoever may be with him.'

Gertrude turned away as Laura uttered her name, and, without being noticed by any one, left the room.

CHAPTER XXXIX.

IN the small, luxurious apartment, hung with prints and crowded with books, which was appropriated as a study, Mr Courtenay was seated in company with General Forester. Both were engaged in writing; the one deeply, with his brows knit, and his head leaning upon his hand; the other carelessly, as if merely for the passing away of a few spare minutes, or, more probably, as a screen to conceal the attention with which he marked the progress of his companion. The door was closed and locked, the curtains were drawn, and the lamp burnt brightly on the table. It seemed an hour devoted to business, but bursts of music and tones of gaiety were sounding faintly from the farther extremity of the corridor; and the roll of carriages and the bustle of departing guests told that a different scene was passing in the other part of the house.

'It is late,' said Edward, laying down his pen with a weary sigh, and looking at his watch; 'will not to-morrow do as well?'

'No time like the present,' was the answer; 'besides, we have a meeting at ten in the morning.'

'It is not a thing to be done in a hurry,' exclaimed Edward; 'if it were only to judge how the sentences should be worded.'

'Oh! that—there is no difficulty in managing the words; let us only have the sense.   May I be allowed to look?'—and he took up the paper, which lay on Mr Courtenay's desk.

'What do you say?' inquired Edward, rather anxiously; 'will it do?'

'Ah, hem! we will see: it is a good commencement.'   Edward beat his foot in irritation.   To be patronised, was more than any ordinary temper could endure.   General Forester went on reading; but the writing was bad—the sentences were interlined—many required consideration.   Edward's eyes were fixed upon him; it seemed as if he would never end.

'You had better let me have it;' and he took the paper from his hand.

'No, no; I understand it perfectly.   It is very well—very right, as far as it goes; but'——

'Well! what?'

'It won't suit.   It is not explicit.'

'Every subject is mentioned which we have ever discussed.'

'Yes; but not your definite opinion.'

Edward pushed aside the table, and rose angrily from his seat. 'I can bear a great deal,' he said, 'but not to be dictated to. I will give my promise upon every point; Church question—manufactures—poor laws; my honour will be pledged upon all; but the manner in which I am to express myself to my constituents is my own affair; and I am, and must be, the best judge of what is right.'   The word 'right' was pronounced with hesitation.

'Then we part,' said General Forester, coolly.   'Put forth such a declaration as this, and two-thirds of your supporters will leave you.   They require, and will have, a positive, open avowal.'

'Require! will have!' repeated Edward.

'Yes; they are strong words, but true ones.   Who will believe that you are intending to vote against all you have hitherto upheld, unless you profess it plainly?'

'Who?—who, indeed?' were the words which rose to Edward's lips.   He walked to the window, and, drawing aside the curtain, looked out upon the bright summer night.

'Time is passing,' said General Forester; 'do you repent?' Edward's gaze was upon the deep blue sky, and he did not answer. 'Mr Courtenay, this is trifling; I am not here to wait your leisure. Am I to consider this paper as the only declaration you intend to give?'

Still Edward paused. From the purity of the heavens, he had turned to the beauty of the earth,—to the fair domain, the outline of which was dimly shadowed forth by the pale moonlight. Let him offend General Forester and his party, and his election was lost. Let his election be lost, and the hope for which he had been willing to sacrifice his honour, the prospect of retaining his property and saving himself from ruin, was lost likewise. General Forester waited in angry surprise, and was about to make another and a last effort, when Edward placed himself again at the table. 'It must be,' he said. 'Yes, you are right; it must be; but the recompense will be ample.' The pen fell from Edward's hand. Why did the thought of recompense make him start with the fear of a coward?

'Half-past eleven,' said General Forester; 'my watch is very correct. I am sorry to hurry you.'

'Some one knocked,' exclaimed Edward, and he turned pale.

'Oh! no; never mind. The door is fastened; we can't be interrupted.' Edward took up his pen again. Another knock, and a louder one. 'No admittance!' exclaimed General Forester. But he had gone a step too far; Edward allowed no one but himself to be master in his own house. His pen was once more cast aside,—his paper carefully covered,—and the door was opened. It was Gertrude, trembling and agitated; her face of care sadly contrasting with the light elegance of her dress, and shrinking with a natural timidity from a task for which her youth and sex rendered her in her own opinion unfitted.

'Edward, I am come—may I see you? Could I speak a few words?' she began.

'Not now—by and by. I am engaged particularly.' He was about to close the door, but she prevented him.

'It is necessary—indeed I must; it is something which must not be delayed.'

'Laura!' exclaimed Edward, in a tone of uneasiness.

'No,' replied Gertrude, though her conscience smote her as she remembered the state in which she had left her.

'Then go, go. I cannot listen to you now.'

'Edward, dear Edward; let me come but for five minutes; it will make me wretched if you refuse.'

'Are you foolish, Gertrude? Don't you see I am engaged? General Forester is here.'

'General Forester? that is but another reason. I must speak to you at once.'

'Ridiculous! absurd!' exclaimed Edward, allowing her to enter. 'If you insist, you shall make your own apology.'

'General Forester will excuse it, I am sure,' said Gertrude, recovering her usual quiet dignity of manner. 'My business is of consequence, or I would not dream of intruding.'

'It will be attended to, I have no doubt,' said General Forester, with a formal bow; 'but perhaps you will not object that mine should be ended first.'

Poor Gertrude felt abashed and confused, but did not offer to retire, and Edward looked at her impatiently. 'You forget,' he said; 'a lady, and a young lady, may surely give way.'

'I would indeed, Edward, if I dared. If General Forester will allow me but a few minutes.'

The General's countenance expressed irritation and contempt.

'I can scarcely ask you to wait,' said Edward; 'this important matter can be nothing but a trifle.'

'My time is not generally at the disposal of every young lady who may require it,' said General Forester; 'however, since you wish it——. You will send, I suppose, when I may be allowed to return.'

He left the room. Gertrude's heart failed her; she stood before her brother mute and trembling. Edward seated himself in pettish silence. 'I am ready,' he said, after a short pause. Gertrude's lips moved, but no sound escaped them. She drew near to the table, and took up the papers, and touched the pens, but no words came to her assistance. 'Gertrude,' exclaimed Edward, 'I am in no mood to bear this trifling.' The allusion dispelled the charm by which Gertrude was bound.

'I know it,' she said; 'it was for that reason I came; only bear with me patiently.'

'Speak!' he replied, hastily; 'I wish for no mysteries.'

'It is not my place,' continued Gertrude; 'but I am forced into it. General Forester is urging you to stand for another election.'

'Well! yes. Why should it distress you? Do you think I shall lose it?' And he tried to laugh.

'I don't know. It is not the election; it is not your success which I care for.'

' Go, Gertrude !' exclaimed Edward ; 'this is unworthy of your sense. What folly has possessed you? If this is all, General Forester had better return immediately.'

' Stay, stay !' exclaimed Gertrude ; 'it is not all. Blame me, laugh at me, if you will ; yet I must speak. Edward, is it true that you are going to sacrifice your principles ?'

' Do you know what you are saying ?' interrupted Edward ; and he held her firmly by the arm, and fixed on her a gaze which made her shudder. ' Even Laura herself should not speak to me in such terms.'

Gertrude's heart beat violently,—she was almost on the point of leaving him. ' They are hard words,' she said, ' but there are none others that I can use. I have been fearfully wretched since I heard it.'

' How can it signify to you ?' he exclaimed, in a softened voice. ' It is a woman's weakness which makes you fear ; you do not understand these things.'

' No,' replied Gertrude, endeavouring to be composed. ' There are many things which I do not understand, but this is not one. You are not fitted for dishonour, Edward ; you could not bear it. It would crush you to the dust ; you would be miserable— miserable for life, and Laura too.'

Edward returned to his seat, and again began writing. ' You will tell General Forester,' he said, without raising his eyes, ' I am ready for him.'

' Edward, I cannot go. I will not, till you have granted me one favour. Wait only till to-morrow.'

' To-morrow !' exclaimed Edward, throwing himself back in his chair. ' Folly ! impossibility ! ignorance ! Listen, Gertrude !' He held her hand, and looked at her with a ghastly smile of despair. ' I am pledged. Now go.' He pushed her from him, and once more rose from his seat.

Gertrude stood thunderstruck. A mist floated before her eyes, and her thoughts were wandering and indistinct. Hopelessness was in her heart, but she forced herself to speak. ' I will hide nothing from you, Edward,' she said ; ' I know all. You are driven to this, because you have no other resource. You cannot bring yourself to declare that you are ruined.'

Edward recoiled from the word. He clenched his hand firmly ; and the veins in his forehead swelled with indignation, as he moved towards the door.

' I am going,' said Gertrude, in the quiet tone of misery, which cannot be expressed. ' I would save you—God knows how willingly ! and not with words only.'

Edward heard, but did not comprehend. He stood with his arms folded, his eyes fixed. At that moment a bustle was heard in the passage, and immediately afterwards a quick knock at the door. Gertrude thought of Laura, and hastened to open it. ' I gave orders not to be interrupted,' exclaimed Edward.

' My mistress, sir,' replied the servant.

' What of your mistress ? Speak instantly.'

The maid looked at Gertrude. ' Is she worse ? What has been done ? ' asked Gertrude, eagerly.

' Miss Edith thinks, ma'am, that some one should be sent for, but she wishes my master to say.'

' What does it mean ? ' exclaimed Edward. ' Gertrude, you have kept it from me. I saw she was unlike herself.'

' You would pardon me if you knew,' began Gertrude, but Edward would not listen. He thrust aside the hand which she had laid upon his arm, and rushed to Laura's apartment.

CHAPTER XL.

THE excitement of Laura's mind during the whole of that eventful day might have affected even a much stronger constitution than hers, and when added to the anxiety, not of days, but of weeks and months previous, its effects were very alarming. When Gertrude left the dancing-room, it could no longer be concealed that Laura was seriously ill. Her voice and manner, so strange and wandering, roused general attention ; and inquiries and surmises circulated quickly through the room, but it was a considerable time before she could be prevailed on to move. Edith entreated, Charlotte insisted, Mrs Courtenay, in great alarm, threatened an immediate visit from a physician, but Laura was inflexible. Mr Dacre stood by, at first afraid of interfering. He could not go away, for he felt as if he was responsible for all that might happen in Gertrude's absence ; but seeing that Miss Forester's presence was painful, he ventured at last to exert the power which he knew he possessed, and, in a tone that sounded like command, suggested, that in cases like the present, relations were the only proper persons to take any active part. Miss

Forester frowned her annoyance, but obeyed ; and withdrew to a distant corner, to express her fears that 'dear Mrs Courtenay was worried. Her sisters were very kind, but it was clear they did not understand how to treat her.' There were few, however to listen. One by one the guests had dwindled away,—some from delicacy, others from fatigue. The dancing had ceased, the lights were burning low, the evergreen leaves were drooping, the sounds of waltzes and quadrilles were exchanged for the tread of the musicians as they stepped over the empty benches with their instruments clattering against the stands. There was a bustle in the anteroom ; a search for shawls and furs ; and a whispered murmur amongst those whose carriages had not been announced ; but by degrees these also ceased. The guests had departed, with the exception of Mr Dacre, Miss Forester, and her father, who was waiting in gloomy silence his summons to the study, and Laura was then induced by mingled force and entreaty to retire. Miss Forester would have followed, but Mr Dacre prevented her ; and in a fit of irritation which could not be concealed, she threw herself back upon the sofa. Mr Dacre seated himself opposite, and General Forester paced the room. No one was inclined for conversation, and few words were spoken, except when Miss Forester occasionally urged upon her father the folly of remaining longer.

Minutes and half-hours passed ; the lights were nearly extinguished ; and the General grew impatient. Footsteps and hushed voices were heard perpetually. Mr Dacre went to the door, and meeting a servant, made inquiries for Laura. 'It is a brain fever, sir,' said the man, in a low voice. 'My master has sent off for advice.' Miss Forester heard the announcement, and the colour forsook her cheek. She said no more about going, but sat still and silent ;—perhaps she was meditating upon her own share in Laura's illness.

They are stern but most salutary truths which are taught by a sick-bed ; and taught, not always by degrees, but often as suddenly and impressively as the visitations with which we are afflicted. Edward had passed through life with scarcely any experience of illness ; he had known but one great shock—his father's death, and this had taken place when he was absent from home ; and since that time, disease and death had never been brought closely to him. And now, with his conscience burdened, his heart distracted with worldly care, he was in a moment, as it were, confronted with them. He placed himself by Laura's bed, but she did not see him; and when he spoke, she seemed not to hear. Her beautiful eyes were glaring and vacant, her mouth was half open, her lips were dark with fever. A gulf seemed suddenly to have opened before him; and in it, in a few short hours, might be entombed all that had made his life desirable. Without his wife, what would wealth or honour profit him? During the first stupefying horror, no one dared to address him; but when his face relaxed from his expression of agony, and he began to inquire what had been done, Charlotte, in ignorance of his tone of mind, spoke to him of hope. He took no notice of her, but immediately left the room. To tell him there was hope, was to tell him also that there was fearful danger. After a short interval he returned; and Gertrude suggested to Edith that she should give up her place by Laura's pillow, and leave him to do anything that might be required. He seated himself, but it was only to gaze for a minute, and then to turn away, as if unable to endure the sight. Gertrude thought of General Forester; but the past and the future seemed suddenly to have vanished from Edward's mind. His only thought was for the arrival of the physician, whose delay seemed longer than was necessary. He came, however, at last; and all felt thankful and relieved, if it were only to be saved from the misery of doubt as to what should be done. The first order given was to send from the room all except those who could really be useful. Jane went willingly; but Mrs Courtenay insisted upon remaining in the dressing-room; and Edith still lingered, though conscious she could do little to assist. Gertrude was uneasy; she would willingly have gone herself, but her long experience of illness made her presence necessary. Edward was becoming impatient: he seemed distressed at the least noise,—and to see any persons about him beckoning and whispering, was more than his irritability could bear; for, besides his anxiety about Laura, he had still on his mind the weight of his other cares. He had not forgotten General Forester, though Gertrude thought he had; but, in that chamber, he could not resolve to follow his guidance. Whilst others were attending upon Laura, he had leisure for meditation. Stationed behind her, he watched all that was passing, and listened to her wandering words; and the sudden change—the possibility of what the end might be—awoke feelings which had long slumbered in his breast. Suffering and sorrow bring us near to the invisible world; and in the presence of saints and angels, and before Him who is the Lord of all, how shall we resolve to sin against our own convictions? Edward thought, and hesitated. He looked at Gertrude, and the word 'dishonour' rang in his ears. He gazed upon the features of her whom he most loved, and the still image of death rose up before him, to warn him of the vanity of earthly hopes. He knew that if the world thought lightly of what he was about to do, yet his own conscience would continually accuse him; and even then, pledged as he was, he asked himself if it would not be possible to give up the election, to forget the offer that had been made him, and again retire into privacy; and if Laura were restored to him, should he not appreciate as he had never done before the happiness of domestic life. But the scene changed. His happiness was to be centered in his home. And his home, where would it be? He was a beggar. He clasped his hands, and bent his head upon Laura's pillow. With a wild unconscious movement she pushed him from her; and then, in a tone which thrilled to his very soul, called upon him to come to her; accused him of unkindness, and prayed him to forgive her.

'Take me, take me,' she exclaimed; 'Gertrude, I deceived him. He is gone. Who says he did not love me?'

Edward leant over in agony. 'Go,' he said, aloud, as the physician would have beckoned him away. 'Leave me, all; you can do nothing.'

'He is right, Edith,' whispered Gertrude; 'some one must go, for all our sakes.'

'Jane and my mother,' began Edith. She was interrupted by Edward, who came up to her as if a sudden thought had struck him, and said, in a hurried under-tone, 'Why do you stay? You did not care for her.'

'O Edward! forgive me; I have done wrong; but do not punish me so cruelly.'

'This is not the place, Edith,' said Gertrude. 'He will not listen to you.'

'He must. I cannot go. It is in vain to insist'——

'Edward, Edward,' again repeated Laura. And Edward groaned in misery.

'You can do nothing now,' said Gertrude, drawing Edith aside; 'if you will take my mother home, and leave Charlotte with me, you shall hear the very first thing. It is madness for us all to waste our strength, when we cannot tell how it may be required.'

'But you, Gertrude, who have had so much to bear.'

‘I must not leave Edward. Everything depends on the next few hours. Things are worse than we imagined. I have spoken to him, but as yet to no purpose; and I must try again. Whatever happens, he must be kept from sacrificing himself.’

‘But there can be no such great reason for being uneasy at this instant.’

‘Yes, indeed there is. I cannot explain, but you must not urge my leaving him.’

Edith still seemed unwilling to consent to the arrangement; she returned to the bed, and Gertrude stole noiselessly from the chamber. Two servants passed her in the gallery, and from them she learned that General Forester was still in the house. She listened at the top of the staircase, and heard his step as he walked the room below, and directly afterwards the drawing-room bell rang. Gertrude waited till a second peal, and then hurried back to the sick-room. Edith was waiting with her mother in the dressing-room, and Edward had given up his place to Laura’s maid, and was seated at the bottom of the bed. Gertrude dreaded to make him angry by speaking, when he longed for silence. She placed herself by him, doubting what to do, but he soon observed her, and inquired eagerly if she wanted anything.

‘Let me speak but two words with you.’

‘Not now,’ he replied, gloomily : ‘spare me; I have had enough.’

‘But it must be now,—General Forester is waiting.’

Edward rose hastily, and signed her to follow him.

‘Your incautiousness is maddening,’ he said, as they stopped at the head of the staircase. ‘Why are my private affairs to be betrayed to every one?’

Gertrude made no excuse. She stood meekly before him, as if really in the wrong, and then said, ‘I know you have much to excuse; but may I take your message to General Forester? He is still here, and of course expects that you will see him again.’

‘Tell him—but no, there is no time. Say that I will leave everything’—— He paused again.

‘Not to him!’ exclaimed Gertrude. ‘O Edward! have pity!’

‘And bring Laura to misery,’ exclaimed Edward. ‘Gertrude, it is but selfishness in you to ask it.’

‘Selfishness!’ began Gertrude, with the proud consciousness of innocence; but the sentence went no farther, and leaning

against the balustrade, she shed tears such as she never shed
before. For the third time the drawing-room bell rang, loudly
and angrily. A servant crossed the hall, and Edward called to
him, 'Is General Forester here still?'

'Yes, sir; he has just rung.'

'Stop; take him this message.' Edward put his hand before
his eyes, and Gertrude, with her hands folded, and her gaze
riveted upon her brother, waited for the next word with an in-
tensity of expectation only endurable because it was blended with
prayer. The dull ticking of the clock told the rapid moments.
To Gertrude they were as the slow passing of an hour. Edward
did not move, and the servant stood patiently below, looking up
into the glimmering darkness of the gallery, when Laura's unconscious laugh was faintly heard. 'Tell him I cannot see him;
he shall hear before ten,' exclaimed Edward. He was gone the
next minute. The message was taken to General Forester, and
Gertrude was left alone.

It was a reprieve—only a reprieve; yet Gertrude was inexpressibly thankful. She felt that it was the answer to her prayer.
She remained still certain that General Forester was gone, and
then went to find Jane, and prevail on her to return to the Priory,
as an inducement to Mrs Courtenay and Edith to go too. When
the house was free, she hoped that Edward might be less
harassed. Jane roused herself from a slumber on a sofa, in a
distant chamber, and objected to being sent away in the middle
of the night; but Gertrude's influence was seldom exerted in
vain, and with some demur she consented. Mrs Courtenay was
obstinate, and Edith very miserable; and it was not until after
a conversation of nearly half an hour, that all parties agreed at
last to order the carriage. The physician was upon the point of
departure also, for Laura was quieter, and all had been done
which could at that moment be required. He spoke cheerfully,
and told of several cases in which, when all hope was relin-
quished, recovery had been granted; but Gertrude read in his
countenance a fear which he would not confess, and even Edward
seemed scarcely comforted by an opinion so doubtful. There
was now, however, a stillness in the house, which in cases of
sickness is almost as necessary to the watcher as to the sufferer.
Laura still lay with a vacant distressed gaze, but her pulse was
less violent, and her manner more composed. That she was in
danger no one could doubt; but after the lapse of more than an
hour, Edward, as he remarked the dangerous symptoms diminish-

ing, although almost imperceptibly, felt that he need not despair. Under other circumstances the blessedness of hope would have been without alloy—but now it brought only a change of care. While Laura's state was so appalling, he forgot in a measure that any other trial awaited him ; but when that ceased, the future in store for them both came distinctly into view. Vacillation would soon be no longer in his power. He had left Elsham for London, on a sudden impulse, because ruin stared him in the face. Without allowing himself time for recollection, he had seen his friends, and pledged himself to give up all that he had hitherto upheld in opposition to them, if only he could be assured of the promised office,—and in a few hours' time he was to profess his weakness publicly. All this he had engaged to do. And when he had done it, what would be his feelings ? How would he enjoy his home, and the society of his family ! With what pleasure would he listen to the praise of his talents ? How would he endure to meet the eyes of those who had hitherto respected him ? Above all, how would he dare to kneel before God and ask His blessing, when bound by a promise to his fellow-creatures to support the very measures which in his heart he believed to be evil ?

Gertrude knew her brother well, when she said that dishonour would crush him to the dust. But there was something more terrible than dishonour which at that moment pressed upon Edward's mind. He had erred, blindly and foolishly, but his conscience was not yet deadened. Memories of the past, recollections of early resolutions, of dreams of goodness, and longings to attain even upon earth the holiness of heaven, rose before him in the gloom of those solemn hours ; and when the morning light stole through the crevices of the window, upon Laura's darkened chamber, Edward in the bitterness of his anguish could almost have been satisfied to be told, that on earth she would never wake to the consciousness that he was a guilty or a ruined man.

CHAPTER XLI.

BUT the hour of final decision rapidly approached. The gray twilight faded before the rising sun, and the distant sounds of busy life broke upon the deep stillness of the dawn. The servants

moved with silent footsteps about the house, unlocking doors, and
opening shutters, and endeavouring, as much as possible, to remove the vestiges of the last evening's festivities. The maid left
Laura's bedside, and crept softly about the room, putting the chairs
against the wall, and smoothing the carpets, and arranging the
glasses and bottles on the stand. Edward envied her occupations. To have gone forth to work for his daily bread would
have been delight compared with the mental suffering he was
enduring. He looked round for Gertrude. She had been resting on the sofa for a considerable time, and he thought she was
asleep, but she had left the room unperceived. He waited long,
expecting her return. Though he could not ask her to forgive
him, he thought he should like to show by his actions that he
was no longer angry, and it was an excuse for delaying the task
of reading over the papers which had been left in the study, so
as to re-write them to suit General Forester's views. Still
Gertrude did not come, but he could not make up his mind to
go, for Laura was becoming more restless. He begged Charlotte
to relinquish her seat, and poured out some medicine himself,
and was about to give it ; but Laura bent her eyes upon him,
and asked him who he was, and the glass dropped on the floor.

'Where is Gertrude?' he inquired, going up to Charlotte
again.

'I don't know. I think she is gone to lie down somewhere
else. She has had no real sleep.'

'Is it late?' said Edward. 'Do you think she will come
back?'

'Half-past seven. I dare say she will stay some time; she
requires rest more than I do.'

Two hours and a half still. But Edward was becoming dreadfully excited. He felt that he must determine at once. Another
hour of indecision would be more than his mind would bear.
The dressing-room was closed, and fancying that he heard some
one move, he softly opened it. Gertrude was there, but Edward
dared not speak to her. She was kneeling before the open
window, her hands clasped in prayer. He gazed upon her for
a few moments, while many thoughts of self-reproach filled his
mind, and was then about to shut the door, when she suddenly
rose. A deep blush overspread her countenance, as she turned
and saw him.

'I am interrupting you,' he said. 'I did not know you were
here.'

'Perhaps I ought not to be,' said Gertrude ; 'but I could not go far from Laura ; and when we are unhappy what can we do besides ?'

'What can you do, you mean?' replied Edward ; and he put his arm round her and kissed her. 'It is not every one that can pray.'

'It must be so horrible not to be able to do it,' said Gertrude, with a sigh. 'Life must be such a burden without it, I have wondered sometimes that any one can keep his senses who does not do it.'

'But there is hope for us now,' said Edward. 'Laura is not worse.'

'No,' replied Gertrude : 'and she has a strong constitution which has never been much tried. There are many things in her favour.'

Both paused ; for they felt that Laura's illness was not then their chief anxiety.

'We shall be happy,' began Edward ; but the word grated upon him.

'Happy ! when ?' asked Gertrude.

'I don't know. Never !'

Gertrude longed to speak ; but she had done her utmost, and now she was resigned.

'There is no happiness for me, Gertrude,' he continued. 'There may be for you.'

'Not for me, without you. I may submit and be grateful, but I can never be happy.'

'Then there is a long life of misery before you,' exclaimed Edward : 'inevitable. Whichever way I act, there is no escape.'

'You are speaking from feeling and not from reason,' said Gertrude. 'In one case I know you must be miserable, and so we all must ; but not in the other.'

'Not miserable !' exclaimed Edward. 'Then you do not know one-half of what is in store for me. Look,' and he drew her to the window, and pointed to the Park and gardens ; 'you think all this is mine—but, Gertrude'—— and his voice sank with agitation—'I tell you, not one tree, not one flower, not one stone upon the whole of the estate is mine, unless I consent to keep my pledge. And when all is gone, what am I to do? Where am I to wander to? Must I return to my mother, and beg her to receive me as a dependent, and give me bread to eat, and feed my wife and child ? I would die first.'

' Is there no alternative?' said Gertrude, gently. ' Your profession is still open to you.'

'And what? Scorn and poverty. How am I to enter upon my profession, when I am penniless? And if I were to do it, how could I bear the taunts and ridicule I should be exposed to? For myself, I could brave anything, but I am not alone : I must think for others.'

' It is a question between the scorn of good men and of bad,' said Gertrude. ' I do not think you have sufficient confidence in yourself, Edward. You do not know how much you could bear, if you felt you had acted uprightly.'

'And Laura is to be punished for my folly! She would curse the day of our marriage.'

' She would endure all things, thankfully and cheerfully,' said Gertrude. ' If ever deep, pure love was felt for any human being, she feels it for you.'

Edward struggled against betraying his emotions. ' I think she loves me,' he said; 'though lately—but I cannot talk of her; she was too good to be thrown away upon one who has deceived her.'

' Yet,' said Gertrude, 'you still can determine to deceive her more. Edward, if you care nothing for your own happiness, still remember hers.'

There was a light tap at the door. Little Charlie's voice was heard entreating that he might come in. Edward rested his head against the window, and Gertrude saw that he could not trust himself to answer. She tried to send the child away with the promise that he should return soon, but he still lingered, petitioning that he might come, only just for one minute. Gertrude doubted, and was going to admit him, when Edward signed to her to stop.

' I have ruined him,' was all he said.

His countenance told the hopeless misery of his mind. Gertrude's heart sank.

' General Forester's servant is coming down the road,' said Edward, in a deep, changed tone.

He roused himself, as if to go, but immediately sank back again to his former posture. Gertrude made no answer, and at that instant the heavy sound of the old church bell was borne towards them on the morning breeze. It was tolling for an early funeral. Edward heaved a heavy sigh, and Charlie's voice was again heard.

'Take him—send him away!' exclaimed Edward, in a voice of agony.

Gertrude opened the door, and the child in a moment was in the room.

'Papa, dear papa!' and he seized his father's hand, and tried to climb up his neck.

'Papa is busy,' said Gertrude ; 'we must not disturb him.'

'Papa will go to church,' persisted Charlie, trying to drag Edward from the window.

'Not to-day,' said Gertrude ; 'another day, perhaps.'

'Is papa naughty?' said the child, and he looked wonderingly in Gertrude's face.

Edward stooped suddenly ; lifted him in his arms, and covered him with kisses ; and when he set him down, Gertrude saw that his little cheek was wet with tears.

'Charlie must not stay here,' she said, coaxingly, as she took him by the hand.

The little fellow rebelled for a few moments, till Gertrude gently insisted, and the door was again closed. But Edward did not notice what was passing. He was listening to the slow, regular toll of the funeral bell, and wrapped in thought. Gertrude listened too, and an overpowering sensation of awe mingled with the bitterness of her feelings. It was as a voice sent to warn them of death, and the judgment that shall follow it. Many minutes elapsed, and neither of them spoke. Edward was the first to break the silence.

'I have been harsh to you,' he said. 'Can you forget and pardon it?'

'It is you who have to pardon,' answered Gertrude ; 'that I should have dared to say so much.'

'Your duty is done now,' replied he ; 'you have but to leave me to my fate. I cannot bring Laura to poverty.'

'But if I were to ask one more favour,' said Gertrude ; 'for the last time—tell me you will not be angry.'

She spoke faintly, and Edward pushed a chair towards her, and made her sit down.

'I have talked of honour,' she continued ; 'but I felt all the time that it was a low, worldly term. O Edward! even honour must so soon pass—it is but a dream ; and if you could keep Allingham, and be happy to the end of your life, it would be such a mere nothing, it seems strange that we can ever think about it. So that, perhaps, if you had only little, and knew that you were exerting yourself,—I mean if you had just enough for Laura and yourself, and were practising in your profession,—you might be really as happy as you have been. And if you could bring yourself to think so, and would take what I have, it would be something to begin upon. It is nothing to what you have been accustomed to, I know'——

Gertrude's voice grew husky, and she stopped. Edward struggled with his rising agitation. Gratitude and astonishment were succeeded by far different feelings. The very offer—the putting it in his power to give up Allingham without involving Laura in absolute poverty, seemed like the completion of the act. He saw himself already bereft of his home—a wanderer upon the world; and the beauty upon which his eye at that moment rested, was but an aggravation to his trial. Gertrude waited in patient expectation, for she knew what must be passing in his mind.

'You will hate me,' he said, at length, in a tone of deep dejection; 'it cannot be otherwise; but I am unworthy of such love.'

'I only ask that you should not reject it hastily,' replied Gertrude; 'that you should think upon it.'

'And can thinking be of any avail? No, Gertrude, no; the time for drawing back is past. But when you would condemn me, remember that I am not acting for myself.'

'You would leave an inheritance to your child,' said Gertrude; 'but if it is purchased by the sacrifice of right, what will be its value? Poverty is hard to bear, but shame and self-reproach are still harder.'

Edward was silent.

'When you have done all that is in your power to retrieve the past,' continued Gertrude; 'when Allingham is gone, and you have entered upon your new life, surely there will be happiness in reflecting that you have resisted a great temptation; in looking round upon the world, and knowing that no human being can cast a slur upon your name.'

'My name!' exclaimed Edward, vehemently. 'Yes, you may well remind me of it. It will be remembered as the last of the Courtenays of Allingham.'

'And if it should be,' replied Gertrude, gently and solemnly, 'it is but a name of Earth.'

Edward threw himself into a chair. His thoughts were to be read in the changes of his countenance. It was as the struggle of life and death, and Gertrude turned aside, that she might not witness his suffering. When he again spoke, his manner was altered. 'I have been blind and thoughtless,' he said; 'but whatever may be the consequences of my folly, I cannot involve you in it. It would be but a miserable reward for affection which can never be forgotten. If I am to bear poverty, it shall be alone. Laura would never endure that you should be injured; and, Gertrude,' he added, in a tone which chilled her with its quietness, 'it may be that she is to be spared the bitterness of my trial.'

Gertrude dared not comfort him. 'Why will you talk of injury?' she said. 'If our positions were changed, how should you feel?'

'It would be injustice,' he exclaimed; 'the world would say it, and you yourself might live to rue the day on which you had urged me to consent. You may marry.'

'And if I do,' she replied, 'I am not worse off than thousands; but I may also die, or '—and her voice changed—'I may choose to appropriate my money for other purposes. My duty, Edward, cannot lie with the future; that is in the hands of God, and with Him I do not fear to trust it.'

She knelt by his side, and threw her arm around his neck, and Edward kissed her pale forehead, with a feeling of reverence and affection too deep for words to have told. 'Gertrude,' he said, 'do not tempt me. You may be about to mar the happiness of your whole life. It is not a common risk which you will run. If I fail in my profession your fortune will be irrecoverably gone.'

'Then let it go,' she exclaimed, eagerly, 'without a thought or a regret,—only with thankfulness that it was bestowed upon those I loved so dearly.' Edward wavered. The vision of a name unstained, a life without disgrace, was nerving him for the sacrifice. 'It is your own lesson,' continued Gertrude. 'Years, —years have passed since it was first taught me. Can you recollect your twelfth birthday and my mother's present of a sovereign? I cried because I wished to have one too, and you came to me, and forced me to accept it, because you said I wanted it more than you did, and that we were both of one family, and what was given to one was for the use of all. O Edward! why are we not children now?'

It was the whisper of an angel's voice, and Edward could not but obey it. He buried his face in his hands, and Gertrude rose and stood by him, motionless as a lifeless statue. There was a long, long silence—a bitter conflict, seen but by one eye—and the trial was over. Half an hour afterwards, General Forester's servant was returning to the Grange, bearing a letter from Edward, in which he stated, that, after deliberation, he felt it would be advisable to relinquish the honour of again standing for the county. He therefore begged General Forester to express, in his name, his grateful thanks to the friends who had hitherto supported him, together with his regret that family circumstances would prevent him from taking any active part in the coming election. The letter concluded with acknowledgments of the General's exertions in his behalf, and an apology for having led him to suppose on the previous evening that he had intended to act differently. When it was gone, Edward realised, for the first time, that, by his own act, he was ruined without hope of redemption.'

CHAPTER XLII.

THE deed was done. Edward repeated the words as he shut himself up in his own room, and Gertrude pondered upon all that was involved in them, as she returned to her task of watching by Laura's bedside. But it is not in moments of excitement that we fully know what sorrow means. There is a greatness in intense suffering which unconsciously ennobles and upholds us. We feel that we are called to act a part above our fellow-creatures, and the knowledge that all which is important to them has suddenly become nothing to us, gives dignity and strength to our minds. And in seasons of distress men are more to be pitied than women. Gertrude, besides the unspeakable relief which her brother's decision had afforded her, found many things to distract and occupy her thoughts. Laura required constant attention, and, at her own request, she agreed to remain with her for several hours, whilst others took their rest. The inquiries of friends seemed incessant, and verbal answers and notes were to be sent in return. Edith came from the Priory, and to her Gertrude could speak without reserve ; and all this, together with the interest of writing to Mr Dacre, and making arrangements for Laura's comfort, served to pass the weary hours. Fatigue and sleep also came to her assistance ; but not so with Edward. He was chilly and uncomfortable, and his head ached, and his limbs were stiff; but he had no thought of rest. From Laura's bedroom to the hall, and from the hall to his study, and from the study to the garden, he wandered without object. The visit of Dr Grant was the only event which seemed left him to anticipate. His bailiff came to consult him upon some farm business, but he was sent away. What good could it be to interest himself in property which would soon cease to be his? The post brought letters, but most of them were upon parliamentary business, and no longer concerned him;—only a few bills were opened in a fit of desperation, and spread out before him, and conned with an abstracted mind, as if the mere looking at them might be the means of diminishing their amount. And during all this Edward's mind was reverting with miserable doubt to Laura's state. He believed her better, and Dr Grant had assured him that if the dangerous symptoms did not increase, he might reasonably entertain hope; but the blessing seemed greater than he could dare to expect. One grief makes us fear another; and, with a self-tormenting spirit, Edward thought over all he should feel when left alone; the bitterness with which he should regard every object connected with her; the loss to his child; the hopelessness for the long life which probably lay before him; till in agony he was about to pray that if she were taken he might not be spared. The prayer was not uttered, for something in his own heart made him tremble lest it should be granted. And so the day wore on, Dr Grant came, and his report was satisfactory; and when he spoke of the possibility that Laura would be restored, a gleam of happiness passed over Edward's darkened heart. But it was momentary. How should he dare to tell her the miserable truth?

It was late in the evening, after a sad and silent dinner with his two sisters, that he resolved upon sending for Mr Rivers, in order to take some immediate steps for the settlement of his affairs. Gertrude heard him say that he was going to write a note, and suggested that the walk might refresh him; and the idea was seized upon with avidity: it was something to do.

'I shall not see you again to-night, probably,' she said, as he took his hat to depart; 'I am going to bed. We have a nurse for to-night, and Dr Grant says she will be sufficient alone.'

Edward held out his hand; he was too wretched to be affectionate, and Gertrude was deeply hurt. She had made a sacrifice of every prospect most valuable to her, and after the first moment it seemed scarcely to be appreciated. Edward had shown her, during the whole day, not the slightest mark of peculiar regard. But a person must be far advanced in goodness before grief makes him thoughtful for others ; and even Edward's kindness of heart was not proof against the numbing effects of his sorrow.

'Don't go yet ; this is the first moment we have had together alone,' said Charlotte, as Gertrude was leaving the room.

'I can do little good by staying, I am afraid,' replied Gertrude.

'Yes, indeed, you can, by telling me everything, and putting me out of my misery. What is Edward going to do ?'

'I can say it to you,' said Gertrude ; 'you are not a person to be overpowered. He must give up all he has and leave Allingham.'

Charlotte was not overpowered, but she was inexpressibly shocked.

'That is the worst, at once,' continued Gertrude. 'It is best for some minds not to be prepared.'

'Prepared !' said Charlotte. 'I have been prepared enough all day, and yesterday too. But it is an absurdity. A man of his fortune ! You must be dreaming.'

'What do you think his fortune is ?' said Gertrude.

'Six thousand a year, of course.'

'Two ; it was never more.'

Charlotte stood in mute astonishment.

'It was mortgaged when he came into possession,' continued Gertrude : 'Edith knew it from the first.'

'That explains, then,' exclaimed Charlotte, interrupting her. 'So many things in Edith's manner have puzzled me for a long time, besides some strange hints she gave me yesterday ; but when did she tell you ?'

'Two or three days ago ; she has had a great deal to bear.'

'And has made other people bear a great deal ; but, however, I don't understand now. Edward may be in difficulties, but what you say is impossible.'

'Just consider,' replied Gertrude. 'He set out with Colonel Courtenay's establishment, which was princely ; married, and new furnished his house. Then came the election.'

'The expenses of which were paid,' said Charlotte.

'So it was understood ; but we both know Edward too well to believe he would accept more assistance than he could avoid. After the election followed the house in town, and parliamentary dinners, and Laura's grand *fêtes;* and open house here in the intervals. No fortune of two thousand a year would stand it.'

'Two thousand a year!' repeated Charlotte, slowly. 'I don't believe it.'

'Whether it is true or not, there can be no doubt of the state of Edward's affairs at this time.'

'And what will he do?' exclaimed Charlotte.

'I don't know, at present. Return to his profession by and by.'

'Don't hesitate,' said Charlotte; 'I am in a mood to hear anything.'

'That is all,' said Gertrude, quietly.

'And enough,' was the reply, in the same tone.

Both were silent for several minutes.

'I am glad you told me, Gertrude,' said Charlotte, at length; 'and not any one else.'

'Why?'

'Because you say it all out in a minute, and don't moralise.'

'It is a case for action, not for moralising,' replied Gertrude.

'If you would give me the world I could not cry,' said Charlotte. 'What is Edward gone to see Mr Rivers for?'

'All sorts of business, I suppose ; but I did not ask him'

'It will half kill mamma,' said Charlotte.

'Yes, I have thought of her; but it must be broken to her gently. We shall see how to manage when the moment comes.'

'And Laura too—does she know anything?'

'She has suspicions ; but nothing like the truth.'

'Wonderful changes,' exclaimed Charlotte. 'No wonder you have looked like a ghost the last day or two. And how horridly people will talk! If one could only change one's name!'

Gertrude could not avoid smiling.

'It is a happy thing that no strangers are here,' she said.

'Because they would not understand? Very possibly not; but you do. I am as unhappy as heart can desire in reality ; yet just now—did you ever hear of a person in a sort of trance knocking his head against a wall and not feeling it ?'

'The waking will come soon enough,' said Gertrude.

'Yes!' and Charlotte sighed from the bottom of her heart. 'This is but the beginning : but we will not sink, Gertrude. No one shall pity us.'

'Not if we can help it; for my mother's sake we must keep up.'

'They must go abroad,' said Charlotte, after some consideration.

'I suppose they must, for a year or so, but not for a continuance.'

'How will they manage to live in England if they have nothing? Edward's profession will not support him at his outset; and he will never hear of being dependent upon us.'

'He will have something,' said Gertrude. 'You know my fortune is a great deal more than I can spend.'

'You are not going to give up your fortune? exclaimed Charlotte.

'Why not? It may as well be used by one member of the family as another.'

Charlotte's firmness was shaken. Her eyes glistened; and, with an earnestness of feeling most unlike her usual cold, light-hearted indifference, she said, as she kissed her sister, 'Gertrude, if I were only certain that I should some day be like you!'

The next moment she dashed her hand across her eyelid; and ran out of the room, declaring that she had been wanted to take the nurse's place a quarter of an hour before.

CHAPTER XLIII.

THREE days had gone by—days of wearisome, anxious watching, and gloom. Edward's time had been divided between Laura's chamber and his own study; he could not summon resolution to go beyond. A barrier had suddenly sprung up between him and the world, in which he had played so busy a part; and all that passed in it was now but 'as the idle wind, which he regarded not.' His note to General Forester had been answered the day after it was sent; but even the cold, sarcastic tone in which the General lamented the unfortunate circumstances that had induced him so totally to mislead his party, nor the information that a personal friend of his own was about to occupy his position and stand for the county, served to excite pain. Some hasty expressions of contempt escaped him, and the note was tossed aside, and thought of no more. Gertrude noticed his manner, and strove, by every means in her power, to interest him. She had determined upon remaining at Allingham with Charlotte, notwithstanding Edith's entreaties that she might share the fatigue, for she could tell, from the few words which now and then dropped from Edward, that he disliked seeing Edith attempt to nurse Laura. He remembered her neglect in former days, and he fancied that Laura herself would dislike it. This decision was a sad trial to Edith, whose only wish now was to atone, as much as lay in her power, for her former conduct; but Gertrude was firm. She had deemed it necessary to tell Dr Grant her opinion, that distress of mind had increased, if not entirely brought on, Laura's illness, and he had so strongly insisted upon the necessity of keeping her free from excitement, whenever the fever should decrease, so as to restore her to consciousness, that Gertrude dreaded to allow any person but herself to remain with her. She entreated Edward to keep himself out of sight, and he obeyed; not because he considered it necessary, but because his spirit was so sunk that he had not energy to resist; and then Gertrude stationed herself in the sick-room, and smoothed the pillow, and administered the medicine, and bore with all the harassing requirements of serious illness, till at length the office of nurse was tacitly yielded to her; and even Charlotte only came into the room now and then to know if anything was wanted. Gertrude was contented at her post, for it occupied her usefully; but it also gave her much leisure for thought, and thought was very bitter. One thing seemed absolutely necessary—that Edward should be told of Laura's debts. To leave her to make the confession herself, when both mind and body were weakened by illness, would be out of the question; but it was not easy to find a favourable moment for the disclosure. He was silent at breakfast, silent at dinner, silent whenever they met in the course of the day. He never mentioned Laura's name, or referred to the past; and Gertrude shrunk from intruding upon his sorrow. Every hour, however, increased her anxiety to speak to him; for Dr Grant became more hopeful at each visit, and spoke confidently of his expectation, that if a tranquil sleep could be produced, Laura might again be fully restored to them.

Gertrude was in the room alone when this opinion was expressed; and Dr Grant was no sooner gone than she hastened to the study. Edward was there engaged in looking over some papers, which, at her entrance, he thrust into a drawer. His countenance did not give her encouragement; and the tone in which he inquired what she was come for, augured ill for the patience with which he would be inclined to hear her. She informed him first of Dr Grant's opinion, and he expressed himself deeply thankful; but when she still lingered, he became restless, and glanced at the door, plainly wishing that she should go. Gertrude felt that the shortest would also be the best way of proceeding, for he was not in a mood to bear circumlocution.

'If Laura should get well,' she began.

'If? You have just told me that Dr Grant has little doubt of it.'

'Just so, and that is the reason I wanted to say a few words.'

'They must be very few then. I am busy.'

Gertrude bore with the ungracious permission, and in a manner of perfect gentleness stated to him briefly, but cautiously, the circumstances which had produced so deep an impression upon Laura's mind; the temptations of her London life; her belief that Edward's fortune was large; Miss Forester's influence and the power which she had obtained by assisting her in her difficulties; the unhappiness which Laura had experienced, whilst conscious that she was deceiving her husband; and the firmness with which at last she had resolved to give up all offers of further help, and confess everything. 'I have told you myself,' concluded Gertrude, 'to save her, and in order that you might know how to act; and now I will go: but you need not trouble yourself with regard to Miss Forester; I have settled her part of the business.'

She was about to leave him, but he caught her hand. The settled gloom upon his countenance had given way to a expression of intense suffering; 'Stay, Gertrude,' he said.

'Not now, unless you have questions to ask.'

'No,' he exclaimed, vehemently, 'it is too clear for questions. If you had been here, Gertrude, all might have been different. It was Edith who threw her into that woman's hands.'

'Edith has suffered much for her error,' said Gertrude.

'It was cruel,' he continued; 'Edith, whom I trusted so entirely! I am not blind to my own faults. I know they have been great,—so great that at times I dare not dwell upon them; but my offences have not been against Laura's happiness. I only loved her too well, and therefore I could not mar her enjoyment by checking it as I should have done ; but Edith neglected and repelled her.'

'You would forgive her,' said Gertrude, 'if you knew her misery.'

'Heaven forbid that I should not forgive !' replied Edward, solemnly; 'but she can never make amends. Did Laura indeed dread my anger? How little she knew !' He stopped, overcome by the ideas which crowded upon his mind. 'It was that one concealment,' he exclaimed, after a pause. 'Fool that I was ! if I had but told her all, she would have warned and supported me. And you, Gertrude,' he added, 'who have done no wrong, must be punished for us all ! Edith thought her selfish,' he continued, 'and accused her to me of selfishness ; but she had not a care for herself. She was idolised in her home, and when they trusted her to me, they thought they were sending her to those who would idolise her too. Gertrude, if you had only seen her as she was when first we married, you would own that it was a harsh spirit which could utter a word against her.'

'There are few to equal her now,' said Gertrude, feeling that it was not the moment to attempt Edith's defence.

'She was perfect,' exclaimed Edward, enthusiastically ; 'and she was happy as she deserved to be. She knew no care till she knew me, and I made her give up all, and promised to cherish and protect her, and then brought her to misery.'

'You will not think it misery by and by,' said Gertrude.

'If it is not so,' he exclaimed, eagerly, 'it will be through your means. Do not judge me hardly, Gertrude. I may seem to you cold and ungrateful, but it is only from wretchedness.' The tone was one of despair, and Gertrude feared to allude again to the former subject, though she knew that something ought to be done immediately for the settlement of the remainder of Laura's debts. But Edward had lately brought himself to think over the details of business, whatever might be the state of his mind. With a calmness which surprised while it pained her he asked for the bills, and said that he would consult Mr Rivers as to the best mode of discharging them. 'It will be the first step,' he said, 'towards freeing myself :—freeing myself, that is, from all obligations but the one which no money can repay.'

The words were common, but the manner in which they were spoken, and the look which accompanied them, sank deeply into Gertrude's heart. She left him, satisfied, and comparatively cheerful, and returned to Laura's chamber. She had not reached

it before the door was very softly opened, and Charlotte's finger
was held up in token of silence. Dr Grant's prescription had
taken effect, and Laura was sleeping. Gertrude beckoned her
sister into the gallery, and then entreated her to leave her alone
in the room ; but Charlotte strongly objected, saying that no one
could tell how long the sleep might last, and that Gertrude was
not equal to such constant fatigue. There was a little pique
mixed with Charlotte's determination ; she did not approve of
wholly giving up the duty of nursing, and she was not unselfish
enough to see that there are times when sitting idle is as great a
virtue as exertion. Gertrude was equally firm, though conscious
that she must appear wilful—perhaps unkind and selfish. It
was essential that Laura's mind should be kept quiet on first recovering its tone, and no one could do this as effectually as herself ; but it was not easy to explain this to Charlotte ; and when
at length the point was yielded, it was with a very bad grace.
Gertrude was extremely vexed. Circumstances had compelled
her to take more upon herself than she would otherwise have
thought of doing ; and it was peculiarly disagreeable to insist
upon anything in which her own gratification seemed involved ;
but there are duties to be performed through evil report as well
as good, and this was one. She crept into the room, and sat down
in the accustomed chair. Laura lay with her head bent down,
her lips apart, and her thin, white hands spread upon the coverlid.
Her breathing was so still that it could scarcely be heard, and a
horrible suspicion crossed Gertrude's mind, as she watched for
some symptom of life. There was not a sound in the house ; her
least movement might disturb, and she dared not summon the
nurse ; and hour after hour she sat in the same posture, her dread
increasing at every instant, till the sun had sunk low in the
horizon, and its parting rays shed a golden light over the room, and
lit up Laura's pallid features with something of an unearthly
radiance. Gertrude trembled ; she rose, leant over her, and
tried to listen again for the breathing, but her nervousness had
become so great that she could hear nothing but the beating of
her own heart. With a faint feeling, from mingled fatigue and
alarm, she tried to reseat herself as before, but her foot touched
the chair, pushed it along the floor, and with the noise, slight
though it was, Laura awoke. The unspeakable relief of that
moment Gertrude never forgot. In the happiness of finding
that her fears were unfounded, she did not even observe that
the glaring lustre of Laura's eye had been succeeded by a quiet,

natural clearness, and when her name was repeated in a sweet, feeble voice, she started as if awakened from a dream.

'Is it very late?' asked Laura, as she looked wonderingly at her sister.

'Not very,' replied Gertrude; 'but you have been asleep some time.'

'Asleep!' repeated Laura, and she glanced restlessly over the room.

'Yes, and ill too; but you must be still; you are not strong enough to talk.'

Laura acquiesced, for even these few words were an effort; but after a few moments she again signed to Gertrude to draw near. 'Did you say I had been ill? Weren't there people about? It is such a trouble to think.'

'Wait till presently,' said Gertrude. 'You must take something now.'

'But only tell me,—Edward,—why is he gone away?'

'Edward is not gone; he is here. I shall go and tell him you are better.'

'But he won't come to me, I know; my head is so dizzy. What is it that is so dreadful?'

'Nothing is dreadful, dearest,' replied Gertrude, 'and Edward will come to you presently, when you are strong enough to see him.'

Laura was silent from exhaustion, and Gertrude was uncertain whether to assist her in recalling what had passed, or allow her to remember it gradually. She seemed, however, too much weakened for thought of any kind, and Gertrude rang for the nurse, that something might be given her; but she would not allow any one else to be told of the amendment, fearing lest Edward's impatience might get the better of his prudence, and mischief might be the consequence. When her strength was a little restored, Laura's mind again began working; and Gertrude, seeing that she would not rest till everything had been explained, sent a message to Edward to tell him that he need no longer be uneasy, but entreating him on no account to come into the room until she sent for him.

'Master won't listen to that,' muttered the old woman, as she left the room; and Gertrude was of the same opinion, and returning to Laura, resolved to say at once all that was necessary, if she found that her sister could bear it. 'You will be better now,' she said, with a smile, as she took Laura's hand, and arranged her pillow.

'No,' said Laura; 'I am not better. I can't remember; it is very unkind in you, Gertrude, not to help me.'

'I will help you now,' said Gertrude; 'you have been ill two or three days; and the people you have been thinking about were at the archery meeting.'

'Yes, yes, I remember,' said Laura, slowly; 'but that was not all. There was something dreadful. Why am I afraid to see Edward?'

'Because you had something to tell him, which you thought would worry him; but I have told him all, and he does not care.'

'Something? I thought he would be very angry.'

'It was about Miss Forester,' said Gertrude, 'and the money she lent you, and the bills from London; but it is all settled. Edward took the matter very quietly, and he will come and give you a kiss whenever you wish to see him. I think, though, you had better lie still a little while first.'

Laura looked distrustful. 'Why should I not see him at once?' she said. 'Are you sure he loves me? Some one said he did not. It was a voice—I heard it always.'

'That was your fancy when you were ill,' replied Gertrude; 'but he will come soon, and tell you himself.'

'Bills?' said Laura, thinking; 'were they long ones?'

'Rather; but don't distress yourself about them. Edward is not at all displeased.'

A slight noise was heard,—the door was opened, and a stealthy footstep approached the bed. Gertrude knew that it must be Edward. She lifted up her finger to stop him, but Laura's attention was attracted.

'Who is it?' she said, quickly, as she tried in vain to rouse herself to see.

'Only be still,' replied Gertrude, laying her hand upon her.

'It was Edward,' said Laura, in an agony of expectation; 'is he gone without speaking? Then he has not forgiven. O Gertrude! why did they not let me die?'

Edward heard the words, notwithstanding the faint tone in which they were spoken, and, regardless of his sister's warning, came forward suddenly. Laura's eyes met his with a fixed, earnest gaze. She held his hand as he bent over her, and whispered words of purest affection and thankfulness, but she could not articulate a reply; and by degrees her feeble grasp was relaxed. her head drooped, and she fainted away.

CHAPTER XLIV.

THE calm which follows a storm may be, and often is, a season of thankfulness and hope ; but it may be also nothing but the lulling of the winds before the gathering of another tempest. And so it was felt at Allingham. All things were returning to their usual course. Laura's good constitution had borne her through the trial of severe illness, and now it assisted her in regaining her lost powers. Day by day some new progress was made, trifling, perhaps, and only marked by the eye of affection, but serving to show that she might in time be restored to her former health. Gertrude seldom left her, and ventured by degrees to talk to her upon the subjects weighing upon her mind. And when her memory grew clearer, Edward himself encouraged her to speak openly. But her confessions, in their simplicity and humility, were often very painful. She told of her vanity and weakness ; and he remembered his own. She entreated him to forgive her deception ; and the sin, not of months, but of years, lay upon his own breast; and she promised amendment, and begged him to guide and teach her, at the very moment when he felt that his own errors had marred his happiness for life. Laura saw that something was amiss, but she attributed it to regret at her own conduct, and this brought deeper expressions of repentance than before ; till Edward was often on the point of acknowledging the truth, without thinking of the consequences, merely to save himself the wretchedness of feeling he was deceiving her. One thing he was obliged to own, that he had declined standing again for the county ; but this, though startling intelligence, did not awaken suspicion, for Laura's mind was not entirely clear as to all that had occurred previous to her illness, so as to enable her to put facts together, and reason upon them. She thought that he must be tired of the responsibility, and perhaps willing to avoid the expense. But this was all ; and her own feeling was that of satisfaction, for, with her newly-formed resolutions, it would be keeping her out of the way of temptation. But the time was fast approaching when concealment would no longer be possible. Edward's embarrassments became more and more pressing, and Mr Rivers urged the necessity of some decisive step being taken, for rumours were afloat, and commented on, and circulated, by all but his own family. Mrs Courtenay, with that happy buoyancy of spirit which can accommodate itself to all circumstances, no sooner learned that Edward had resolved upon giving up the election, than she declared it was by far the best thing that could have been done. It had always been too much for him ; and now he would be able to live quietly at Allingham with dear Laura, and they should see so much more of him. She quite looked forward to the winter, and he would be able to give such nice parties ; though, to be sure, she never went to any of them, for fear of taking cold ; but it was pleasant to think other people were enjoying themselves. The observations were made to Charlotte, whose reply was brief and unceremonious ; and Edith, who was present, also escaped as quickly as possible, to go to her own room.

'There is but one comforting thought in the whole of the business,' said Charlotte, following her, 'and that is, that if Edward is not member, no other of his party will be. I care not one iota about politics, but I could not bear the notion of his being thrust aside, and no one missing him.'

' But how do you know no one else will be ?'

' Because there is a split amongst them. Mr Dacre, or some one, was saying so this morning ; and there is to be an opposition. There would have been none if Edward had stood. And I saw General Forester ride past just now, as I was standing at the lodge gate, and I thought he looked as black as November.'

''That accounts for General Forester's being so anxious about Edward,' said Edith ; ' but, however, it does not signify to us now. Public affairs are all very well when there is nothing else to think of, but that is not the case with us.'

' And will not be for many a long day. I wish Edward would settle something. This living with a sword hanging over one's head is not agreeable.'

' How can you talk so lightly, Charlotte !' exclaimed Edith.

' No, it is not lightly ; it is sober truth. But there is no good in putting on a sad face ; misfortunes are never the less for our being doleful about them. Life to me is very like a furze brake ; you must be scratched, go which way you will ; but if you step out boldly, and make up your mind not to care, you are sure to be better off than you expected.'

' We are in the midst of a very thick furze brake just at present,' said Edith.

' Yes, very ; but we shall see our way out of it by and by.'

'I wish Jane knew it,' said Edith ; 'I really think she ought to be told.'

'What for?—to make her uncomfortable before there is any occasion? Just leave her to me ; I understand her better than you do, and I will tell her when it is necessary.'

'But she will be annoyed at being the only ignorant one,' said Edith.

'We cannot help that. For all our sakes she must be kept quiet as long as possible. You know what she is like when things go wrong.'

Edith did know from bitter experience. A vision of dark looks, sharp words, and a fit of hysterics, presented itself; and, following Charlotte's counsel, she said no more about telling Jane.

But though Edith and her sisters were so regardless of public affairs, Edward still felt some interest in them. He received the information of the progress of the election with an air of proud indifference ; but when at length the news reached him of the defeat of his former friends, he felt a momentary satisfaction; for it proved that his own importance had been greater than he imagined. If he had stood, no one would have ventured to oppose him. He was, however, too wretched and too penitent to dwell upon the idea ; and, after a little exertion, so disciplined his mind, that even the report of some hasty expressions made use of by General Forester against him, scarcely excited his indignation. The General had, in truth, considerable cause for annoyance. With Edward's retirement and the downfall of his party was involved the loss of his own position. He was no longer the friend and adviser of the county member, possessing influence and occasionally patronage, and the change was keenly felt. His ambition had been low, but earnest ; and in the bitterness of his disappointment, he accused Edward of inconsistency, and even duplicity. Miss Forester shared his feelings, though in a different way. The enjoyments of the last four years were now at an end. Under any circumstances she felt that her intimacy with Laura must cease, and with it much of the pleasure derivable from luxuries and amusements, which to her were the grand objects of her life. But Miss Forester's selfishness did not render her wholly callous to the misery that might be the result of Mr Courtenay's embarrassments,—the report of which was now very generally believed. She had some regard for Laura,—deeper than she herself was aware of,—and her anxiety during her illness had been sincere ; and when she remembered that she had done her utmost to encourage the thoughtlessness which seemed about to bring such fatal consequences, something like repentance arose in her heart. She did not dare offer her society or assistance ; but if they had been sought, her mind would have been relieved from a burden of unusual weight.

It was a day of exquisite beauty when Laura was carried out of doors, and laid on a sofa under the colonnade. The season had been unusually fine, and the garden, instead of being burnt up by a scorching sun, retained very much the appearance of early spring. Laura, her mind relieved from great care, felt as if she had never before enjoyed the loveliness of her home. She delighted in the sunshine, the birds and flowers, the lights and shadows upon the lawn, and the soft, warm breeze that fanned her cheek. She could not believe that the summer was so nearly gone, and appealed perpetually to Edward to join in her ecstacies.

'Now that you have given up the election,' she said, 'we shall have so much time together, and I intend to make you fond of gardening ; and in September it will be such delicious weather for riding. I suppose by that time I shall be strong enough to bear it. Edward, dearest, don't be so grave, it makes me un-happy. Do teach him to smile, Gertrude.'

'I would if I could, you may be sure,' said Gertrude, attempt-ing to smile herself ; 'but he is obstinate. I see Mr Dacre coming,' she added ; 'but I shall not let him talk to you now ; you have had enough excitement for to-day.'

This was perfectly true ; but Gertrude was not sorry to have an excuse for a *tête-à-tête*, for it was her chief comfort. This day, however, she had less satisfaction than usual ; Mr Dacre was looking very ill, and walked feebly ; and Gertrude fancied she could see the effects of thought and anxiety for her brother. He was not a person to take a half interest in a character like Ed-ward's ; and perhaps the consciousness that his own strength was rapidly diminishing, and that, in all human probability, he should never live to witness the effect of the change of circumstances upon Mr Courtenay's mind, served to increase his care, and made him peculiarly watchful for the little indications of firmness and resolution, which he fancied he discovered in the course of their conversations. Laura followed Gertrude with her eye, till she had joined Mr Dacre, and taken his arm, and turned into the shrubbery ; and then, looking at Edward, she said—

'We are alone now, Edward; there can be no reason for not speaking out. Why are you so changed?'

'I have had enough to change me,' he replied, 'if it were only fear for you.'

'Yes, my illness; but not other things,—you tell me you have forgotten them; and if I thought you had not, I should never forgive myself.'

'Forgotten!' he exclaimed; 'if everything were but as easy to forget as that, I should indeed be a fortunate man.'

'But am I the cause of your vexation?'

'Yes;' and then checking himself, he added, in as indifferent a tone as he could assume, 'you must always be, since you are dearer to me than anything on earth.'

Laura looked agitated and excited, and Edward was frightened.

'It is all nothing,' he said, carelessly; 'every one has moods. Don't you think you have been here long enough?'

'I have not been out ten minutes. You never used to have moods.'

'Yes, frequently; only you don't remember.'

'There are a great many things I don't remember,' said Laura; 'but it will all come again in time, I hope. What should you say, Edward, if it did not?'

'Why ask?' he said, anxiously. 'Do you feel worse?'

'Not exactly, but I think sometimes it would be very disagreeable always to feel as I do at present.'

A deeper gloom overspread Edward's countenance.

'You want change,' he said, and paused. 'Will you go abroad?'

The tone was startlingly abrupt, but Laura did not remark it.

'Really, are you in earnest?' she exclaimed, and her eyes sparkled with almost childish delight.

'Will you go?'

'Yes, everywhere with you; but abroad would be so very delightful! You have often promised you would take me again, and there has always been some reason against it.'

'There is none now,' he replied, in the same gloomy voice.

'And the season of the year would be so good,' continued Laura, 'if we set off at once. September is always fine, and deliciously cool. Do you remember what torrents of rain we had when we were in Normandy, four—nearly five—years ago? How time passes! Ah, Edward, we were very happy then!'

'Are you not happy now?'

'Yes, if you are; but there is something in being very young, and not having known what care meant. And all was so new to me. Only Allingham, I think, is pleasanter and dearer every year.'

Edward suddenly left her side, but immediately returned.

'Are you very fond of Allingham?' he asked.

'What a question! Is there any other spot on earth which has half its charms?'

'Will you leave it?'

There was that in his voice which made Laura look up into his face, and shrink from the expression which she saw there.

'What do you mean?' she exclaimed. 'You frighten me, Edward. Why are you so strange?'

Edward felt that he had done wrong, but he could not retract.

'Tell me, Laura,' he said, 'if you had united your fortunes with those of a man whom the world thought wealthy,—if he deceived you for years, and suffered you to act wrongly, and set you the example, and then brought you and your child to ruin, —how should you feel?'

Laura gazed on him, bewildered and alarmed.

'You would hate and despise him,' continued Edward, vehemently; 'and with justice. But if he loved you, Laura,—loved you,—idolised you,—felt that life was only endurable when shared by you,—if his deception was the result of an affection so great that it would have ransacked the whole world to gratify your slightest wish,—could you forgive him?'

'Who? What?' exclaimed Laura. 'You, Edward! Is it real?'

'Yes,' said Edward, bitterly; 'you may well ask "is it real?" Who would believe that the man whom hundreds honoured,— the man who dared to seek your love,—could act a part so base? Yet, Laura, I am he,—most miserable,—most unworthy.'

He cast himself on the ground beside her, and as he bent his head on her hands, scalding tears of anguish fell upon them. A mist seemed suddenly to vanish from Laura's eyes. The dim past came vividly before her, and the rumours which before her illness had been so little regarded, returned clearly to her recollection.

'Edward, dearest,' she said, gently; 'this is not the posture for you. If sorrow is at hand, who shall teach me to bear it if you fail?'

Edward clasped her hands convulsively.

'Why should you fear to tell me all?' continued Laura. 'Am I not your wife? Is not our existence one?'

'Yes,' he exclaimed, rising suddenly; 'and therefore the more wretched! Laura, you little know what is before you. I am ruined. Allingham can no longer be your home.'

He bent upon her a steadfast gaze, as if to read her inmost thoughts; but she did not shrink from it. The sight of his grief had nerved her, and not a muscle of her countenance moved; only the faint tinge of red forsook her cheek, and her voice slightly shook as she said—

'My home is in your heart. Whilst you are spared to me, all trials will be light.'

'And can you, indeed, say so?' exclaimed Edward. And bending over her, he imprinted a long, fervent kiss upon her brow.

' 'But you have never felt privation, and how will you bear that Charlie's lot in life should be so different from that to which he was born?'

'If it is your lot,' replied Laura, 'you will teach him to support it nobly; and for myself, I am not, Edward, what I was. I have lived many years within the last few months, and life can never again be the light and valueless thing I once thought it. If you could give me boundless wealth, it could not make me happy; and I trust I should not wish it for my child.'

'But the shame,—the ridicule,' exclaimed Edward.

'Let them come. I have deserved them, if not for this, for other and worse follies. Only tell me all that has happened.'

Edward hesitated, for Laura sank back on her sofa exhausted.

'I would rather hear it now,' she said, earnestly; 'and you would rather too.'

'Yes, but I can bear delay. The worst suffering is past.'

Laura, however, again entreated, and Edward then confided to her the whole state of his affairs, together with the weakness which had caused him to conceal from her the heavy claims upon his estate, when first they married.

'It is this which lies heaviest on my conscience,' he said. 'It was the root of all other errors. And, Laura, if you have ceased to respect me '——

Laura stopped him.

'Do not recall my own faults. Love might be your excuse, Edward, but I fear could not be mine.'

Edward heaved a bitter sigh. His wife's humility and strength

of character were as so many reproaches for the part he had
acted towards her.

'I would rather you should speak hardly of me,' he said. 'I
could bear anything but this; and I feel you must be miserable.'

Laura's eyes filled with tears as she answered—

'O Edward! is affection indeed of so little worth in your
estimation? When I vowed to love, to honour, and obey you,
was it for your money and your position? If you had been poor
and homeless, to have been your wife would have been greater
happiness than to have been united to the wealthiest noble in
the land. And now, what have I done that you should doubt
me?'

'Doubt you!' exclaimed Edward. 'No, never for one
moment. You are my hope—my comfort—my precious in-
estimable treasure! You will endure with an angel's patience;
but it will still be endurance, and I shall be the cause. And,
Laura, there is one thing yet untold. What if our only prospect
of subsistence, until I can rise in my profession, should be by
dependence?'

Laura's cheek flushed crimson.

'You would not consent,' she said, eagerly.

'Not if Gertrude entreated,—if she said that her happiness
depended on it?'

Laura looked at him, to discover his meaning, and then burst
into tears. At that instant Gertrude returned.

'I have done it,' exclaimed Edward, in a frightened voice, as
he hastened towards her. 'I can't tell what possessed me.
Why did you leave us, Gertrude?'

'You have not told her all?' said Gertrude, alarmed in her
turn.

'Yes—all. I could not help it. It was agony to be with her
longer, and deceive her.'

'And she has borne it—how?'

'Nobly!—wonderfully! I never understood her, or appreciated her, till to-day. But go to her, Gertrude; she can consent to all but what you would do; and I cannot consent
either.'

He walked into the house, and Gertrude quietly seated herself by her sister's side. Laura tried to raise herself, and when
Gertrude put her arm round her to assist her, she leaned her
head on her shoulder, and sobbed with the weakness of a child.
Gertrude kissed and soothed her, and strove to restore her to

composure; but her presence only seemed to increase Laura's distress; though once, when she attempted to leave her, Laura caught her hand, and signed to her to remain.

'I cannot think of it,' she said, at length, in broken words, 'for you to suffer. I could beg my bread rather.'

'We will not talk of it now, dearest,' said Gertrude. 'When you are better you shall hear all I have to say, and no one shall force you to do anything against your will; but Edward must carry you to your room. He has done enough mischief for to-day.'

'I would bear all pain—all imaginable pain,'—whispered Laura, 'rather than you should' ——

'Yet you will not agree to the only plan which will save me from it.'

Laura was going to answer, but Gertrude would not give her the opportunity; and summoning Edward, insisted upon her being left without disturbance for several hours.

CHAPTER XLV.

EDWARD had said that his worst trial was over, and so perhaps it was. There was at least no longer anything to conceal—no necessity for appearing cheerful when his heart was sinking in despondency. But there was also, now, no pretext for further delaying his ultimate intentions. Before the winter, Allingham must be left; and in Laura's delicate state, a few weeks might make a considerable difference in the prudence of travelling; for this was the final arrangement. A twelvemonths' residence abroad would give Mr Rivers time for settling Edward's affairs, and enabling him to return to his country with freedom and honour; and he would then take the necessary measures for again resuming his profession. And all this sounded easy; but how much was involved in it! How many bitter remembrances, and self-accusations for the past!—how many sad visions for the future! It required all Edward's newly-strengthened principles to teach him to submit to the duty before him. If there had remained any hope of a competency, however small, out of the wreck of his fortune, he might probably have been tempted to continue abroad for the remainder of his life, rather than brave the observations which must follow his intended line of conduct. But to be dependent upon Gertrude, to feel that he was depriving her of her right merely to gratify his own weakness, was impossible; and if, for a moment, his resolution wavered, Laura was at hand to warn and support him. Trial, with her, was indeed working its great end, repentance and amendment. Her step was slow, and her eye dim, and her whole bearing thoughtful and sometimes sad, but not in Edward's presence. With him she was cheerful, contented, sanguine; occupied only in endeavouring, as far as lay in her power, to smooth the rugged path upon which he had entered. If she could not actively exert herself, she could write for him, and think for him; she could discuss his plans, and brighten his dark prospects by hopeful smiles, till even in the midst of his grief Edward sometimes felt that a spring of happiness had opened in his desert life which might make amends for all that he had lost. But this was but seldom. Too heavy a burden lay upon his conscience to be cast suddenly aside. His offences were errors in the eyes of his fellow-creatures, but they were sins before God, and the sins of years, in the face of warnings and instructions; and years must pass before he could hope to enjoy that peace of mind which long-confirmed habits of watchful obedience alone can give. The plans were at length definitely fixed; the day of departure, the route, the place of destination. Edward had committed his affairs without reservation to Mr Rivers, in the certainty that all would be done which talent and integrity could effect, and two things only remained to be thought of; the one, the best mode of breaking the intelligence to Mrs Courtenay; the other ——

'Gertrude will not consent to it,' said Edward, when Laura first proposed it. 'To leave her home for a twelvemonth! I think you can hardly ask it.'

'She will tell us at once if it cannot be,' replied Laura; 'and it might be less painful than remaining behind.'

'That will not weigh in the scale,' said Edward. 'But you must write to her. It is not fair to take a person by surprise in these cases.'

The note was written. It was urgent and affectionate, begging that, if it were possible, Gertrude would agree to accompany them.

'If it were merely a question of pleasure,' wrote Laura, 'I should hesitate in asking, knowing the claims you already have at home; but, dearest Gertrude, there are many things in which

you are become necessary to us both.   It is not a common case,
Edward will have much to encounter, and I feel myself so overwhelmed when he is miserable, I scarcely know how to comfort
him.   Pray think of it.   If it is not right, I will be contented;
but I cannot resist proposing it, even if you should be obliged
to say no.'

The idea was not new to Gertrude's mind.   She had observed
with anxiety Laura's delicacy of constitution since her illness, and
often dreaded the consequences of the fatigue and distress of mind
which must attend her journey; but the duties of her home were
primary, and, for a long time, her decision wavered.   She knew
that she was useful to Laura, but she still felt doubtful as to leaving her mother until aware of the effect which the intelligence of
Edward's circumstances might have upon her.   If Edith could go
instead—but no, Edith could never regain her lost place in Edward's affection.   He had seen and acknowledged to Gertrude his
injustice in accusing any but himself of having led Laura into
error, and his manner to Edith had lately been peculiarly kind,
as if to atone for the harsh words he had spoken; but the love
that has once been chilled can never be restored to its former
warmth.   And Edith felt this, daily and hourly.   It was the most
bitter drop in her cup of sorrow, for it was the consequence of
her own actions.   In the doubtful state of her mind Gertrude had
recourse to Charlotte, whose quick yet cool judgment she had
learned especially to appreciate since it had been lately called into
action.   'What new mischief is there?' was the observation
with which her request for a few minutes' private conversation
was received.

'Not mischief at all as yet,' replied Gertrude; 'but I want
your advice.   Edward and Laura go next week.'

'And they wish you to go with them?—exactly what I said
they would.   Edith and I were talking of it only last night.'

'And what did Edith say?'

'She is in the passage.   I will make her come and tell herself.'

Poor Edith looked so very unhappy, that Gertrude did not like
to drag her into the conversation, but Charlotte began without
mercy.   'Now, Edith, give your own opinion.   Is it best for
Gertrude to stay at home with us, or go abroad with Edward and
Laura?'

'I don't know—I don't care.   Why should you ask me?' said
Edith.

'Because you are a party concerned.   If Gertrude goes, the

care of mamma and Jane will fall upon our shoulders : do you feel equal to bearing it ?'

'Should you very much object ?' said Gertrude, gently.

Edith appeared extremely distressed.

'Well !' exclaimed Charlotte, 'if you will not speak, I may as well do it. Go, by all means, Gertrude. I shall hate it cordially, and be wretched till you come back ; but still, go. If I were you, I should dislike such short notice ; but that is not my affair '

'My mother !' said Gertrude. 'That weighs with me most. I know if we ask her to consent, she will ; but the whole thing will be a shock to her. I cannot think what she will say.'

'She has a notion already,' said Charlotte. 'The rumour has been mentioned by visitors, though she has always contradicted it, and I took an opportunity, yesterday, to say that I thought it very probable Edward and Laura would spend the winter abroad, and she opened her eyes, and said that it would be a very good thing, and that it might make Laura quite a different person.'

'But the circumstances ?' said Gertrude.

'Why say anything about them ? Nothing will be done with Allingham for some time, and when she has once become accustomed to their absence she will feel it much less. It must be broken to her gently at all events.'

'But she must hear of it all soon,' said Gertrude.

Charlotte looked annoyed. 'I see how it is, Gertrude,' she said ; 'you distrust us ; you think we shall not take care of my mother ; but,' she added, more gravely, 'I think you might give us credit for having learned something within the last twelve months.'

'I was really thinking only of myself,' replied Gertrude. 'I could not agree to the notion unless mamma did; but even if she were to consent, I could not go with any comfort if I fancied she had anything dreadful hanging over her head, to be told her when I was away.'

'Then tell her at once yourself,' exclaimed Charlotte ; 'you have no time to lose.'

'That is the difficulty : perhaps it would be better ; but we must decide immediately.'

'Yes, a week is a very little time for you to settle everything, if you are going. But how will you manage ?'

'I am not sure,' said Gertrude, 'whether it would not be the best way to say everything at once. I don't mean suddenly : but one trouble neutralises another, and the selling Allingham will swallow up all minor evils. Mamma will scarcely care for my going when she thinks of Edward.'

'If it is to be done,' said Charlotte, 'the sooner the better. I should infinitely prefer myself sitting down in a dentist's chair, which I used to think the acme of human misery ; however, you are a person of courage, Gertrude.'

'I do not feel at all courageous just at this minute,' replied Gertrude. 'I must consider about it quietly alone first.'

She walked to the door, and Edith followed her. 'Did you think me cross just now?' she said. 'It was very foolish and wrong, but I think I was jealous. Five years ago, Edward would not have asked you to go abroad with him.'

Gertrude wished to say that the time might come when he would feel again as he had once done, but she had little hope of it, and Edith, having made her confession, hurried away.

Mrs Courtenay was in her little room, as usual ; but not, as usual, busied in doing nothing. She was knitting a pair of woollen socks for a poor old woman in Elsham, and a book lay open beside her. 'I was just looking out the place where we left off, my dear,' she said, 'and thinking I would go on by myself. What kept you so long?'

'I have been talking to Charlotte and Edith,' replied Gertrude.

'Well? but you have been with them ever since breakfast. What can you have to say to each other?'

'We were talking of Edward and Laura,' said Gertrude. 'You know they have some idea of going abroad.'

'Yes; Charlotte told me so yesterday; but is it settled? How quick they are in all their plans?'

'It is Edward's way generally,' replied Gertrude ; 'and now, I believe, he has particular reasons for it. It is rather necessary he should make some change ; he has been at such heavy expenses.'

'So he has, poor fellow ! As your dear father used to say, people don't go into Parliament for nothing.'

'No, indeed, they don't,' said Gertrude ; 'and Edward has been particularly pressed lately.'

'Has he, indeed?' and Mrs Courtenay looked up from her work rather frightened.

'I think you must have seen he was worried,' continued Gertrude : 'and that has been the cause.'

'Ah! very likely; nothing is so troublesome as money matters. When I first married I always had a headache whenever I thought about them; and at last your father took them out of my hands entirely.'

'If Edward goes abroad,' said Gertrude, 'he will probably stay some time.'

'Yes, I dare say, when he is once there, he will wish to see everything—all young people do. But, my dear, I don't like to think about it. It made me very nervous when Charlotte told me yesterday. Some one called at the time, and I thought it was merely a notion of hers, not of any consequence. He won't be going just yet, though?'

'Next week, I rather think.'

Mrs Courtenay laid down her work. 'Next week! Gertrude, my dear! you are dreaming. He can't—it is impossible—he won't be ready.'

'He does not like to delay,' said Gertrude, 'because of Laura. Travelling later in the season will be inconvenient on her account.'

'To be sure, I forgot. But, my dear, what will he do with Allingham? Not trust it with Mrs Dickson, I hope? I don't know why, and I have no wish to say a word against her, but I can't help thinking she cheats him.'

'Allingham is a very large place,' said Gertrude; 'too large for a man who desires to economise.'

'So it is, dreadfully expensive! I forget how many servants the Colonel used to say it required, but it was an immense number; and Edward, poor fellow, is so fond of having things in style.'

'Perhaps it would be better if he were to let or sell it,' said Gertrude, pronouncing the last word with hesitation.

'Better, my dear!' repeated Mrs Courtenay, and she placed her spectacles on the table, in utter astonishment and horror. 'Better to let or sell Allingham! Why, it has been in the family for I can't tell how many years. It came to them just when the last wall of the Priory that stood near here was pulled down. The house then was an old place, all full of gables and chimneys; and old Mr Courtenay, Samuel Courtenay, that was, your great-great-grandfather, had it taken down, and built up again as it is now. I have heard your father talk of it a hundred times, and he always had a notion that some day or other it would come into his part of the family. He and the Colonel never liked each other very much.'

'It would not be desirable, I grant,' said Gertrude, 'but if it were right, dear mamma, you would be the last person to object.'

'My dear, you are not serious.   Right! how could it be right?'

'It would be better to sell it,' said Gertrude, 'than to live in it and run in debt.'

'But who talks of running in debt?   Edward has a very handsome fortune,—ten times better than he had any reason to expect when your father died.'

'It was not so large as people imagined,' said Gertrude; 'and, at all events, he has had immense claims upon it; and I think, if he were to go abroad, he would most likely decide upon doing something with Allingham during his absence.   Mr Rivers strongly advises it.'

'Mr Rivers, my dear! advise!   What are you talking of? Mr Rivers is no relation.'

'No, but he has the whole management of the property, and knows what would be most prudent.   And, dear mamma, if they did go away, they still will be tolerably near you, because Edward would most probably live in town.   He thinks sometimes of trying his profession again.'

Mrs Courtenay looked at Gertrude, and then rubbed her eyes. 'I don't know,' she said, 'it is a very strange world; things come so suddenly.   Has he only thought of it all since yesterday?'

'Oh yes, he has been planning it for some time, but he has only just decided; and what made me think of talking to you about it this morning was, that Laura has written me a note to ask if I would go abroad with them for a twelvemonth; and, of course, I could not consent unless you did.'

This last request was the completion of the shock.   Mrs Courtenay threw herself back in her chair and gasped for breath.

'Abroad ; all of you gone! to leave me.'

'It would not be very long,' said Gertrude.   'Time passes so quickly, and I think you would be more comfortable about Laura if I were with her, and you would hear much oftener.   Edward is an extremely bad correspondent.'

'Yes, to be sure, Laura looks very thin ; but, my dear, what shall I do?   If you are not here, who will read to me?'

'Edith will, I am certain,' said Gertrude; 'and one thing, dear mamma, their being abroad will accustom you to their absence ; you will not care so much for Edward's giving up Allingham.'

This was the important point which Gertrude felt it necessary to insist on, as it was clear her mother by no means realised it. ' It will be a very great trial for us at first,' she continued ; 'but if he can sell Allingham, he will be freed from all his encumbrances,—his debts, I mean ; and he will begin life, as it were, afresh ; for he will go to the bar, and he is certain of doing well, as far as any man can be, he is so clever.'

A glimpse of the truth was dawning upon poor Mrs Courtenay's mind. She obliged Gertrude to repeat her words, and questioned and wondered, till the facts were clearly brought to view, and then her burst of grief was terrible to witness. The whole pride of her heart was centered in Edward. From the day of his birth till that hour she had looked upon him as something almost more than mortal, and the idea of distress ever reaching him in his journey through life had never yet entered her mind. Gertrude felt for her mother's sorrow, the more because it was so hard to comfort. Her mind was not equal to listening to reason at such a time. She wrung her hands and cried,—one moment entreating that they should all give up everything,—that they should leave the Priory, and live upon nothing, rather than Edward should suffer ; and the next declaring that the report must be untrue,— it was only what ill-natured people thought, and she wondered Gertrude could attend to such nonsense. With unwearied patience Gertrude listened and sympathised, but she did not attempt explanations. She knew that the feeling could not be lasting from its very violence, but she felt thankful that the truth was known ; and when Mrs Courtenay at length lay upon the sofa, silent and still, because her strength was exhausted, Gertrude alluded to the only point which she had not yet mentioned, and which she had purposely kept back, in the hope that it might be some slight consolation.

' We will do something for him, dear mamma,' she said ; ' he can have aunt Heathfield's fortune, instead of me, and that will make him comfortable now, and by and by he may be a rich man again.'

' Ah ! my dear, yes. Poor fellow ! Who could think it ? Your aunt's fortune was little enough.'

Gertrude felt a pang of disappointment, though she reproached herself for it. She did not wish to be praised for a common act of duty ; but she forgot that no one but Edith, herself, and Mr Dacre understood the full extent of the sacrifice—how her bright day-dreams had been destroyed, and how overpowering had been

the first feeling of disappointment.   Yet she continued the subject
for nearly an hour ; and, at the end of that time, had in some
degree reconciled her mother to the arrangements, and obtained
permission to accompany Edward and Laura.

That day at the Priory was more painful than any which had
yet passed.   Jane, who could no longer be kept in ignorance,
went to her own room and refused to see any one.   Mrs Courtenay
cried incessantly ; Edith sat by, the image of blank despair ; while
Charlotte and Gertrude discussed the proposed journey, and the
preparations required.   The tone of the conversation was not
agreeable to Gertrude's feelings.   Charlotte was extremely useful,
sensible, and practical ; she thought of everything, obviated every
difficulty, suggested plans, which none but her own peculiarly clear
head could have devised ; even insisted upon making considerable
sacrifices for her sister's comfort ; but it was all done cheerfully,
and poor Gertrude was wretched.   The idea of going abroad,
which at another time would have been a delight, was now full of
gloom.   She fancied herself in a foreign country, amongst people
who could neither understand nor sympathise with her,—Edward
miserable, Laura ill.   She thought of her mother's distress at
home, and Edith's loneliness, and the desertion of Allingham, and
the trial it would be to them to see it inhabited by another family.
It seemed equally hard either to go or to stay.   And then came
other thoughts, of the church and Mr Dacre.   She had schooled
herself into submission, but the vision had never ceased to haunt
her.   Even in the midst of all her late anxiety, it had been with
her,—in fancy and in dreams ; and before she returned it would
in all probability be reality.   Some necessary steps had already
been taken, and now that the Allingham property was to be sold,
there would be no difficulty in determining the site.   It was a
painful interest which Gertrude felt whenever Mr Dacre had
lately alluded to the subject.   She longed to hear everything,
and yet when she had heard, she almost wished that it had never
been introduced.   From any other person it would have been
overpowering, but Mr Dacre's perfect consideration and gentleness softened the trial ; and even when suffering most, she felt as
if she had never before sufficiently estimated his character.   And
of him, when they were so soon to part for many months, Gertrude thought much and anxiously.   He had been a friend when
friendship was above all things needed, and he had understood
and sympathised with feelings so sacred and private, that she
could not have mentioned them in words.   When she returned to

England, would he be waiting to welcome her, or was it more than probable that, before a year had gone by, his troubled life would be over? That his health was sinking there could be no doubt; it was the general remark, and he himself frequently spoke of it, but the knowledge had never pressed so heavily upon her before; and when Edith mentioned it as they sat together, after the remainder of the family were gone to rest, Gertrude turned from the idea with a hasty assent and began talking of other things.

CHAPTER XLVI.

THE evening was clear, soft, and motionless; no breath of wind stirred the leaves; the song of the birds was stilled; the hum of the insects had nearly ceased. A few bright, flaky clouds were gathering around the setting sun, which, as it slowly sank to its repose, lit up the western horizon with a broad, golden belt, melting through scarcely perceptible shades from brilliant orange into a dim, shadowy green, and rising again from the most delicate azure to the deep purple of the overhanging sky. It was an hour for sweet yet solemn thoughts, for chastened memories of earth, and tranquil hopes of heaven—a time when holy influences seem hovering near, hushing to rest the cares of the busy world, and shedding a secret charm over the homes of earth unfelt and unthought of in the dazzling lustre of day. And Edward and Laura stood together for the last time beneath the colonnade at Allingham. The parting words had been said, the last farewells taken. It was their own request that their few remaining hours should be alone. And who could venture to intrude upon such sorrow? Who that has felt the bitterness of parting for years, even with the prospect of return, from scenes endeared by associations with all that life holds most precious, could wish to disturb the grief which must fill the heart, when the parting is brought upon us by our own folly, not for years, but for ever? And it seems vain at such a time to say that happiness may be found in any place. Perhaps it may, and so may kind words and voices of affection; but do we therefore feel the less when forced to relinquish all which we have hitherto prized? And the beauty of nature, and the scenes of home, are not senseless and inanimate. There is a spirit enshrined in each object on which our eyes have long been accustomed to dwell, for we have hung upon it hopes and fears, thoughts of love, and dreams of enjoyment; and when the hour of separation draws nigh, they will crowd around us like the ghosts of by-gone days, to mock us with the remembrance of pleasures which may never again be ours.

It was not a moment for words; deep feeling is, and must be, silent; but Laura clung to her husband's arm as she tearfully gazed on the gorgeous sky; and when a sigh escaped him in the anguish of his soul, she turned to him with the same smile which had once possessed such power to lead him from the right path, and whispered, as she laid her hand upon his, 'Mine still for ever.' Edward dared not speak, but he threw his arm round her, and pressed her to his heart, and then slowly and sorrowfully they went forth together. Through the walks, and shrubberies, and terraces—by the green lawns, and the radiant flowers, which shone mistily in the evening light—not one spot was left unvisited, though Laura's weary step told that her strength was nearly gone, and Edward, in anxious apprehension, urged her to return. The task was at length over. Laura again stood under the colonnade, and cast a lingering look upon the garden.

The sun had sunk, and by the pale streak of light which marked where his path had been, the evening star now glittered in solitary beauty. Edward raised his hand and pointed to it. 'Will it be as lovely in a foreign land?' he said.

'Not to our eyes,' replied Laura; 'but shall we murmur, Edward? Is there not much left us?'

Edward thought for a few moments. 'Yes,' he said; 'this same hour might have come, and I might have been alone.'

'And Charlie,' said Laura, 'and Gertrude, and the consciousness that no one will have suffered but ourselves; that no slur can be cast upon our name. We have much to be thankful for.'

'Much, everything, while you are spared,' he exclaimed earnestly.

'And our child,' said Laura; 'will you not come and look at him?'

Edward hesitated. 'Go alone,' he said. 'Why should I be reminded that I have injured him?'

The tone was so wretched that Laura could not press him. She entered the house, but Edward immediately followed her. The hall presented a dreary contrast to the beauty without. It was filled with boxes and trunks, and the few servants who had not been dismissed were collecting the remaining articles for the travelling bags, and discussing in an under-tone the reasons for their master's movements. Laura passed up the splendid staircase, and through the long gallery, hung with family portraits, till she reached her own luxurious apartment. The furniture had been chosen to suit her particular taste, and involuntarily she stopped and looked wistfully at the tables and chairs, the glasses and couches, with which it was adorned. It was not a sigh of regret, but of affection, which escaped her; but Edward heard it, and it cut him to the heart.

'You will come,' said Laura, opening a door which led into her little boy's sleeping-room.

And Edward went. Laura bent over the bed and in the delight of a mother's heart, forgot as she gazed upon her child's fair forehead, and long, dark eyelashes, and rounded cheek, flushed with the rosy tint of health, that life could have any trials whilst he was with her; but to Edward's mind they were more vividly present at that instant than they had ever been before. He stood apart, his arms folded on his breast, and his features rigid with the effort to control his feelings; but when Charlie moved in his sleep, and softly murmured his name, his stern self-command gave way, and for the first time, unmindful of Laura's presence, his grief burst forth without restraint.

Who may tell the wretchedness of the remainder of that dreary evening? The comfortless tea taken in Laura's room, because she was too tired, and too sick at heart, to go down-stairs. The pain with which Edward looked at the smallest article with which he was to part. The trial of searching over Laura's own books to see which it would be best to keep, and then the last walk through the long, dark rooms, partly from a wish to see them once more, and partly with the view of deciding whether it would be desirable to give up two or three favourite pieces of furniture. It was one protracted suffering, yet neither of them could forego it. The drawing-room was the last place they visited. It had not been used since the night of the dance, and Laura shuddered as she recollected the splendid misery of the archery party. Everything in it was to be sold: Laura's inlaid work-table (Edward's present on her last birthday), her chess-table, and flower-stand, and Mosaic cabinet; even the enamel miniatures, and collections of drawings by modern artists. It was her own especial request. Since a sacrifice was necessary, she desired it might be complete. Gertrude indeed had urged that her mother was anxious to spare the several articles which were especially valued, but Laura was resolved. They were luxuries, she said, and from henceforth her duty was to live without them. Yet she could not resist going round to each, and turning over the drawings, and opening the drawers of the cabinet; and Edward moved mechanically wherever she did. 'This rubbish had better be thrown away,' she said, as she took out some old papers. 'Let us just look through the cabinet. We should be sorry to leave things which people may remark upon.'

'They must have been here an immense time,' observed Edward, unfolding a roll. It was the plan for the church. He had never seen it since the night preceding the nomination-day of his election. Laura looked at it now attentively, with far different feelings from those which she then had.

'The mistake was great,' said Edward, answering what he felt must be in her thoughts. 'If this had been my object, how different things would have been!'

'You did what you imagined your duty,' said Laura.

'No,' he exclaimed, firmly, though sadly; 'I made my duty suit my will, not my will my duty.'

'But how could you have known what was your duty?'

'External circumstances—property—my own doubts—the opinion of a man like Mr Dacre: but repentance has come too late.' And heaving a deep sigh, he cast the paper aside, and leaning his head upon the cabinet, remained buried in thought.

With that one sin came the remembrance of many others. The doubtful acts which, though not encouraged, had been allowed in order to secure his election; the weakness and irresolution which had induced him so frequently to act against his conscience, in compliance with his wife's wishes, and which had been the cause of Miss Forester's influence; and an offence, little thought of at the time, and long since forgotten, but which now, by some mysterious power, returned upon him in all its reality—the selfishness which had urged him to meditate an act of cruelty, only not carried into effect, because the hand of death anticipated his purpose. Was it superstition which made him read in the trial of that hour, when he was bidding farewell to his home, something of retribution for the hardness of heart which would have inflicted a similar suffering on a fellow-creature? They were bitter thoughts; and if Laura could have known the secrets of his soul, she might have heard his earnest confession in the words of one who also had wandered far astray: 'Father, I have sinned against heaven, and before Thee, and am no more worthy to be called Thy son.'

'There is no use in staying here longer,' he said, at length. 'My sisters will take care that nothing is left which ought not to be. I have spoken to them about it—and it is late. Remember we must set off early to-morrow.'

Laura still lingered; past hours of happiness crowded upon her memory, and her heart was full; but she looked at her husband, and recovering herself in an instant, she said quietly, 'I think we have done all that was necessary;' and led the way from the room. The timepiece in the hall was striking ten, and Edward insisted upon her going immediately to bed. He feared the fatigue of the next day, and he thought she might be able to sleep; but for himself he knew it would be vain to expect it; and many times in the course of the long night, as Laura awoke from her broken slumbers, she heard him pacing the adjoining room, and groaning in the anguish of a repentant spirit, over the desolation which his own sins had caused.

And on that evening there were other farewell looks and parting thoughts arising from the same circumstances, but mixed with better, happier feelings. Gertrude walked with Edith and Mr Dacre on the Priory terrace, and watched the golden sunset, and welcomed the pale, evening star, and knew that the morrow would see her far away from the scenes and the friends she loved so well; but her heart was thankful and at peace. She had endeavoured to conquer the vain regrets for Edward's suffering, from the hope that it might be the beginning of a new and holier life; and she could look back on the events of the last few months with the consciousness that, with all her faults, she had acted with a single heart. Purity of intention is the great secret of peace; and after a long conversation with Edith, in which she received a strict promise that all other ordinary duties should give way to the paramount obligation—her mother's comfort— Gertrude enjoyed with melancholy pleasure her last conversation with Mr Dacre. She spoke to him of the church, of her weakness, her disappointment, the difficulty of submission; and, if he had allowed it, she would again have begged his forgiveness for her hasty unkindness. And then she entreated that he would himself write to her a detailed account of the plans for the building and the progress made. Mr Dacre listened with the deepest interest, and entered into all her feelings ; but when she alluded to the future, his manner changed. 'He would write,' he said, 'whilst he was able ; but a year was a long time, even for the strongest to calculate upon.'

Gertrude understood him, and a choking sensation arose in her throat.

'You will be in my thoughts,' he said,—'all of you, every day. My prayers may comfort you, when my fingers are powerless.'

Gertrude felt a gratitude which she could not speak. She had often longed to ask him to remember her thus. 'I little imagined,' she said, 'that my first visit to the Continent would have been so unjoyous. It was one of my childish dreams of perfect happiness.'

'And it is in this way that the greater number of our early wishes are granted,' replied Mr Dacre, 'and at length we learn the meaning of our disappointments ; we fear to wish at all. So at least, I think you will feel, if you ever reach my age.'

'I have begun to feel it now,' said Gertrude. 'At this moment I am not aware that I have any great wish.'

'Not for Edward ?' inquired Edith.

'No, not even for him, beyond the desire that he may act rightly. Which of us would venture to restore Allingham to him if the means were in our power ?'

'My mother would,' said Edith.

'Poor mamma !' exclaimed Gertrude. 'It is a worse trial for her than for any of us ; but she will be better when to-morrow is over.'

'She was sadly upset this afternoon when Edward and Laura came over to see her,' said Edith. 'I think she fancied it was the last visit, from their manner, though they did not exactly say it.'

'It will have been the last,' said Gertrude. 'The carriage is to come for me first to-morrow morning. We agreed about it before they went away.'

'Then I shall not see you again ?' said Mr Dacre, in a peculiarly suppressed voice, as he directed his steps towards the entrance-gate.

'We start early,' replied Gertrude, 'but is it impossible ?'

'It could do no good,' he said, 'and you will have enough farewells without my adding to the number.'

Gertrude felt he was right, but she could not force herself to acknowledge it. They reached the gate in silence. 'You will think of me in my long, weary journey?' said Gertrude, as Mr Dacre lingered, unwilling to open it.

'And you of me in mine, if such should be the will of God? It may be a long, but not, I trust, a weary one.'

'Why—why should you say it?' exclaimed Gertrude; and her cheek was pale, and her lip quivered. 'I told you I had no great wish; but I have one,—that we may meet again.'

'And it will be granted,' he said, solemnly, 'though many years may pass first.'

Gertrude's tears came in spite of her utmost efforts. 'It may be on earth,' she said.

'Yes, and if not '——. He took her hand and pressed it to his lips. 'May God's blessing be with you through life!'

Gertrude would have spoken, but he had turned away. For a few minutes he pursued his path rapidly, but then his strength flagged; and when she looked at his tall, attenuated figure, and feeble steps, Gertrude felt as if the decree had already gone forth, that she should see him on earth no more.

CHAPTER XLVII.

ALL who have experienced the oppression of that moment when we first awake to consciousness upon a day of heavy trial, will understand the weight upon Edward's heart, when the light broke into his chamber, and roused him from the deep slumber which had followed his long hours of watchfulness. It was a glorious morning. The sun shone brilliantly in the unclouded sky, and the freshness of the early dew was lying on the smooth turf; insects were humming on the window, and straggling sunbeams dancing on the many-coloured carpet and damask furniture. The luxury and beauty of his home struck Edward with the vividness of a scene which is gazed on for the first time. He thought that he was leaving happiness for ever. Other scenes might be as fair,—other spots as fitted for enjoyment; but, even were they his, where would be the associations which had made Allingham so dear? and when would the buoyancy of spirit be restored to him which had enabled him to enjoy them? The answer came from the depth of his heart—' Never !'   And Gertrude awoke yet earlier, with the knowledge that much was still left her to think of.   Her last evening had been occupied with her mother, whose anxiety for Edward had increased daily as the time drew near for his journey.   Understanding little or nothing of business she could not persuade herself that his ruin was complete, and harassed herself with the idea that it would still be possible, by some great personal sacrifice, to save him.   Edward, when the notion had first been hinted to him, rejected it without a moment's hesitation ; but Mrs Courtenay would not be convinced, and with all a parent's partiality for an only son, she would have given up all herself, and overlooked the privations entailed upon every other member of her family, to save him from suffering.   Gertrude's sacrifice she scarcely considered.   Nothing indeed would have satisfied her but the complete restoration of his fortune, and it was not until Gertrude had reasoned, and entreated, and repeated the same arguments again and again, that she had been persuaded, late on the preceding evening, to give up the idea of their all leaving the Priory, and agreed only to make such alteration in their style of living as would enable him to live with greater comfort abroad, and to begin his profession upon a competency, when the year of exile was expired.   And even this Gertrude knew must not be hinted to her brother.   Whatever was to be done must pass through her hands, and this formed an additional reason for being contented to go with him.   There were so many ways in which he might be assisted without his delicacy being wounded, which no one but a member of his own family could discover.   Mrs Courtenay was, however, at length convinced, apparently, if not really, and Gertrude was relieved at finding that her mother's tears ceased, and that she became more tranquil.   She bade her good night with the earnest request that she would not think of rising early the next day.   It would only make her ill, and the rest of the family uncomfortable, and she promised to go to her room the last thing.   Mrs Courtenay assented, but the next morning, before Gertrude was dressed, she heard her mother's voice, inquiring whether the coffee was ready, and sending the footman to the lodge, to look down the road, and see whether the carriage was coming.   Gertrude left the conclusion of her packing to Charlotte, and went down-stairs. Jane and Edith were writing directions, and Mrs Courtenay, whose sorrow and nervousness were conquered for the moment by the interest of providing for her daughter's comfort, was cutting some meat at a side-table. ' I thought you would never come, my dear,' she exclaimed ; ' your coffee is quite cold, and you will have no time to eat.'

' I want very little, thank you,' said Gertrude. ' I am not at all hungry.'

' Oh ! but my love, just consider, you are going such a long journey ; you will make me very unhappy if you don't ; and I ordered the chicken to be dressed expressly, for I thought poor Edward and Laura might come without any breakfast, and then perhaps they would finish here.'

' I scarcely think they will be ready in time,' said Gertrude, ' and they wish me to go to them. Perhaps it will be the best arrangement.'

The knife and fork dropped from Mrs Courtenay's hands, and all the grief which had been for the time suppressed burst forth again. Lamentations, sighs, tears ; but in the midst of all she still insisted upon Gertrude's eating.

' Don't attempt it,' whispered Jane ; but Gertrude saw her mother's eyes fixed upon her, and forced herself to do the only thing which she knew would satisfy her.

' You will write to me ?' said Edith, in an under-tone. ' All my comfort will go with you.'

' Not all, dearest ; and I am sure you may make things better.'

' I will try it ; but I don't understand it as you do.'

' Attention,' said Gertrude,—' attention to other persons' ways and habits. I think that is the secret.'

Edith looked very desponding. At that instant Charlotte entered. ' Done at last ! ' she exclaimed, holding up the keys. ' I would not have taken the trouble for any other human being.'

' Just in time,' said Jane ; ' I hear the carriage.'

Mrs Courtenay went into the hall with the faint hope of seeing Edward.

' We shall hear from Boulogne ? ' said Jane.

Gertrude promised that she would not delay a single hour if she could possibly avoid it. They should have a detailed account of everything. And anxious to shorten the parting, she hurried out of the room, followed by her sisters.

' This time twelvemonth, dear mamma,' said Gertrude, as she threw her arm round her mother's neck,—' we must look forward to that.'

Mrs Courtenay seated herself in a chair, and cried bitterly; and Gertrude felt inclined to repent her decision. The servants crowded into the hall; she could scarcely speak to say good-bye to them, and almost wondered at herself for feeling so much. 'My mother!' was her last word to Edith, as she held her hand.

'You may depend on us both,' said Charlotte.

Gertrude stood up in the carriage till it had turned the corner of the road, and then gave up her mind to Allingham.

And much indeed there was to prepare for; but the drive was short, and before she had summoned up all the thoughts which she trusted might support herself and others in the coming trial, the carriage stopped. Edward and Laura were awaiting her arrival in the hall; and little Charlie, standing by his nurse, was expressing in broken accents his wonder and delight at the novelty of the scene. Edward leaned against a marble pillar, with a countenance which told but too plainly the tale of his broken rest and his morning's agony of mind. He looked at all that was passing, but he gave no orders; even then he felt himself a stranger in his own halls. And Laura was at his side, silent and trembling; only occasionally she stroked her child's glossy hair, or in a faint voice inquired if every direction had been attended to. There were few servants present, and of those few, none who had any peculiar interest in their master. All whom he had most valued he had provided with other situations before parting with them. The housekeeper had taken upon herself the whole authority, and moved and spoke with an air and tone which, a few months before, would have insured her immediate dismissal. Edward was not insensible, though he appeared so. He heard every word, and saw every action, and each symptom of indifference or inattention was felt with the keenness of a broken spirit. Gertrude greeted him briefly. She expressed no fear lest he had been kept waiting, but assisted in collecting the few things that were not already packed, and then going up to her brother, she said, 'The carriage is ready.' Edward sprang forward as if he dared not think. With perfect calmness he assisted Laura to put on her cloak, and tied his child's hat, and walked round the hall to see that nothing was left behind, and then, placing Gertrude and Laura in the carriage, he seated himself with Charlie by his side, and drawing his travelling cap over his forehead, closed his eyes, Gertrude held her sister's trembling hand. Laura sat upright, and her breath was quick and faint. It seemed as if her earnest gaze was seeking to retain the impression of every tree and fence, —every winding of the road; and onward the carriage rolled, rapidly and easily, each turning of the wheel robbing them of some spot endeared by memory and affection. It was but the work of a few minutes. They reached the Park gate. The lodge-keeper, an old, gray-headed servant of the family, came forward to express his wishes for his master's prosperous journey. Edward raised his head, and tried to thank him, but the tone was strained and unnatural; and Laura bowed her gratitude,—she could do no more. And the greeting was over. Edward, in a hoarse voice, called to the postilion to proceed, and then once more the carriage rolled on, and Allingham was left for ever.

CHAPTER XLVIII.

ABOUT half-way up the ascent of a wide, heath-covered hill, distant nearly two miles from the village of Elsham, stands a small church of modern date, in the decorated style of the fourteenth century. The beauty of the situation, commanding an extensive view over the valley of Elsham, backed by the Allingham woods, might alone excite admiration; but a more rare and perhaps more interesting subject for observation, is to be found in the building itself. The deep porch, with its massive door and ornamented hinges, the flowing tracery of the windows, the rich mouldings, the buttresses surmounted by carved pinnacles, the trefoil parapet, the spire rising from a tower of exquisite proportions, all tell that the hand of taste as well as of piety has been busied in erecting a fitting temple for the worship of God. And to those who have gazed on it with pleasure, it may perhaps add something of a deeper interest to know that he who dedicated no small portion of his worldly substance to be thus employed for his Maker's honour, was summoned to his great reward before he had been permitted to witness the full completion of his work.

About three weeks previous to the day fixed for the consecration of Torrington church, Mr Dacre breathed his last, after an illness of a few hours; his final request being that no alteration might take place in the arrangements which he had made. He had no regrets, no longings: the praise of man could be nothing

to him, who for so many years had sought only the favour of
God. Some thoughts, indeed, there were of one, who in the
course of a few days was about to return to her home, and
whose voice it would have soothed him once more to hear; but
they were thoughts of comfort and peace, for Gertrude's frequent
letters from abroad had relieved him from many sources of
anxiety. She had told him of Edward's increasing stability of
character, of Laura's improving health, and her own perfect
satisfaction in all that had been done. She was not, she said,
resigned merely, but grateful. Edward's peace of mind had
been lightly purchased by the sacrifice of her own inclinations,
and all that she desired was to know that the task which had
fallen into Mr Dacre's hands had been fulfilled according to
his wishes. To have received the assurance from her own lips
would, indeed, have been a blessing; but Mr Dacre had learned
most perfectly the lesson of submission, and when he was told
that a few hours must, in all human probability, terminate his
existence, he turned from the prospect of an earthly meeting,
to the hope of one upon which no parting should follow. And
as Mr Dacre had lived, so he died,—humbly, thankfully, and in
faith,—his hands crossed upon his breast, and his lips moving
in prayer to the Saviour, in whose merits alone he trusted; and
when the last breath was drawn, not one of those who viewed
the smile which rested upon his worn features, dared, even for
an instant, to indulge the wish that would have recalled him
from his deep repose.

It was a bitter trial for Gertrude when the intelligence first
reached her. She was then on her way to England, and the
latest accounts had been so good, that he had buoyed herself up
with the idea that the foreboding tone of their last interview had
been merely the effect of passing circumstances—that they might
meet again, and that, perhaps, it might be granted to her to be a
comfort to him in his last days. She thought of her home, and
longed to be restored to it; but the remembrance of the voice
now silent, which she had hoped would join in welcoming her,
cast a melancholy shade over every anticipation of pleasure.

The arrangements of Edward's property had by this time been
made. Allingham had passed into other hands; and, with no
fortune but that of a name unstained, and resolution strengthened
by trial, he was about to recommence his career in life. Gertrude
stayed with him till he was settled in London, in a small house, in
a quiet street, with two servants,—no carriages, no luxuries,

nothing but the necessaries of life ; and when she had seen him smile, as Laura occupied herself with domestic affairs. and laugh at the deficiencies of his establishment, her mind was happy. If he had no false shame, she had little doubt of his ultimate success. And Edward was hopeful also. He knew his own powers, but he did not trust to them. If the blessing of God went with his endeavours, they would prosper—if not, the wisdom of ages could not help him. And the blessing of God rests upon a pure intention, a heart which will shrink from evil, at whatever risk, under whatever temptation. With Allingham in his possession, purchased by the relinquishment of a single principle of right, his happiness would have hung upon a thread, which a single instant might sever ; and this he now unhesitatingly acknowledged.

The moment was a happy, though a trying one, when Gertrude once more found herself seated in the drawing-room at the Priory, her mother questioning her about Edward, and her sisters crowding round her, as around a newly-found treasure. But the pleasure was quickly damped,—an allusion to Mr Dacre brought back the full remembrance of her loss. Yet it was only when by herself, or with Edith, that she ventured to give way to her grief, for Edith alone had known and appreciated him truly. To hear his name mentioned carelessly was a profanation scarcely to be endured ; but it was a trial to which she was daily subjected. A person of Mr Dacre's character and fortune could not die without leaving many causes for curiosity and speculation.

Every one turned to General Forester, as the party most interested in the event ; and the General attended at the opening of the will, with a self-important manner, but ill concealed by an affectation of regret. Yet he might have spared himself any anxiety. He was remembered, so was his daughter, so were Edward, and Gertrude, and Edith, and the housekeeper and servants, with kind expressions and small legacies, but the bulk of Mr Dacre's fortune was gone. He had disposed of it during the latter part of his life, in favour of some public institutions in India, and the church had swallowed up the remaining portion, which he had reserved for his own especial need. He was a rich man, but he died poor ; no one knew how poor, but those who had witnessed the increasing abstemiousness of his habits, and the denial of what to many would have been only necessaries, after he had decided upon the building and endowment of his church   General Forester's disappointment was keen, and plainly shown.   Miss Forester affected indifference, but not with her usual success.   The last year had robbed her of much of the interest of her existence ; and middle age was creeping upon her before she had forgotten the follies of youth.   The Grange was distasteful, the Priory odious, Elsham insipid.   She spoke of travelling, and her father seconded the idea.   He thought it might amuse, and relieve *ennui;* but it was a delusive fancy.   Happiness lies in our own hearts, and they who seek it elsewhere will assuredly seek in vain.

It was with an involuntary feeling of satisfaction that Gertrude heard of their intention to leave the Grange, at least for two years.   Every association connected with them was full of pain. She could not endure Miss Forester's inquiries after Laura, or the tone in which she alluded to Mr Dacre, as her late dear uncle ; and when, about a fortnight after her return, she understood that business had called both the General and his daughter to town, and that it was thought they would not return again, the relief was not to be expressed.   Yet, notwithstanding Gertrude's many subjects for regret, there were some changes in her home circle which were a source of never-ceasing thankfulness.   Mrs Courtenay's mind was not, indeed, enlarged, but she had become less excitable, less dependent upon luxuries, and estimated more deeply the importance of religious duties ; and Edith and her sisters were more united, more willing to take a common interest in the poor, and to exert themselves in the schools.   Edith was considerate, and Charlotte softened, and Jane less wrapped up in herself.   The difference was not very marked, but it could not be hidden from Gertrude, for trial had brought with it thought, and thought was maturing into practice ; and as Gertrude watched these dawnings of a better spirit, she thought that no affliction could be overwhelming, which brought such blessings in its train. Yet, when the day of the consecration arrived, the spring of her past sorrow seemed opened afresh.   Since her return she had never summoned courage to walk to the Heath ; and when she stood, for the first time, with Edith before Mr Dacre's church, the memories which flashed like lightning upon her mind were sad almost to tears.   Allingham and its beauty, Edward's ruin, her own disappointment, Laura's illness, seemed again realities ; and Mr Dacre seemed still near her,—she almost heard his grave, quiet tones, and saw his deep-searching eye, and sweet though sad smile ; and then she looked upon the beautiful building before

her, raised as if by magic in the wilderness, and it was a dream—
a phantom. Edith drew her into the church, for the crowd was
pressing on. Through the stained windows was gleaming a misty
light, and upon the clustered pillows rainbow hues were flickering ;
and dimness rested upon the dark oak roof and the raised chancel
—a dimness which was, as it were, the shadow of heaven. The
building was the type of the spiritual temple of God, and His
peace seemed resting upon it. With soothed and tranquil hearts
Gertrude and her sister took their places, where, retired and unobserved, they might join without distraction in the services of
the day. By degrees the church was filled, the rustling murmurs
ceased, and the procession of the bishop and clergy moved down
the narrow aisles. And then was heard the solemn acknowledgment of the sovereignty of the Lord of Heaven, and the encouragement to those who, with clean hands and pure hearts, would
seek to rise up in His holy place ; the exhortation to pray faith-
fully and devoutly for the blessing of God ; and the entreaty that
He would vouchsafe to be present with those who were there
gathered together ; that He would accept their service and bless
it with success ; that He would sanctify those who in that house
should be dedicated to Him by baptism ; that He would keep for
ever, and preserve in the unity of His Church, those who should
there renew their vows ; that He would fill with His heavenly
benediction whosoever should in that place receive the blessed
sacrament of the body and blood of Christ ; that He would give
strength for the performance of the marriage vow ; grace to the
hearers of His holy Word ; steadfastness of faith, seriousness, and
sincerity to the penitent ; and to all such a portion of His Holy
Spirit, that, after serving and worshipping Him below, they might
finally be received into His presence.

The service proceeded. The appointed psalms, the lessons,
with the solemn words in which Solomon dedicated the Temple
of Jerusalem, the daily prayers, in which the needs of the Church
are intended to be continually represented before the throne of
grace ; the entreaty that the people of God might be filled with
an awful apprehension of His Divine Majesty, and a deep sense
of their own unworthiness ; the assertions of the Apostle of the
mysterious privileges by which Christians are made the temples
of the living God ; and the awful warning against profaning the
dwelling-place of the Most High.

The sermon followed ; and when it was ended, and the final
prayers were read from the altar, Gertrude's heart beat quickly.

There was one most fervent petition for unity, and then the bishop paused. He, for whom the next prayer should have been offered, was beyond the reach of intercession. Lonely and childless, he had passed to his eternal rest, and the kindness which he had showed for the house of his God was written among the deeds which shall be blessed, not on earth, but in heaven. For him there was no need to seek 'the peace that passeth understanding.'

Gertrude and Edith were among the first to leave the church. They did not pause, or speak, or look back, till they had reached a still, sheltered spot, far from the road which they believed all others would take ; and then Edith drew a long breath, and, in a low, half-broken voice, said—

'Gertrude, was it a sinful wish? The prayer was uttered for no one ;—it might have been for you.'

Gertrude's answer was firm. 'Yes ; and at that moment a thought of self might have arisen, and the offering would have been marred.'

On the north side of the altar in Torrington church there is inserted in the floor a small brass plate, inscribed with Mr Dacre's name, and the date of his birth and of his death. It is all that remains to tell of him who founded and endowed the beautiful edifice which is now the admiration of the beholder, and the centre of instruction and blessing to the neat and orderly population which has sprung up around its walls. But there needs no earthly monument to remind those who once dwelt within reach of his bounty, of the friend thus granted for their aid. In the cottage and the hovel, in sunshine and in gloom, beneath the summer's sun and by the winter's hearth, his name is yet remembered and beloved ; and when years have gone by, and the great and the powerful have sunk into oblivion, it may be that the light of his example shall still linger upon earth ; for 'the memory of the just is blessed.'

THE END.

PRINTED BY BALLANTYNE, HANSON AND CO.
EDINBURGH AND LONDON

POPULAR WORKS ON NATURAL HISTORY.

By the REV. J. G. WOOD, M.A.

With Numerous Illustrations.

***

HOMES WITHOUT HANDS:

A Description of the Habitations of Animals, classed according to their Principle of Construction. With about 140 Vignettes on Wood. 8vo, 10s. 6d.

INSECTS AT HOME:

A Popular Account of British Insects, their Structure, Habits, and Transformations. 8vo, Woodcuts, 10s. 6d.

INSECTS ABROAD:

A Popular Account of Foreign Insects, their Structure, Habits, and Transformations. 8vo, Woodcuts, 10s. 6d.

BIBLE ANIMALS:

A Description of every Living Creature mentioned in the Scriptures. With 112 Woodcuts. 8vo, 10s. 6d.

HORSE AND MAN:

Their Mutual Dependence and Duties. With 49 Illustrations. 8vo, 14s.

STRANGE DWELLINGS:

A Description of the Habitations of Animals, abridged from "Homes without Hands." With Frontispiece and 60 Woodcuts. Crown 8vo, 5s. Popular Edition, 4to, 6d.

OUT OF DOORS:

A Selection of Original Articles on Practical Natural History. With 6 Woodcuts. Crown 8vo, 5s.

COMMON BRITISH INSECTS, BEETLES, MOTHS, AND BUTTERFLIES:

With 130 Woodcuts. Crown 8vo, 3s. 6d.

PETLAND REVISITED:

With 33 Woodcuts. Crown 8vo, 7s. 6d.

***

POPULAR WORKS.

WORKS BY DR. G. HARTWIG.

THE SEA AND ITS LIVING WONDERS. 8vo, with many Illustrations, 10s. 6d.

THE TROPICAL WORLD. With about 200 Illustrations. 8vo, 10s. 6d.

THE POLAR WORLD: A Description of Man and Nature in the Arctic and Antarctic Regions of the Globe. Maps, Plates, and Woodcuts. 8vo, 10s. 6d.

THE ARCTIC REGIONS (extracted from the "Polar World"). 4to, 6d. sewed.

THE SUBTERRANEAN WORLD. With Map and Woodcuts. 8vo, 10s. 6d.

THE AERIAL WORLD: A Popular Account of the Phenomena and Life of the Atmosphere. Map, Plates, and Woodcuts. 8vo, 10s. 6d.

LADY BRASSEY'S A VOYAGE IN THE "SUNBEAM." With Map and 65 Wood Engravings.

> CABINET EDITION. Crown 8vo, 7s. 6d.
> SCHOOL EDITION. Fcap. 8vo, 2s.
> POPULAR EDITION. 4to, 6d. sewed; 1s. cloth.

HOWITT'S VISITS TO REMARKABLE PLACES. With 80 Illustrations engraved on Wood. Crown 8vo, 7s. 6d.

SIR SAMUEL BAKER'S EIGHT YEARS IN CEYLON. Woodcuts. Crown 8vo, 5s.

SIR SAMUEL BAKER'S RIFLE AND THE HOUND IN CEYLON. Woodcuts. Crown 8vo, 5s.

LIFE OF THE DUKE OF WELLINGTON. By the Rev. G. R. GLEIG, M.A. With Portrait. Crown 8vo, 6s.

MEMOIRS OF SIR HENRY HAVELOCK, K.C.B. By JOHN CLARK MARSHMAN. Crown 8vo, 3s. 6d.

THE WIT and WISDOM of the REV. SYDNEY SMITH. Crown 8vo, 3s. 6d.

THE WIT and WISDOM of the EARL of BEACONSFIELD. Collected from his Writings and Speeches. Crown 8vo, 3s. 6d.

THE BEACONSFIELD BIRTHDAY BOOK. Selected from the Writings and Speeches of the Right Hon. the Earl of Beaconsfield, K.G. With 2 Portraits and 11 Views of Hughenden Manor and its Surroundings. 18mo, 2s. 6d. cloth gilt; 1s. 6d. bound.

LONDON: LONGMANS, GREEN, & CO.

GENERAL LISTS OF WORKS

PUBLISHED BY

MESSRS. LONGMANS, GREEN, & CO.

PATERNOSTER ROW, LONDON.

—oo꞉ꙮ꞉oo—

HISTORY, POLITICS, HISTORICAL MEMOIRS, &c.

Arnold's Lectures on Modern History. 8vo. 7s. 6d.
Bagwell's Ireland under the Tudors. Vols. 1 and 2. 2 vols. 8vo. 32s.
Beaconsfield's (Lord) Speeches, edited by Kebbel. 2 vols. 8vo. 32s.
Boultbee's History of the Church of England, Pre-Reformation Period. 8vo. 15s.
Bramston & Leroy's Historic Winchester. Crown 8vo. 6s.
Buckle's History of Civilisation. 3 vols. crown 8vo. 24s.
Chesney's Waterloo Lectures. 8vo. 10s. 6d.
Cox's (Sir G. W.) General History of Greece. Crown 8vo. Maps, 7s. 6d.
    —   —   Lives of Greek Statesmen. Two Series. Fcp. 8vo. 2s. 6d. each.
Creighton's History of the Papacy during the Reformation. 2 vols. 8vo. 32s.
De Tocqueville's Democracy in America, translated by Reeve. 2 vols. crown 8vo. 16s.
Doyle's English in America. 8vo. 18s.
Epochs of Ancient History :—

        Beesly's Gracchi, Marius, and Sulla, 2s. 6d.
        Capes's Age of the Antonines, 2s. 6d.
        —   Early Roman Empire, 2s. 6d.
        Cox's Athenian Empire, 2s. 6d.
        — Greeks and Persians, 2s. 6d.
        Curteis's Rise of the Macedonian Empire, 2s. 6d.
        Ihne's Rome to its Capture by the Gauls, 2s. 6d.
        Merivale's Roman Triumvirates, 2s. 6d.
        Sankey's Spartan and Theban Supremacies, 2s. 6d.
        Smith's Rome and Carthage, the Punic Wars, 2s. 6d.

Epochs of Modern History :—

        Church's Beginning of the Middle Ages, 2s. 6d.
        Cox's Crusades, 2s. 6d.
        Creighton's Age of Elizabeth, 2s. 6d.
        Gairdner's Houses of Lancaster and York, 2s. 6d.
        Gardiner's Puritan Revolution, 2s. 6d.
        —   Thirty Years' War, 2s. 6d.
        —   (Mrs.) French Revolution, 1789–1795, 2s. 6d.
        Hale's Fall of the Stuarts, 2s. 6d.
        Johnson's Normans in Europe, 2s. 6d.
        Longman's Frederick the Great and the Seven Years' War, 2s. 6d.
        Ludlow's War of American Independence, 2s. 6d.
        M'Carthy's Epoch of Reform, 1830–1850, 2s. 6d.
        Morris's Age of Queen Anne, 2s. 6d.
        —   The Early Hanoverians, 2s. 6d.
        Seebohm's Protestant Revolution, 2s. 6d.
        Stubbs's Early Plantagenets, 2s. 6d.
        Warburton's Edward III., 2s. 6d.

Freeman's Historical Geography of Europe. 2 vols. 8vo. 31s. 6d.

London : LONGMANS, GREEN, & CO.

Froude's English in Ireland in the 18th Century. 3 vols. crown 8vo. 18s.
— History of England. Popular Edition. 12 vols. crown 8vo. 3s. 6d. each.
Gardiner's History of England from the Accession of James I. to the Outbreak of the Civil War. 10 vols. crown 8vo. 60s.
— Outline of English History, B.C. 55–A.D. 1880. Fcp. 8vo. 2s. 6d.
Grant's (Sir Alex.) The Story of the University of Edinburgh. 2 vols. 8vo. 36s.
Greville's Journal of the Reigns of George IV. & William IV. 3 vols. 8vo. 36s.
— — — Reign of Queen Victoria, 1837–1852. 3 vols. 8vo. 36s.
Hickson's Ireland in the Seventeenth Century. 2 vols. 8vo. 28s.
Lecky's History of England in the Eighteenth Century. Vols. 1 & 2, 1700–1760, 8vo. 36s. Vols. 3 & 4, 1760–1784. 8vo. 36s.
— History of European Morals. 2 vols. crown 8vo. 16s.
— — — Rationalism in Europe. 2 vols. crown 8vo. 16s.
— Leaders of Public Opinion in Ireland. Crown 8vo. 7s. 6d.
Longman's Lectures on the History of England. 8vo. 15s.
— Life and Times of Edward III. 2 vols. 8vo. 28s.
Macaulay's Complete Works. Library Edition. 8 vols. 8vo. £5. 5s.
— — — Cabinet Edition. 16 vols. crown 8vo. £4. 16s.
— History of England :—

Student's Edition. 2 vols. cr. 8vo. 12s.	Cabinet Edition. 8 vols. post 8vo. 48s.
People's Edition. 4 vols. cr. 8vo. 16s.	Library Edition. 5 vols. 8vo. £4.

Macaulay's Critical and Historical Essays, with Lays of Ancient Rome In One Volume :—

Authorised Edition. Cr. 8vo. 2s. 6d. or 3s. 6d. gilt edges.	Popular Edition. Cr. 8vo. 2s. 6d.

Macaulay's Critical and Historical Essays :—

Student's Edition. 1 vol. cr. 8vo. 6s.	Cabinet Edition. 4 vols. post 8vo. 24s.
People's Edition. 2 vols. cr. 8vo. 8s.	Library Edition. 3 vols. 8vo. 36s.

Macaulay's Speeches corrected by Himself. Crown 8vo. 3s. 6d.
Malmesbury's (Earl of) Memoirs of an Ex-Minister. Crown 8vo. 7s. 6d.
Maxwell's (Sir W. S.) Don John of Austria. Library Edition, with numerous Illustrations. 2 vols. royal 8vo. 42s.
May's Constitutional History of England, 1760–1870. 3 vols. crown 8vo. 18s.
— Democracy in Europe. 2 vols. 8vo. 32s.
Merivale's Fall of the Roman Republic. 12mo. 7s. 6d.
— General History of Rome, B.C. 753–A.D. 476. Crown 8vo. 7s. 6d.
— History of the Romans under the Empire. 8 vols. post 8vo. 48s.
Noble's The Russian Revolt. Fcp. 8vo. 5s.
Pears' The Fall of Constantinople. 8vo. 16s.
Seebohm's Oxford Reformers—Colet, Erasmus, & More. 8vo. 14s.
Short's History of the Church of England. Crown 8vo. 7s. 6d.
Smith's Carthage and the Carthaginians. Crown 8vo. 10s. 6d.
Taylor's Manual of the History of India. Crown 8vo. 7s. 6d.
Walpole's History of England, 1815–1841. 3 vols. 8vo. £2. 14s.
Wylie's History of England under Henry IV. Vol. 1, crown 8vo. 10s. 6d.

BIOGRAPHICAL WORKS.

Bacon's Life and Letters, by Spedding. 7 vols. 8vo. £4. 4s.
Bagehot's Biographical Studies. 1 vol. 8vo. 12s.

London : LONGMANS, GREEN, & CO.

Carlyle's Life, by Froude. Vols. 1 & 2, 1795–1835, 8vo. 32s. Vols. 3 & 4, 1834–1881, 8vo. 32s.
— (Mrs.) Letters and Memorials. 3 vols. 8vo. 36s.
De Witt (John), Life of, by A. L. Pontalis. Translated. 2 vols. 8vo. 36s.
English Worthies. Edited by Andrew Lang. Crown 8vo. 2s. 6d. each.
    Charles Darwin, by Grant Allen. | Marlborough, by George Saintsbury.
Grimston's (Hon. R.) Life, by F. Gale. Crown 8vo. 10s. 6d.
Hamilton's (Sir W. R.) Life, by Graves. Vols. 1 and 2, 8vo. 15s. each.
Havelock's Life, by Marshman. Crown 8vo. 3s. 6d.
Hullah's (John) Life. By his Wife. Crown 8vo. 6s.
Macaulay's (Lord) Life and Letters. By his Nephew, G. Otto Trevelyan, M.P.
    Popular Edition, 1 vol. crown 8vo. 6s. Cabinet Edition, 2 vols. post 8vo.
    12s. Library Edition, 2 vols. 8vo. 36s.
Mendelssohn's Letters. Translated by Lady Wallace. 2 vols. cr. 8vo. 5s. each.
Mill (James) Biography of, by Prof. Bain. Crown 8vo. 5s.
— (John Stuart) Recollections of, by Prof. Bain. Crown 8vo. 2s. 6d.
—   —   Autobiography. 8vo. 7s. 6d.
Mozley's Reminiscences of Oriel College. 2 vols. crown 8vo. 18s.
—   —   — Towns, Villages, and Schools. 2 vols. cr. 8vo. 18s.
Müller's (Max) Biographical Essays. Crown 8vo. 7s. 6d.
Newman's Apologia pro Vitâ Suâ. Crown 8vo. 6s.
Pasolini's (Count) Memoir, by his Son. 8vo. 16s.
Pasteur (Louis) His Life and Labours. Crown 8vo. 7s. 6d.
Shakespeare's Life (Outlines of), by Halliwell-Phillipps. Royal 8vo. 7s. 6d.
Southey's Correspondence with Caroline Bowles. 8vo. 14s.
Stephen's Essays in Ecclesiastical Biography. Crown 8vo. 7s. 6d.
Taylor's (Sir Henry) Autobiography. 2 vols. 8vo. 32s.
Telfer's The Strange Career of the Chevalier D'Eon de Beaumont. 8vo. 12s.
Trevelyan's Early History of Charles James Fox. Crown 8vo. 6s.
Wellington's Life, by Gleig. Crown 8vo. 6s.

MENTAL AND POLITICAL PHILOSOPHY, FINANCE, &C.

Amos's View of the Science of Jurisprudence. 8vo. 18s.
— Primer of the English Constitution. Crown 8vo. 6s.
Bacon's Essays, with Annotations by Whately. 8vo. 10s. 6d.
— Works, edited by Spedding. 7 vols. 8vo. 73s. 6d.
Bagehot's Economic Studies, edited by Hutton. 8vo. 10s. 6d.
— The Postulates of English Political Economy. Crown 8vo. 2s. 6d.
Bain's Logic, Deductive and Inductive. Crown 8vo. 10s. 6d.
    PART I. Deduction, 4s. | PART II. Induction, 6s. 6d.
— Mental and Moral Science. Crown 8vo. 10s. 6d.
— The Senses and the Intellect. 8vo. 15s.
— The Emotions and the Will. 8vo. 15s.
— Practical Essays. Crown 8vo. 4s. 6d.
Buckle's (H. T.) Miscellaneous and Posthumous Works. 2 vols. crown 8vo. 21s.
Crozier's Civilization and Progress. 8vo. 14s.
Crump's A Short Enquiry into the Formation of English Political Opinion. 8vo. 7s. 6d.
Dowell's A History of Taxation and Taxes in England. 4 vols. 8vo. 48s.
Green's (Thomas Hill) Works. (3 vols.) Vol. 1, Philosophical Works. 8vo. 16s.

Hume's Essays, edited by Green & Grose.   2 vols. 8vo. 28s.
—   Treatise of Human Nature, edited by Green & Grose.   2 vols. 8vo. 28s.
Lang's Custom and Myth : Studies of Early Usage and Belief.   Crown 8vo. 7s. 6d.
Leslie's Essays in Political and Moral Philosophy.   8vo. 10s. 6d.
Lewes's History of Philosophy.   2 vols. 8vo. 32s.
List's Natural System of Political Economy, translated by S. Lloyd, M.P.   8vo. 10s. 6d.
Lubbock's Origin of Civilisation.   8vo. 18s.
Macleod's Principles of Economical Philosophy.   In 2 vols.   Vol. 1, 8vo. 15s. Vol. 2, Part I. 12s.
—   The Elements of Economics.   (2 vols.) Vol. 1, cr. 8vo. 7s. 6d. Vol. 2, Part I. cr. 8vo. 7s. 6d.
—   The Elements of Banking.   Crown 8vo. 5s.
—   The Theory and Practice of Banking.   Vol. 1, 8vo. 12s.
—   Elements of Political Economy.   8vo. 16s.
—   Economics for Beginners.   8vo. 2s. 6d.
—   Lectures on Credit and Banking.   8vo. 5s.
Mill's (James) Analysis of the Phenomena of the Human Mind.   2 vols. 8vo. 28s.
Mill (John Stuart) on Representative Government.   Crown 8vo. 2s.
—   —   on Liberty.   Crown 8vo. 1s. 4d.
—   —   Essays on Unsettled Questions of Political Economy.   8vo. 6s. 6d.
—   —   Examination of Hamilton's Philosophy.   8vo. 16s.
—   —   Logic.   2 vols. 8vo. 25s.   People's Edition, 1 vol. cr. 8vo. 5s.
—   —   Principles of Political Economy.   2 vols. 8vo. 30s.   People's Edition, 1 vol. crown 8vo. 5s.
—   —   Subjection of Women.   Crown 8vo. 6s.
—   —   Utilitarianism.   8vo. 5s.
—   —   Three Essays on Religion, &c.   8vo. 5s.
Miller's (Mrs. Fenwick) Readings in Social Economy.   Crown 8vo. 2s.
Mulhall's History of Prices since 1850.   Crown 8vo. 6s.
Sandars's Institutes of Justinian, with English Notes.   8vo. 18s.
Seebohm's English Village Community.   8vo. 16s.
Sully's Outlines of Psychology.   8vo. 12s. 6d.
Swinburne's Picture Logic.   Post 8vo. 5s.
Thompson's A System of Psychology.   2 vols. 8vo. 36s.
Thomson's Outline of Necessary Laws of Thought.   Crown 8vo. 6s.
Twiss's Law of Nations in Time of War.   8vo. 21s.
—   —   in Time of Peace.   8vo. 15s.
Webb's The Veil of Isis.   8vo. 10s. 6d.
Whately's Elements of Logic.   Crown 8vo. 4s. 6d.
—   —   — Rhetoric.   Crown 8vo. 4s. 6d.
Wylie's Labour, Leisure, and Luxury.   Crown 8vo. 6s.
Zeller's History of Eclecticism in Greek Philosophy.   Crown 8vo. 10s. 6d.
—   Plato and the Older Academy.   Crown 8vo. 18s.
—   Pre-Socratic Schools.   2 vols. crown 8vo. 30s.
—   Socrates and the Socratic Schools.   Crown 8vo. 10s. 6d.
—   Stoics, Epicureans, and Sceptics.   Crown 8vo. 15s.
—   Outlines of the History of Greek Philosophy.   Crown 8vo. 10s. 6d.

MISCELLANEOUS WORKS.

A. K. H. B., The Essays and Contributions of. Crown 8vo.
    Autumn Holidays of a Country Parson. 3s. 6d.
    Changed Aspects of Unchanged Truths. 3s. 6d.
    Common-Place Philosopher in Town and Country. 3s. 6d.
    Critical Essays of a Country Parson. 3s. 6d.
    Counsel and Comfort spoken from a City Pulpit. 3s. 6d.
    Graver Thoughts of a Country Parson. Three Series. 3s. 6d. each
    Landscapes, Churches, and Moralities. 3s. 6d.
    Leisure Hours in Town. 3s. 6d. Lessons of Middle Age. 3s. 6d.
    Our Little Life. Essays Consolatory and Domestic. Two Series. 3s. 6d.
    Present-day Thoughts. 3s. 6d.   [each.
    Recreations of a Country Parson. Three Series. 3s. 6d. each.
    Seaside Musings on Sundays and Week-Days. 3s. 6d.
    Sunday Afternoons in the Parish Church of a University City. 3s. 6d.
Arnold's (Dr. Thomas) Miscellaneous Works. 8vo. 7s. 6d.
Bagehot's Literary Studies, edited by Hutton. 2 vols. 8vo. 28s.
Beaconsfield (Lord), The Wit and Wisdom of. Crown 8vo. 3s. 6d.
    — (The) Birthday Book. 18mo. 2s. 6d. cloth ; 4s. 6d. bound.
Evans's Bronze Implements of Great Britain. 8vo. 25s.
Farrar's Language and Languages. Crown 8vo. 6s.
French's Nineteen Centuries of Drink in England. Crown 8vo. 10s. 6d.
Froude's Short Studies on Great Subjects. 4 vols. crown 8vo. 24s.
Lang's Letters to Dead Authors. Fcp. 8vo. 6s. 6d.
Macaulay's Miscellaneous Writings. 2 vols. 8vo. 21s. 1 vol. crown 8vo. 4s. 6d.
    — Miscellaneous Writings and Speeches. Crown 8vo. 6s.
    — Miscellaneous Writings, Speeches, Lays of Ancient Rome, &c.
        Cabinet Edition. 4 vols. crown 8vo. 24s.
    — Writings, Selections from. Crown 8vo. 6s.
Müller's (Max) Lectures on the Science of Language. 2 vols. crown 8vo. 16s.
    — — Lectures on India. 8vo. 12s. 6d.
Smith (Sydney) The Wit and Wisdom of. Crown 8vo. 3s. 6d.

ASTRONOMY.

Herschel's Outlines of Astronomy. Square crown 8vo. 12s.
Neison's Work on the Moon. Medium 8vo. 31s. 6d.
Proctor's Larger Star Atlas. Folio, 15s. or Maps only, 12s. 6d.
    — New Star Atlas. Crown 8vo. 5s. Orbs Around Us. Crown 8vo. 5s.
    — Light Science for Leisure Hours. 3 Series. Crown 8vo. 5s. each.
    — Moon. Crown 8vo. 10s. 6d.
    — Myths and Marvels of Astronomy. Crown 8vo. 6s.
    — Other Worlds than Ours. Crown 8vo. 5s.
    — Sun. Crown 8vo. 14s. Universe of Stars. 8vo. 10s. 6d.
    — Pleasant Ways in Science. Crown 8vo. 6s.
    — Studies of Venus-Transits. 8vo. 5s.
Webb's Celestial Objects for Common Telescopes. Crown 8vo. 9s.
    — The Sun and his Phenomena. Fcp. 8vo. 1s.

THE 'KNOWLEDGE' LIBRARY.

Edited by RICHARD A. PROCTOR.

How to Play Whist. Crown 8vo. 5s.
The Borderland of Science. Cr. 8vo. 6s.
Nature Studies. Crown 8vo. 6s.
Leisure Readings. Crown 8vo. 6s.
The Stars in their Seasons. Imp. 8vo. 5s.
Home Whist. 16mo. 1s.
Star Primer. Crown 4to. 2s. 6d.
The Seasons Pictured. Demy 4to. 5s.
Strength and Happiness. Cr. 8vo. 5s.
Rough Ways made Smooth. Cr. 8vo. 6s.
The Expanse of Heaven. Cr. 8vo. 5s.
Our Place among Infinities. Cr. 8vo. 5s.

London : LONGMANS, GREEN, & CO.

CLASSICAL LANGUAGES AND LITERATURE.

Æschylus, The Eumenides of. Text, with Metrical English Translation, by J. F. Davies. 8vo. 7s.
Aristophanes' The Acharnians, translated by R. Y. Tyrrell. Crown 8vo. 2s. 6d.
Aristotle's The Ethics, Text and Notes, by Sir Alex. Grant, Bart. 2 vols. 8vo. 32s.
— The Nicomachean Ethics, translated by Williams, crown 8vo. 7s. 6d.
— The Politics, Books I. III. IV. (VII.) with Translation, &c. by Bolland and Lang. Crown 8vo. 7s. 6d.
Becker's *Charicles* and *Gallus*, by Metcalfe. Post 8vo. 7s. 6d. each.
Cicero's Correspondence, Text and Notes, by R. Y. Tyrrell. Vol. 1, 8vo. 12s.
Homer's Iliad, Homometrically translated by Cayley. 8vo. 12s. 6d.
— — Greek Text, with Verse Translation, by W. C. Green. Vol. 1, Books I.-XII. Crown 8vo. 6s.
Mahaffy's Classical Greek Literature. Crown 8vo. Vol. 1, The Poets, 7s. 6d. Vol. 2, The Prose Writers, 7s. 6d.
Plato's Parmenides, with Notes, &c. by J. Maguire. 8vo. 7s. 6d.
Sophocles' Tragœdiæ Superstites, by Linwood. 8vo. 16s.
Virgil's Works, Latin Text, with Commentary, by Kennedy. Crown 8vo. 10s. 6d.
— Æneid, translated into English Verse, by Conington. Crown 8vo. 9s.
— Poems, — — — Prose, — — Crown 8vo. 9s.
Witt's Myths of Hellas, translated by F. M. Younghusband. Crown 8vo. 3s. 6d.
— The Trojan War, — — Fcp. 8vo. 2s.
— The Wanderings of Ulysses, — Crown 8vo. 3s. 6d.

NATURAL HISTORY, BOTANY, & GARDENING.

Allen's Flowers and their Pedigrees. Crown 8vo. Woodcuts, 5s.
Decaisne and Le Maout's General System of Botany. Imperial 8vo. 31s. 6d.
Dixon's Rural Bird Life. Crown 8vo. Illustrations, 5s.
Hartwig's Aerial World, 8vo. 10s. 6d.
— Polar World, 8vo. 10s. 6d.
— Sea and its Living Wonders. 8vo. 10s. 6d.
— Subterranean World, 8vo. 10s. 6d.
— Tropical World, 8vo. 10s. 6d.
Lindley's Treasury of Botany. Fcp. 8vo. 6s.
London's Encyclopædia of Gardening. 8vo. 21s.
— — Plants. 8vo. 42s.
Rivers's Orchard House. Crown 8vo. 5s.
— Rose Amateur's Guide. Fcp. 8vo. 4s. 6d.
— Miniature Fruit Garden. Fcp. 8vo. 4s.
Stanley's Familiar History of British Birds. Crown 8vo. 6s.
Wood's Bible Animals. With 112 Vignettes. 8vo. 10s. 6d.
— Common British Insects. Crown 8vo. 3s. 6d.
— Homes Without Hands, 8vo. 10s. 6d.
— Insects Abroad, 8vo. 10s. 6d.
— Horse and Man. 8vo. 14s.
— Insects at Home. With 700 Illustrations. 8vo. 10s. 6d.
— Out of Doors. Crown 8vo. 5s.
— Petland Revisited. Crown 8vo. 7s. 6d.
— Strange Dwellings. Crown 8vo. 5s. Popular Edition, 4to. 6d.

THE FINE ARTS AND ILLUSTRATED EDITIONS.

Dresser's Arts and Art Manufactures of Japan. Square crown 8vo. 31s. 6d.
Eastlake's Household Taste in Furniture, &c. Square crown 8vo. 14s.
Jameson's Sacred and Legendary Art. 6 vols. square 8vo.
     Legends of the Madonna. 1 vol. 21s.
         — — — Monastic Orders 1 vol. 21s.
         — — — Saints and Martyrs. 2 vols. 31s. 6d.
         — — — Saviour. Completed by Lady Eastlake. 2 vols. 42s.
Macaulay's Lays of Ancient Rome, illustrated by Scharf. Fcp. 4to. 10s. 6d.
The same, with *Ivry* and the *Armada*, illustrated by Weguelin. Crown 8vo. 3s. 6d.
Moore's Lalla Rookh, illustrated by Tenniel. Square crown 8vo. 10s. 6d.
New Testament (The) illustrated with Woodcuts after Paintings by the Early
     Masters. 4to. 21s. cloth, or 42s. morocco.
Perry on Greek and Roman Sculpture. With 280 Illustrations engraved on
     Wood. Square crown 8vo. 31s. 6d.

CHEMISTRY, ENGINEERING, & GENERAL SCIENCE.

Arnott's Elements of Physics or Natural Philosophy. Crown 8vo. 12s. 6d.
Bourne's Catechism of the Steam Engine. Crown 8vo. 7s. 6d.
     — Examples of Steam, Air, and Gas Engines. 4to. 70s.
     — Handbook of the Steam Engine. Fcp. 8vo. 9s.
     — Recent Improvements in the Steam Engine. Fcp. 8vo. 6s.
     — Treatise on the Steam Engine. 4to. 42s.
Buckton's Our Dwellings, Healthy and Unhealthy. Crown 8vo. 3s. 6d.
Crookes's Select Methods in Chemical Analysis. 8vo. 24s.
Culley's Handbook of Practical Telegraphy. 8vo. 16s.
Fairbairn's Useful Information for Engineers. 3 vols. crown 8vo. 31s. 6d.
     — Mills and Millwork. 1 vol. 8vo. 25s.
Ganot's Elementary Treatise on Physics, by Atkinson. Large crown 8vo. 15s.
     — Natural Philosophy, by Atkinson. Crown 8vo. 7s. 6d.
Grove's Correlation of Physical Forces. 8vo. 15s.
Haughton's Six Lectures on Physical Geography. 8vo. 15s.
Heer's Primæval World of Switzerland. 2 vols. 8vo. 12s.
Helmholtz on the Sensations of Tone. Royal 8vo. 28s.
Helmholtz's Lectures on Scientific Subjects. 2 vols. crown 8vo. 7s. 6d. each.
Hudson and Gosse's The Rotifera or 'Wheel Animalcules.' With 30 Coloured
     Plates. 6 parts. 4to. 10s. 6d. each.
Hullah's Lectures on the History of Modern Music. 8vo. 8s. 6d.
     — Transition Period of Musical History. 8vo. 10s. 6d.
Jackson's Aid to Engineering Solution. Royal 8vo. 21s.
Jago's Inorganic Chemistry, Theoretical and Practical. Fcp. 8vo. 2s.
Kerl's Metallurgy, adapted by Crookes and Röhrig. 3 vols. 8vo. £4. 19s.
Kolbe's Short Text-Book of Inorganic Chemistry. Crown 8vo. 7s. 6d.
Lloyd's Treatise on Magnetism. 8vo. 10s. 6d.
Macalister's Zoology and Morphology of Vertebrate Animals. 8vo. 10s. 6d.
Macfarren's Lectures on Harmony. 8vo. 12s.

London: LONGMANS, GREEN, & CO.

Miller's Elements of Chemistry, Theoretical and Practical. 3 vols. 8vo. Part I. Chemical Physics, 16s. Part II. Inorganic Chemistry, 24s. Part III. Organic Chemistry, price 31s. 6d.

Mitchell's Manual of Practical Assaying. 8vo. 31s. 6d.

Northcott's Lathes and Turning. 8vo. 18s.

Owen's Comparative Anatomy and Physiology of the Vertebrate Animals. 3 vols. 8vo. 73s. 6d.

Payen's Industrial Chemistry. Edited by B. H. Paul, Ph.D. 8vo. 42s.

Piesse's Art of Perfumery. Square crown 8vo. 21s.

Reynolds's Experimental Chemistry. Fcp. 8vo. Part I. 1s. 6d. Part II. 2s. 6d. Part III. 3s. 6d.

Schellen's Spectrum Analysis. 8vo. 31s. 6d.

Sennett's Treatise on the Marine Steam Engine. 8vo. 21s.

Smith's Air and Rain. 8vo. 24s.

Stoney's The Theory of the Stresses on Girders, &c. Royal 8vo. 36s.

Swinton's Electric Lighting : Its Principles and Practice. Crown 8vo. 5s.

Tilden's Practical Chemistry. Fcp. 8vo. 1s. 6d.

Tyndall's Faraday as a Discoverer. Crown 8vo. 3s. 6d.
   — Floating Matter of the Air. Crown 8vo. 7s. 6d.
   — Fragments of Science. 2 vols. post 8vo. 16s.
   — Heat a Mode of Motion. Crown 8vo. 12s.
   — Lectures on Light delivered in America. Crown 8vo. 5s.
   — Lessons on Electricity. Crown 8vo. 2s. 6d.
   — Notes on Electrical Phenomena. Crown 8vo. 1s. sewed, 1s. 6d. cloth.
   — Notes of Lectures on Light. Crown 8vo. 1s. sewed, 1s. 6d. cloth.
   — Sound, with Frontispiece and 203 Woodcuts. Crown 8vo. 10s. 6d.

Watts's Dictionary of Chemistry. 9 vols. medium 8vo. £15. 2s. 6d.

Wilson's Manual of Health-Science. Crown 8vo. 2s. 6d.

THEOLOGICAL AND RELIGIOUS WORKS.

Arnold's (Rev. Dr. Thomas) Sermons. 6 vols. crown 8vo. 5s. each.

Boultbee's Commentary on the 39 Articles. Crown 8vo. 6s.

Browne's (Bishop) Exposition of the 39 Articles. 8vo. 16s.

Colenso on the Pentateuch and Book of Joshua. Crown 8vo. 6s.

Conder's Handbook of the Bible. Post 8vo. 7s. 6d.

Conybeare & Howson's Life and Letters of St. Paul :—
   Library Edition, with Maps, Plates, and Woodcuts. 2 vols. square crown 8vo. 21s.
   Student's Edition, revised and condensed, with 46 Illustrations and Maps. 1 vol. crown 8vo. 7s. 6d.

Cox's (Homersham) The First Century of Christianity. 8vo. 12s.

Davidson's Introduction to the Study of the New Testament. 2 vols. 8vo. 30s.

Edersheim's Life and Times of Jesus the Messiah. 2 vols. 8vo. 42s.
   — Prophecy and History in relation to the Messiah. 8vo. 12s.

Ellicott's (Bishop) Commentary on St. Paul's Epistles. 8vo. Galatians, 8s. 6d. Ephesians, 8s. 6d. Pastoral Epistles, 10s. 6d. Philippians, Colossians and Philemon, 10s. 6d. Thessalonians, 7s. 6d.
   — Lectures on the Life of our Lord. 8vo. 12s.

Ewald's Antiquities of Israel, translated by Solly. 8vo. 12s. 6d.
   — History of Israel, translated by Carpenter & Smith. Vols. 1–7, 8vo. £5.

Hobart's Medical Language of St. Luke. 8vo. 16s.
Hopkins's Christ the Consoler. Fcp. 8vo. 2s. 6d.
Jukes's New Man and the Eternal Life. Crown 8vo. 6s.
— Second Death and the Restitution of all Things. Crown 8vo. 3s. 6d.
— Types of Genesis. Crown 8vo. 7s. 6d.
— The Mystery of the Kingdom. Crown 8vo. 3s. 6d.
Lenormant's New Translation of the Book of Genesis. Translated into English.
    8vo. 10s. 6d.
Lyra Germanica : Hymns translated by Miss Winkworth. Fcp. 8vo. 5s.
Macdonald's (G.) Unspoken Sermons. Second Series. Crown 8vo. 7s. 6d.
Manning's Temporal Mission of the Holy Ghost. Crown 8vo. 8s. 6d.
Martineau's Endeavours after the Christian Life. Crown 8vo. 7s. 6d.
— Hymns of Praise and Prayer. Crown 8vo. 4s. 6d. 32mo. 1s. 6d.
— Sermons, Hours of Thought on Sacred Things. 2 vols. 7s. 6d. each.
Monsell's Spiritual Songs for Sundays and Holidays. Fcp. 8vo. 5s. 18mo. 2s.
Müller's (Max) Origin and Growth of Religion. Crown 8vo. 7s. 6d.
— — Science of Religion. Crown 8vo. 7s. 6d.
Newman's Apologia pro Vitâ Suâ. Crown 8vo. 6s.
— The Idea of a University Defined and Illustrated. Crown 8vo. 7s.
— Historical Sketches. 3 vols. crown 8vo. 6s. each.
— Discussions and Arguments on Various Subjects. Crown 8vo. 6s.
— An Essay on the Development of Christian Doctrine. Crown 8vo. 6s.
— Certain Difficulties Felt by Anglicans in Catholic Teaching Con-
    sidered. Vol. 1, crown 8vo. 7s. 6d. Vol. 2, crown 8vo. 5s. 6d.
— The Via Media of the Anglican Church, Illustrated in Lectures, &c.
    2 vols. crown 8vo. 6s. each
— Essays, Critical and Historical. 2 vols. crown 8vo. 12s.
— Essays on Biblical and on Ecclesiastical Miracles. Crown 8vo. 6s.
— An Essay in Aid of a Grammar of Assent. 7s. 6d.
Overton's Life in the English Church (1660–1714). 8vo. 14s.
Rogers's Eclipse of Faith. Fcp. 8vo. 5s.
— Defence of the Eclipse of Faith. Fcp. 8vo. 3s. 6d.
Sewell's (Miss) Night Lessons from Scripture. 32mo. 3s. 6d.
— — Passing Thoughts on Religion. Fcp. 8vo. 3s. 6d.
— — Preparation for the Holy Communion. 32mo. 3s.
Smith's Voyage and Shipwreck of St. Paul. Crown 8vo. 7s. 6d.
Supernatural Religion. Complete Edition. 3 vols. 8vo. 36s.
Taylor's (Jeremy) Entire Works. With Life by Bishop Heber. Edited by the
    Rev. C. P. Eden. 10 vols. 8vo. £5. 5s.
Tulloch's Movements of Religious Thought in Britain during the Nineteenth
    Century. Crown 8vo. 10s. 6d.

TRAVELS, ADVENTURES, &c.

Aldridge's Ranch Notes in Kansas, Colorado, &c. Crown 8vo. 5s.
Alpine Club (The) Map of Switzerland. In Four Sheets. 42s.
Baker's Eight Years in Ceylon. Crown 8vo. 5s.
— Rifle and Hound in Ceylon. Crown 8vo. 5s.
Ball's Alpine Guide. 3 vols. post 8vo. with Maps and Illustrations :—I. Western
    Alps. 6s. 6d. II. Central Alps, 7s. 6d. III. Eastern Alps, 10s. 6d.
Ball on Alpine Travelling, and on the Geology of the Alps, 1s.

London : LONGMANS, GREEN, & CO.

Bent's The Cyclades, or Life among the Insular Greeks. Crown 8vo. 12s. 6d.
Brassey's Sunshine and Storm in the East. Crown 8vo. 7s. 6d.
—   Voyage in the Yacht 'Sunbeam.' Crown 8vo. 7s. 6d. School Edition,
            fcp. 8vo. 2s. Popular Edition, 4to. 6d.
—   In the Trades, the Tropics, and the 'Roaring Forties.' Edition de
            Luxe, 8vo. £3. 13s. 6d. Library Edition, 8vo. 21s.
Crawford's Across the Pampas and the Andes. Crown 8vo. 7s. 6d.
Dent's Above the Snow Line. Crown 8vo. 7s. 6d.
Froude's Oceana ; or, England and her Colonies. 8vo. 18s.
Hassall's San Remo Climatically considered. Crown 8vo. 5s.
Howitt's Visits to Remarkable Places. Crown 8vo. 7s. 6d.
Maritime Alps (The) and their Seaboard. By the Author of ' Véra.' 8vo. 21s.
Three in Norway. By Two of Them. Crown 8vo. Illustrations, 6s.

WORKS OF FICTION.

Beaconsfield's (The Earl of) Novels and Tales. Hughenden Edition, with 2
    Portraits on Steel and 11 Vignettes on Wood. 11 vols. crown 8vo. £2. 2s.
    Cheap Edition, 11 vols. fcp. 8vo. 1s. each, sewed ; 1s. 6d. each, cloth.
Black Poodle (The) and other Tales. By the Author of ' Vice Versâ.' Cr. 8vo. 6s.
Brabourne's (Lord) Friends and Foes from Fairyland. Crown 8vo. 6s.
Harte (Bret) On the Frontier. Three Stories. 16mo. 1s.
—   —   By Shore and Sedge. Three Stories. 16mo. 1s.
In the Olden Time. By the Author of ' Mademoiselle Mori.' Crown 8vo. 6s.
Melville's (Whyte) Novels. Cheap Edition. 8 vols. fcp. 8vo. 1s. each, sewed ;
    1s. 6d. each, cloth.
The Modern Novelist's Library. Crown 8vo. price 2s. each, boards, or 2s. 6d.
    each, cloth :—

By the Earl of Beaconsfield, K.G.
    Lothair.
    Sybil.
    Coningsby.
    Tancred.
    Venetia.
    Henrietta Temple.
    Contarini Fleming.
    Alroy, Ixion. &c.
    The Young Duke. &c.
    Vivian Grey.
    Endymion.
By Bret Harte.
    In the Carquinez Woods.
By Mrs. Oliphant.
    In Trust, the Story of a Lady
        and her Lover.
By James Payn.
    Thicker than Water.

By Anthony Trollope.
    Barchester Towers.
    The Warden.
By Major Whyte Melville.
    Digby Grand.
    General Bounce.
    Kate Coventry.
    The Gladiators.
    Good for Nothing.
    Holmby House.
    The Interpreter.
    The Queen's Maries.
By Various Writers.
    The Atelier du Lys.
    Atherstone Priory.
    The Burgomaster's Family.
    Elsa and her Vulture.
    Mademoiselle Mori.
    The Six Sisters of the Valleys.
    Unawares.

Oliphant's (Mrs.) Madam. Crown 8vo. 3s. 6d.
Payn's (James) The Luck of the Darrells. Crown 8vo. 3s. 6d.
Reader's Fairy Prince Follow-my-Lead. Crown 8vo. 5s.
Sewell's (Miss) Stories and Tales. Cabinet Edition. Crown 8vo. cloth extra,
    gilt edges, price 3s. 6d. each :—
    Amy Herbert. Cleve Hall.   A Glimpse of the World.
    The Earl's Daughter.   Katharine Ashton.
    Experience of Life.   Laneton Parsonage.
    Gertrude. Ivors.   Margaret Percival.   Ursula.

London : LONGMANS, GREEN, & CO.

Stevenson's (R. L.) The Dynamiter. Fcp. 8vo. 1s. sewed ; 1s. 6d. cloth.
—   —   Strange Case of Dr. Jekyll and Mr. Hyde. Fcp. 8vo. 1s. sewed ; 1s. 6d. cloth.
Sturgis' My Friend and I. Crown 8vo. 5s.

POETRY AND THE DRAMA.

Bailey's Festus, a Poem. Crown 8vo. 12s. 6d.
Bowdler's Family Shakespeare. Medium 8vo. 14s. 6 vols. fcp. 8vo. 21s.
Dante's Divine Comedy, translated by James Innes Minchin. Crown 8vo. 15s.
Goethe's Faust, translated by Birds. Large crown 8vo. 12s. 6d.
—   —   translated by Webb. 8vo. 12s. 6d.
—   —   edited by Selss. Crown 8vo. 5s.
Ingelow's Poems. Vols. 1 and 2, fcp. 8vo. 12s. Vol. 3 fcp. 8vo. 5s.
Macaulay's Lays of Ancient Rome, with Ivry and the Armada. Illustrated by Weguelin. Crown 8vo. 3s. 6d. gilt edges.
The same, Annotated Edition, fcp. 8vo. 1s. sewed, 1s. 6d. cloth, 2s. 6d. cloth extra.
The same, Popular Edition. Illustrated by Scharf. Fcp. 4to. 6d. swd., 1s. cloth.
Macdonald's (G.) A Book of Strife : in the Form of the Diary of an Old Soul : Poems. 12mo. 6s.
Pennell's (Cholmondeley) 'From Grave to Gay.' A Volume of Selections. Fcp. 8vo. 6s.
Reader's Voices from Flowerland, a Birthday Book, 2s. 6d. cloth, 3s. 6d. roan.
Robinson's The New Arcadia, and other Poems. Crown 8vo. 6s.
Shakespeare's Hamlet, annotated by George Macdonald, LL.D. 8vo. 12s.
Southey's Poetical Works. Medium 8vo. 14s.
Stevenson's A Child's Garden of Verses. Fcp. 8vo. 5s.
Virgil's Æneid, translated by Conington. Crown 8vo. 9s.
—   Poems, translated into English Prose. Crown 8vo. 9s.

AGRICULTURE, HORSES, DOGS, AND CATTLE.

Dunster's How to Make the Land Pay. Crown 8vo. 5s.
Fitzwygram's Horses and Stables. 8vo. 10s. 6d.
Horses and Roads. By Free-Lance. Crown 8vo. 6s.
Lloyd, The Science of Agriculture. 8vo. 12s.
Loudon's Encyclopædia of Agriculture. 21s.
Miles's Horse's Foot, and How to Keep it Sound. Imperial 8vo. 12s. 6d.
—   Plain Treatise on Horse-Shoeing. Post 8vo. 2s. 6d.
—   Remarks on Horses' Teeth. Post 8vo. 1s. 6d.
—   Stables and Stable-Fittings. Imperial 8vo. 15s.
Nevile's Farms and Farming. Crown 8vo. 6s.
—   Horses and Riding. Crown 8vo. 6s.
Steel's Diseases of the Ox, a Manual of Bovine Pathology. 8vo. 15s.
Stonehenge's Dog in Health and Disease. Square crown 8vo. 7s. 6d.
—   Greyhound. Square crown 8vo. 15s.
Taylor's Agricultural Note Book. Fcp. 8vo. 2s. 6d.
Ville on Artificial Manures, by Crookes. 8vo. 21s.
Youatt's Work on the Dog. 8vo. 6s.
—   —   —   —   Horse. 8vo. 7s. 6d.

SPORTS AND PASTIMES.

The Badminton Library of Sports and Pastimes. Edited by the Duke of Beaufort and A. E. T. Watson. With numerous Illustrations. Crown 8vo. 10s. 6d. each.

> Hunting. by the Duke of Beaufort, &c.
> Fishing, by H. Cholmondeley-Pennell, &c. 2 vols.
> Racing, by the Earl of Suffolk, &c.

Campbell-Walker's Correct Card, or How to Play at Whist. Fcp. 8vo. 2s. 6d.
Dead Shot (The) by Marksman. Crown 8vo. 10s. 6d.
Francis's Treatise on Fishing in all its Branches. Post 8vo. 15s.
Jefferies' The Red Deer. Crown 8vo. 4s. 6d.
Longman's Chess Openings. Fcp. 8vo. 2s. 6d.
Peel's A Highland Gathering. Illustrated. Crown 8vo. 10s. 6d.
Pole's Theory of the Modern Scientific Game of Whist. Fcp. 8vo. 2s. 6d.
Proctor's How to Play Whist. Crown 8vo. 5s.
Ronalds's Fly-Fisher's Entomology. 8vo. 14s.
Verney's Chess Eccentricities. Crown 8vo. 10s. 6d.
Wilcocks's Sea-Fisherman. Post 8vo. 6s.
Year's Sport (The) for 1885. 8vo. 21s.

ENCYCLOPÆDIAS, DICTIONARIES, AND BOOKS OF REFERENCE.

Acton's Modern Cookery for Private Families. Fcp. 8vo. 4s. 6d.
Ayre's Treasury of Bible Knowledge. Fcp. 8vo. 6s.
Brande's Dictionary of Science, Literature, and Art. 3 vols. medium 8vo. 63s.
Cabinet Lawyer (The), a Popular Digest of the Laws of England. Fcp. 8vo. 9s.
Cates's Dictionary of General Biography. Medium 8vo. 28s.
Doyle's The Official Baronage of England. Vols. I.–III. 3 vols. 4to. £5. 5s. ; Large Paper Edition, £15. 15s.
Gwilt's Encyclopædia of Architecture. 8vo. 52s. 6d.
Keith Johnston's Dictionary of Geography, or General Gazetteer. 8vo. 42s.
Latham's (Dr.) Edition of Johnson's Dictionary. 4 vols. 4to. £7.
— — — — — — Abridged. Royal 8vo. 14s.
M'Culloch's Dictionary of Commerce and Commercial Navigation. 8vo. 63s.
Maunder's Biographical Treasury. Fcp. 8vo. 6s.
— Historical Treasury. Fcp. 8vo. 6s.
— Scientific and Literary Treasury. Fcp. 8vo. 6s.
— Treasury of Bible Knowledge, edited by Ayre. Fcp. 8vo. 6s.
— Treasury of Botany, edited by Lindley & Moore. Two Parts, 12s.
— Treasury of Geography. Fcp. 8vo. 6s.
— Treasury of Knowledge and Library of Reference. Fcp. 8vo. 6s.
— Treasury of Natural History. Fcp. 8vo. 6s.
Quain's Dictionary of Medicine. Medium 8vo. 31s. 6d., or in 2 vols. 34s.
Reeve's Cookery and Housekeeping. Crown 8vo. 7s. 6d.
Rich's Dictionary of Roman and Greek Antiquities. Crown 8vo. 7s. 6d.
Roget's Thesaurus of English Words and Phrases. Crown 8vo. 10s. 6d.
Ure's Dictionary of Arts, Manufactures, and Mines. 4 vols. medium 8vo. £7. 7s.
Willich's Popular Tables, by Marriott. Crown 8vo. 10s.

London : LONGMANS, GREEN, & CO.

Spottiswoode & Co. Printers, New-street Square, London.